"Sarah introduces many issues: race relations, the presence of Jews in the Choctaw Nation, the Lighthorsemen, the educated and civilized Choctaw, a few greedy white people, the struggle for women to have equal rights and be able to pursue careers, the political issues of the Nationals and the Progressives, the confusion and separation of the two tiered system for lawbreakers for the white man and the Indian in Indian Territory, morality, integrity, doing what is right and the Gospel message. These issues are all woven into the story of the Teller family. So much intrigue and mystery."

Beverly Hardy Allen, author of
Back Then: A Choctaw Family's
Noble Legacy of Perseverance

"Sarah's writing is excellent, and the story—captivating. This book is absolutely beautiful. Well done."

Kathi Macias, author of _Red Ink_
www.KathiMacias.com

"The eagerly awaited second book in Sarah Elisabeth Sawyer's _Choctaw Tribune_ series certainly does not disappoint! Choctaw siblings, Matthew and Ruth Ann Teller, are at it again, dedicated to reporting the real truth all while publishing a small town newspaper in early Indian Territory. Will it cost them everything this time? Even their lives? Only God knows...

"Those who love history and have a curiosity for what it was like before Oklahoma Statehood are going to love this book. I know I did!"

Shelia Kirven, Tribal Member
Choctaw Nation of Oklahoma

TRAITORS

A Novel

SARAH ELISABETH SAWYER

ROCKHAVEN PUBLISHING

TRAITORS

RockHaven Publishing
P.O. Box 1103
Canton, Texas 75103

Scriptures taken from the *Authorized King James Version*, Holy Bible. Used by permission. All rights reserved.

This is a work of fiction. Names, characters, places, and incidents are fictitious or used fictitiously. Any resemblance to real persons, living or dead, is coincidental and unintentional.

Editors: Lynda Kay Sawyer, James Masters

Interior Design: Sarah Elisabeth Sawyer

Cover Design: Kirk DouPonce (www.DogEaredDesign.com)

Author Photo by R. A. Whiteside. Courtesy of the National Museum of the American Indian, Smithsonian Institution

ISBN-10: 0-9910259-4-6
ISBN-13: 978-0-9910259-4-7
LCCN: 2016956013

To my aunts

Sherry and Judy

Strong supporters on my journey

He shall redeem their soul from deceit and violence: and precious shall their blood be in his sight. Psalms 72:14

CHAPTER ONE

Indian Territory, August 1893

RUTH ANN URGED HER CHOCTAW paint mare, Skyline, into a lope to stay alongside her brother Matthew. There hadn't been reported killings in the area lately, but it didn't hurt for them to stay close together.

They took the northern road toward the Kiamichi foothills. Since the sawmill was several miles from the nearest train depot, riding was the best option. They could take the timber road and shortcuts no iron horse could.

The dawn wasn't cool, but with only a few sunrays splashing across the land, the intense August heat was kept in check for now. Ruth Ann wore a wide straw hat for protection from the sun to come.

Their mother had packed ample food for them on top of the full breakfast she'd laid out in the pre-dawn hours. The stout picnic basket was strapped over Matthew's saddlebag behind him. A scabbard held his Winchester in front.

Ruth Ann envied the functionality of his saddle. Her sidesaddle barely held her, and was mostly covered by her brown riding skirt. At nineteen years old, she no longer had the option of riding astride like in the days of being a young girl instead of a young lady.

They slowed to give the horses a walking rest, and Ruth Ann fought a yawn. Matthew grinned. "I warned you it would be a long day."

"Humph. You should have talked to me last night instead of in the dark of morning. But I'm glad you did. This is the most important investigation you've done for the *Choctaw Tribune*."

She tried to brush aside the cobwebs in her mind. "Um, who did you say this man is?"

Matthew laughed. "You were asleep when I got home last night, little *luksi*. The man's name is Will Hocks, superintendent of a timber operation on Blackjack Mountain, and he knew Mayor Warren before he came to Indian Territory. He answered my telegram that he's willing to talk if I rode up to his office at the sawmill."

Matthew took off his hat and dropped it on the horn of his saddle. He ran his hand over his head and rubbed the back of his neck. His dark brown hair brushed his collar. He claimed he'd been too busy lately for a haircut, so his hair was shaggier than normal, and bits fell over his eyes when he turned his head. Ruth Ann wanted to brush the strands back or cut them off, but he wouldn't be still for either. If he waited until he had time for a cut, it would grow out to his waist. That might make him closer to what people thought Indians looked like, even though his skin was lighter than hers. The ruddy tone gave him another advantage besides not being female. He could easily move from native to white circles. Like a chameleon, he could blend in wherever he needed to.

Not to mention he was a good-looking twenty-three-year old, if one judged from the coy glances young women gave him. Ruth Ann just saw his stubborn jawline so much like their daddy's when he was alive.

Matthew urged his gelding, Little Chief, into a lope.

They stayed at a good clip while they could. Their ride would slow in several places at narrow trails, cutting through the woods and creeks often until they gained the well-groomed timber road. Timber roads were the better ones in Choctaw Nation since they had to bear the burden of heavy wagons, hauling tons of timber from the mountains. Choctaw timber.

When they were able to ride side by side again, Ruth Ann continued her questions. "Who's running the timber operation Mr. Hocks supervises?"

"Mr. Robert Barnes."

Ruth Ann almost pulled her mare to a halt, but forced herself to keep a steady pace. She needed to stop letting things catch her by surprise. And if they did, not show it.

"How…interesting. Mr. Barnes is ambitious, but this is a bit much, even for him."

"The federal government thinks so. They filed an indictment on him of illegally cutting timber in the Choctaw Nation since he's a white man."

"Indictment? Was he arrested?"

Her thoughts went to her friend, Sissy Barnes. How would Sissy take it if her father was arrested? Knowing the Barnes family, Ruth Ann figured they would be cool and calm.

There had been a shootout at the Barnes mansion last winter when one faction in the Choctaw election took offense to the Barnes' support of the other faction. Ruth Ann knew about it firsthand; she and Matthew had been there during the fight, which ended with no one seriously hurt. After something like that, an arrest writ couldn't be much of a bump in Robert Barnes' road.

Matthew sank back in the saddle and brought Little Chief to a walk. Skyline matched the pace. "He was arrested and taken to Fort Smith, where he posted bail and went home. But the officials are trying to get the operation shut down until things are sorted out in federal court."

Ruth Ann took a deep breath, inhaling a mix of dusty horseflesh and the strong fragrance released by the pines.

The forest they approached was patient looking. The trees had stood for dozens, even hundreds, of years, offering a haven in the Choctaw Nation. Timber. What would the land be without it?

Did Mr. Barnes have a right to sell their timber? He was a white man who had come to Indian Territory after the War, and married a full-blood Choctaw woman. Intermarried whites were granted citizenship and access to the community-held land of the tribe. But there had been so many abuses of the tribe's natural resources by white and Choctaw alike. Which brought them back to the problem at hand—Mr. Warren, the white man who had founded the town of Dickens where the Tellers now lived.

Gazing at the trees undisturbed even by a harmless breeze, Ruth Ann asked, "What's the right thing, Matt?"

Her brother's sigh was followed by a long pause. She turned her gaze to the trail and saw where it would narrow to single file width. If Matthew didn't answer soon, he wouldn't have another chance for awhile. Still, Ruth Ann knew he wouldn't hurry, even if it meant an hour passed before they could talk again.

But he didn't wait that long. "One problem at a time, Annie. Right now, we're going to talk to a man who had dealings with Thaddeus Warren back in the '70s. If I can glean anything helpful about the timber operation itself or the charges against Mr. Barnes, I will. But we can't set the world right in a day."

Matthew took the lead before the trail narrowed, and left Ruth Ann to her own thoughts about right and wrong.

Several hours later, in the foothills of Blackjack Mountain, the sawmill came into sight. A heavily laden wagon was on its way out the timber road. The driver dipped his head in greeting at Matthew and Ruth Ann and he clucked to the mule team hauling out the milled boards. Another man sat shotgun on the spring seat, the butt of his gun settled on his thigh with the barrel pointed skyward.

They created a curtain of dust. When it settled, Ruth

Ann blinked away specks and made out the hustle of business. Men operated saws that blazed in the open pavilion, sawdust choking the air.

But Ruth Ann realized her presence had drawn attention. Some lumberjacks glanced inconspicuously at her, others openly stared. She resisted the urge to reach down and rearrange her long skirt. Her mama cautioned her that men wouldn't hesitate to take a second look at a pretty Choctaw girl like her. Her dusty rose lips and brown dove eyes didn't help her appearance as a serious reporter.

She kept Skyline close to Matthew.

If Matthew noticed the looks sent their way, he gave no indication of it. He rode straight for what looked like an office where a man had stepped out on the porch and watched their approach.

Matthew reined to a stop. "I'm Matthew Teller. Is Will Hocks around?"

The man lifted his chin toward the open door. "Inside. He's expecting you."

Ruth Ann slipped off the saddle, happy to get down from her perch. She landed safely between Skyline and Little Chief where she settled her skirts before tying her horse to the hitching rail.

There were no steps for the high platform. Before Ruth Ann could worry over how to mount gracefully, Matthew hopped onto the platform with a thud and reached his hand down to her. She took it and felt his strength when he pulled her with ease onto the wood platform. She breathed a quiet *yakoke* and followed him to the door.

The man casually dropped an arm across the doorframe, blocking their way. He glanced past Matthew to Ruth Ann with a smirk. "Maybe your lady friend would like to wait out here. Be glad to show her around."

Matthew stared at the man until he dropped his arm and shrugged. Matthew motioned Ruth Ann ahead of him and she gladly dodged through the doorway. She heard him say, "My *sister* stays with me."

Ruth Ann found herself in a dim, narrow hallway and having to lead the way. She didn't hesitate—much—as she strolled through the dark corridor, seeing light near the end and to the right past a closed door. She aimed for the light, Matthew's footsteps behind her. This office and storage building seemed hastily assembled like the sawmill itself.

She stepped through the doorway into a tight space that boasted two windows, allowing filthy sunshine through to light the interior. The windows were shut, the air stale. But which was worse, the stifling heat or choking on sawdust? At least the open skylight allowed a breath or two of air.

A man sat behind the desk and glanced up without a smile, noted Ruth Ann and bent over his ledger again. "I expected Matthew Teller to look a whole lot more like a man."

Flushed, Ruth Ann moved further into the office, being careful not to disturb anything while she made room for Matthew to squeeze in beside her. The room was a fire trap with its papers and books scattered across the desk and overflowing onto every square foot of the rough-hewn wood floor.

Matthew removed his hat, leaned over the stack of boxes in front of the desk, and offered his hand. "Matthew Teller from the *Choctaw Tribune*, and my sister, Ruth Ann Teller. Pleasure to meet you."

The man laid aside his pencil and gripped Matthew's offered hand, gave it a quick shake and resumed his work. "Will Hocks. Have a seat."

Ruth Ann glanced around. The only other chair in the room was buried beneath at least twenty pounds of paper.

Matthew noted it too. "Thank you, sir, we'll stand. It's a long ride up here."

"So it is."

Matthew handed his hat to Ruth Ann, who was thankful to have something to do with her hands, even if just pinching the rim of the sweaty felt hat. Matthew had a tablet and pencil to keep his hands occupied. A list of questions was scrawled on the first page.

"Mr. Hocks, I understand you were partners with Thaddeus Warren in '79. How would you describe—"

"Let's skip the formalities, all right? I'm a busy man, and one with a grudge, so I'll do the talking."

Ruth Ann darted her eyes between the two men, contrasted in many ways. Hocks was older, older even than Mayor Warren, and worn out like a mule who plodded along in the traces because that was what he knew and it took little effort to move forward as long as he didn't have to leave his rut. While Matthew was dressed for the long, hot ride, he still had a professional air with his pressed pants, shirt and jacket. Hocks wore a simple red plaid shirt that must be in its tenth season, summer and winter.

Yet he held himself like a boss, asserting his authority as he took the conversation like that old mule taking the bit in his teeth and going where he pleased.

"I knew Warren back East, and I didn't like him then, but he had something I didn't—a way into Indian Territory, biding time until the government divided up the land. Those who got here early stood to make a killing and settle in like kings of the country. Turned out, there were other whites luckier than us."

Matthew halted his note-taking. "What was Warren's way in?"

Hocks leaned back and eyed Matthew as if discerning whether the young reporter was truly ignorant or baiting him. "The old Choctaw squaw...er, woman he married." He said this without glancing at Ruth Ann but she still felt she'd been looked at.

"The woman was old and needed someone to take care of her. Warren was more than obliging, provided she marry him legally. She didn't have any kin looking after her and lived way out alone. I reckon if any Choctaws got wind what he was doing, they'd have butchered his...well, I reckon it wouldn't have happened. But it did and he kept her in a sorry state while he plowed through as many rights as he could without getting his head blown off."

While Mr. Hocks told the story, Ruth Ann drifted into the wall behind her as if she could vanish from the conversation. Hocks would speak more candidly if not for her. But she couldn't help that. She was a reporter and folks would get used to a woman writing the harder stories. Still, she didn't want to get in Matthew's way.

The rough boards behind Ruth Ann were splintered and they poked through her thin sleeves, but she resisted scratching her arms. She would be still like the Grandmother. She would be patient and wait for her time of usefulness to come.

Hocks continued. "That's when I met up with Warren again near Wilburton. He was digging for coal in the Kiamichi Mountains and so was I, only he had a right because of the marriage. He invited me in and kindly let me do all the work. I remember the first time I went to that shanty he lived in. Never forget it."

Hocks jerked open his desk drawer and pulled out a cigar stub. Ruth Ann put her fingers on her throat. It constricted at the very thought of cigar smoke in the tight space.

Thankfully, Hocks simply clenched the stub between his teeth. "Sorriest sight I'd ever seen, and that's saying something, son. I was in the War Between the States, but this was just rotten. A poor old squaw—pardon me—an elderly Choctaw woman, all stove up and mostly blind trying to stump her way around that shanty. Though she was mostly laid up in bed. And I do mean she was laid up and did everything in that bed, not the chamber pot."

Hocks bit off the end of the cigar and shot it in the spittoon placed on a teetering stack of books. "I reckon that's when I took a strong disliking to Thaddeus Warren. He wasn't just a greedy man who would go through people's rights to get what he wanted. He's a downright, stinkin'…"

Apparently Ruth Ann hadn't been successful at blending with the wall because Hocks glanced at her and bit on the cigar. "Well, he's a skunk. Cut and ran with the coal profits we'd dug out of the hills. I couldn't do anything unless I wanted to take after him with a gun and then the U.S. marshals would be after me. I couldn't press charges since all the work I'd done was illegal. Looking back, it didn't amount to much, but when you sweated blood drops to get it… Anyway, I tracked him awhile but he left Indian Territory and went back to the States. Heard he got into scheme after scheme. Married that fancy woman, er, lady, he has now. Came back into the Choctaw Nation using his old marriage license like a free pass. Never thought it would get him this far."

While Matthew scribbled a note, Ruth Ann pushed away from the wall. "What was his Choctaw wife's name? What happened to her?" All Ruth Ann knew was that the woman had died from an unknown cause.

Hocks eyed her as he had Matthew, deciding whether she really wanted to know. "Bascom. Rachel Bascom. She died in her own filth."

Ruth Ann's stomach tightened and she put a palm over it.

Taking up his pencil, Hocks gave a quick nod. "Now if you'll excuse me, I have work to do."

Matthew looked up from his tablet. "When was the last time you saw Thaddeus Warren?"

"1879. Got no desire to see him again in this lifetime."

Hocks went back to his ledger, but Matthew asked, "What about this timber operation? I understand Robert Barnes is having legal troubles."

The supervisor raised his eyes, not his head. "You asked your last question, son. Good day." He nodded to include Ruth Ann before adding a column to his ledger.

Matthew led the way from the office and down the dark corridor. Outside, the blinding sunlight confirmed how dim and depressing the office had been.

Ruth Ann dreaded the long ride home. It was hard to talk with all the dust and narrow trails. They'd soon reach Daniel Springs where they could get refreshed with cool mineral water. Until then, Ruth Ann had to settle into a boring ride.

But it wasn't to be.

◆ ◆ ◆

Matthew hadn't been to Daniel Springs in a while. Some people called the place Medicine Springs because of the healing minerals in the water that worked miracles on sore muscles and other ailments. Known as a meeting place for Choctaws, the springs were the best stop on a dusty ride through the foothills. There was a cleared out patch of ground with plenty of trees left for shelter. Logs had been hauled around the main spring and set haphazardly around areas where fires warmed travelers who gathered on cool nights.

When he was a boy, Matthew had sat around these fires on many occasions. His father and Uncle Preston would bring him and his brother, Philip, here. The reasons varied from temperance meetings to wolf hunting to Bible readings. The days and nights were always long. It seemed no man ever slept. Even when things quieted in the circle, someone would start chuckling and, as though they all remembered why, everyone chuckled until the circle rolled round with laughter. Whatever the funny story was, no one ever said.

Matthew brought Little Chief to a slow walk as they neared the springs.

"What are you smiling about?" Ruth Ann asked, matching his pace.

He glanced at her, realizing a grin had crept onto his lips as he reminisced. "Nothing. Springs sure look good about now."

Ruth Ann huffed at his explanation, but there was nothing more to say. Some things he just couldn't share with her. Besides, any talk of Daddy or Philip would sadden her. She still grieved for them five years after they'd been killed by outlaws. He still grieved too. But it was another feeling that made him pull his thirsty horse up short of the springs.

Ruth Ann sighed. "What now?"

Matthew motioned her to be quiet with a quick wave of his hand. He leaned forward, raising up in the stirrups. Three riders loped into sight on the trail ahead.

Two of the riders wore hats to shade their eyes against the afternoon sun but the third wore only a bandana wrapped around his head. The man couldn't keep his horse in a straight line, jerking the reins first to the right then the left, bumping into the rider next to him, pulling up on the reins, then kicking his sweaty horse's ribs to get it moving again.

The man was plain drunk.

The trio looked like Choctaws, but that didn't ease Matthew's mind. Their expressions were hard. He nudged his gelding in front of Ruth Ann, which put him between her and the fast approaching men.

One called out, "You! You Matthew Teller? Heard you was comin' up this way. We want to talk to you."

The drunk man slurred, "Sure do."

The three men halted close to Matthew. He faced them by turning sideways in his saddle, blocking their sight of Ruth Ann.

The first man settled his arms crossway on his saddle horn. "Heard tell you'll be coverin' the elections come fall. You haven't written too kindly about the Progressive party and how them stinkin' Buzzards need to fly on back to the hills. Whose side are you on, Matthew Teller?"

The drunk man spit to the side. "You got no call to be sidin' with that white skunk Barnes and his full-blood crew. They only lookin' for their own profit."

The man in the middle jumped in. "You been up to see Barnes' sawmill, ain't you? He's rippin' our timber right out. No wonder he don't want no U.S. soldiers here. He can steal from us and we can't touch a white man! Time's come all that changed. We gonna have them here, we gonna make them live by the law."

Matthew sat still while they spewed and ranted. When they hesitated at his silence, he figured at least some of the charges needed answering. "My newspaper doesn't take sides except for truth. You Progressives go shoot up a Nationalist's mansion like last winter, I'm going to report it. A Nationalist murders Progressives in their own homes, I'm going to report it. What I don't do is put in people's minds that this makes one side's way right and the other's dead wrong. Folks need to decide based on facts—"

"Coward!" The drunk man tumbled off his saddle. But he landed on his feet and shooed his horse away. He leaped forward and grabbed the butt of Matthew's rifle, which was exposed in his front-facing scabbard. The man yanked the rifle free, jumped back and aimed the barrel at Matthew's face.

Matthew started to grab for the barrel but halted. Ruth Ann was behind him. If he moved the wrong way, she would be in the line of fire. Besides, his own Winchester was already leveled on him. There was nothing he could do but die.

"Hey now!"

"Hey!"

The other two men scrambled off their horses and one grabbed the barrel of the rifle and shoved it upward. The gun went off, the blast ringing through the foothills and in Matthew's ears with a sound he knew would stay with him a long, long time.

One of the men grabbed the drunk's shoulder, pulling him back. "We didn't come to do no shooting."

"Come on, now. We ain't killing anyone today. Come on."

The man holding the barrel released his grip. With a swagger, the drunk shoved the rifle back into its place in Matthew's scabbard. Through the thick leather, Matthew felt the hot barrel against his leg.

He sat stiff and nodded to the men. "You had your say. Now you best move on."

The drunk man caught his horse and mounted. The other two, noticing Ruth Ann, tipped their hats her direction, said, "Good day, ma'am," and mounted up.

They rode off the way they'd come, and Matthew wondered if they planned to lay an ambush. He and Ruth Ann would turn back to take another trail near the timber road.

Ruth Ann's long, shaky breath behind him broke the silence, but when Matthew turned to look at her, she was holding herself together fine. She even smiled a little.

"That's not the first time you've had your hide saved."

Matthew shook his head and took another look down the road to satisfy himself that the riders had cleared out. Then he nudged Little Chief toward the springs. "Get a long drink. We likely won't be home before dark."

They dismounted at the smaller spring and dropped reins to let the horses drink. Matthew and Ruth Ann went to the main spring and filled their canteens, neither saying anything about the incident. Ruth Ann didn't pepper him with concerns. For once, he had to wonder what she was thinking.

As he drank the cool, iron-flavored water, Matthew observed his sister from the corner of his eye. She was a good Choctaw girl. Even now, with hair falling from her bun onto her sweaty neck and her dress dusty from the ride, she held herself with a strong, yet womanly air. Plenty enough beauty to catch any man's eye, white or red.

Sometimes Matthew had to remind himself his little sister wasn't little anymore. She was a full-grown woman, and he couldn't treat her like a brother. He wondered how often he'd done that since Philip's death. Ruth Ann had her own role to fill, and she was doing a fine job. Matthew just needed to make sure she didn't get hurt.

Ruth Ann caught him looking at her. "What?"

He feigned an excuse. "You all right? You must have been scared."

She didn't meet his eyes. "There's a lot of killing all over Indian Territory these days. Daddy and Philip…I suppose I'll think on it more later…"

Matthew put his arms around her and pulled her head to his chest. Her tears blended with the sweat already soaking his shirt.

She rested heavy against him and whispered, "I guess I should say there's nothing more powerful than the press except God Almighty, but right now, I'd say God Almighty is Who gives our press any power. Only He could keep us covered with so many miracles."

Matthew rubbed his chin in her mussed up hair. "*Ome.*"

He would make sure his little sister had something safe to do in the coming days.

CHAPTER TWO

RUTH ANN FOUGHT AGAINST THE yawn that threatened to split her mouth wide open. She ducked her head behind Mrs. Warren's plumed hat where the woman sat on the church pew in front of her. Ruth Ann lifted her fingers, intertwined with a pencil, to cover her mouth. She gave in to the smallest yawn she could manage, but it still ended in an audible sigh.

The plumed hat shook. Mrs. Warren stopped midsentence and turned with a frown.

In the sudden stillness, attention from the small gathering of ladies in the church was on Ruth Ann. Mrs. Anderson and Beulah had amused smiles, while Mrs. Warren and Mrs. Maxwell wore irritated frowns.

Pastor Rand stood in front of the pulpit rather than behind it like on Sunday mornings. Though a slender man, he had a hearty soul. His face wasn't as red as when he delivered a sermon, and his lips were turned up in a bright smile. He seemed glad for any kind of disruption and cleared his throat. "Well now, Miss Ruth Ann, I will pardon the offense of your fatigue this time, so long as it is not repeated during my next sermon."

Ruth Ann smiled and ducked her head. This meeting was a welcome break after what had happened the day before at Daniel Springs, but the dull talk was putting her to sleep.

The droning of Mrs. Warren's voice picked up again. The woman was going on and on about the education system—or lack of—in Indian Territory.

"Why, last week on the train to St. Louis I never saw one schoolhouse, not a one mind you. Every white family in the territory suffers their children to stay home and work, and those who do want to send them off to school, why, there just aren't any."

When Mrs. Warren took a breath, Mrs. Anderson, the doctor's wife, interjected. "And the schools that do exist cost an exorbitant amount."

Mrs. Warren sniffed, perturbed by the interruption. "We cannot let this deplorable condition go on in our town."

Ruth Ann straightened in the pew, pencil and tablet poised for what might be worth reporting at this, the first meeting called by Pastor Rand of the Concerned Citizens of Dickens. Only women had shown up. They would represent their families with suggestions for the betterment of the town while their menfolk worked. Besides, most men didn't care.

Ruth Ann came as a reporter for the *Choctaw Tribune*, trusting her mother, Della, to present any comments for the Teller family. Della, who sat beside Ruth Ann, had said nothing so far. She continued her latest sewing project, head down. But Ruth Ann knew she listened.

Few ladies had been able to say much anyway. Mrs. Warren had dominated every discussion, asking and then answering her own questions about how backward and dangerous and volatile and corrupt Indian Territory was. She made snide remarks about Choctaws in particular, who held such a ridiculous claim to this land, and how that would eventually change.

Pastor Rand had tried to politely interrupt her. Near fifty years old, he was experienced with handling sticky situations, but it was no use. Mrs. Warren was indignant and would rebuke him before continuing her diatribe.

Now, at last, Mrs. Warren seemed to be coming to a point. "My husband—who you all know as the fine mayor of Dickens—has graciously consented to pay for bringing a teacher for the white children of our town and surrounding area. This is most generous of the mayor, considering we have no children of our own. But he believes in the right of education for white children, not just the Indians, who've always enjoyed such privileges."

This brought a hard cough from Ruth Ann. For a white woman to call Indians "privileged" was ironic, but pointing that out was, well, pointless. Especially with Mrs. Warren, who kept her chin raised and eyes forward on Pastor Rand as though challenging even him.

He sighed. "That is generous, indeed, coming from you. I mean, well, as you said, I'm certain the families around here will appreciate it."

Without pausing, Pastor Rand looked anxiously around the room. "Are there other suggestions we can work on as a committee for the betterment of the town? Mrs. Anderson? Yes, you have the floor."

While the doctor's wife talked about sanitation issues, Ruth Ann stared at Mrs. Warren's plumed hat. It bobbed as the woman went from nodding to bending her head and dabbing away sweat on her upper lip. Mrs. Warren must bathe three times a day. There was no other way for her to stay fresh and clean smelling this time of year.

When Mrs. Anderson finished, Mrs. Warren took a deep breath as though preparing to speak. Beulah Levitt shot her hand in the air.

Pastor Rand acknowledged the young Jewish woman seated across the aisle from Ruth Ann. "Yes, Miss Levitt, isn't it? It's a pleasure to have you here."

This was the first time Beulah had come inside the church. She and her father held their traditional Jewish services at home, being the only Jews in the area. But what they lacked in numbers, Mr. Levitt made up with gracious dignity and Beulah with fiery spirit. They had carried these things with them throughout their immigration journey from op-pressed Russia to New York to Kansas and finally, Dickens, Indian Territory.

Though Jewish, the Levitts didn't have all the typical traits associated with their people. Beulah's deep blue eyes and long blonde hair let her blend in white society, but she still possessed the distinct nose that reminded Ruth Ann of the deep pride Beulah held for her people.

Beulah sat with her back straight, chin up in her com-manding way. But there was a childish gleam in her eyes. "I would like to offer two free group singing lessons a week for children. With enough help from those on the committee, I wish to put on choir concerts, the first taking place right after harvest time. A Thanksgiving performance."

From the excited nods around them, Ruth Ann knew the idea was a success. She'd known it would be from the first time Beulah shared the idea with her. Ruth Ann had offered support along with the promise they would promote the op-portunity in the *Choctaw Tribune*.

These kinds of undertakings had worked like a salve be-tween her and Beulah since the pain they'd experienced over the lynching of two men down in Paris. Beulah had expressed beliefs about other races that shocked Ruth Ann, and their relationship hadn't been the same. Ruth Ann still struggled with those memories, but she let God use time to work His healing.

Mrs. Warren cleared her throat and her hat bobbed as she shifted to raise her hand. Pastor Rand looked everywhere but her direction. "Anyone else? Mrs. Teller, did you have something to add?"

Della had not stirred, but Ruth Ann recognized the re-spect the pastor had for her mother. It was as though he did not want the meeting to close without her input. Della had always proven faithful and her wisdom was respected, espe-cially among the churchgoers present. With a few exceptions of course.

After a moment of silence, Della lowered her sewing to

her lap and raised her head. A hint of a smile was on her lips. "These are all good works. It is good for all to have an education. Even the Indian knows this."

Ruth Ann was sure the pastor put his hand over his mouth to hide a smile.

Della continued. "There is one thing left to do. We should pray."

Pastor Rand dropped his hand and showed his smile while Mrs. Anderson nodded. Mrs. Warren made a puffing sound and raised her hand high.

Pastor Rand slowly acknowledged her. "Yes, Mrs. Warren?"

"Before I was *interrupted*, I was going to announce a teacher has already been solicited. He comes with the highest recommendations and an excellent pedigree. His name is Lance Fuller, and he will arrive by train in two weeks. We should prepare a welcome for him—"

"Good." Pastor Rand nodded. "Are there any objections to making Mrs. Warren head of that committee? Very well. Shall we end with prayer?"

Before Ruth Ann bowed her head, she saw the plumed hat shake with indignation before it jerked down. She sighed. At least she wouldn't be on Mrs. Warren's list of desirable committee members.

The church emptied quickly, everyone with things to do. As soon as they were in the blazing sunshine, Beulah started enlisting Ruth Ann's help with teaching the children's choir. Mrs. Anderson also seemed to want to talk, but Ruth Ann avoided meeting her eyes. She was a busy young woman these days with the newspaper. Matthew entrusted her with more and more important articles to write. The Concerned Citizens of Dickens meeting was supposed to be a break from the more intense—and dangerous—work.

Ruth Ann walked with her mother and Beulah toward the newspaper office. A shrill voice halted her.

"Oh, Miss Teller! I need to speak with you a moment!"

Ruth Ann managed a tentative smile as she faced Mrs.

Warren. The lady made no small show lumbering down the five steps of the church porch.

"Hello, Miss Teller! Do slow down for an older lady." Mrs. Warren puffed when her too small laced-up boot landed on the hard-packed dirt.

Ruth Ann hadn't moved since the lady called her. She folded her hands patiently in front of her. She'd grown far more patient in the past year with people like Mrs. Warren.

Beulah had not. She whispered teasingly, "You are on your own, my friend."

She excused herself and strolled away. Mercifully, Ruth Ann's mother stood by her side.

Mrs. Warren pulled a huge white handkerchief from her reticule, making Ruth Ann wonder if the handbag could hold anything else. She also wondered how many handkerchiefs the Warrens owned. She never saw Mayor Warren without his signature white cloth waving about.

Catching her breath, Mrs. Warren straightened the plumed hat and smiled tightly. "Well now, aren't we looking fine and...civilized this afternoon."

The latter word was probably not one she'd intended to use, but it could have been worse. Ruth Ann knew she had a definite Choctaw look even dressed in her business-like outfit of muted gray with a trim skirt and jacket. Her cinnamon skin would blend in with most ethnic groups. Excluding white.

Mrs. Warren bubbled on with a quick nod to Della. "You have raised a sensible young...woman, here, Mrs. Teller. You must be proud."

Mrs. Warren reminded Ruth Ann of grape dumplings. Appealing, but when not contained, they made a mess. Mrs. Warren had trouble containing her many layers of clothing. Something always flapped out of place, always skewed or lopsided. Like her hat. Her cloth belt. The light shawl she wore around her shoulders even with the sweltering temperatures that must have exceeded one hundred degrees. But despite her haphazard appearance, Mrs. Warren acted as though she were the finest lady in town.

Straightening her shawl and hat, Mrs. Warren stared down her nose at Ruth Ann. "Child, oh, that is, Miss Teller, I want you to join me on the welcoming committee for the new teacher."

Each word seemed to leave a bitter taste in Mrs. Warren's mouth, making the loose skin around her lips pucker. Ruth Ann wondered who had forced her to make this request. Pastor Rand? No. He would not be that cruel to Ruth Ann. The mayor? But what reason could he have for wanting a young woman he despised welcome his new teacher? Perhaps the man was Indian.

No. Impossible.

Before Ruth Ann could respond, Mrs. Warren barreled on. "I do so appreciate your willingness. As a female reporter, I know you're concerned about the welfare issues of our town. And lack of education is the most tragic we face!" Mrs. Warren scowled. "I shall let you know when we are to meet the train."

Hat wilting sideways and her shawl off one shoulder, Mrs. Warren turned and marched toward her house off Main Street. She'd likely be in a cool bath in ten minutes.

With a heavy sigh, Ruth Ann trailed along behind Della who had turned to go the other direction of the crossroad instead of continuing down Main Street to where their home lay at the other end. She was going to walk Ruth Ann to the newspaper office.

Ruth Ann waited for her mother's thoughts. Mrs. Warren's comment about her being a female reporter brought again to mind that perhaps the mayor had had a say in the request. The last time he spoke to Ruth Ann, he was in a rage and insisted a woman's place was in the kitchen. That Ruth Ann was a disgrace, reporting on political and social issues that should be covered by men only.

It wasn't until they reached the newspaper office that Della spoke. "You can say no."

There was a valuable lesson rolled into those simple words, and Ruth Ann knew it. Still, she said, "I suppose it won't hurt. After all, I *am* a reporter and a new teacher for the white children is newsworthy. It's not exactly legal, but who wants to deny children an education? They'll grow up poor in mind and body if someone doesn't do something."

Della nodded. "It will be good for them, and good for you to know who this man is and what his character is. You discern those things well."

Ruth Ann grew warmer, but it wasn't from the heat or the praise. She didn't feel it was deserved. More than once she failed on judging character. Her mother's faith in her added apprehension but at the same time, she was grateful for her confidence.

"I will, Mama. I will do well."

Della smiled and reached out to take her daughter's hand. She squeezed tight. "God knows."

Ruth Ann squeezed back and tried to smile, but her lips quivered. She heard an echo of the words in her father's voice. There was pride in that voice, too. He would add, "That's my good girl. That's my good Choctaw girl."

Della released her hand and turned back toward Main Street.

The print shop was quiet, save for the sounder clacking in the telegraph office and violin music near the back. The front desk—used for greeting customers and handling trans-actions of the *Choctaw Tribune* and the Levitt Repair Shop and Music Studio—sat empty. There was no sign of Mr. Levitt at his workbench that ran half the length of the back wall. The printing press stood to the right of the bench along with the makeshift desk for the *Tribune*.

Mr. Levitt had more repair projects come in by the day, and custom furniture orders. Though his stack of work was enormous, he never got in a rush. Even before his bout of heart failure that put him in bed four weeks, Mr. Levitt worked with patience and perseverance. Right now, though, Ruth Ann assumed Beulah had sent him home to rest in the heat of the day.

Beulah was perched on the end of the workbench, lost in

the mournful violin tune she played. A quick glance to Ruth Ann's right showed Matthew in the telegraph office. The office was a lean-to built on the side of the large building.

With a few swift strokes, Beulah ended the tune and jumped up. She set aside her violin in its case on the bench. "From the look on your face, I would say the chat with old battle-axe Warren was less than pleasant."

Ruth Ann shook her head at her friend's colorful description and set her tablet and reticule on the makeshift desk of the *Choctaw Tribune*. She managed to keep the desk cleaner than when they were in the storage shed before it burned, but Matthew still made a mess of any area when she had her back turned.

She began to re-stack newspapers and separate Matthew's scattered notes from where she kept her own. "Mrs. Warren wants me on the welcoming committee for the new teacher."

"Do tell." Beulah's voice took on a fascinated tone. "And what do we know about this man?"

The clacking in the telegraph office had stopped and Matthew emerged from the office. "His name is Lance Fuller, he was educated at Harvard, he's the son of an old friend of Warren's—Richmond Fuller—and he's a white man in his mid-twenties, never set foot in Indian Territory before."

Ruth Ann frowned and shook her head. She'd never have the knack for digging up information that Matthew had.

Beulah played along, testing Matthew's knowledge. "And what of his marital status, Mister One-Who-Knows-All?"

Matthew joined them at the desk and riffled through the newspapers Ruth Ann had just stacked. "He's unmarried and…here's an article on his bachelorhood that made society news in New York, where he's from. The article didn't include a photograph. Likely to protect his identity from amiable young ladies such as yourself."

Ruth Ann tucked her chin and kept her eyes down, reading through her meeting notes a third time.

Beulah accepted the newspaper eagerly. She elbowed Ruth Ann. "Think, you will be among the first to make an impression on this eligible newcomer. My, does this not speak most highly of him?"

Matthew tapped Ruth Ann's shoulder with a rolled up newspaper. She lifted her eyes, keeping her face and her scowl down.

"If you can pull yourself away from this thrilling news, I have something to discuss on our, um, sideline investigation."

This brought Ruth Ann's head up in anticipation. But Beulah moved away, eyes still on the newspaper. She hadn't taken an interest in real news stories since the lynchings in Paris. When a man was arrested for a vicious murder and tortured to death by the locals, rumor spread that the man was black. This brought out Beulah's beliefs that in order for Jewish people to survive, they needed to align themselves with the superior race—a race that tended to exclude other races, though she was confident tribes like the Choctaws had proven their intelligence.

Ruth Ann was shocked by these revelations because of her own belief that it didn't matter the color of a person's skin. What mattered was the condition of their heart. But even after discovering the tortured criminal was a white man, the damage had been done. Having immigrated to America from Russia when she was fifteen, Beulah had her own fears and struggles and perspectives. Her own father had yet to convince her otherwise.

Since the incident, Beulah kept conversation with Ruth Ann light, even giddy, never offering a chance for serious discussion. It kept their friendship intact. Someday they would revisit the pain and find a way to healing. But for now, Beulah stayed well out of newspaper business, though she might have guessed Matthew was working on something important. Something he'd asked Ruth Ann not to mention to anyone.

Ruth Ann leaned forward on her toes toward Matthew, who stood on the other side of the desk. He watched Beulah walk away and lowered his voice.

"The mayor doesn't do much these days without my knowing, like the new teacher he so graciously hired. But I need your help with something."

She gave an enthusiastic nod. "Anything to get me away from Mrs. Warren. Maybe you could conveniently have something for me the day the new teacher arrives?"

But Matthew shook his head. "Actually, that's what I need your help with."

At Ruth Ann's frown, he planted both fists on the table and leaned closer to her, putting them eye level. His hair fell over one eye. "If we're going to expose Mayor Warren's scheme, we need a lot more evidence and witnesses than we have. You could be the key to getting close to Mrs. Warren herself. Women tend to spill things when they think they have a sympathetic ear."

Ruth Ann frowned. "I don't want to be deceitful."

"Be your sweet self. That will win her over."

Ruth Ann smiled shyly and started to brush Matthew's hair away from his eyes, but he jerked back and straightened with a grunt. He tapped her nose with the newspaper. "Just don't do the same with that new teacher. I'm keeping Daddy's shotgun handy."

He dodged the jab Ruth Ann shot at his stomach. The sounder clattered again, and Matthew went to the doorway of the telegraph office. "You just worry about getting all the right and wrong in the world sorted out."

CHAPTER THREE

THINGS BECAME EERILY PEACEFUL FOR Ruth Ann after the harrowing ride back from the sawmill, and the committee meeting with too many commitments.

Matthew wrote a simple article about the shooting incident. He countered the newspaper reports that tried to disguise the amount of violence in the Choctaw Nation. He also admonished people to take action to keep peace.

Ruth Ann wrote about social issues in Dickens, worked the telegraph, and helped Beulah in her children's choir venture, during which she endured teasing from her friend about the new teacher set to arrive soon.

She made time to help Pastor Rand and Mrs. Warren prepare the church to serve part-time as a school. Most Indian children went to the nearby Choctaw boarding schools. This would be the only white school within fifty miles on this side of the Red River.

With all the work, she had little chance to befriend Mrs. Warren like Matthew hoped. It was hard for Ruth Ann to be sweet with the haughty woman. When Mrs. Warren wasn't giving orders or making another demand of the *Choctaw Tribune*, she avoided Ruth Ann, though the needs were endless.

Articles about the new school, special flyers, books and supplies donated. But when Ruth Ann asked about the complications of a white school in Indian Territory, Mrs. Warren lifted her chin and acted as if the question was coming from a heathen Indian.

It tested Ruth Ann's patience. She wasn't sensitive about being Choctaw, but to be scorned for it was unnerving. Especially since they lived *in* the Choctaw Nation, a fact Mrs. Warren ignored.

It was pleasant to spend time with Beulah as they rounded up ragtag children from their summer fun to turn them into an organized group of singers. But the first gathering disbanded even as it was being formed, and ended in boys tussling and little girls crying. Beulah didn't lose heart. She brought them together again and they actually made it through the chorus of *Oh! Susanna*.

Fortifying herself with determination like Beulah and patience like Pastor Rand, Ruth Ann was prepared for the new teacher's arrival. Or so she thought.

Ruth Ann stood quietly in the group assembled at the train depot to welcome Lance Fuller to Dickens, Indian Territory. Among those gathered were Mayor and Mrs. Warren, Pastor Rand and other prominent whites—Dr. and Mrs. Anderson, and Mr. Maxwell, editor of the *Dickens Herald*, the rival newspaper. Even the cocky Sheriff Banny showed up. He wore his long black coat and six-shooter with ties on the holster like a gunfighter. His presence should have brought a sense of security, but Ruth Ann knew Jake Banny was a thinly veiled criminal who had no business wearing a badge. He'd threatened her family more than once. But she wasn't bothered by his presence today. Most people no longer bothered her like they once had. Perhaps they'd changed. Or perhaps she was the one who had changed.

Still, Ruth Ann wished Matthew had come. He'd been

gone a great deal lately, leaving her to manage the office and tend local responsibilities. She didn't mind, but did miss him being around. And she worried fiercely when he wasn't in sight.

A whistle sounded as the southbound train huffed down the tracks. A large crowd had gathered on the platform. Some wanted a glimpse of the new teacher, others waited to board or greet returning family. The St. Louis-San Francisco Railway—known as the Frisco—was heavily used. It made three runs a day to St. Louis, Missouri, and three to Paris, Texas.

The train screeched to a halt. After all the fuss and preparation, Ruth Ann was ready to be done with this business. Greet the young man if she must, then slip away. Best yet, not meet him at all. She negotiated her way to the back of the welcoming committee.

Mr. Maxwell crowded near the front, his chin lifted as though to show off his pointed salt and pepper beard. He was a tall man, and accustomed to making crowds part when he needed to get a story. This was big news for the town. Ruth Ann edged forward again.

She spotted Lance Fuller before he descended the steps of the passenger car. He wasn't what she expected, although she wasn't sure what she'd expected. But he didn't fit the image in her mind of a teacher—slicked back hair, stern eyes behind spectacles, and a wooden ruler to smack an obstinate child's hand.

The real-life Lance Fuller had a hopeful look on his face, his eyes bright and sharp as he looked around the full platform. He wore a brown suit and derby hat, though nothing set him apart as a big city man from New York. In all, the impression he made on Ruth Ann was…gracious. She wondered if he was. She made notes.

Lance Fuller came down the passenger car steps and Mayor Warren stepped forward to pump the newcomer's hand. "Lance, my boy! Good to see you. You remember Susan?"

The mayor motioned to his wife who clung to his left

arm though she was jolted by her husband's jerky movements. Thaddeus Warren was a hefty man, his round belly pooched enough to make a nice shelf. His face was pulled tight with a stiff smile. Brown age marks spotting his skin showed he was a seasoned traveler of life. Was this just another season for him? Ruth Ann thought of Rachel Bascom, the elderly Choctaw woman.

"Thaddeus, it's good to see you." Lance Fuller turned to Mrs. Warren. "The climate in Indian Territory suits you, Susan. Your color is stunning compared to the drabness of the northeast."

Gracious. Yes, that was the word for him. Ruth Ann made notes. Glancing over the words, she realized she'd already written *gracious* twice.

Before she could scribble away the evidence, she heard her name spoken. Mrs. Warren's voice bubbled from the flattery she'd been given. "Ruth Ann? Yes, here she is. This is our lovely town reporter who writes all the quaint stories, Ruth Ann Teller. *Miss* Teller, that is."

Ruth Ann raised her head at the emphasis on her marital status. She found herself looking up into Lance Fuller's eyes—a hazy blue sky color. He stepped toward her, close enough for a whiff of his cologne amidst the dust and sweat around them. His face was clean shaven, skin smooth as if he'd taken a razor to it an hour before arriving. He removed his hat to reveal ash blonde hair. Though close cut, it was combed to one side in a natural wave.

Lance Fuller smiled at her. "I'm pleased to meet you, Miss Teller. I understand you've helped a great deal with the school arrangements and organizing a children's choir with your friend."

And where is that friend now? Ruth Ann trembled at the attention suddenly on her. Why hadn't Beulah come? Ah yes. She had a violin student and had told Ruth Ann it would be unfair for the teacher to meet so many lovely young ladies at the same time.

With everyone's gaze on her, Ruth Ann shifted her pencil

onto her tablet, holding it in place with a stiff thumb. She shook his hand and fumbled for a polite greeting. "Welcome to Dickens, Mr. Fuller. I—I hope you find success here."

She tried not to blush when he continued to smile at her.

Mayor Warren cleared his throat and clasped Lance Fuller's shoulder. "Come on, we'll show you around. The Andersons have refreshments at their home."

The group dispersed and Mrs. Warren tucked herself close to Ruth Ann. She dabbed her lips with her white handkerchief, the feathers on her plumed hat tickling Ruth Ann's cheek.

Leaning close, Mrs. Warren whispered, "Run along to the Andersons and freshen up. We'll be there shortly."

Ruth Ann wondered if something in her appearance was out of place and if so, why would Mrs. Warren care? Either way, she'd had enough heat and fake pleasantness for one day.

Before Mrs. Warren flounced away, Ruth Ann replied quietly, "I need to go to the newspaper office. I'm behind on a deadline." Which was true. She'd promised Beulah she'd print copies of song pages before the choir rehearsal that afternoon.

Bidding a flustered Mrs. Warren good day, Ruth Ann left the platform as graciously as she could. She'd be careful not to use the word *gracious* in her article about the new teacher.

♦ ♦ ♦

At the newspaper office, Ruth Ann finished printing copies of *Oh! Susanna*, one of the Stephen Foster songs Beulah had chosen for the Thanksgiving choir performance. But to Ruth Ann's ear, the little choir of sixteen was far from ready to perform anytime in the next year. Maybe two.

Beulah was not discouraged. While Ruth Ann handed out the pages, she handed out instructions.

"Tommy, move to the right. No, not on top of Glenrose! Now, Neches, keep your chin up—the floor has no interest in hearing you. Dorothy, sing out, you have a fine voice. All right, everyone look at me!"

Beulah clapped her hands and the children turned their attention to her. No one questioned her when she was in this mood. But she also had an openness that made everyone want to do their best, even this ragtag choir in front of her father's workbench.

Mr. Levitt had kindly taken his work out back to make room for the brief choir rehearsal. Even Beulah's commanding presence wouldn't hold the children long. The chance of a swim hovered in every child's mind.

Beulah raised her hands like the choir director she was. She kept time as she sang:

> *I came from Alabama,*
> *With a banjo on my knee,*
> *I'm going to Louisiana,*
> *My true love for to see*

The children stared at Beulah. Perhaps they were in awe of her beautiful voice, although they looked confused. Ruth Ann bent near Glenrose Jessop and pointed at the correct place on the page. Glenrose didn't even glance at it, keeping her eyes on Beulah as instructed.

> *It rained all night the day I left,*
> *The weather it was dry,*
> *The sun so hot I froze to death;*
> *Susanna, don't you cry*

When no one joined in, Beulah cleared her throat. "Now, sing along, children. Do not be afraid."

The oldest boy, twelve-year-old Neches Jessop, shrugged his shoulders. "Don't know the song, ma'am."

"Oh, you will pick up the tune soon enough. Now, *sing!*"

Her exuberance was met with blank stares and bare feet rubbing on top of one another. One girl, maybe six years old, stuck three fingers in her mouth and glanced up at the big children around her. No one else moved.

Beulah started the song again, but halted with a frown. "Come now, children. One brief projection will not hurt you one bit. I have heard you whoop and holler like wild Indians—" She glanced at Ruth Ann with an apologetic wince. "Surely you can make an effort to raise your voices for the sheer joy of singing!"

Neches shuffled his feet and looked at his hands but not at the paper. "Can't, ma'am."

"Why, of course you can! You all can."

"Can't read them words, ma'am."

For the first time since she'd hatched the idea of a choir, Beulah gave Ruth Ann a desperate look.

Ruth Ann moved to stand before the children, hands clasped in front of her. "Well, now, I have wonderful news!"

She looked at the summertime faces of the children, tan and dirt streaked. The few Choctaws in the group could likely read but were shy and kept to the back. Actually, most of the children kept shifting positions, each trying to be the one at the back.

Ruth Ann mustered an encouraging voice. "You've probably heard your parents talk about your new teacher. He will teach you to read and write and do arithmetic and about the history of the world. Isn't that exciting?"

Neches shrugged. "Who wants to know about the world? Won't never see it."

Before she could explain, Tommy pointed toward the large picture windows of the shop. "Is that him? That our new teacher?"

Ruth Ann spotted Lance Fuller across the street in front of the tailor shop. Mayor Warren waved his hands around, pointing out different businesses.

She recognized the mischievous look in Beulah's eyes. "I do believe it is! Ruth Ann, lead the children in a familiar hymn. Children, sing loud. We want to give him a warm welcome!"

Before Ruth Ann could stop her, Beulah was across the shop and out the door. She called to Lance Fuller and the mayor before the door closed behind her.

Ruth Ann turned back to the children with a quivering smile. "Shall we sing *Marching to Zion?*"

The prospect of performing for someone excited the children. The boys puffed out their chests and sang with gusto, the girls joined in with sweetness to offset the sour notes. Ruth Ann winced and tried to get them on key. The bell over the door jingled. To her dismay, the children sang louder. She brought the hymn to a halt as soon as possible.

Still wanting to encourage the children, she smiled at their bright faces and silently clapped her hands before turning around. Lance Fuller stood there with a grin and Beulah beamed at her little choir.

He laughed. "That is the finest greeting I've ever had. Well done." He glanced over to include Beulah but his eyes settled on Ruth Ann.

She quickly introduced him. "Children, this is your new teacher, Mr. Fuller. We need to encourage other children in the area to come to school and to join the choir. Will you help Mr. Fuller make this a proud year for Dickens?"

The children chorused their agreement and circled around Lance Fuller as he asked each one for their name. Ruth Ann breathed a sigh of relief. These children desperately needed an education. Someone was here to give it to them.

With Lance Fuller making a wonderful impression on the children, Ruth Ann slipped into the telegraph office. She needed to check on her cousin, Peter, who was minding the telegraph for the day.

The fifteen-year-old had taken a liking to living in town. Uncle Preston let him explore that interest so long as he kept up his ranch work three days a week. And stuck with his education, which should include a few more years at boarding school before college. But Peter had convinced his father to let Matthew tutor him. Peter learned quickly, which made school boring. He had an aptitude for the telegraph wire, mastering it twice as fast as Ruth Ann had.

But today, the sight inside the telegraph office made Ruth

Ann question her cousin's intelligence.

On the desk in the small office, a checkerboard showed a close game. But there was no one in the office except Peter. He bent over the board in concentration, tapping his chin with one finger.

Ruth Ann frowned. "Peter, what on earth are you—"

"Shhh!" His hand paused with a black checker in mid-air. He placed it on the board and gave a satisfied nod. Then he worked the sounder, pecking out a telegram. Ruth Ann deciphered the last part.

Beat that!

The sounder clattered with a reply and she realized it was from station Tn up the line. It was operated by their good friend, Daniel, though he was more commonly referred to as "D." In the reply, she caught something about a young whippersnapper not beating him three times in a row.

Ruth Ann laughed. "Are you playing checkers over the wire with D?"

Without looking up, Peter frowned, moved a red checker and muttered, "Gotta have something to drown out that caterwauling."

"Peter Abraham Frazier! You know better than to—"

"He's right." A quiet voice came from someone close to Ruth Ann's ear. Too close.

She jumped to the side of the doorway and faced Lance Fuller. He smiled and kept his voice low. "The young man's right. But I have confidence in your and Miss Levitt's abilities to turn those raw voices into a heavenly choir."

Peter cleared his throat, game forgotten as he stood. He combed his fingers through his brown hair—a shade lighter than most in their mixed-blood family—and came around the desk. He put himself between Lance Fuller and Ruth Ann.

"So you're the new white teacher. I'm Peter Frazier."

Ruth Ann rolled her eyes at her young cousin's sudden protective nature. She pushed him back with her shoulder. "This is Lance Fuller, and white, Choctaw, it doesn't matter. Children need an education so they don't grow up so poor and helpless. Now mind the telegraph."

The sounder clattered. Ruth Ann knew it was just from D, but she wanted Peter busy again.

He wasn't put off. "I hear Boston is fine this time of year. I suppose this heat is a shocker for you."

Lance Fuller never lost his smile. "I haven't been up there this summer. I'm from New York."

"Well, that explains everything."

Lance Fuller cocked his head, amused, then turned to Ruth Ann. "Mrs. Warren asked me to invite you to the dinner at 6:30."

The idea of dinner with the affluent citizens of Dickens didn't sit well with her. It was a lion's den. But she remembered Matthew's request to uncover what she could of the mayor's dealings. An invitation to his home for dinner…would she have a better opportunity?

These were the thoughts fixed foremost in Ruth Ann's mind and not the hopeful look of Lance Fuller when she answered. "Please thank her for the invitation. I will be prompt."

"Wonderful. If it's all right, I'll come by and escort you over."

Ruth Ann's stomach churned. Peter inserted his shoulder at her chin. "I'll see she's there on time."

Her apprehension turned to indignation at her cousin's high and mighty tone. She put her hand on his shoulder and squeezed until he gritted his teeth.

She smiled. "Thank you, Mr. Fuller. I will see you this evening."

The last sour notes of the choir rang out, followed by Beulah's applause and dismissal. The children stampeded through the front door, hollering farewells to the new teacher.

He waved and leaned toward Ruth Ann confidentially. "It's Lance. Mr. Fuller is how one addressed my father."

With that gracious smile, he bid them all good day and donned his derby hat on the way out.

Beulah came over to Ruth Ann and Peter. "Well, I would say you did a fine job of welcoming the teacher, my friend.

Mrs. Warren must be pleased."

Ruth Ann mustered an indifferent smile in response to Beulah's teasing and Peter's scowl. "All in a day's work."

At least she hoped that was all.

CHAPTER FOUR

"WHO WILL BE THERE?"

Ruth Ann sat at the small oak vanity while she worked on her coiffure and tried to answer her mother's questions about the evening. Della was behind her, standing on a stool to hang the washed curtain over the attic bedroom window.

Ruth Ann murmured between the pins in her mouth, "Likely the Andersons, the Maxwells…"

From the frown on Della's face that reflected in the mirror, Ruth Ann knew she hadn't understood a word. But Ruth Ann didn't want to be too clear or she'd be forced to admit even Sheriff Banny might be at the dinner. The mayor was scheming something and she'd have to play along to find out what it was.

When her hair tumbled from the top of her head again, Ruth Ann dropped her hands with an irritated sigh. She'd been trying to get it in a new style like Beulah had shown her in the *Ladies Home Journal*, but it wasn't working. According to the ad: *The Newport knot, when properly made, is very soft and graceful.* Beulah had offered to help fix her up for the evening, but Mr. Levitt wasn't feeling well when the shop closed. Beulah went home with him. Matthew hadn't returned yet, and Ruth

Ann felt abandoned in her mission.

Della fluffed the curtain and stepped off the stool. She turned with a chuckle. "Pretty Choctaw girl. All want you at their dinner table with young men."

Ruth Ann's cheeks warmed. "Not you too, Mama. This is strictly business. I'm a reporter and was invited for the same reason as Mr. Maxwell."

Della kept chuckling and Ruth Ann had to smile at that comparison between her and the editor of their rival newspaper. "All right, maybe not the exact same reason, but I have a chance to expose whatever the mayor is up to by winning Mrs. Warren's confidence."

Della took the hairpins from her and tucked them in her pocket. She went to work on the long, black locks with brown undertones. "Be careful that's all you win."

Ruth Ann fidgeted with the combs on the vanity. The shell or the silver? She hadn't decided which to match with her brown dress. She'd chosen this outfit as her most businesslike one.

"I'm trying, Mama. Trying to please everyone, but do what's right."

Della heated the hair iron over the lamp, then wrapped a thin strip of hair around the jaw of the tongs. Ruth Ann closed her eyes. So much trouble for a hairdo. She was exhausted from the effort.

Her mother worked patiently. "Just please God. That takes care of everything."

Minutes later, Ruth Ann felt a final tug on her hair. A hand on each side of her head brought her face up and her eyes opened to meet her mother's in the mirror. Ruth Ann's hair was in a perfect Newport knot with bangs curled back from her oval face, shell comb in place. Just like in the magazine. But it was the care in her mama's eyes that shone with the true beauty. She took Della's hand and nestled her cheek in it.

"*Yakoke*, Mama."

The tender moment was broken too soon by a knock on

the front door. Ruth Ann scrambled to her feet, trying to hold her head carefully while Della tugged and adjusted her sleeves and skirt. The knock sounded again. Why hadn't Peter answered it? He'd stationed himself in the front room, ready to pounce on her escort.

She sighed, picked up her reticule, and looked at her mother. Della chuckled and patted her arm. "Patience. Peter is learning too."

Learning at Ruth Ann's expense. Not answering the door right away might not agitate Mr. Fuller, but it agitated her. Still, Ruth Ann tucked her mother's words in her heart and descended the stairs that ended next to the stove in the kitchen. From there, she could see Peter sauntering to the door as a third knock sounded. She took a moment to straighten her brown jacket and glance up at Della on the stairs behind her to receive a nod of approval.

Ruth Ann moved through the kitchen and into the front room while Peter let Lance Fuller in. The teacher had changed from his traveling clothes, opting for a simple suit of gray, his hazy sky eyes bright like when he'd disembarked from the train that morning.

He nodded to her. "A pleasure to see you again, Miss Ruth Ann. You look lovely this evening."

Before things could shift from business to personal, Ruth Ann turned and introduced him. "Mrs. Della Teller, my mother. And you remember my cousin, Peter?"

Peter responded by lifting his hat from the rack and motioning at the open door. "We'd best be going. Getting on suppertime and Aunt Della has mine waiting already."

Lance Fuller glanced between them, perhaps amused, but Ruth Ann held herself steady. "My cousin will see us to the Warrens and home again."

He nodded and offered his arm, but she hesitated and turned back to give her mother a quick hug and kiss. Then she took a deep breath and settled her hand on the offered arm—lightly. Peter remained rigid by the door, his eyes on Lance Fuller.

This didn't appear to bother the young man, who began a conversation once they were on the porch. "I've heard a great deal about your brother, Matthew. When does he get back in town? I'm anxious to meet him."

Ruth Ann thought of the reports he might have heard from Mayor Warren and Mr. Maxwell. It was unlikely they had said anything favorable. The leading men of Dickens despised everything Matthew stood for.

But before she could respond, Peter came to her other side and answered. "He'll be home tomorrow, though I wonder why you'd want to meet Matt after the things your friend must have said."

Ruth Ann started to reprimand her cousin, but stopped. She would let Lance Fuller answer for himself. That might tell her more about him than a whole evening in his company.

Instead of becoming defensive, he gave a genuine laugh. "The rumors make me want to meet him all the more. Anyone who can stand up to my…to the mayor, I'd like to shake his hand."

Ruth Ann noted the bump in his reply and tucked it away in her thoughts. "My brother stands for truth. That's why he started the *Choctaw Tribune*, and what makes him unpopular with a great many people."

Without warning, images of the confrontation at Daniel Springs overcame Ruth Ann and she caught her breath. Matthew had nearly been killed right in front of her.

It was a moment before she realized she'd halted and closed her eyes. When she opened them, the concerned face of Lance Fuller came into view, and on her left, she saw the uncertain, boyish look of Peter.

She chuckled to ease her tense muscles. "I'm sorry. Matthew and I had a close brush with death not long ago over tribal politics."

"I'd like to hear about it sometime." Lance Fuller resumed his place next to her, nearer this time, Ruth Ann was sure. She leaned closer to Peter. The Warren's stately home loomed ahead.

♦ ♦ ♦

"Such a joy to have you this evening, my dear."

Mrs. Warren embraced Ruth Ann at the door like she was a long-lost daughter. Ruth Ann greeted the hostess the best she could for all the nerves tingling through her body. Before entering the front hall, she bid Peter *chi pisa la chike* with him making a strict promise he would return for her soon.

Inside, the home was indeed stately for a dwelling in Indian Territory in 1893. It seemed the Warrens wanted to rival the fine homes south of the Red River in Paris, Texas. While their home was far from a mansion like the Barneses and other Choctaw families had built, it still spoke of prosperity and optimism in the growing civilization crowded by whites.

No sounds of conversation came from the parlor to Ruth Ann's left. "Am I early?"

Mrs. Warren stiffened. "Not at all, my dear." She motioned toward the parlor. "We decided not to overwhelm poor Lance with too many dinner guests. Besides, you two hardly had a chance to get acquainted."

Heat came up Ruth Ann's neck, and she smiled weakly.

The parlor was lit by wall sconces and a pair of cranberry oil lamps set on each side of the matching sofa with its cloth buttons. Across from the sofa sat two mustard colored armchairs with mahogany wood trim. The floor was carpeted and a carved mantel graced the fireplace that held a low fire to ward off the chill of the evening. The night had the feel of autumn to it.

But there was another kind of chill in the air. Mayor Warren stood by the fireplace with one arm propped against the mantel as though posing for a photograph. His suit and lifted chin would have made him quite dignified, but Ruth Ann had seen him in his harsher moods.

Where was the other company? Why was she singled out? It had to be the *Choctaw Tribune*. Mayor Warren wanted to flatter her to get something. It was a devilish assumption, but

Ruth Ann had experiences upon which to base her judgment.

The mayor lowered himself from his elevated position and turned to face her, thumbs hooked in his vest pockets. "Good evening, Miss Teller." The polite words sounded forced.

Ruth Ann nodded. "Good evening, sir."

She allowed awkward silence to fall. It wasn't her place to make someone comfortable in their own home.

Surprisingly, Mrs. Warren came to the rescue. "Well, isn't this fine, Thaddeus? Two lovely young people in our home under such good circumstances."

She went to a tray set on the low tea table in front of the sofa. "A teacher for the first school here in Dickens, and the local newspaper in support. Who knows what we'll have next? Oh yes, the children's choir. Lance says it's coming along well, isn't it, Ruth Ann?"

Ruth Ann accepted the teacup and the seat offered to her, wondering how she'd make it through dinner. Lance Fuller sat in the other armchair, looking at ease in his benefactor's home. The aroma of roast and potatoes filled the house and she heard sounds of kitchen work. Who prepared meals in the Warren home? She'd learn a great deal about the leading citizens this night, if she didn't get sick before dinner was served.

She took a sip of tea while she tried to remember where the conversation was. "Beulah—Miss Levitt—is an excellent teacher, and the children are loyal to her. I think the choir will do well." She shifted and raised her teacup, using it as a buffer between her and the mayor as she addressed him. "I understand you are fully funding the school and…"

Ruth Ann had meant to thank him, to say how kind it was of him, but she faltered. Dark shadows edged around the mayor's eyes. He tilted his head forward and frowned. Knowing she might spill the tea with her trembling hand, she slowly lowered the cup onto the saucer.

Thumbs still hooked in his vest that barely buttoned over his paunch, the mayor resumed a pompous air. "I know what kind of vicious hogwash your brother will write about the school. Well, there's not a thing he can do about it or my town. Whites—or intruders as your kind likes to call us—are here to stay. No newspaper or arrogance or legalities can run us out."

Mrs. Warren gasped. "Thaddeus!"

Lance Fuller frowned and rattled his teacup back onto the tray. "Really, sir."

Ruth Ann clanked her teacup and saucer on the table and rose. She met the mayor's stormy gray eyes, noting the pride in them. "I can't think of anything more vicious than what Will Hocks told us about the treatment of a certain Choctaw woman near Wilburton in 1879."

The darkness vanished from Mayor Warren's face and his skin paled three shades. His eyes bugged like a dying fish on a riverbank, mouth gaping. Then his face reddened, blooming up from his neck. When it reached his eyes, they turned red as well.

Ruth Ann covered her mouth. How could she have been so foolish! In a few words, she'd ruined Matthew's investigation.

She took a step back. Her backside toppled a high round table by her chair, and whatever had been on it rolled across the carpeted floor. She didn't dare pause to see the mess.

Ruth Ann nodded to Mrs. Warren, who had jumped to her feet, but for once was speechless. "Pardon me, ma'am. I'll be going now."

Her words sounded pathetic, unsophisticated. But it didn't matter. There was no use pretending anything. She rushed from the parlor to the front hall where she retrieved her reticule and fumbled with the door handle.

She bolted through the door and tried to pull it closed. It was stopped by another hand. She caught a glimpse of Lance Fuller's face before she hurried across the porch in the coming darkness.

Whatever chance Ruth Ann had of getting information for Matthew was gone in one horrible outburst. Whatever

Lance Fuller's reason for following her could only make things worse.

Ruth Ann scurried down the steps, him right behind her. She was too embarrassed to look back, uncertain which was worse—her gaff or her rudeness at walking out before dinner. Tears wouldn't be long in coming. The last thing she needed was a witness.

When Lance Fuller followed her to the empty Main Street, she halted and kept her head down. "Please. I just want to go home."

"I just want to see you get there."

She raised her head. "Thank you, but I know the way."

"Ruth Ann." He stepped closer and took her elbow. "I don't blame you for being upset. I've known…I've known Mayor Warren a long time and he's not the most gracious man. I hope my association with him hasn't damaged my reputation in your eyes."

Ruth Ann hesitated before slowly pulling her arm from his hold. He dropped his hand. She tried to think of something godly or even philosophical to say, but couldn't. "Good evening, Mr. Fuller."

Much to her relief, he didn't follow her, and Ruth Ann made her way down the dark yet familiar Main Street of Dickens.

The mayor's house was on the crossroad from Main and Ruth Ann was thankful it wasn't more than three blocks from her own home near the railroad tracks.

But when she passed the hotel, she sensed another presence before someone leaped from the shadows at her.

A scream lodged in Ruth Ann's throat before she recognized Peter's shadowed face. She clenched her reticule with both hands to keep from striking him. "Peter Abraham Frazier! How dare you frighten me like that!"

Peter remained serious, something she hadn't expected. "You didn't think I was going to leave you all alone with them, did you? Didn't figure you'd last a whole evening with those vultures."

Ruth Ann pushed past him and strode down the dirt road toward home. "Don't be cynical."

But she had no explanation for her early departure. She was humiliated, a complete failure. She'd have to confess to Matthew, but Peter couldn't begin to grasp the complexities of social structure outside of their own people. Any more than she could.

Feeling like a traitor, Ruth Ann lifted her skirts and broke into a run.

◆ ◆ ◆

Ruth Ann opened the telegraph office early the next morning. Beulah was early as well. She bustled in and plopped down across the desk from Ruth Ann in the tiny room with its window shelf ready to open for customers.

"Well, do tell!" Beulah brought her voice down when Ruth Ann winced. "My dear Ruth, are you ill?"

Ruth Ann dipped her head and scribbled notes for her next article. She couldn't concentrate on it. "I made a fool of myself."

She rubbed the heels of her hands against her eyes. She didn't want to tell Beulah too much that would compromise the investigation—again—so she simply said, "It was terrible. The mayor and I got into a spat before dinner and I left in such a rush I knocked over a stand. Now I have to apologize to Mrs. Warren for my rudeness. Mr. Fuller too, I suppose."

She stole a look at Beulah's sympathetic head shake. "You wouldn't feel up to delivering a batch of cookies with me, would you?"

The head shake continued. "Dear friend, there are some things you must face alone." The shaking stopped and Beulah winked. "This, however, is not one of them."

Ruth Ann sighed in relief, but before the two could begin plotting the day, the sounder went off with a message. She raised her eyebrows as she jotted it down, her mouth opening in wonder.

"What is it, Ruth?"

"Special delivery. Shortest I've ever made." She handed the message to her friend and held her breath.

Beulah took it and cocked her head. "To Beulah Levitt: Greetings to you and your father from the Zadok family in Chicago." She gasped and read faster. "A letter is forthcoming. You must visit and see the World's Fair before it ends. Details to come. Edith Zadok."

Before Beulah finished, her voice took on a high-pitched tone that ended in a squeal. "Ruth! Our old friends from Kansas! We lost touch with so many…"

She lowered the telegram and grinned. "The Zadoks in Chicago…and the World's Fair! You must go with us, Ruth. Ah, so many plans to make! Please send Edith a reply. I must tell my father."

Beulah popped up and disappeared through the door leading into the print and repair shop. Mr. Levitt would be working at his back bench. Ruth Ann listened to Beulah's excited chatter and shook her head with a smile. She sent a confirmation to Edith Zadok, then received the next incoming message.

Hello there, my little R.A.! Going to Chicago, are we?

She answered the message from D, the operator twenty-two miles up the line. They enjoyed chatting over the wire when things were slow.

Not me, though I sincerely hope Beulah and her father can make the trip.

I went to a world's fair once. Don't miss it if you can help it.

Maybe someday. Tell about your experience.

For the next few minutes, D regaled Ruth Ann with stories of the Centennial International Exhibition of 1876 in Philadelphia. She was so engrossed she forgot about anything important, until the bell over the front door jingled.

A moment later, Matthew appeared in the doorway of the telegraph office.

CHAPTER FIVE

IT WAS APPARENT MATTHEW HAD stopped at home this morning. With fresh clothes and a clean shave, he looked the part of a serious newspaper publisher. Except for his expression. It was relaxed, boyish. He stuck his hands in his back pockets and leaned against the doorframe. He looked every bit like her big brother, dark hair falling across his forehead.

"It'll be all right."

Embarrassed, Ruth Ann stood and faced the floor. Their mother or Peter must have told him what happened. Likely the latter. The rascal had probably spilled everything before leaving for the farm. She hadn't seen Peter that morning, but he must have seen Matthew.

"I'm sorry. Really."

"For what?" There was tenderness in Matthew's voice. Nothing hostile.

Ruth Ann muttered, "For what I did."

Matthew crossed the distance to her. "Whatever it was, it'll be all right."

She raised her eyes to his innocent smile. "You really don't know?"

"It doesn't matter, Annie. I knew the moment I walked in something must have happened, but we'll take it one problem at a time like always. So, what is it now?"

With a nervous chuckle, Ruth Ann took a step away from Matthew and opened the window of the telegraph office. It didn't alleviate the stuffiness, but at least she wasn't so close to him. Matthew crossed his arms and cocked his head, waiting patiently as always.

"Oh, well, I had a dinner invitation from the Warrens and thought it was a large gathering to get acquainted with the new teacher, but it turned out to only be me, and the mayor and I exchanged some unpleasant words, mine including the name of a certain man who told us about an incident in Wilburton in '79…"

Matthew dropped his crossed arms. "You didn't."

Ruth Ann dragged her fingers along the shelf by the window and picked at splintered pieces. She peeked at Matthew's shocked expression.

He rubbed his hands together as if to keep from hitting something. "Well."

That one word sliced her heart. The truth hung between them: She couldn't be trusted with newspaper business. Not something this serious. Not only had she failed to gain Mrs. Warren's confidence and learn anything useful about the new teacher, she had given away Matthew's hand. Now the mayor knew they were after the truth. What would he do to stop them?

The magnitude of what she'd done overcame her. She feared she would vomit, but thankfully, there was nothing in her stomach.

Brisk footsteps from the main shop brought Ruth Ann's attention to the doorway. Beulah appeared with a quick hello to Matthew before turning to her.

"I am sorry, but I must take my father home. The exciting news from the Zadoks overwhelmed him with joy. He says he is fine, but I want him in bed with a cool compress. I will not be able to go with you on your errand this morning."

Beulah looked truly sympathetic. Ruth Ann waved her friend away. Mr. Levitt's condition was still fragile after his heart failure at the lynching last spring. He'd shown his fortitude since then, but it came in small doses. "Tell your father to rest."

Matthew looked at nothing and questioned absently, "Exciting news?"

Beulah must have heard him. "Oh!" She spun back. "Papa will not be able to make such a trip in the near future. You must go with me, Ruth. And you, Matthew. We must have an escort." She nodded resolutely before leaving.

The sounder broke the silence, but it was for a station down the line. Matthew turned back to Ruth Ann, a reporter's look in his eyes. "You said you were the only one invited to dinner?"

And with that, Ruth Ann knew her blunder was forgiven. She wanted to cry.

Matthew pulled a small tablet from his back pocket and flipped through the pages. "Why would you be the only one…"

He jerked his head up and stared at her.

Ruth Ann felt like a specimen under a scientist's microscope. "I—I don't know. Mrs. Warren said something about getting acquainted…"

"Mama told me Lance Fuller was there, that I should talk to you about what happened. What happened?"

Her mother wasn't referring to her blunder, the only thing she'd thought about. Well, almost. The other was too personal. It had nothing to do with newspaper business, but Matthew acted like it did.

Ruth Ann shrugged and dropped into the chair by the table that held the sounder. "Nothing happened. He seems like a pleasant young man, but I learned nothing useful. I'm working on the article about his arrival now."

It lay in front of her, scant looking. Ruth Ann resisted the urge to cover it. She should have been able to fill half a page with facts about the new teacher's arrival. But she only had two short sentences.

"Did Fuller walk you home?"

That was one victory at least. "He wanted to, but I told him no."

Matthew moved toward the window shelf and leaned against the wall. He rubbed the back of his neck. "Where does Beulah want us to go?"

Ruth Ann laughed a little. The money and time involved made such a trip silly to consider. "To visit her Jewish friends in Chicago, and see the World's Fair."

"Interesting." Matthew traced a dusty line down the window. "Buffalo Bill's Wild West Show is there, camped right outside the fair. He's one of the few white men the Lakota Chief Sitting Bull trusted. So they say."

Something was working in Matthew's brain. But the sounder interrupted with a message for their station.

Ruth Ann took it and the knot in her stomach tightened. "Of all things." She sighed, then added before he had to ask, "It's for Mrs. Warren."

Matthew pushed away from the window with his shoulder. "I'll take it to her."

She shook her head. "No. I need to go and apologize for leaving so abruptly. And for knocking over the side table..."

Matthew raised an eyebrow as though wondering what all she hadn't told him yet. "Sounds like you'll need a peace offering. Better see if the bread Mama was baking is ready."

◆ ◆ ◆

It was a shorter trek than normal for Ruth Ann. Instead of going down Main Street and turning right onto the crossroad where the Warren home lay, she took a route that led her clear of Main Street. She didn't want anyone to see her going to the Warren home with a basket of bread on her arm and a red face. Out the back door of the Teller home, she cut through the grass behind the false front buildings on the south side of the booming town of Dickens and picked her way through the overgrowth. She scolded herself for being a coward and hoped the price to pay wasn't a skirt full of chiggers.

But Ruth Ann was soon on the side road where the Warrens had built their home. She mounted the steps cautiously. The house seemed to watch her every move, judging her worthiness. She wished she'd accepted her mother's offer to accompany her, or waited until Beulah could come. But this was her task.

Ruth Ann tapped on the door, then waited without fidgeting until it opened. But it wasn't Mrs. Warren who greeted her. The dark face of Mabel appeared and Ruth Ann relaxed. Mabel was a maid and cook at the hotel. She was a cheerful woman, even though she had to work for the arrogant Sheriff Banny, who owned the hotel.

At least Ruth Ann discovered whose meal she'd missed out on the night before. She returned the smile of the tender looking older woman who greeted her with exuberance. "Well, come on in here, Miss Ruth Ann Teller. Weren't expectin' you, but it good to see your sweet face. You go on in the parlor, I'll see if I can fetch Mrs. Warren."

"Thank you, Mabel."

There were no other sounds in the house. The parlor looked undisturbed by Ruth Ann's presence the night before. The high round table by the armchair was set upright with a doily and flower vase with a single bud gracing its center.

Ruth Ann sat in the armchair and remained still to avoid disrupting the perfect order in the room. Instead of placing the basket on the floor, she set it in her lap and absently ran her fingers around the sturdy piece of art. She had dyed the stripped outer skins of cane and wove them into a practical yet attractive basket as the Grandmother had taught her. Her daddy had called it art. He always exaggerated when praising her. How she missed that.

It was Ruth Ann's mother and the Grandmother who had taught her the essentials of being a young woman, including respect for another's home. Failing to do so in this home summoned an ill feeling in her stomach as she waited.

And waited. And waited. The only sound was a clock ticking on the mantel.

Tick-tock. Tick-tock.

Time ticked into a quarter of an hour, then twenty minutes. Finally, she heard steps in the back of the house and Mrs. Warren appeared in the doorway.

The woman held herself with a regal air, wrapped in a light robe with her hair pinned tight at the base of her head. But she must have been sleeping hard. Red marks lined one side of her face, perhaps from an embroidered pillow she'd fallen asleep on. Dimness in a room with drawn curtains must have prevented Mrs. Warren from seeing the redness. "Well, what do you have to say for yourself?"

Ruth Ann averted her eyes from the marks, embarrassed for the woman. She stood, set the basket in the armchair, and lifted the loaf of bread wrapped in a cloth. She kept her eyes down to keep from staring at the indentations in Mrs. Warren's cheek. "I'm sorry, ma'am. It was rude of me to run out. I hope you'll accept my apology and this as a gesture of my sincerity."

When Mrs. Warren didn't move from her rigid position to accept the offered loaf, Ruth Ann set it on the low tea table between the armchairs and the sofa. From this new angle she noticed a porcelain figurine beneath the sofa.

"Oh." Ruth Ann dropped to her knees and fished it out.

Mrs. Warren huffed. "Such a heathen."

It was harder to scramble up than Ruth Ann thought it would be, but she managed, and settled the figurine on the low table.

Mrs. Warren gasped, strode forward and scooped up the white dressed figurine with a pink sash painted around her waist. Soft pink cheeks highlighted the expression of an innocent young lady.

"Why…why, this has been missing since…" Mrs. Warren stiffened but not as much as before. "It…it must have been on the table you knocked over…"

Her voice weakened and she met Ruth Ann's eyes, truly met them as though seeing her as an equal. "It went missing a week ago, after we entertained several guests. I had taken it from the mantel to show someone and set it on the tea table. It must have gotten knocked off...I couldn't believe someone would have *stolen* from us..."

She turned and lowered herself onto the sofa. It groaned. Uncertain what to do, Ruth Ann settled beside her and waited.

Mrs. Warren held the figurine in two hands, though it was small enough to fit in her palm. She turned it over, tracing the porcelain sash, the cheeks, the flared skirt. "My mother gave this to me for my twelfth birthday. It's the only thing I have from her."

The deep sadness left Ruth Ann with nothing to say. And that seemed right. She didn't move, didn't blink. Time was an element of its own, used by God for many things—respect, understanding, healing. Whichever was taking place now, she would wait to find out.

Tick-tock. Tick-tock.

Mrs. Warren sank deep into the sofa cushions and exhaled. She seemed smaller, not the plump woman who acted sophisticated in spite of her topsy-turvy ways. The red marks on her face had faded to pink lines.

Finally, she lifted her gaze to Ruth Ann. "You and your mother are very close, aren't you?"

Ruth Ann nodded. It wasn't the time for her to speak.

"I always wanted to be close to my mother. But my...but her *husband* was always between us." Mrs. Warren lifted her chin. She was closing the door on personal feelings.

But before she closed off, Ruth Ann leaned forward. "I'm sorry. Has your mother passed? My father was killed almost five years ago. I don't believe I'll ever stop missing him."

Mrs. Warren stirred and dropped her gaze. "Mother has been gone since I was younger than you."

Her thumb hovered over the face of the porcelain lady as though she wanted to stroke it, but was afraid of destroying its frail existence. "You never stop missing them. You only wish for better memories."

In those words, Ruth Ann absorbed a depth of hurt she never would have imagined the boisterous Mrs. Warren to harbor. In all her rudeness, this was someone suffering in silent anguish and unspent grief.

She reached out a hand and covered Mrs. Warren's that held the figurine. "You have one good memory to hold on to. And maybe...maybe I could help you remember more."

Ruth Ann bit her lower lip. What was she offering? To befriend a woman who thought she was a heathen Indian?

But Mrs. Warren didn't pull away. She laughed softly, the sound filled with unshed tears. "If only there were enough good memories to overshadow the bad."

There was a rustling sound at the parlor doorway and Ruth Ann looked up to see the flare of a worn skirt. A voice that tried to sound distant called, "Want I should bring in the tea tray, Mrs. Warren?"

Snapped back from her grievous thoughts, Mrs. Warren bristled and pulled away. "That won't be necessary, Mabel."

She stood, strode to the mantel and set the lady with the pink sash in place as though it were a minor thing. She peered down her nose at Ruth Ann. "Your apology is accepted. Now run along home. I'm sure your mother is waiting for you."

Despite her cool words, the depth of Mrs. Warren's pain was no longer hidden from Ruth Ann. She accepted the dismissal with a nod. When she picked up her basket, she spied the telegram inside. She laid it on the low table. The telegram was from Mrs. Warren's sister in St. Louis, a notice of a linen sale. "Good day, Mrs. Warren."

"Mabel will see you out."

Ruth Ann's last glance back showed the pink lines on Mrs. Warren's cheeks had faded. But the marks were still there.

◆ ◆ ◆

Despite Ruth Ann's renewed efforts to befriend Mrs.

Warren, the woman remained aloof. At church, she didn't have any requests for the school opening the next day.

Lance Fuller did.

The Teller family called *chi pisa la chike* to relatives who had come in from Uncle Preston's farm. Then Ruth Ann turned to repack the large picnic basket from the meal that had followed the service. From the corner of her eye, she saw the new teacher coming toward them.

Lance Fuller had his gracious look when he nodded to Della. "Good to see you, Mrs. Teller. Would you be available to see about a shirt I need mended? It's for social gatherings. Thaddeus said I can expect events in the near future."

Though he spoke to her mother, Ruth Ann felt his attention on her. Matthew moved from his conversation with Pastor Rand and stepped toward them.

Della nodded and lifted the blanket from the grass. She gave it a hearty shake. "Bring it tomorrow. I will see what I can do."

Lance Fuller snagged one end of the blanket and helped fold it. Della thanked him as Matthew came to her side. He nodded to the teacher. "I'm Matthew Teller. How was your first week in Dickens?"

"Pleasant." There was a smile in his voice and Ruth Ann's cheeks burned. "The people are remarkable, not at all what I expected on the frontier. I've met several of the children, thanks to your sister. By the way…"

He sidestepped Matthew to put himself closer to Ruth Ann. "Miss Teller, could I impose on you to come by the school in the morning? The children adore you, and it would help to have you introduce me. Would that be convenient?"

Before Ruth Ann could think, Matthew cut in. "I have an important assignment in the morning for Ruth Ann."

He glanced at her, and she frowned. He'd used her full name, and Ruth Ann couldn't determine what that meant. Was he worried she'd give away more secrets? She didn't have any. Matthew hadn't shared his latest findings from his trip, and though they'd been busy, she suspected her loose tongue was the reason.

Matthew studied her a moment then turned back to Lance Fuller. "If she's willing, though, I can hold the work." He nodded at her. "But I'll need you in the office straight afterwards."

Ruth Ann sighed. Matthew would keep a close eye on her awhile. He had a right. She'd made a blunder only time would eradicate. Hopefully, the story about the mayor's schemes would still come out even though he knew their plans. Or rather, Matthew's plans now.

Lance Fuller waited expectantly and she nodded without meeting his eyes. "I suppose I could...I mean, I'd be happy to." *I wish you'd asked Beulah instead.* "I'm sure the children will be excited." *I hope they come.*

He looked relieved and Ruth Ann wondered if he was nervous. Surely not. Mrs. Warren had extolled his credentials. He was well-educated and had taught at one of the finest boarding schools in New York.

Yet when Ruth Ann bid him good day, she detected a definite unease. Hopefully he'd get past whatever it was. Those children needed a strong and steady hand.

CHAPTER SIX

IT WAS A LONG HAUL across the Red River from Texas using Hawkins Ferry. The ferry chugged slowly toward the Choctaw Nation side of the river. The twenty minute ride was the longest of Frank Bean's short career as a whiskey runner with this gang.

The men watched the woods to see if Lighthorsemen— the Indian police—waited in the shadows. Minutes passed slow like molasses dripping. Frank didn't take any comfort that four other men rode this run. Of the five gang members, none were worth the bullets it would take to kill them. Two of the men were already as drunk as boiled owls.

The other two Frank might could count on—Cub Wassom and Lester Cotten. Lester had a few drinks in him, but still looked like he could shoot straight. And there was Cub Wassom—drunk or sober, Frank had never seen a man as mean or as fast with a gun. Frank never wanted to be on Cub Wassom's wrong side, though he wondered if it was any better on the man's right side. He was a young cuss, but he dominated the others like a wild stallion. It was easy to peg Cub as a mixed-blood Indian—Choctaw—by his dark skin and long hair which he let hang loose down his back.

Frank—the only white man—had been with the gang two months running whiskey. They occasionally found a lone traveler to relieve of valuable property. Nothing too dangerous, but Frank had seen young Cub Wassom put three men in their graves during that time. One had been a fellow gang member.

Lester Cotten was the only one who could calm their leader when things got heated. He wasn't much older than Cub, but he had an easy personality as if not many things— right or wrong—bothered him. He was taller than Cub and Frank, making them form an arch if anyone saw them from the riverbank.

Frank had a feeling Cub and Lester had been through thick scrapes together. They didn't talk much, but there was a kinship between them. Lester could say more to Cub than any man without getting his head blown off. Like now.

Cub Wassom stood rigid by his big paint pony's head, holding the reins loose in his hands and watching the woods. Lester swayed on his feet and jabbed an elbow at him. "What say we head north toward Wilburton next?"

Cub Wassom's lip curled up. "Don't need that Dan Holder anymore, Lester. He's turned old and yellow, and besides, we're doing just fine on our own. If we ride any special direction, it'll be east, deep into Choctaw Nation."

The ferry dipped in the current and Frank's knees dipped with it. He sank his fingers in his horse's mane and glanced at his partners. He hoped Lester wouldn't rile Cub. He had a feeling the man was key to them making it out of this run alive.

Lester Cotten snorted. "You mean over to Dickens and your gal and boy."

Frank glanced toward the woods and swallowed. A disturbance brought his attention back to the two men. Cub Wassom had dropped his reins and grabbed Lester by the collar. He gave him a shake.

"You bet. No one to keep me from them now!"

Lester batted Cub's arm, but the outlaw didn't let go. "Touchy, aren't you? But I got no desire to be anywhere near the Teller family. I had enough of that back when."

Cub snorted and released Lester. "Then why you want to go crawlin' back to Dan Holder? I thought you was done up with him after what he did to your buddy."

Frank wondered what they were talking about but didn't ask. He wasn't that big of a fool.

Lester pulled away and grabbed a crock jug tied to his saddle. The run had been a good one. Each man's saddle was loaded with full jugs, though if the ferry ride lasted much longer, the other two men would have all the whiskey downed. The two drunks were near the back of the ferry, still mounted on their horses but swaying like they might topple into the river. Frank knew Cub would let them drown out of sheer cussedness. Likely Lester, too. And Frank? He wanted to be on the winning side.

After a long drink, Lester offered the whiskey to Cub, who scowled. Lester shrugged and shoved the jug at Frank, who stood on his other side. "Here, this will brace you for the run. You won't believe what you see anyway when Cub starts pumping off that Winchester."

Frank took the jug, uncertain whether to drink to please Lester, or not drink to keep from Cub Wassom's judgment. He had seen the man serve out deadly sentences on men who riled him. Frank hadn't wanted to throw in lots with men as hardened as these two, but the money was worth it. At forty years old, Frank had grown tired of trying to earn a living with an honest life. But he wasn't ready to die just yet.

Cub paid no attention to him. He nodded toward the woods. "Mount up and get ready to ride…"

"Like the devil is on your tail," Lester finished, taking the jug again for a final swig before tying it tight on his saddle. He mounted. Cub and Frank mounted at the same time, never taking their gazes off the woods. Frank wondered what it meant to die. He should have taken that drink.

Cub glanced at Lester. "Maybe we will make that run north. Things are kinda hot down here."

Lester nodded, though he watched the woods. He was as sober looking as Frank had ever seen him. Lester withdrew his Winchester from his scabbard. Cub did the same. Frank did too, taking a moment to look back at the other riders. They didn't realize the potential mortal danger coming with the fast approaching bank.

Before the ferry landed, Cub Wassom gave a wild yell and spurred his big paint off the side. The horse thrashed through the water. Lester whooped and followed. Frank made the leap behind him. The other two men yelled curses. But Frank ignored everything except staying as close to Cub and Lester as possible. They charged toward the woods at the top of the bluff.

The other two lashed their horses to chase them down, but to Frank's surprise, Cub and Lester pulled up short of the bluff. The other two charged up it.

From the woods, three men galloped out, firing six-shooters. The drunk men shouted, "Choctaw Lighthorse!"

Lester turned his horse in a circle and grumbled, "What'd you expect, a tea party?" He spurred his horse up the other side of the bluff and disappeared into the trees.

Frank's horse reared and he flipped off the backend and landed hard. His horse galloped after Lester. Frank picked up his rifle and looked up to see one of the Lighthorsemen aiming at him.

He ducked but the next shots came from behind him. Cub Wassom rode up to Frank while firing at the Lighthorsemen. He released his trigger grip to offer a hand to Frank.

He gripped Cub Wassom's wrist and hoisted himself up behind him on the big paint pony. Cub fired two more shots before spurring his horse up the bluff. Frank looked back through the choking gun smoke to see two Choctaw Lighthorsemen staggering around the dead whiskey runners and their horses. The lawmen were injured, though still on their feet. But the third lay flat out. Cub's aim had been deadly.

That was all Frank saw before trees blocked his view. He turned his attention to hanging tight to Cub Wassom.

CHAPTER SEVEN

THOUGH EARLY MORNING, THE temperature had turned back warm. High enough to raise a sweat on Ruth Ann's upper lip as she trekked to the church. She had a civic duty to perform.

Civic duties had interfered with her work at the telegraph and newspaper lately, but Ruth Ann was determined not to fall behind. She stayed up later each night to read the Eastern newspapers Matthew subscribed to, and got up earlier each morning to tend the animals and household duties before hurrying off to face the mounting work at the *Choctaw Tribune*. Now, she had another civic duty to fill her morning—introducing the new teacher to his pupils.

Ruth Ann nodded in greeting to those she passed on the boardwalk. Most offered a polite nod in return, but more than once she was ignored. Folks still held prejudices against a female being in a man's world of reporting on political and criminal stories. Maybe someday that would change. At least she didn't have rotted fruit hurled at her like women in her position twenty years ago.

The boardwalk ended and she drifted onto the dirt road to avoid the high grass surrounding the church building. The church stood aways past the last building in Dickens in a field off the road. A dirt path took her to the steps. She mounted them, but hesitated at the open doors. At the front of the room, Lance Fuller shuffled through books and papers.

Ruth Ann took a moment to turn and stare back at Dickens, a town so young, yet with an old soul. It had seen its share of tragedies and triumphs, sadness and joy. She had been in the middle of them. And that connected her to every building and every person in the town, whether they had been there from the beginning or not.

From the church porch, she could see the Levitts' small house. How much she'd endured alongside the Jewish father and daughter! Their friendship had withstood fires, shootouts, lynchings, prejudices. But Beulah had shocked Ruth Ann with her sharp criticism of blacks when Ruth Ann was reporting on the lynchings. Though the two young women had held onto their friendship, the divide was still there and Ruth Ann wondered when it would fester again.

Lined up even with the side of the church but across the field was the backside of the *Choctaw Tribune* and Levitt Repair Shop. They would already be open for the day: Matthew at his desk, Peter at the telegraph, Mr. Levitt on his workbench, and Beulah darting from one project to the next. She was busier than ever with choir rehearsals and private students and even repair jobs. She tried to ease the burden on her still recovering father. Despite their differences, they made a remarkable team.

But Beulah was still headstrong and independent. She had sent a letter to her friends in Chicago, accepting the invitation to visit on the condition two friends could accompany her on the trip instead of her father. The letter was already on the train before she announced this to Ruth Ann, who protested. There wasn't a chance of them all going. But so far, Matthew hadn't objected. It was another thing for them to discuss as soon as Ruth Ann finished with...

"Oh! Good morning, Miss Ruth Ann!"

Lance Fuller's voice sounded strained. When Ruth Ann

entered the church, she noticed his red face that had nothing to do with the warm morning. Was he nervous about teaching?

He stood behind his new desk, a simple oak table Mayor Warren had purchased from Mr. Levitt. The pulpit had been set by the wall. Pastor Rand had promised to move it before and after Sunday service each week.

When Lance Fuller came around the desk to greet Ruth Ann, he bumped the corner and sent a precariously stacked set of books tumbling. He tried to stop the avalanche, but ended up on his knees in the mess.

"Oh." Ruth Ann kept her exclamation as quiet as she could.

The teacher looked up, face crimson. He chuckled, then laughed heartily. Hands on his knees, he shook his head. "Well, I ruined my introduction. I was going to do that *after* the children arrived."

Ruth Ann smiled and set her reticule in a pew. She knelt by the scrambled books and began stacking them on the floor. "I saw three students coming this way when you called."

Lance Fuller added a book to her stack, but his eyes weren't on it. "Thank you for coming, Miss Ruth Ann. You've been a lovely part of being in Dickens. I appreciate your help."

"Oh, it's just my civic duty. I mean, actually, Mrs. Warren asked me…" She stammered and rose with a stack of books.

He stood with the rest of the books and placed them in the middle of his desk. He took the ones from her, brushing her hand. Ruth Ann quickly withdrew it.

"Susan is persuasive," he said. "But maybe in the future, it'll be your own idea."

Ruth Ann was relieved to hear shouts and laughter of children outside the door. She chuckled to shift the focus. "The children won't come willingly. You'll have to call them in."

"Of course." But Lance Fuller didn't move. He stared at the jumble of papers on his desk near a handbell and his fingers twirled a pencil on the smooth oak surface.

He didn't have the look of a frontier schoolteacher, dressed like a businessman instead. And he didn't have the confidence of someone who could earn the trust and respect of the wild children of Dickens.

But Lance Fuller's pedigree was flawless. He had been top in his class and went on to teach two years at a private boarding school in New York before accepting this invitation for what Mrs. Warren had described as the "mission-like" opportunity the thoughtful young man sought.

He was thoughtful now, but Ruth Ann had a feeling he wasn't thinking about the poor, uneducated children now under his charge. What was it?

When Lance Fuller continued to twirl the pencil on the desk, Ruth Ann cleared her throat. "Most of the children have never been to school, but deep down they're eager to learn. It's like a well. You have to draw that desire up. It's deeper down in some than others. But it's there. Splash them with cool water the first time and they'll learn from you the rest of the year."

Ruth Ann didn't know why she felt she needed to inspire the teacher. But he lifted his face with a smile.

"Thank you for the encouragement, Miss Ruth Ann. I'll try not to disappoint you."

She took a step back and retrieved her reticule. She faced him with chin lifted. "I'm not the one you need to please. That would be your benefactor, Mayor Warren, and more importantly, the children. I only came to give you an introduction."

Lance Fuller's face reddened again and he quickly nodded. "Of course. I meant no offense. It will take time to, um, adapt to all your social customs in Indian Territory."

Ruth Ann had been outside the Territory for school and newspaper business. His familiar comment was not due to a gap in their social customs. But she let it be.

"Beulah wants to have a choir practice after your last lesson. Is that all right?"

"Yes. Yes, of course."

When he still didn't move, Ruth Ann picked up the handbell and went out on the porch. She rang the bell to summon the twenty children in the churchyard. It was their first day of school and Ruth Ann wanted to see them have a prompt start. There was no time for dilly-dallying.

◆ ◆ ◆

It was late in the morning before Ruth Ann made it to the newspaper office. She had spent an hour at the school, getting the children settled in the church pews, distributing the scant supply of books, taking roll. For all of Mrs. Warren's talk, there was a sore lack of supplies. The children had to share tablets, pencils, books.

But scant supplies weren't her only disappointment.

Lance Fuller had been at a complete loss about what to do. Ruth Ann doubted he even had a lesson plan. After Ruth Ann quieted the children and introduced him, they launched into questions about school and why they should be there at all. Ruth Ann answered those questions while he darted panicked looks around the room.

Finally, Ruth Ann admonished the children to study hard and be successful with their lives. She fled the church, closing the door firmly behind her. She'd done all she could.

Ruth Ann was winded by the time she pushed through the door of the newspaper office. She slammed the door behind her and leaned her head back against it, eyes closed. She sucked in a deep breath of the ink and wood-tainted air.

"Ah, you look as though you just escaped a monster's lair, dear Ruth. Or was it twenty little monsters?"

Ruth Ann shook her head and opened her eyes. Beulah was seated at the front desk, sheets of music spread across it. Ruth Ann chuckled and started to tell her about the morning, but her gaze drifted to the right and further back where Matthew sat behind his makeshift desk. He wasn't writing. He wasn't reading. He was staring at her.

Beulah followed her gaze. She leaned closer to Ruth Ann and whispered in a voice they all knew Matthew could hear, "Caution, my friend. Your brother is in a mood this morning. And this monster is full grown."

Matthew frowned. Ruth Ann moved to Beulah's desk, feeling the need to tiptoe, but she resisted. "Mr. Fuller said you can hold choir practice after school, but don't be late. I doubt he'll be able to hold them a second past their last lesson."

"I cannot wait to hear all about it." Beulah glanced over her shoulder and Ruth Ann followed her gaze. Matthew hadn't moved.

"But I think you had better talk to him first. We do not want him growing into a grouchy old man back there."

Ruth Ann reluctantly left Beulah and approached the desk near the printing press. She'd soon write an article about the new school, and her words would be inked and pressed onto paper that would find their way to places she'd never been. At least, they would if Matthew wasn't too upset with her about…she didn't know what. Perhaps for being at the school too long?

When she reached him, Matthew stood and went to the door by the workbench. Mr. Levitt sat there, his small hand wrapped around a clock as he worked on the intricate piece. He lifted his eyes to look over his spectacles and a smile lifted the corners of his thin lips. "Good morning, Ruth Ann."

Relief touched her heart at the gentle greeting on this chaotic day. "Good morning, Mr. Levitt. You look well."

Though he wasn't his former self yet, Mr. Levitt had made great strides in recovering. His wispy, whitish-blonde hair was slicked down with oil to keep it from falling in his eyes. His skin was paler than it had been when the Levitts first arrived in Dickens and his cheeks sagged in ways they hadn't before his heart failure, but thankfully, his lips had a light pink hue again.

Matthew opened the storage room door and stood waiting for her. Ruth Ann went through to the room that housed everything from Mr. Levitt's projects to printing paper, and included a corner Beulah kept cleared out for her music lessons.

But Ruth Ann knew this wasn't where Matthew wanted to stop. She opened the back door and stepped out into the shade behind the print shop.

Overturned wood crates littered the area and the grass was beaten down. To the casual observer, it was a shabby spot. Here, behind the buildings that made up this side street off Main, there was nothing but the wind blowing through the field that gradually gave way to the churchyard where the children would soon break free for a recess.

The privacy made it a favorite spot of Matthew's for writing articles or reading his Bible. It also seemed to be his favorite place to scold Ruth Ann.

But what had she done now? He'd forgiven her for the blunder at the Warrens. She was doing as he'd asked, offering friendship to Mrs. Warren and keeping up with the new teacher.

Ruth Ann grew hopeful. Maybe he didn't plan to scold her. Maybe he wanted to share his latest findings with her.

But the expression on his face said otherwise.

Sighing, she dropped onto a wood crate. The splintered planks felt familiar, but not in a comforting way. She'd get sore quick. Matthew was never in a hurry when he had something to say.

He sat across from her on another crate, this one turned on its end. To her surprise, he started right in, though he watched the church in the distance as though drawing his words from there. "I expected you back earlier."

That was it? He wanted to lecture her for being late? Ruth Ann opened her mouth to respond, but Matthew kept talking.

"I don't blame you. Lance Fuller is a charming young man."

Ruth Ann gasped. The last time Matthew had talked to her about being careful with men was when she'd formed an attachment to D before she knew he was a kind, but much older, married man. It was exciting to chat with someone she couldn't see, imagine all sorts of admirable things about him. This was nothing like that, and Matthew knew it!

"Honestly, Matt, we've been through this. The telegraph thing with D was different and yes, exciting. But I will never be that silly again. I can't believe you think—"

"I don't."

The smile on Matthew's face made Ruth Ann want to whack him. But she restrained herself, instead narrowing her eyes in the most ladylike scowl she could muster.

"What do you mean then?"

Matthew leaned forward and put his elbows on his knees. He clasped his hands together and stared at them, humor gone. "You're a fine young woman, Annie. It's no wonder men look your way. Now hold on, don't fuss. I'm not blaming you, you're modest as you should be. But at your age, knocks on the door are serious. I have a sharp eye on Lance Fuller for more than one reason. He's a white man."

Ruth Ann tried to sort through her confusion. "I know that. He's never even been west of the Mississippi."

This wasn't a comfortable conversation to have with Matthew. She'd rather have it with her mama. She brought her voice down, soft. "I have no inclinations toward Lance Fuller. He seems like a nice young man, and I have no prejudice because he's white. But...but there's more to it..." Ruth Ann sighed in frustration. "Matthew Teller, you are the worst person in the world to talk to."

His smile came back. "I know, I'm all business. And sadly, that's what I see here. There's more news on the Dawes Commission from the council meeting this week."

How infuriating! How could Matthew shift from something about romance to a news story that had nothing to do with...

A rock settled in Ruth Ann's stomach. The tips of her fingers rose to her lips and she couldn't speak.

Matthew nodded, but didn't look at her. "It's not an uncommon ploy, hasn't been for some time—white men with the sole intention of marrying into the tribe to get at our resources. There's no stopping the Dawes Commission. Our land will be divided by allotment. Everyone will get an equal share according to the value of the land. It won't happen for some years still, but it's coming fast like the Frisco over there barreling down the tracks."

Before he finished, the train coming into Dickens let off a whistle as it neared the Dickens depot. From the back of the print shop, Ruth Ann couldn't see the mighty steam engine billowing its smoke above the treetops nor the long line of passenger cars, freight cars and caboose. But she envisioned the bustle at the depot, the spectacle that took place with the arrival of the train. People disembarking, loading, working, loitering.

Within minutes, the train sounded its whistle once more and was off. The sound of steel on steel grew faint. The train had come and gone, like the ways of life. Nothing remained except the change.

Matthew rubbed his chin. "I don't like this school set up by Warren. He's trying to cover up something. I think Lance Fuller is involved, but I haven't found anything except good reports about him." He dropped his hand. "I'm not trying to be cynical, Annie. Maybe it's because of all the things we know. Maybe it's me being a protective brother. Fuller is charming everyone in town. I just want you to know there's a lot more under the surface than on top."

Ruth Ann bowed her head, then raised it. "Do you really think that's why Lance Fuller is here? Why he seems to...to show me special attention?"

Matthew looked toward the church. "I can't say for sure. But I do know the mayor, and any close friend of his I'd keep a fair distance from." He met her eyes, and his own twinkled. "Unless you're a newspaper reporter. Then you have to set aside your own safety for the sake of a story."

Ruth Ann frowned. This was no joking matter. She had no intention of allowing Lance Fuller to court her, but she wasn't sure how to play this game Matthew hinted at. "Just what do you want me to do?"

Matthew grew serious again. "Be careful, Annie. Be real, real careful. You'll have to use your own judgment and wisdom in each situation."

Ruth Ann sighed. He gave her nothing definite. But then, what in life was definite?

Her heart heard her father's whisper. *God knows.*

"Tell me about the council meeting. Any more shootings?"

For the next half-hour, they discussed the changes in the Choctaw Nation and the violence those changes bred. Officials expected trouble at the tribal election next month.

Their talk turned to issues outside Indian Territory. Matthew expressed his desire to cover a broader range of news in the *Choctaw Tribune*. The U.S. stock market had crashed earlier that year, causing widespread panic through the States. Indian Territory wasn't impacted as much, but it was still big news. As was the Chicago World's Fair that had opened in May.

Ruth Ann laughed. "Beulah insists we go with her right after the elections in October. She's determined I see a big city and get a taste of international life. Next thing you know, she'll want me to travel abroad."

"You could." Matthew's response caught her off guard. She shook her head at the ridiculous notion, but he countered, "Why not? Choctaws have traveled the country and the world. Chief Peter Pitchlynn met Charles Dickens on a riverboat going up the Ohio. The Barneses have talked of taking a trip to Europe someday. I don't see why we can't go to the World's Fair in Chicago."

Ruth Ann gaped at her brother, filled with a sudden rush of excitement.

Matthew grinned. "We're doing all right financially. We could shut the newspaper down for a week, make the trip, and come home with a month's worth of international stories to tell. I want to get an interview with Buffalo Bill Cody. The man fascinates people, but I want to see what he's really like with Indians."

Ruth Ann kept from squealing as she listened to his reasoning. The World's Fair! Exotic, breathtaking, mindboggling. "We have to take Mama! She'll love it."

Matthew eyed her and she sighed. "Well, we could convince her she'd love it. The trip would be good for her. She needs...she needs to go more places."

Sadness claimed Ruth Ann's heart. Before Daddy and Philip died, their mother was perfectly content to stay home and rear her children. But things had changed. Della needed to be part of a broader world. And what could be broader than Chicago during the World's Fair?

Matthew wiped sweat from his forehead. The day was heating up. "You work on convincing Mama. I'll work on arranging how to get things situated enough to leave for a week."

"Peter will be a big help..." Ruth Ann winced. Peter would love to go. But he was young, younger than her anyway. He would have other opportunities. Besides, knowing her cousin, he'd be just as thrilled to be left in charge of their business an entire week.

Something needled at the back of Ruth Ann's mind and she dropped her gaze. "I'm sorry, truly, truly sorry about losing my temper with the mayor and giving away your investigation. I'd do most anything to go back and sew my lips shut!"

A gentle hint of forgiveness was in Matthew's voice when he replied, "It's all right, Annie. You'll make up for it."

She smiled but still didn't raise her head. "Well, are you going to tell me your latest findings about him or not?"

Matthew stood and paced between the crates. "I would if I had any. I've talked to everyone, and most are scared. I can't find a record of Rachel Bascom and Thaddeus Warren being married in Fort Smith, yet there was a marriage certificate filed at Skullyville. That's Warren's only ace, but it's enough to protect him for now. I can't get anything else to budge."

Matthew cocked his head at Ruth Ann and she nodded in understanding. "I need to get close to Mrs. Warren. I'll try, but she doesn't like me."

He shrugged. "Keep trying. We don't have much else."

What he didn't say was how difficult his investigation had become because of her blunder. The mayor had been seen calling on several key people, likely making threats or doling out bribes for their cooperation. The case was sealed tight. Unless...

"Matt, there is someone who *does* like me..."

Matthew slapped a palm on the upright crate. "No. With what I know, I wouldn't trust Lance Fuller with minding a mule, much less getting close to my sister."

"I wasn't thinking of anything like that! But, well, he does need help with the children, and we're doing the choir and all...Oh, don't look at me like that! I'm not a fool, and I can keep my eyes sharp for anything that might cut the strings Mayor Warren is pulling this town by." Ruth Ann stood, her back straight. "This is still Choctaw Nation. I have to do what I can. And there's nothing more powerful than the press, except God Almighty. Don't you forget that, Matthew Teller."

"Humph." Matthew opened his arms for a hug. It was far too warm and they were talking too much business for that, but Ruth Ann hugged him anyway. As long as she had her brother, she had the courage to climb any mountain in the world.

God knows.

CHAPTER EIGHT

IN SPITE OF A SHAKY start, the school progressed through September. The children returned day after day, some eager to learn, some shy, some looking to make trouble with the new teacher. One of the troublemakers was a youngster named Stephen Austin Jessop.

At thirteen years old, he was already a strapping boy growing into an angry young man. Ruth Ann didn't know much about his family, only that they lived on a farm two miles south of town. She did know Stephen Austin—yes, he had to be called by both names—was intelligent but cared nothing about learning.

During the school day, he roved the cemetery by the church or took off into the woods where he disappeared for hours. He came back when school ended and snatched his three younger siblings—Neches, Glenrose and Belle—from the choir rehearsal, shouting at Beulah that they needed to tend their chores at home.

At the end of the fourth week, Beulah urged Ruth Ann to go to the school and help with choir rehearsal. With white students and Choctaw children who weren't at boarding school, the choir had grown to twenty-six. Beulah insisted she needed help wrangling them, especially the older boys who would rather be on the farm. In truth, Ruth Ann knew Beulah was capable of managing with the help of the teacher, but Lance Fuller was the real reason she wanted Ruth Ann along.

She didn't decline the invitation. Somehow, she'd rectify her blunder with Mayor Warren and help Matthew reveal the truth. If that meant careful maneuvering around the two people closest to the mayor, so be it.

The choir session went smoothly, helped by the presence of three adults the children expressed genuine affection toward. The choir was absent of the older boys, who got away as fast as they could, promising to return for their younger siblings. Except Stephen Austin Jessop—he took his siblings with him.

When the last note faded, Beulah praised the children and freed them for the weekend. The stampede for the door was deafening, drawing laughter from the adults.

Lance Fuller shook his head and moved into one of the pews where he gathered books and homework assignments that had been discarded or forgotten. "Thank you, ladies, for your assistance. I wouldn't have survived without you, nor would my students. But I do have yet another favor to ask."

Beulah and Ruth Ann had started on another aisle, sorting music sheets from arithmetic assignments. Beulah stopped and smiled at the teacher, but Ruth Ann kept working. "Yes?"

"I'm concerned about the Jessop children. Hardly any of my students come from educated families, none rich by any means. In fact, I've never seen poorer people than in this territory."

Ruth Ann halted and raised her eyebrows. Beulah lifted her chin with civic pride. "This might seem like a backwoods country to you, Mr. Fuller. However, Indian Territory boasts fine amusements and even wealth. Have you seen the Barnes mansion? Not to mention—"

"No offense intended." Lance Fuller raised his hands in surrender. "Dickens is a fine young town. It's the poverty among the white children of tenant farmers I find shocking, the Jessops in particular. Their clothing, while clean for the most part, is deplorable. None have shoes and the winter months are coming. I'm concerned about Stephen Austin. He refuses to stay inside, though he's as smart as they come. There's so much potential for these children, but we must have the parents' cooperation. I want to call on the Jessops, but it'd be helpful if you ladies accompany me and provide introductions. I doubt Stephen Austin carried high praise of me back home."

Beulah nodded. "We could take the Teller's buggy and make a day of it. I do not have a clue where the Jessops live, but we have an experienced guide." She turned to Ruth Ann, who felt trapped under two pairs of eyes.

But wasn't this the opportunity she'd hoped for? "I haven't met the Jessop parents. I don't believe they come to the church, but I do know where they live. They're tenant farmers on Mr. Perkins' ranch, a Choctaw. I need to ask my mother though…"

Beulah turned back to Lance Fuller with a firm nod. "I am certain she will agree. Shall we pay the call in the morning?"

Meeting time and place arranged and music sheets gathered, Ruth Ann and Beulah left the church. Ruth Ann tried not to drag her feet. It was, after all, the opportunity she needed to help with redemption.

Besides, what could be so awful about spending the morning with Beulah and Lance Fuller, and paying a call on the Jessops?

◆ ◆ ◆

A chilly morning breeze sent the three companions out the next morning. Della had given permission to use the family buggy, and Matthew wasn't around to make objections. Ruth Ann was sensible and made sure she positioned herself and Beulah on the back seat. Lance Fuller took the front seat and the reins and soon they were halfway down the dusty road to their destination.

The chit-chat was mundane until Beulah said, "Have you been to the Columbian Exposition, Mr. Fuller? The World's Fair in Chicago?"

Ruth Ann's stomach dropped.

He cocked his head as though forming his answer. "Well, actually, no. I've never been to Chicago. I did go to the Centennial International Exhibition in Philadelphia, Pennsylvania, when I was a boy." When he relaxed his shoulders, Ruth Ann realized he'd been tense. "Are you ladies going to the Columbian Exposition? It closes at the end of October, I think."

Beulah scooted to the edge of her seat and grasped the back of his bench. "I received an invitation to visit friends and they insist we come for the fair. My father is too ill to travel, and I cannot go alone, so I have corralled Ruth Ann and her brother into accompanying me."

Ruth Ann frowned behind Lance Fuller's back and shook her head at Beulah.

"Is that not the right word? Corralled?"

The problem wasn't her Russian friend's word choice. Ruth Ann knew where the conversation was headed.

"Would you care to join us, Mr. Fuller? School must break for the children to help with harvest."

Lance Fuller turned in the seat enough for Ruth Ann to see his smile. "That's a kind invitation, Miss Beulah. I'll consider it."

From the tone of his voice, Ruth Ann knew he'd already considered and decided. There would be another party joining the trip, someone that would set her nerves on edge.

The road curved sharply. Ruth Ann gathered her wits. "The turnoff is ahead, on the right. You can hardly see it."

The turn was overgrown and Lance Fuller had to slow the buggy considerably to make it. A loose branch caught on the wheel and dragged along with them. Beulah pulled her skirt close as branches snagged at it.

"Sorry, ladies."

Ruth Ann had never actually been down this road. It was

pointed out to her as the one leading to the dwellings of three white tenant families that kept to themselves. The Choctaw who had claimed the land let them work it for a share of the crops they produced. Those white families were poor and un-educated, the kind Mrs. Warren referred to when she announced plans for a school.

The road was barely wide enough for a buggy, and holes created by spring rains had never been filled. There was no way around them, and Lance Fuller apologized with each jerk of the buggy.

The woods thinned. Ahead was a shanty in a yard littered with rocks and scrub brush.

Lance Fuller pulled the buggy to a halt a hundred feet from the shanty. The yard had enough craters to bust all four wheels off the buggy. "I think we'd better walk from here."

Ruth Ann descended in a hurry, not wanting to wait for him to help. Beulah was behind her, one hand on the back of the front bench, the other on Ruth Ann's shoulder. "Careful, Ruth, haste makes waste—"

A shot rang out. The buggy horse bolted and yanked the carriage forward. Beulah gasped and lost her balance. She tumbled onto Ruth Ann and knocked them both to the hard-packed dirt road.

Ruth Ann cried out when her shoulder landed hard on a rock before she could roll to ease the fall. Beulah's larger frame was tangled around her.

Two more shots came from the shanty and the buggy horse broke into a run. Lance Fuller tried to slow her by turning her head sharply. Too sharply. Before Ruth Ann could shout a warning, the buggy tipped onto two wheels.

Dirt stinging her eyes, she realized she was sprawled on her stomach. She wiped her fallen hair from her face and saw the buggy on its side. The horse pranced and eyed the now strange object it was attached to.

Her senses warned her to run, but when she tried to push herself up, she realized Beulah was on her back. In a moment, though, her friend scrambled off, breathing hard. "Are you well, my friend? Ruth?"

Ruth Ann blinked and looked at Beulah's face. She gasped at the sight of blood trickling from her friend's forehead. "Beulah, you're hurt! You—"

"A keen observation." Raising up on one elbow, Beulah winced and glanced toward the shanty. Ruth Ann followed her gaze. A young woman appeared in the doorway, carrying a Winchester. She lifted her skirt and ran toward them.

Beulah shook Ruth Ann's injured shoulder, which caused hot pain throughout her body. "I believe we should run."

Ruth Ann knew they had no chance of making it to the woods. Even if the woman was a poor shot from a distance, she was closing to a range from which she couldn't miss.

The pop of a small pistol sounded behind them. Ruth Ann ducked her head but Beulah sat up straight. "Lance!"

Ruth Ann saw him bring the small barrel of a derringer down from where he'd fired the warning shot into the sky. He leveled the gun on the young woman, who had halted a dozen yards from Ruth Ann and Beulah.

Lance Fuller looked unsteady on his feet but held firm. "Drop the rifle."

The woman held the gun loosely in one hand, the rifle barrel pointed at the dirt. "I mean no harm. It wasn't me shooting, it was…well, no more trouble now. Just put away that pea shooter so I can help these ladies." She moved forward again.

Ruth Ann pushed herself to a sitting position and glanced at Lance Fuller. He slowly lowered the pistol and pocketed it in his rumpled gray suit coat. A torn piece of his pant leg flapped in the breeze like a flag of surrender.

Then he moved briskly forward to help Ruth Ann and Beulah to their feet. "Just who shot at us?"

The young woman ignored the question as she prodded the skin around Beulah's swelling cut. "Doesn't look too deep, but I have something that'll take the sting out if you're willing."

"Oh, I am willing. I love the excitement in Indian

Territory!"

Ruth Ann shook her head and started to straighten her twisted skirt. She gasped when pain gripped her shoulder.

"Are you all right, Ruth Ann?" It wasn't Beulah who gently touched her shoulder. It was Lance Fuller.

Ruth Ann pulled away and bumped into the young woman who had moved closer and now glided her hand over the raw pain. She frowned. "Doesn't seem broken, but better have Takba look at it. She'll fix you up."

Beulah slipped an arm around Ruth Ann's waist, though Ruth Ann suspected they both needed support. Beulah wobbled when she took her first step. "Who is Takba?"

The young woman glanced at Lance Fuller, who seemed hesitant. She abruptly handed him her rifle and tucked herself on Beulah's other side. She grabbed the taller woman's arm and looped it around her shoulder. The young woman must have been stronger than she looked. "Takba helps with the young'uns and whatever needs doing around the house. I can't keep up with everything."

Beulah asked, "And who are you?"

"Amarillo. My pa gave us all Texas names."

"Your pa?" Lance Fuller studied the quiet shanty they neared.

"You must be the new teacher. Sorry for the welcome, we don't get many friendly visitors out this way."

Ruth Ann felt dizzy and leaned against Beulah. "It was Stephen Austin who shot at us, wasn't it?"

Amarillo looked sharply at her, but didn't miss a step. "He's a good boy, he just takes on thinking he's the man of the house, but his britches aren't big enough yet."

Amarillo had distinct mannerisms, but she didn't sound uneducated. In fact, there was a refinement about her that puzzled Ruth Ann, considering the shanty they now approached.

It was weathered like it had stood many seasons. The door was hinged but crooked, not set right in the frame. Even closed, large gaps showed at the top and bottom. The front window, the one the bullets had flown from, was glassless with a gunnysack covering it. Ruth Ann imagined the window was boarded over in the winter, making the inside of the shanty dark and sad.

When Amarillo released her hold on Beulah and moved toward the door, Ruth Ann noted the young woman's appearance. Her worn calico dress might have been pink at one time. The color had been washed to a dull tan, the tiny flower print all but absorbed in the worn threads. The skirt was patched in several places like it had been worn in thorny work. But Amarillo was really a lovely young lady when she didn't have a rifle in hand. Her face was tan from more hours in the sun than not, but no freckles dotted her clear complexion that highlighted her blue eyes. Her hair was a honey-blonde like all the Jessops Ruth Ann had seen, though Amarillo's was the longest. In a braid, it still reached her waist.

Ruth Ann glanced at her companions before they entered the shanty and realized she wasn't the only one who noticed the natural beauty of the tenant farmer's daughter.

When Amarillo pushed the door open, there was a scurrying sound near the window. A stampede of small footsteps ended in a far corner. Ruth Ann couldn't see the children until her eyes adjusted to the darker interior.

Amarillo spoke to the corner. "Neches, set that chair up and dust it off. Glenrose, you bring a bucket of fresh water from the spring, then finish the washing. Belle, stop crying. Run up to the north field and fetch Takba. Tell her I need help tending injuries. Neches, go on and find your brother and tell him I'll hang him by the thumbs if he doesn't get back here right now and help this man get that buggy up. Go on."

The children crashed into each other. They took off in three directions, one through a back door, the other through the window, and the third, Belle, whimpered as she squeezed by and out the front door.

The sound of a baby crying filled the silence. Amarillo directed Beulah to a cot along the wall, and motioned for Ruth Ann to take the chair.

Beulah perched on the cot. "I would love to have your brothers and sisters stay for choir rehearsals after school. Perhaps we could arrange—"

"I'd like to see that, too." Amarillo turned toward the tiny potbelly stove in the back corner and stocked it with kindling. "But the young'uns would rather get their chores done so they can go roam down at the creek than anything else."

Glenrose, a shy girl of ten, reappeared at the back door. Her knuckles were white around the handle of the water bucket as she puffed with the strain.

Lance Fuller—who had stood in shock as he absorbed his pupils' living conditions—hurried forward and took the bucket. Glenrose let go and ran out the back door. Lance Fuller settled the bucket on the table next to Ruth Ann. Their eyes met and she saw the sorrow in his. He hadn't been prepared for how destitute his pupils really were. Perhaps he had wanted to believe they were scruffy at school because their parents hadn't cared to dress them properly. Whatever illusions he'd had were shattered. The floor beneath them—well-swept, packed dirt—spoke the truth.

Amarillo dipped water from the bucket and filled a pan on the stove. She glanced over her shoulder at Lance Fuller as he watched her. "You might see about your horse, mister. No sense leaving the poor thing tethered in the sun."

"Oh!" Ruth Ann jumped to her feet and winced at the pain in her shoulder, but she still went to look out the door. In the distance, the Teller's horse stood calmly, still hitched to the overturned buggy.

Lance Fuller came to her side. She stepped back to allow him to pass, but instead found he was looking at her. He hesitated, then said softly, "I'll take care of the horse. Of everything."

He glanced back at Amarillo before he went out, leaving Ruth Ann to wonder what the latter half of his promise meant.

A shuffle at the back door drew her attention. Little Belle, the six year old, stood there with two dirty fingers stuck in her mouth.

A woman appeared behind Belle, pulled her fingers out of her mouth and smacked her hand. The little girl wailed and ran out the door.

The woman straightened and Ruth Ann felt the back of her neck tingle and her knees weaken for no reason. Perhaps it was surprise. Perhaps it was the way she was immediately lost in the woman's deep, dark eyes that seemed to hold a thousand secrets. Perhaps it was because Ruth Ann sensed the woman called Takba was Choctaw. *Takba*. A Choctaw word for bitter.

The baby wailed again.

CHAPTER NINE

THE HOUSE WAS QUIET, A break from Della's children and nephew. They came and went on an irregular basis to inform her of news or find a meal or bring a general need that a mother was happy to fill. Della would have it no other way.

But she was busy herself this Saturday after Ruth Ann left to visit the Jessops. Della had finished her shopping early before the usual crowd bore down on the stores. The kitchen was stocked and she had the material she needed for the projects she worked on now.

Della had claimed the side room near the front door for her sewing space. Their bedrooms upstairs in the attic left this room free for her to work in. It was the right size for her business that bought groceries when the latest controversy or disaster consumed any profits from the *Choctaw Tribune*.

She spread a bright blue silk across the table set in the middle of the room. She didn't check the measurements jotted down on a note that came with the order. Instead, she used her memory of taking the measurements earlier that week. Scissors in hand, she cut a straight line down her mark.

Many women had nervously observed Della when she took measurements, and always questioned how she could do it without notes. She would chuckle and go on her way. When the garment was complete, they praised how perfect the fit was.

For Della, it was a matter of feel rather than numbers. An exact measurement would not necessarily result in a good fit. There was no room in exactness for give and take in the right places that made a garment not only fit well, but become a part of the person.

It was the same with life. Someone's character needed to be a part of them, with give and take in certain situations. But only in the right places. In the wrong places, it would cause a tear and ruin the garment.

This was the understanding she'd reared her children with. Now, she prayed for the wisdom they needed to live it.

"Dear *Chihowa*, watch over my Ruth Ann. Your Ruth Ann. She is precious in Your sight…"

A sound near the front door pricked Della's ear. Someone was coming up the porch steps at a hesitant walk. It wasn't one of her children, and certainly not her rambunctious nephew, Peter.

Della laid aside the scissors on her way out and closed the door behind her. She never left it open when they had guests. When she worked on a project, things just wouldn't stay in place and the room was a mess. It was her weakness.

When a knock sounded at the door, Della was waiting on the other side. She opened the door to the sunshine of late morning.

Few things surprised Della anymore. This was an exception.

Mrs. Warren stood on the porch, dressed from head to toe in style. She would have resembled a picture in the *Ladies Home Journal* except for the scowl on her face. And her hat was pinned too far back. Her belt was crooked. And…

Della stopped herself from her critical evaluation. "Good morning, Mrs. Warren." She motioned for her to come in.

But Mrs. Warren hesitated, fidgeting with her reticule clenched in both hands. "I, oh, I can't stay. I'm not here on a social call. That is, I need a blouse made, right away. The first school board meeting is Monday and I simply must have something new to wear, you know." Her nose went up. "The tailor refused to even *try* and have it ready for me."

Della motioned again for the woman to enter. "You need to come in."

Pity for the woman kept her from making an embarrassing remark about taking the woman's measurements on the porch in front of people passing by.

Even with the words unspoken, Mrs. Warren's cheeks reddened, and she hurried across the threshold. She glanced back as though wondering if anyone had seen her.

"I really can't stay. I must return home very soon. I have other errands to attend…"

Della turned but instead of going to her sewing room, she headed to the kitchen.

The woman's voice rose behind her. "Mrs. Teller, I really am in a hurry."

"Come." Della went to the stove and stirred the coals. The kettle was still warm. She moved it onto the burner over the coals and added more water.

Mrs. Warren waved her hands. "I don't have time for tea! I need to make this as quick as possible before someone…"

Della lifted two tea cups from the cabinet beside the stove and set them on the table. She nodded toward the chair across from where she seated herself. "Sit. Please." She needed a few minutes to observe her client's movements in order to make a well-fitted blouse.

Mrs. Warren bristled, her shoulders tense. "As I said…" She spoke slowly, as though Della might have trouble understanding English. "…I do not have time for a social call."

When Della didn't move, Mrs. Warren sighed, plopped into the chair and spoke faster. "I declare, you're like your daughter. Or I suppose she's like you. I wouldn't know. I never had a child, much less one like her."

She plunked her reticule on the table and leaned over it. She stared hard into Della's eyes. "Just what is it that makes you Indians think you're better than us?"

Della raised one eyebrow. The accusation was interesting. But she didn't respond.

The tea kettle whined. Della stood and lifted it off the stove. She poured the steaming tea through the strainer for each cup, then tapped the strainer. She put everything away before taking her seat again. The sugar dish sat in the middle of the table. Della removed the lid and slid the dish closer to Mrs. Warren.

Sighing, Mrs. Warren spooned a heaping dose of sugar into her cup. Her arms moved widely, something Della's experienced eye caught. "I suppose that was a harsh thing to say. But land sakes, you people act like you own this world. I know we aren't part of the States yet, but you must adjust. This isn't the Wild West anymore. You Indians must assimilate into our culture or...or perish." Her voice trailed away. From the way she avoided Della's eyes, Della suspected Mrs. Warren was repeating her husband's words.

"I don't mean to be offensive, Mrs. Teller, but you people are a wear on the civilized mind. Your ways are so...well, so *strange*. Your codes, your humor, your religions. Why, I can't sort it all out. You Choctaws are just...*different*." She took a sip of the tea, her eyes down.

Della observed her guest, absorbing the words, the meanings behind them, the trail of thoughts. She spoke gently. "Do you mean we are different in a good way, a bad way, or both?"

Mrs. Warren's tea cup clattered in her saucer. She glanced up to meet Della's eyes briefly. Della didn't know which startled Mrs. Warren most—that Della spoke the English language well, or her direct question.

After a few seconds, Mrs. Warren stumbled through her response. "I suppose both. I can't say that everything you do is bad...I mean, well, it's both."

Della chuckled and rose with her empty tea cup. "Then we are the same in different ways."

Mrs. Warren gasped and covered her mouth properly. Della headed for her sewing room. It was time to take the measurements.

They exchanged only necessary words as the work was done. Mrs. Warren didn't remark on Della not jotting down the measurements. Perhaps she realized it was one of those ways different about Della.

As they finished, there was another sound at the front door. Della recognized the footsteps. She left the sewing room but stayed clear of the front door. It was flung open by someone who was home.

Matthew almost plowed into Della. "Oh, sorry. I thought I'd write here awhile…" He saw Mrs. Warren and his eyebrows went up. "Good morning, ma'am."

"I was just leaving." Mrs. Warren lifted her chin, trying to gather her arrogant air again. But much of the air had been lost.

They bid polite goodbyes with Mrs. Warren reiterating the importance of her blouse being done by Monday morning. Della made no promises, though the woman didn't seem to notice. Della would finish her other work, then start the blouse at sundown on Sunday. It would be ready by Monday morning.

When Mrs. Warren was gone, Matthew cocked his head. "Why would she come groveling to you…?"

Della gave him a stern look. He shrugged. "Mind if I write at the table?" He held up a tablet, the first page a mess of scribbles. Had he still been in school, Della would make him sit down and neatly rewrite every word ten times.

He continued. "There's too much noise in the shop. Peter and D are playing checkers and the constant clacking drives me crazy."

He followed Della when she reentered her sewing room where she took up the blue silk. She measured and cut and listened to Matthew talk for half an hour about his article on the upcoming election, and another one about the Dawes Commission.

She smiled to herself. This day was good.

♦ ♦ ♦

After stabling the horse and buggy in the Teller's barn and ensuring Ruth Ann didn't need a doctor, Lance walked Beulah home in the dwindling light of evening. The young woman chatted about the adventure they'd had. She reminded him about the Thanksgiving choir performance, and admonished him to make plans to join her and her friends on a grand adventure to the World's Fair in Chicago.

Lance wasn't paying much attention, though he did note the twinkle in her eye at the end. She really wanted him to go. She'd like to see him close to Ruth Ann Teller, wanted happiness for her friend. How different that was from Uncle Thaddeus' reasons. If they only knew Lance's thoughts this evening weren't of the lovely Ruth Ann. Another face filled his mind's eye.

He bid Beulah good evening and headed home, if he could call it that. His uncle would expect a report of the week. Thaddeus was more nervous than ever. Matthew Teller had spent the day making rounds and asking too many questions.

Lance winced. Ruth Ann's brother had better quit while he could, or someone would see to it that he did. But Lance couldn't warn them. His own situation was precarious enough.

The darkness around the house was fitting. It shadowed truth. No one knew his real identity, or his relation to Thaddeus Warren. Almost no one.

Boots scraped across the porch and Lance froze on the middle step. "Who's there?" He squinted at the shadows shifting in the evening light. The scraping stopped.

"Pretty green, aren't you?"

Lance frowned and took the final step onto the porch so he could face the sheriff of Dickens, Jake Banny. "Maybe I wrongly assumed you keep this town safe."

Banny shifted into the fading sunlight. The lanky gunslinger spent too much time around the Warren home. Lance hated his arrogance. It was always there, whether the man was trying to be polite or intimidating. His expression never changed. His face had a look of rage as though daring someone to poke it. Lance was tempted to, but he restrained himself and moved toward the door. He had spent the day with three lovely young ladies, being shot at and thrown from a buggy. He had no desire to hear what Banny had to say.

But Banny stepped in front of the door and put his hand on the frame, blocking the way with his arm. "You should show respect for authority, boy."

"I'm no boy." Lance grabbed Banny's wrist and yanked down, clearing the doorway.

Surprise flashed across Banny's face, but he quickly recovered. He twisted his wrist free and seized Lance's jacket with both hands and jerked him forward and around. He shoved Lance back and slammed him into the door. He braced one arm across Lance's throat, choking him.

Lance clawed at the arm to make a show of trying to resist. Let the sheriff think he'd won. For now.

Banny leaned close, his breath foul. "*Boy*, you've got a few things to learn about respect, like when to show it and when not to. The Tellers and their friends don't get any. You'd best remember why you're here. You let things get out of hand, and…" The arm pressed tighter and Lance gasped for air. "And boy, I'll have to teach you a few things."

Banny pushed off and took a step back. He tipped his hat. "See you later, boy."

Lance rubbed his throat. Banny walked away, though he never fully turned his back on him. It was a habit Banny probably applied in every situation. Always had to look over his shoulder.

Like you have to now.

The harsh accusation took more wind out of Lance. He leaned his head back against the door, eyes closed, breathing slowly. At least for a moment.

The sound of the doorknob didn't give him enough warning before the door was jerked open. Lance stumbled back and into his Aunt Susan's arms.

"Good grief gracious!" Susan Warren pushed away from

him and tripped on her skirt hem. Lance regained his footing and steadied her. She pressed her hands over her heart.

"What on earth! First all the bumping and thumping and then you plow me over and—"

She halted when her husband stepped into the front hall. He slowly folded his newspaper, a copy of the *Choctaw Tribune*. Susan dropped her eyes.

Sighing, Lance closed the door, sealing him in the private world of Thaddeus Warren. His world now.

Thaddeus stared at Lance. "You're late. What happened?" His sharp gaze went to Lance's pant leg, where the old Choctaw woman Takba had crudely sewn the rip. It was the best she could do while he had still been wearing the pants.

Lance did feel like a boy under his uncle's scrutiny. "A little accident." He wondered what stories would go around town about the incident, or what might end up in the *Choctaw Tribune*. "What was Banny doing here?"

"*Sheriff* Banny. Show some respect."

Lance stiffened. "*Sheriff* Banny accosted me on the porch, choking me between threats. What was he doing here?"

Susan gasped, then whimpered at the look her husband shot her. "You both need a better understanding of our delicate position here. If this plan unravels, we all unravel. Banny. Me. You." He said this to Lance, but his gaze bore down on Susan.

Lance stepped closer to her. "I'm doing what you want, getting close to Ruth Ann Teller. What's the complaint?" He glanced at Susan, who had hunched over, head low and trembling.

Thaddeus twisted the newspaper in his white-knuckled fists. "I said get close, not chummy. If either of you get weak-kneed—" he glared at Susan "—our little secrets will seep out. You wouldn't want that, either of you." His hard-set eyes met Lance's. It was worse than Banny's arm against his throat. It was just as difficult to breathe.

Dickens was Lance's chance to start over. He had been

brought here to get land, get riches. He had just wanted to get away. His last chance lay with this man and his schemes. Good old Uncle Thaddeus. Liar, thief, opportunist.

What a chance.

When the silence lasted long enough, Lance touched his aunt's arm and shifted his feet. "It's been a long day. I think we should all retire."

Thaddeus dropped his hands to his sides, still clenching the ruined paper in one. He glared at his wife. "We have a few things to discuss. Goodnight...Lance."

Even in private, they used that name. It was careful, safe. And it left him with no grasp on who he really was.

Lance Fuller. It was a handsome sounding name, the kind that belonged to someone with prestige, yet was friendly. The kind of name everyone liked and admired and wished was their own.

He wished it was his own.

Lance strode up the stairs, two at a time. Inside his room, he pressed himself against the door. He unbuttoned his shirt with one hand. Slowly. One button at a time.

He froze when the sharp crack of bare skin on skin came from downstairs.

The soft crying sounds were familiar. He'd heard them all his life, how his father had treated his mother. Each time, he swore he'd do something.

Thomas Warren had sworn that. Lance Fuller was a fake, a nonexistent creature. There was nothing he could do. No one in Dickens or anywhere could know who he really was. Especially not Ruth Ann Teller or her newspaper brother. If they found out he was Thomas Warren, nephew of Thaddeus Warren, he was finished for good.

When he closed his heart against the truth and the sounds from downstairs, all he could see was the dusty but determined face of Amarillo Jessop. And all he could hear was the cry of a baby no one talked about.

◆ ◆ ◆

Further north in the Choctaw Nation lay a secluded spot just right for hiding out. But in the darkness behind the cabin, Frank Bean heard an approaching horseman. He dropped the kindling he'd gathered and eased to the corner of the cabin, though he knew it was too late to warn Cub and Lester who were on the front porch. But those two didn't need warning. They were already walking into the moonlit yard. The rider had emerged from the trees, and since Cub hadn't already shot him, Frank figured the man was known to him.

The scrawny man was all bones and joints, like he could fold himself up and slip inside a small trunk. Judging from his mashed down hair and flighty eyes, Frank wondered if he often did just that to hide out. The man clutched the mane of his bareback horse, barely able to keep himself astride while he hissed something to the outlaws.

Lester responded to whatever the man had said. "Look here, Al Percy, why don't you weasel on back to the man and tell him we're not interested. I don't care how much money you got in that bag."

Frank came up quietly behind his two partners, though he knew they were aware of his presence. It was the man on horseback, Al Percy, who was alarmed when he saw him. "Who's that? I've never seen him before!"

Cub glanced over his shoulder and met Frank's eyes. Frank's heartbeat quickened. Even if by some twist of nature a rattlesnake saved your life, he was still a deadly snake.

"A friend."

Percy shoved a set of saddlebags off his horse's withers. "I can't go back with that. You either do the job or get blamed for taking the money and running."

Frank wondered if those were the boldest words the man had ever spoken.

Cub Wassom chuckled softly. Lester looked at him and shook his head. "You know I don't want no part of killing another Teller man. I'll quit you first. Dan Holder still has a place for me."

Lester glanced at Al Percy. The scrawny man licked his

lips. "I don't know anything about Holder."

Cub reached down and scooped up the saddlebags. "Of course you don't, Al. Just like you don't know nothing about what's in these bags, right?" He jerked his head at Lester. "Why don't you go on back with Al to Holder's hideout? I'll take care of this one. I got Frank to do half the job." Cub looked back at Frank again.

It was one of those moments when a man had to commit to something he knew would set his life down a path that couldn't be changed. No going back.

Frank nodded.

He didn't know what was expected of him, but he knew one thing. Cub Wassom had saved his life. Rattlesnake or not, Frank would ride with him to the death.

CHAPTER TEN

CONTROVERSY SURROUNDS
UPCOMING ELECTIONS

By Matthew Teller

With the election for Choctaw Nation national officers this first week of October, hot blood steams with threats and violence. Three fistfights between the National and Progressive parties occurred in Talihina over the weekend. Word of a shooting near Springstown was reported, but there are no known injuries at this time.

Ruth Ann's fingers flew over the type pieces to set the article in English. She'd set it in Choctaw later that afternoon. In either language, it wasn't an encouraging article, but it was simple and direct. That was the power behind the *Choctaw Tribune.*

Facts filled the article: when, where, how the election results would be announced during the general session of the council at the council grounds in Tushkahomma. Matthew had wrapped up the article with admonishment against violence and drinking.

Ruth Ann bit her lip at the memory of the Winchester aimed in Matthew's face by a drunk at Daniel Springs. She wanted to add two final words to the article:

Be civilized.

♦♦♦

They arranged for the prolonged stay at Tushkahomma to cover the current session of the General Council. Matthew wanted to be among the early arrivers and stay until everything ended. That would involve at least three days.

Ruth Ann was surprised she didn't encounter resistance when she said she wanted to go. Matthew replied with, "Can't be any more dangerous than buggy rides with that teacher."

In truth, Lance Fuller was one reason Ruth Ann wanted out of town. She needed a break from him and from Beulah. Lance Fuller was not courting Ruth Ann, but Beulah kept giving her looks as if he were.

But it was Peter's spy report that made her jittery. He had gotten word that Lance Fuller and Sheriff Banny had been chummy since the teacher's arrival. A friend of the sheriff—and someone who lived under the same roof with the Warrens—deserved the healthy dose of caution Ruth Ann spooned out. Whatever dangers she might face at the council grounds didn't outweigh the situation in Dickens.

Peter would be left in charge of the telegraph, the home chores, and responsible to note newsworthy happenings. Ruth Ann knew the final task would be mostly undone. Peter didn't keep a reporter's eye on things; he leaned more toward gossip. That was why he enjoyed the wire.

With final preparations in place, Ruth Ann went to bed with thoughts of the adventure ahead. She had seen a great deal as a reporter for the *Choctaw Tribune*. What did this trip hold?

♦♦♦

At the depot, folks gathered to see the Tellers off like they were going to war. Matthew thought it was a bit much. Beulah fussed over them, saying how she wished she was going. Della gave them extra long hugs. Peter pumped Matthew's hand and reassured him for a fourth time he would take care of everything in Dickens, not to worry about a thing. Even Lance Fuller had slipped away from the schoolhouse during the noon meal break, but Matthew gave him a warning look. Fuller stayed in the background after a brief exchange with Ruth Ann.

The northbound Frisco pulled up to the depot. Della pressed a pouch into Matthew's hand. "You never know."

Matthew felt coins in the bag. He pocketed it and bent to give his mother another kiss on the cheek. "*Yakoke*."

The busyness of the depot as people disembarked from the train gave him a private moment with her. He winked in Peter's direction. "Don't let that rascal break too many things I'll have to fix when I get back."

His cousin had positioned himself between Ruth Ann and Lance Fuller as she said another goodbye to Beulah.

Della put a hand on Matthew's cheek and he knew from the look in her eyes she was not taking the moment lightly. But she said nothing. Her hand slid down his arm and to his hand. She held it.

He nodded as though he understood her motherly concern. In truth, he didn't understand. He didn't understand a great deal about women even though he lived with two. But he understood enough to love them as they were. His father had taught him that.

Ah. His father. That was his mama's concern. Daddy and Philip went away on a trip and never came home. Though it had been nearly five years, grief could show itself fresh, especially for women in a moment like this.

Matthew had his moments, too. He kissed his mother's cheek a final time. "We'll be careful, Mama. *Chi pisa la chike*."

She murmured, "*Ome*," agreeing with the phrase that didn't say "goodbye." There was no word for goodbye in their native tongue. Only, *I will see you again.*

Matthew turned and grabbed the two carpetbags that bulged with more than enough supplies for the short trip. He would have taken a small bag himself, but Ruth Ann's "necessaries" and the food Della had packed for them took up her bag and half of his. "Come on, little *luksi*, or the train will leave without us!"

Ruth Ann pulled herself from Beulah's hug, shook a finger in Peter's face, and wrapped her arms around Della again. Matthew just knew all the women were going to cry.

He went to the train steps and whistled. Della released Ruth Ann with a little push to send her off on the journey. The train let out its own whistle. Matthew motioned with the heavy carpetbag for Ruth Ann to mount the steps.

"Hurry up, unless you want to take the night train."

This put enough fear in his sister to make her scurry up into the passenger car.

They were on their way. Off to war, from the looks on everyone's faces.

◆ ◆ ◆

The first part of the ride found Ruth Ann and Matthew contemplative. At least she was. Matthew had his nose buried in a newspaper. He claimed the only time he had to *read* the news was when traveling or late at night. This time he held a copy of the *Indian Citizen,* which sided with the Nationals in the political debates. Another paper sided with Progressives. The *Choctaw Tribune* maintained a neutral position which didn't win them friends on either side, and made enemies on both.

Ruth Ann took inventory of their fellow travelers who boarded and disembarked at each stop. Immigrant coal miners, Texas cowboys, Eastern businessmen, families traveling from Paris, Texas, to St. Louis and beyond to see relatives or friends. It wasn't easy to pick out the Native people among them.

A boy dressed in a sailor suit and straw hat pressed his

nose against the window across the aisle from Ruth Ann. He looked at a woman who was reading a magazine. "Mother, where are we?"

"I told you, dear. Indian Territory. Now sit and don't crinkle your suit; Grandmother will be displeased." She never glanced up from her magazine.

The boy swiveled his head and caught Ruth Ann's gaze. His eyebrows scrunched together and he looked around the rest of the passenger car. "But where are all the Indians?"

Matthew smirked behind his newspaper. Ruth Ann shook her head. He had eyes and ears on all sides of his head.

She turned her attention to the countryside of the Choctaw Nation flashing by. Where, indeed, were all the Indians?

The encounter with Takba came to mind. Her eyes had pierced Ruth Ann's soul, staring as though she knew just who Ruth Ann was. It had sent a chill up her spine and caused her to jerk involuntarily. She rubbed her shoulder at the memory. Whoever the woman was, she'd helped. Ruth Ann still felt twinges in her shoulder at night if she lay on it, but otherwise, her injury didn't bother her like it should have. In fact, she'd neglected to tell her mother about it until Della poked at the bandage and torn sleeve.

Ruth Ann, Lance Fuller, and even Beulah had sat quietly under the woman's care. Takba hadn't said much. Neither had Amarillo. It was a quiet visit for people with so many things to discuss. None of the children returned to the house. Only the cry of a baby disturbed the quiet, but no one asked about that either. Once, Amarillo slipped behind a blanket hanging on the wall into what must have been a lean-to on the side of the house. The crying stopped and she emerged before long without a word.

Takba, who appeared to be full-blood Choctaw, tended them. Her movements were quick and intense, as though ready to be rid of the visitors.

None of them spoke on the way home. It wasn't until Dickens came into view that Beulah blurted, "Well, that certainly was interesting!"

They had not accomplished what they'd set out to do.

Ruth Ann wondered who the Choctaw woman was. The odd way she kept the room in silence, and the way she could heal...

But it was a mystery for another time. There was a whole new story ahead.

The train approached the Springstown stop. Ruth Ann tried to get a good look at the platform through the glass window of the passenger car. As in Dickens, the people here used the arrival of a train as an excuse to gather and gossip, pick up mail and loiter.

She recognized someone who was making his way through the crowd with absolute certainty of where he was headed. Pepper Barnes. He glanced at the windows of the passenger car and their eyes met.

"Oh." Ruth Ann leaned back in her seat, wishing she hadn't been staring.

"What is it?" Matthew lowered the newspaper and looked out the window, but he couldn't see the platform from where he sat next to Ruth Ann.

"Oh. Nothing." Ruth Ann slid lower in her seat. She watched the door of the passenger car. But she shouldn't have done that either.

Pepper Barnes came through, carrying a small travel bag. He was dressed in a brown suit, complete with vest and a gold watch chain looping from one pocket to another. He wasn't hard looking, but not pleasant either. Strictly business. Most people would assume his dark skin was from the summer sun. Even though he had a white father, his mother was full-blood Choctaw and his skin would stay dark through winter. It helped him fit in with the National party he belonged to, a party of mostly full-bloods. He fit in many places. His handsome features didn't hurt either.

Matthew followed her gaze and spotted Pepper. Ruth Ann saw Matthew's frown before it slipped away.

He folded the newspaper and stood as Pepper approached. Matthew greeted him cordially, but coolly.

"*Halito, chim achukma?*"

"*Vm achukma.*"

Pepper removed his hat and motioned to the empty bench across from them. "Mind if I join you?"

To Ruth Ann's dismay, Matthew nodded. She pushed herself up straight in the seat and tried to smile politely. Pepper took a seat directly across from her.

He slid his bag under the bench and returned the smile, though it was tight. "I suppose you're headed to Tushkahomma too."

The train jerked into motion and Ruth Ann glanced at Matthew to defer the conversation to him. But she wasn't sure the two could hold a civil discussion, and the conductor certainly would not appreciate a fistfight on his train. That was what happened the last time these two young men were together. They'd argued over tribal politics right in the middle of the mansion shoot-out last winter and destroyed more furniture than the bullets had.

But Matthew eased back in his seat, seeming comfortable. "Thought we'd check into a few other happenings while we're there."

"Like Bob Carney's court hearing?"

"Oh?" The way Matthew said this, Ruth Ann knew he wasn't surprised. She, however, was clueless.

Though she had wanted to remain a shadow, she asked Pepper, "What hearing is that?"

Matthew glanced at her. He probably thought they'd discussed it, but lately, he hadn't told her everything.

Pepper remained stiff as he addressed Ruth Ann. "You don't know about the charges filed against my former employee, Bob Carney, for leasing tribal land to intruders? His hearing is tomorrow. I'm going to…see about a few things before then."

Not knowing what that meant, Ruth Ann decided to ease out of the conversation she shouldn't have gotten into. "Oh." She shifted to look out the window.

The two young men kept the conversation on other topics: *How's the rest of the family? Sissy is back at school in Sherman for the semester; yes, things are going well in Dickens, Mama is fine; been somewhat a dry spell going into fall; still looks to be a good harvest; heard about the new white teacher you have.*

This was when Ruth Ann took an interest in the conversation, though she kept her attention on the mountainous country they were entering. Tushkahomma wasn't far.

Matthew nodded. "Lance Fuller held the first classes at the beginning of September. Some folks object strongly to a white school, though."

Ruth Ann knew from his tone he was asking if Pepper Barnes was someone who strongly objected. She hoped the attentions of Lance Fuller toward her wouldn't enter the conversation.

Pepper shrugged. "Education is important. Still, can't trust most white men that come here. They're always looking at what they can siphon from the Nation."

Like timber? Ruth Ann bit her lip at the irony. Pepper's father, Mr. Robert Barnes, was white, a man who came into the Territory after the War. He married a Choctaw, which gave him access to the resources held in common by the Choctaw Nation. Whether he was "siphoning" those resources, or just doing good business was something the court at Fort Smith, Arkansas, would decide soon.

Mr. Barnes made no bones about his dislike for most men, in particular whites and mixed-bloods who tried to swindle the Indians. In the fight over the election for chief, Mr. Barnes sided with the Nationals, the political party mostly made up of full-blood Choctaws. Mr. Barnes was in a class of his own. No one put limits on him.

Thankfully, Matthew didn't voice any of Ruth Ann's thoughts. Instead, he turned the conversation to the Barnes horse breeding operation that included a purebred strain of Choctaw horses. Still, there was an underlying argument ready to happen between the young men who had known one another their whole lives.

Ruth Ann tried to relax. The next few days would be

tense enough without adding the Barnes conflict. But she didn't have to endure it long. The train let out a long whistle, alerting the next stop of its arrival.

Tushkahomma. The seat of the Choctaw Nation.

CHAPTER ELEVEN

THE DEPOT SAT AT THE end of a row of buildings settled in a cleared out area of the town. The mountain served as a backdrop. The Kiamichi Mountains and the Potato Hills sent a great deal of timber to Tushkahomma to be milled and carted off by the railroad.

When the Council House had been built in 1884 two miles north, a community sprang up around it. Chief McCurtain had proposed building five homes close to the stately building for elected officials, but that never came about. When the St. Louis-San Francisco Railway laid track two miles south, the businesses moved there. The new Tushkahomma was largely a timber town that included three hotels.

This depot didn't have frivolous bustle. It was all business. Men in patched flannel shirts, like Ruth Ann had seen at the sawmill when they visited Will Hocks, hustled by as the train puffed to a halt. She craned her neck to look back at the flatcars about to be loaded with milled boards.

Matthew jostled her when he stood and lifted their hefty carpetbags. "Come on, Annie, there'll be time for gawking later."

Ruth Ann turned with a frown and met Pepper's eyes. He

wasn't moving, allowing her to leave first.

It was one thing for Matthew to talk to her like a little sister in private. It was another to do it in front of a young man, even someone she'd known from childhood.

Matthew made his way down the aisle with the two large carpetbags. Ruth Ann followed, aware of Pepper Barnes right behind her.

On the platform, she took another look at the flatcars, astonished by the amount of timber taken from the hills. This was only one load. Hundreds went out every year. Men like Mr. Robert Barnes were getting wealthy.

Pepper stood near her arm, Matthew on the other side. Pepper motioned with his bag toward two wagons parked alongside the platform. The drivers were seated on the spring seats. "I'll see if we can get a ride to the Council House."

Matthew nodded, but Ruth Ann didn't think it was a good idea. The men looked like they were in an argument.

"You Buzzard, you don't know nothin' about nothin'! You ought to—"

"And you got room to talk, you half-breed Polecat. You not dry behind the ears yet and you think—"

"Better than being wet in the ears and can't hear nothin'!"

Ruth Ann deciphered the conversation, such as it was. The Progressive party was known by their opponents as "Polecats" and the Nationals as "Buzzards."

The younger man—a Polecat—took off his hat and shook it in the other's face. "I'd rather be half-blood and half sense than be full of nothin'. You gonna ruin what we got left. You—"

The older man, a Nationalist, used his long reins to swat the hat out of his hand. "Young pup! Was your daddy buried on the long trail from Mississippi? You want blood spilled today?" His hand went to the Winchester leaning in the floorboard by his foot.

Ruth Ann gasped and stepped back but Matthew dropped the carpetbags and went to the edge of the platform,

Pepper at his side. "Hold it, both of you! You want to shoot each other, do it where innocent women and children don't have to watch. Better yet, settle this in a way that honors the Choctaw blood in your veins."

Ruth Ann noticed Pepper's right hand deep in his pocket. Did he have a pistol?

The two wagon drivers glared at Matthew. The younger one hopped from his wagon and retrieved his hat from the dirt. He swatted it like it was his worst enemy, muttering something Ruth Ann thankfully couldn't hear.

Matthew took a deep breath. "Now, would one of you gentlemen give us a ride out to the Council House?"

The older man swished something around in his mouth and spit dangerously close to the man on the ground. The younger man jerked his head up with a scowl but the older man was still looking at Matthew. "Who're you voting for?"

"That's a private question."

"Then find your own way." He slapped the reins across the backs of his tired mules. They started forward as though sleepwalking. The driver gave his opponent a final dirty look.

Pepper turned to the Progressive party member who had climbed back onto his wagon seat. "How about it? Will you give us a ride out?"

The man spit like he'd been holding it in a long, long time. "Mind your own business!"

He moved his wagon away but headed toward town rather than the road the older man had taken toward the mountain.

"Guess we walk." Matthew sighed and retrieved the bags. He finally noticed Ruth Ann. She must have looked as drained as she felt because he quickly added, "After we get hotel rooms, drop these bags and freshen up." Quieter, he said, "Sorry you had to see that."

Ruth Ann shook her head but didn't trust herself to speak. Being a reporter in this territory required fortitude. The only way to get it was to keep being knocked around until she learned not to fall.

Since it was late in the afternoon, Matthew opted to spend the rest of the day in town. This was fine with Ruth Ann, who wanted to remain in the Roebuck Hotel while he made contact with people. But she accompanied him through the grueling evening hours.

They went to the houses near town and interviewed folks they'd never met who were well acquainted with the *Choctaw Tribune*. This surprised Ruth Ann. Strangers knew her by name because of her columns and articles. Some were appreciative. Others were not.

◆ ◆ ◆

The next morning, they rented a buggy—one that might have been in a wreck itself—and drove north to the Council House. Pepper was already out that way, staying at the home of a friend.

Ruth Ann had not attended the election for chief last year. In fact, she hadn't been up this way in some time and she leaned forward for that first glimpse of the magnificent structure.

The wood-lined road they'd traveled opened to a well-kept lawn that led to the Council House. Vacant buildings surrounded it, remnants of the community that used to be. People used the buildings to camp in during hearings or elections. Most were already filled with campers, entire families, who staked out their spot early. No wonder Matthew had wanted to arrive yesterday. The hotels in Tushkahomma were filling too.

The Council House in the center of the lawn commanded attention. Built from local material, the three-story red brick building with its mansard roof made a statement about the progress in Choctaw Nation. The ornamental wrought iron lining the rooftop was like a crown settled on what the *Indian Journal* of Muskogee had said was "the finest structure in Indian Territory." It had ample room for the two branches of the council, executive offices, Supreme Court, and offices of government officials. Wide steps led to the large double doors. Anyone who climbed those steps knew to show respect for the halls of Choctaw legislation and justice.

Matthew stopped the buggy near the steps. Ruth Ann hopped off the spring seat and leaned back to see the top of the structure again.

"You here to vote?"

The voice had a familiar ring, and Ruth Ann's heart pounded. She glanced around though she knew the question was directed at Matthew, who paused on the steps.

A man stood at the corner of the Council House, a Winchester settled in his arms. He wasn't drunk today, but that didn't relieve Ruth Ann. This was the man who had almost shot Matthew at Daniel Springs.

Matthew looked over at the man. Ruth Ann held her breath. *No speeches, Matt. Not unarmed and with no one but me to help.*

Her brother stayed casual. "I'll vote. Everyone should instead of..." He stopped and glanced Ruth Ann's way. Maybe her presence would keep him safe.

The man's hand drifted over the lever of his rifle. He gripped it, finger on the trigger, though he kept the barrel pointed skyward. "Be sure you vote right. You be sure to do that."

Matthew nodded with a tight smile. "I plan to, come Election Day."

With a low wave, he motioned for Ruth Ann to go up the steps and on through the double white doors of the Council House. She happily obliged.

To her relief, it was pleasantly cool inside. Ruth Ann breathed in the scent of the wood floors and coffee brewing somewhere. The long entry hall welcomed her, with its ceiling that stretched fourteen feet high. Doors lined both sides and led to the various offices of the elected officials. But the first room to the left was the courtroom. That door opened continuously with men in suits going in and out with determined expressions. A hearing must be about to take place.

She wanted to shake herself. Of course. Bob Carney's trial. Pepper was probably inside, making it the last place she cared to be.

Matthew nudged her to the side from where she had stood blocking the front doorway. "Why don't you go in the courtroom and take notes? I have people to talk to before noon."

"You're going to leave me?"

"If you can't handle it, I won't."

She swatted at his arm, but he was already heading down the long hall. She watched him go, wanting an idea where he would be in case she needed him. At the end of the hall, Matthew bounded up the first part of the staircase leading to the second floor. He slowed to exchange casual greetings with the men descending. He made the turn for the next part of the steps and disappeared.

Ruth Ann took a deep breath and waited until the courtroom doorway was clear before she boldly stepped through. She crashed right into Pepper Barnes.

"Oh!"

"Oh. Ruth Ann." Pepper sidestepped her and hurried for the front doors.

It took a little doing to refocus her thoughts, but Ruth Ann was determined. How hard could it be to cover a trial?

She took a quick inventory of the room and its occupants. Near the door where she'd entered stood the judge's stand. It faced the room and the tables set up for the accused and their prosecutors. Rows of wood pews filled the other half of the room. Ruth Ann took a seat on the back row.

Pepper reentered and joined the prosecutor's table. The preliminaries started and Ruth Ann took notes. No one paid her any mind.

Midway through the morning, she stifled a yawn. Matthew hadn't returned, and she had a terrible hunch he'd left her in the courtroom to stow her away while he took care of business. She fought her droopy eyelids until the third witness for the prosecution was called.

"Will Hocks."

Ruth Ann jolted upright in her seat and stared at the swearing in of the next witness. Mr. Hocks!

The white foreman stood at the head of the Choctaw court, tugging on his starched collar. He wore a suit coat too small for his muscular frame. It was buttoned dangerously at his chest and his shoulders all but poked through the material. He still wore his work pants. But the mismatched outfit didn't distract from the deathly serious expression on his face. He didn't want to be there and the audience agreed.

Someone whistled and called out, "White men not allowed to testify in our court!"

Other men shouted their agreement. The judge banged his gavel. Ruth Ann watched the disgruntled expressions around her. Things were already tense because of the election in two days. These men were on one side or the other. This could bring those tensions to the surface, and who knew what would happen?

But the Lighthorse at the hearing moved around the room, and a dissatisfied quiet ensued. The judge gave a final rap with his gavel.

The defense attorney stood and Ruth Ann noted a smirk on his dark features. "No objection to this witness, Your Honor."

Hocks was sworn in and seated on the witness stand. Ruth Ann held her breath as the prosecutor established Hocks as foreman of the Springstown timber operation. That drew more catcalls from the audience. Everyone knew who the owner was. Mr. Robert Barnes.

A few questions later, the prosecutor brought out his reason for calling this witness. "Mr. Hocks, would you please describe your last conversation with the accused?"

Drops of sweat glistened on Hocks' forehead, reflected by the sunlight coming through the large windows. Ruth Ann figured he would rather be trapped under a felled tree than sitting before this crowd, saying things one side or the other wouldn't like.

Hocks cleared his throat. "Carney, Bob Carney that is, he came to me a month or so ago and wanted to lease me land in the Potato Hills. I said no thanks, that I was manning the Springstown operation. He laughed and said that would go under soon enough. He said he could fix us both up, that the timber in the hills was ours for the taking. He'd already helped himself to quite a bit with the help of white men like me."

By this point, the men in the audience made such a ruckus it nearly drowned Hocks' words. The judge banged his gavel, but it took several minutes for the crowd to simmer down. Ruth Ann noticed a few Choctaws stand and line up by the long side wall of windows. Their arms were crossed and they scowled with something deeper than irritation.

"Mr. Hocks, what was your response to this man?"

"I told him to beat it, that I was loyal to working for…well, that I didn't have any interest in partnering with someone to sell out his own people."

The prosecutor took his seat amid more catcalls before the defense attorney stood. He still had his smirk.

"Mr. Hocks, wouldn't it be fair to say that your boss, Mr. Robert Barnes, is selling out the Choctaw Nation for his own gain?"

"Objection, Your Honor!"

"And isn't it true that Mr. Barnes is facing charges for stealing Choctaw timber?"

"Your Honor, Mr. Barnes isn't the one on trial!"

"Isn't he?" The attorney raised his hand. "I withdraw those questions, Your Honor, and ask this: Mr. Hocks, in 1879, did you conduct illegal mining operations in the Kiamichi Mountains?"

Ruth Ann squirmed. She wasn't sure if Mr. Hocks had noticed her. She started to duck behind the burly man seated in front of her, but she wanted to see every expression. Though the prosecutor prevented the last question from being answered, she could tell from Hocks' face that the question hadn't bothered him. Apparently his past life was no secret, and he didn't care if the whole Choctaw Nation knew about it.

Despite efforts by the defense attorney to discredit the witness, Hocks and the prosecutor stood their ground and kept things from becoming a circus. The grumbling in the audience settled to a low buzz, and Mr. Hocks was soon dismissed from the witness stand. He bolted for the door. Pepper followed him. The judge called for a recess.

While most people lingered in the courtroom, Ruth Ann hurried to stuff her pencil in her reticule as she bumped her way through the crowd to the door. In the hall, there was no sign of Mr. Hocks or Pepper. They must have gone outside. She went through the door and spotted them at the bottom of the steps, talking to Matthew.

Slowing her heart and her breath, Ruth Ann descended the steps in a ladylike fashion while wondering what she was missing in the exchange. She caught a snippet from Hocks, whose back was to her.

"You talk to him, if you can find the rabbit hole he's hiding down. He knows. That's all I'm gonna say."

There was a quick exchange between Hocks and Pepper. Then Hocks turned and saw Ruth Ann. He gave her a quick nod. "I would advise you to stop messing around in politics. Ain't safe for a lady. Or a man."

He glanced at Matthew briefly enough to send a cold chill over Ruth Ann. "Good day, ma'am."

Hocks gave a curt tip of his hat before turning away. He yanked the tiny suit coat off and headed down the road toward Tushkahomma. The road that would lead him back to his timber operation.

CHAPTER TWELVE

THOUGH THE OCTOBER DAYS STILL had length to them, Ruth Ann hardly found an evening stroll through a cemetery appealing. But Matthew wanted to visit the cemetery before more people arrived. And he had that pondering look which told Ruth Ann she was in for disturbing news.

The Tushkahomma cemetery held graves of prominent Choctaw families. It wasn't the oldest cemetery, not as old as the one in Doaksville where David Folsom, one of the district chiefs during the Removal, rested. Her people had been through much in the past sixty years.

A cemetery stroll at sunset made Ruth Ann shiver even in the warm evening air that refused to give way to autumn just yet. But at least here, no one would overhear their conversation.

Matthew halted by the headstones of the McCurtain family and motioned to the fenced area. "Quite a story here. This whole area." He waved to include the faint light coming from the Council House across the rolling field from them.

Ruth Ann hugged herself. She needed to prompt him into spilling whatever he was going to say. There was no sense being caught in the cemetery after dark. "Quite a story going on now."

He looked down at her with his amused smile and she bristled. "Come on, Matt, what did you find out? What did Mr. Hocks mean about...whatever he said?"

Matthew sighed, serious again. He scrubbed a hand over the evening whiskers on his chin. "We've been betrayed, Annie. The Choctaw people, especially the ones around Dickens. Sold out. Or should I say, leased out."

Somewhere in the woods edging the west side of the cemetery, a coyote yipped a sharp accusation. "What do you mean? Who do you mean? Mr. Carney?"

"I wish it were, then we'd have him. Whoever it is knows he's a dead man if the Nationals find out he leased land to a white man for a townsite. That's far worse than selling off timber." Matthew dropped his hands and sank them in his back pockets. "Hocks knows, but he doesn't want to talk. I think it's someone who goes back to his dealings with Warren. This leased land business will lead to disaster for the Nation if it's not stopped, but Hocks didn't give me much. He just said to talk to someone named Al Percy. But I plan to have a long talk with Hocks after the election. On the way home, I'm taking off at Kosoma depot and riding over to the sawmill."

Ruth Ann didn't miss his use of the singular pronoun. "We, you mean. I want to know too."

Matthew eyed her. "I don't think you should go, Annie. Not this time. Whichever way the election comes out, there'll be trouble. The back roads will be loaded with angry, trigger-happy men who don't take care what they're aiming at."

"Then you shouldn't go either. You bleed as red as I do."

Something flickered across Matthew's face, a distant thought. Or maybe it was a final shadow caused by the fading sunlight. Either way, it was gone when he said quietly, "Maybe so."

He wasn't responding to what she'd just said. But Ruth Ann didn't know what her brother meant. His eyes were distant. It was almost as though she stood next to a stranger.

Ruth Ann shivered and elbowed him. "It's time we headed back to town. Tomorrow will be a long day."

Her brother came back to himself and she slipped her arm through his. He pulled her close and they walked silently from the Tushkahomma cemetery. Whatever lay ahead, they would face together.

God knows.

◆ ◆ ◆

The hearing ended the next morning with Carney found guilty of partnering with a white man to sell off tribal resources for personal gain. There was celebration but also grumbling. Other Choctaws were committing greater atrocities in the Nation, but it went ignored. There were rumors that the judge had a personal vendetta against Carney—something about him marrying then abandoning the judge's sister—and that was the reason justice was served in this case.

On the other side they said it wasn't justice, that any Choctaw had a right to tribal resources, which was true. Sort of. Ruth Ann grew tired of trying to figure it out. So much depended on who was in leadership at the time.

The hearing elevated tempers on the council grounds as the election drew closer. The crowd grew and fistfights were common. There was even a gunshot, though someone said it was just from excitement.

Ruth Ann stayed close to Matthew. Maybe that man from Daniel Springs wouldn't take a shot at the publisher of the *Choctaw Tribune* if a woman stood next to him. Matthew was caught up in his own reporting and didn't seem to notice his constant shadow. She'd always been there anyway, especially since Philip's death.

Election Day saw the largest and most temperamental crowd to gather since, well, since the election for chief that spawned the local wars of 1892. Ruth Ann had experienced one of the battles at the Barnes mansion shootout.

The Barneses wouldn't be left out this time either.

The family arrived and caused a stir in the crowd arguing

outside the Council House. Ruth Ann was relieved to see Sissy wasn't with them. The young woman had returned to school in Sherman, Texas.

The presence of Mr. Barnes made the crowd separate with jeers cast his way. Pepper met up with his father. After a brief exchange, Mr. Barnes looked Ruth Ann's way and smiled.

With Mrs. Barnes—a graceful Choctaw woman—on his arm, he headed to where Ruth Ann stood with Matthew's back to her under the shade of a sturdy elm. Autumn hadn't claimed the tree's leaves yet, so it provided a shelter from the early October sun.

But sweat still broke out on Ruth Ann's lips. She poked Matthew's back, interrupting his conversation with a mixed-blood named Sam Mishaya. He followed her gaze to the approaching Barnes family. Robert Barnes walked with his signature limp, a keepsake from his time in the Civil War. But he had always walked tall and straight. His wife, Abby Barnes, was a picture of refinement, of social class yet with an air of grace and humility. With her long black hair folded up in the traditional way, her fashionable dress, and her white husband, she was a contrasting figure.

Matthew excused himself from Sam Mishaya and turned with a polite smile. They exchanged greetings, and Mrs. Barnes crushed Ruth Ann in a motherly embrace. "Look at you! What a fine lady you are. How is your mama?"

Mr. Barnes pumped Matthew's hand longer than necessary. "Well, son, what are your predictions? Think these Pole-cats have a chance of winning?"

The man Matthew had been talking with, Sam Mishaya, answered. "Better chance than any Buzzard."

Pepper moved to his father's side. "No one was talking to you."

"We'd be better off stringing up Barnes next to Carney. No account, blood sucking—"

Mr. Barnes stepped in front of his wife and Ruth Ann. "You got vile words for me, you say them in private. I don't let no man talk that way in front of my wife."

"She's the only reason you can come in thievin' and actin' like you one of us. You nothing but a filthy—"

Mr. Barnes' fist finished the sentence and Mishaya landed on his backside. Despite his age, the Civil War veteran could move with the speed of any youngster. He even beat out his own; Pepper hadn't moved as fast as his father, although he tried.

Sam Mishaya leaped up and tried to charge, but Matthew grabbed his arm, swung him around and pinned Mishaya's arm behind his back.

"Hold it, Mishaya! We need unity among our people, not prejudices."

Mishaya struggled to get free. Matthew shook him. "I said, hold it! Go calm down."

Matthew released him and Mishaya stumbled. He glared at Mr. Barnes and wiped the blood from his lip. Ruth Ann saw Barnes brace for an attack, but it didn't come.

The bloody lip turned up into a smile. "Sure, Matthew Teller. Whatever you say. You know so much."

Sam Mishaya strode away. Ruth Ann had witnessed the man's temper before, some years back when he'd lost an election for a Choctaw senate seat. He wasn't the kind of man she'd care to have looking after the affairs of the Nation.

Mrs. Barnes held a handkerchief under her nose against the swirling dust. She looked at Matthew. "I think you do."

Mr. Barnes relaxed his posture, slapped his son's back, and nodded to Matthew. "I see your father in you, Matthew Teller. He'd be proud." He pointed at the retreating form of Mishaya. "But you need to know when to stay out of another man's fight."

Ruth Ann muttered, "That's one thing he'll never learn."

Her quiet words made Mr. Barnes chuckle. "Well, Ruth Ann, it keeps life from getting dull. Can't say it will help when a fellow comes courting you, though."

Whether he was joking or not, Ruth Ann wasn't sure. Surely he wasn't somehow referring to Lance Fuller. But Mrs.

Barnes' eyes shined with hope and Ruth Ann wanted to hide behind the trunk of the elm. Did they still think something would bloom between her and Pepper?

But Matthew was on to other subjects. He dusted off his suit coat and addressed Mr. Barnes. "I understand you'll have the results from Fort Smith any day now."

Pepper beat his father to this punch. "We expect to hear from the lawyers today. My father will be cleared of all charges soon."

Ruth Ann cocked her brow at the confident air of Pepper and Mr. Barnes. Despite Carney's guilty verdict, and the fact they had helped convict him, they seemed confident of the results from Fort Smith. Mr. Barnes believed his timber operation followed tribal law to the letter, whereas Carney had brought in white investors to lease land to.

Mr. Barnes had said from the beginning he was confident his lawyers would get him off. He said Judge Isaac Parker was the best, and he'd do things right. Ruth Ann wouldn't want to sit in the judge's seat. She couldn't say for certain what was right, and she wasn't sure Matthew could either. But her brother reported news; he didn't sit in judgment.

They spent the rest of the day in idle chitchat, and Ruth Ann stayed in the background as much as possible.

U.S. troops were camped out around Tushkahomma to keep an eye on things during this session of the General Council. The *Indian Citizen* had reported "an appalling number" of political assassinations on both sides in September. Martial law had been declared because of the wars and feuds caused by the 1892 elections, and Ruth Ann prayed for a peaceful session this time to relieve the federal troops from the Choctaw Nation.

With evening came the poll results from the districts in the Choctaw Nation. Each time a rider was spotted, people stirred around the Council House. Tension mounted. It was hard to hear the results called out from the Council House steps, and hard for the Lighthorsemen to keep the crowds from stampeding up the steps.

Thankfully, Matthew didn't insist on being near the front. He found a place to stand in the bed of a wagon, Ruth Ann at his side. They could watch the hundreds of Choctaws press and shout, fight and celebrate as the hours rolled on. Only the Council House itself stood stable. All else descended into chaos.

But there was no doubt of the outcome when darkness fell. The Nationals were in the lead by an overwhelming margin. At least, so the poll booths said. The Progressives accused the Nationals of tampering with ballots and threatening voters. The din rose and Ruth Ann swayed in the bed of the wagon, tired from several hours of straining to see everything.

Matthew leaned close to her and said over the shouts, "Time you went back to the hotel, Annie. It's mostly over now."

"Not hardly." Ruth Ann spotted a man in the crowd passing a whiskey bottle to his companion.

A fist pounded the side of the wagon near where she stood. She jerked, then recognized Mr. Barnes in the darkness.

"We did it! One step closer to ousting them Polecats before they ruin the Nation. We'll get Chief Jones next. You wait and see." He beamed and nodded to Ruth Ann. "But it's getting late for the womenfolk and I don't want you around what's coming when they make the official announcement. Pepper's taking his mother back to town. I'd advise you go with them."

Matthew nudged Ruth Ann toward the back of the wagon. She hissed, "I'm a reporter, and I need to stay for the whole story."

He took her elbow and urged her along. "You leave now, Annie, and I'll…" He pondered a compromise. She was surprised when it came. "I'll let you ride along to see Hocks." He said this in a low tone where Mr. Barnes wouldn't hear.

Ruth Ann's legs trembled with fatigue. She would gladly trade the bed of the wagon for her hotel bed. She allowed Mr. Barnes to help her off and escort her through the increasingly hostile crowd.

He kept a careful eye on those they passed, many of whom sneered at him. "Don't worry about your brother. He's a good Choctaw man and can take care of himself from foes on either side."

Mr. Barnes had meant to encourage her, but for Ruth Ann, his words were a harsh reminder that neither side was fond of the *Choctaw Tribune* since it reported the wrongdoings on both sides rather than slanting the news in anyone's favor. But Ruth Ann wasn't worried about Matthew. He could take care of himself without her around. Couldn't he?

On the other side of the large Council House, Pepper and Mrs. Barnes greeted her and the three set off for the two-mile walk to Tushkahomma.

Ruth Ann had plenty to think on, but little she wanted to say. Pepper carried a lantern and Mrs. Barnes kept conversation going from where she walked between the young people. "Things will settle down now that the elections are over. We could certainly use a peaceful spell!"

Pepper shook his head. "The fight's just begun, with Dawes running around, getting ready to divide our nation. If the Progressives have their way, it'll be the end of the Choctaw Nation with them lining their pockets with our money."

He swung the lantern to fully light them all and looked directly at Ruth Ann for the first time since the train. "Your brother doesn't understand how important it is to get on the right side and fight. He's doing more harm than good with his newspaper. You're not helping either. You should—"

"Robert Barnes, Jr.!" Mrs. Barnes—a genteel woman—smacked her son's shoulder with the back of her hand. "Don't speak to a lady that way ever again."

Pepper stared straight ahead and said nothing.

Ruth Ann wasn't sure how to respond, but the exchange left her anxious. Did Pepper Barnes view her as less than a lady because they'd known one another their whole lives? Or was it because she'd become a reporter and was no longer the feminine young woman she should be? She'd known the dangers of being a woman reporter, but was losing the right to be treated as a lady one of them?

After a good walk, the lights of Tushkahomma showed the remainder of their way to the Roebuck Hotel. Ruth Ann thought of Matthew. People in the politics of the Choctaw Nation were being shot down, assassinated in their own homes or offices. If an old friend like Pepper thought the *Choctaw Tribune* did more harm than good, what of that mob that Matthew planted himself in the middle of at the Council House grounds?

Chihowa, please protect him. Please. I want to see my brother to-morrow.

CHAPTER THIRTEEN

MATTHEW DIDN'T RETURN TO THE hotel that night, but he did return. Ruth Ann was so relieved to see him in the hall of the hotel the next morning, she gripped him in a hug. When he started to pull back, she held on a moment longer.

No shootings had taken place at the general council session, and it looked like the martial law was over. The federal troops were leaving the council grounds.

After breakfast in the busy hotel dining room, Ruth Ann and Matthew boarded the southbound Frisco and rode down to Kosoma. Ruth Ann didn't see the Barneses on the train. Since Ruth Ann and Matthew didn't have horses, it was better for them to take the train to Kosoma, rent horses and ride east to the sawmill.

At Kosoma, Matthew asked the station master to stow their luggage until evening, then he sent Peter a wire telling him to expect them home on the evening train. They left Kosoma on rented horses for the ride through the foothills to the Barnes sawmill. That was where they'd find Hocks, and hopefully learn the identity of the Choctaw who'd betrayed them by leasing land to Warren to build a town in the Choctaw Nation.

When Ruth Ann asked Matthew why they couldn't check court records for the lease, he said the records had been lost in a fire. Only two people would have copies of the lease now—Warren and the traitor.

They skirted the town of Finley and kept a good pace toward Blackjack Mountain. The road was wide for hauling timber to the railroad and well-maintained to prevent problems for the heavy wagons. Other than the choking dust, Ruth Ann had no complaints of taking a peaceful ride away from civilization.

The road curved upward toward a large outcrop. Matthew stretched back in the saddle with a moan. "Man, I'll be glad to get home and sleep and eat Mama's cooking and write—"

The report of a rifle sounded from the outcrop a split second before the bullet found its mark. Matthew jerked.

Ruth Ann screamed when her brother tumbled from the saddle, his horse dancing wild-eyed. When Matthew hit the ground, the horse took off.

She slid from her sidesaddle. Her knees buckled. She landed hard on the dirt road, but kept a grip on the reins. She knew the shot had come from the outcrop just ahead of them, and the horse was the only shield they had on the open road. But she couldn't hang on. Her horse reared and the leather reins burned her sweaty palms when they slipped through.

Ruth Ann scrambled to Matthew's side. He lay face down in the dust.

He's pretending. He's pretending so the shooter will go away. He's only pretending...

She grabbed his shoulder and shook it. She gripped hard and rolled Matthew onto his back. She screamed again. Blood spurted from the hole in his left shoulder. Or was it over his heart? Dirt had mixed with the blood to create an ugly paste. Was he breathing?

Another rifle shot sounded, and Ruth Ann vacillated between wanting to die and wanting to live. *Mama can't lose us both...*

Two more shots rang out along with thundering hoofbeats coming down the road.

Ruth Ann knew she wanted to live. She had to live.

She scrambled around for a weapon and found a fist-sized rock. She stood and flung it at the approaching rider who came around the curve ahead. Not able to see if she'd hit her target, Ruth Ann wiped away her tears, her hair fallen from its bun and in her eyes. The rider waved a Winchester over his head and she saw his face. Pepper Barnes.

She grabbed another rock.

"Hold it, Annie! It's me, Pepper!"

He yanked his horse to a stop in front of her. The dust he stirred stung Ruth Ann's swollen eyes. Pepper leaped off his horse, Winchester in one hand. He moved toward her and took the rock from her grip. He glanced over his shoulder.

"I chased him off, but I don't know how far he'll run. Got to get you out of here."

Ruth Ann dropped to her knees again by Matthew. The blood had spread over his chest, his white shirt soaked to crimson red.

Pepper jumped over him, knelt, and pressed his free hand against the blood. "His heart's still beating, Annie. We'll get him to a doctor. There's not one in Finley, but Springstown isn't far, but we only have one horse so…"

A faint rustle sounded behind Ruth Ann. Pepper tossed his Winchester to his right hand and aimed behind her. She turned to see a woman emerge from the woods by the road.

"Takba."

Ruth Ann's own voice sounded strange. She cleared her throat. "Takba."

It was as though the name would explain everything, would explain the woman's appearance so far from the Jessop farm.

Pepper lowered his rifle. "You know this woman?"

Takba, the Choctaw woman with the gift of healing, didn't hesitate. She crossed the road and squatted at Ruth Ann's side. "He's a bad man."

Ruth Ann knew instinctively that Takba wasn't talking about Matthew. Or Pepper. But that was as far as her thoughts would carry her.

Takba lowered the bag that had been strapped across her back, and removed a small towel from it. She withdrew items from the bag and laid them on the towel: small brown bottles, a clay bowl, bandages.

"I don't know who you are, but we have to move." Pepper addressed the woman, but he looked to Ruth Ann.

She shrugged, though she was numb in her own body. "She has to do something. We won't make it to Springstown."

Matthew won't. Ruth Ann knew this to the core of her being.

Pepper scrubbed the blood from his hand on his pant leg and surveyed the woods where Takba had emerged. "I'm going to look around, make sure he didn't come back. I think I hit him in the leg. Then I'm going for help. Some of the lumberjacks have cabins around here. I'll find a wagon."

Pepper was talking in bits and pieces, at least it seemed so to Ruth Ann. She nodded as though she understood everything.

When Pepper rode away, Ruth Ann watched Takba. "How can I help?"

"Hold his head."

Confused, Ruth Ann turned and cradled Matthew's head in her lap. He was so limp, his face an odd white despite his Native blood and a season of summer sun. His eyes were closed, his lips parted but little breath came through them.

She finally comprehended Takba's words. She was to hold her brother close when he died.

The understanding overcame her, and Ruth Ann shook violently. She wailed and cupped herself around her brother.

CHAPTER FOURTEEN

RUTH ANN SWAYED IN THE back of the rocking wagon, watching. She had watched the old woman, Takba, remove a bullet from her brother's chest. She had watched Pepper return with three men and a wagon from the sawmill. She had watched them load her unconscious brother into the wagon bed, and watched Pepper instruct the driver to take the road to Springstown and the Barnes mansion.

Now she watched her brother's still face touched by the sun when the trees ended. Takba sat on his other side, hand planted firmly over the wound she'd bandaged. Her eyes were on his face as well. Ruth Ann held his head in her lap.

Pepper sat beside Ruth Ann, his arm around her shoulders. It was an odd feeling, him so close, comforting her. He was strong, strong as her brother. In many ways, he was like a brother, not afraid to treat her like herself, instead of a porcelain figurine. He wasn't afraid to speak his mind to her. He treated her as an equal.

Ruth Ann leaned her head on Pepper Barnes' shoulder and he moved closer where they knelt in the bed of the jolting wagon. She missed her daddy. She missed Philip. She missed Matthew. Pepper was as close to a brother as she had.

But he wasn't her brother.

With the next jolt of the wagon, Ruth Ann pulled herself upright and leaned over Matthew's drained face, and away from Pepper Barnes. It sounded like Pepper sighed.

It was a long ride.

When they arrived at the Barnes mansion, Mrs. Barnes came out on the porch. She was wearing the same dress as the day before, looking like she'd just arrived on the afternoon train from Tushkahomma. The driver shouted what happened as he slowed the wagon to a gentle stop. Mrs. Barnes cried out but then started shooting orders like a Gatling gun. A rider was sent for the doctor. Offspring sent to prepare the guest bedrooms. Hired hands sent to fetch a board to use as a stretcher. The cook sent to prepare food. Mr. Barnes sent to wire Della and fetch her from the train as soon as she arrived. Everyone obeyed and soon, Matthew was settled in an upstairs room.

As for Ruth Ann, Mrs. Barnes made a half-hearted attempt to send her to bed. Whatever frightened expression she may have had, Ruth Ann's determination was clear—she was not leaving her brother's side.

An hour later, Ruth Ann still watched. The doctor had removed Takba's bandages and examined the wound. He was satisfied with the work of the old woman. However, Takba was nowhere to be found. She'd disappeared when they arrived at the Barnes mansion.

Things settled down under Mrs. Barnes' direction. The doctor left, the cook cleared away the uneaten food, the hired hands went about their work, and Ruth Ann watched the room empty of all but Mrs. Barnes.

Mrs. Barnes stood on the other side of the bed and watched Ruth Ann. "We've done all we can, and the doctor says he has a fine chance of pulling through. With his stubborn streak, I'd say the chance is mighty fine."

She came around to Ruth Ann, lifting an afghan from the end of the bed. She laid it across Ruth Ann's lap and tucked it snugly around her waist. She bent low to give her a solid hug. "Your mother will be here soon."

Ruth Ann returned the hug weakly. "*Yakoke.*" Her voice cracked. She gripped her hands in her lap.

Mrs. Barnes patted Ruth Ann's shoulder. "Rest. I'll be back." She left the room. It was as silent as a tomb.

But it wasn't a tomb. Ruth Ann stared at Matthew's face, determined not to miss the moment when his eyelids flickered and his lips turned up in a grin at the sight of his little sister so worried about him. He'd laugh and say how a bullet couldn't stop a stubborn reporter, that nothing was more powerful than the press short of God Almighty. He'd say he was proud of her, and that he expected her to run things until he was back on his feet.

How would she manage that? What did any of it matter now? Someone had gotten what they, and many others, wanted. To stop the *Choctaw Tribune.* But Ruth Ann would not allow that. For the sake of her people, she would fight.

Ruth Ann leaned forward and combed Matthew's dirt and sweat-matted hair over his eyelids, smoothed the strands together then brushed them to the side. Now that he was finally still enough for a haircut, she had nothing to cut it with. She took Matthew's cold hand and squeezed it. No response. But soon. Soon he would be back to her and tell her what she needed to do. Give her the courage to fulfill her purpose in life.

God, our gracious God, I ask thee, I beseech thee to spare my brother's life…

Ruth Ann shook her head. The words were as lifeless as she felt. She whispered, "Oh my *Chihowa*, You know how scared I am, how helpless. There's no reason for You to care for me, but, oh, You do! Please, Lord. Don't let us face the world without Matthew. Mama, she couldn't take it, I couldn't either. I know I said the same thing about Daddy and Philip, but there wasn't a chance to pray then. There wasn't a chance to…" Ruth Ann's breath caught on her tears. *A chance to say goodbye*.

Was that why Matthew had survived so far? Was it merely a chance to say goodbye before he slipped a heartbeat away into eternity?

Ruth Ann rested her forehead on her hands, both clenching Matthew's still hand, and sobbed. She cried until feeling came back to her body. She ached from crying, from the rough wagon ride, from her tense posture. But it was good to feel something, even pain. At least she knew she was still alive herself.

Something scratched her skin, causing it to itch. She lifted her head and blinked her eyes to clear the black edges.

Again. Something stabbed the back of her hand. A fingernail. It left a red mark.

Gasping, Ruth Ann stared at her brother's face. His eyelids flickered, then went still again. They didn't open, he didn't smile, he didn't whisper teasing words to her. But his eyelids had moved, and so had his finger.

Ruth Ann pressed the back of her itching hand to his cheek. "I'm here, Matt. You hang on. There's a lot of work to do. You need to wake up before you miss the greatest front page story the *Choctaw Tribune* ever printed."

There was no response other than the irregular rise and fall of Matthew's chest as he breathed.

It was everything.

Ruth Ann had no idea how lost she was until her mother found her hours later, still seated at her brother's bedside. Beulah was a blurry figure in the background.

Ruth Ann wailed in her mama's arms, drawing from her the love and care Matthew needed. But there was no end to her mama's love. It flooded through Ruth Ann like a river and carried her along in its current. She stayed in the rush of the love as she moved with Della to Matthew's side. The river of love would overcome him, too. And if it made him as alive as it had Ruth Ann, they would all laugh together soon.

CHAPTER FIFTEEN

WELL INTO THE NEW MORNING, Dr. Caldwell returned to Matthew's room and examined him. The doctor had seen his fair share of shootings as a white man in Indian Territory. He had been caught in the Barnes mansion during the shootout last winter.

Dr. Caldwell announced Matthew's condition had stabilized, though he hadn't regained consciousness. The doctor put his stethoscope back in his medical bag. "Give him another day or so and you won't be able to pin him in that bed. A strong constitution comes in handy for surviving a plug so close to the heart, but it's the devil when it comes to following doctor's orders to recover."

Beulah harrumphed and bobbed her head. "Do not worry, Doctor, he has women just as stubborn who will see he follows orders."

Ruth Ann leaned back in the leather chair that had become so familiar to her. She was becoming aware of many things now that Matthew's face had some red in it again.

This room had been turned into a guest room back when the eldest Barnes son married and moved. It was furnished with a large bed standing against the wall opposite the door.

On either side, oversized leather chairs had made the vigilance pass with comfort for her and Della. The dresser was from a Sears and Roebuck catalogue, a fine piece to complement the cowhide rug that finished out the masculine decor.

Also coming to Ruth Ann's attention were the people in the room for the doctor's visit. Beulah had ridden the train up from Dickens with Della, though she'd stayed in the shadows during the family reunion. She hadn't tried to get Ruth Ann or Della to retire to the other guest room, and Ruth Ann was grateful for Beulah's understanding and strong presence.

Mr. and Mrs. Barnes conversed with the doctor on the details of Matthew's needs and assured him Matthew would receive the best care.

Last in the room was Pepper Barnes. He stood in the shadows near the door. He'd said little during the whole affair once they'd gotten on the road to Springstown. But his eyes said a great deal. Whenever they met Ruth Ann's, she sensed he had something to say but was holding off. There was something deeper in him than concern for what had happened. Some secret that Ruth Ann had a burning desire to uncover.

Sometime in the night, her thoughts had shifted from pure concern for her brother's life to questions. The main one that rang in her head all the night and morning was unspoken by anyone so far: who had shot Matthew?

From the look in Pepper's eyes, he knew. Ruth Ann would find out even if he didn't want to tell anyone. He had to tell her. She would make sure of it.

"I'll check on him this evening." The doctor repacked the rest of his medical supplies. "Oh, and let me know if you track down that medicine woman. I'd like to know what she used to stop the bleeding. Never saw anything work like it."

He moved to the door and Della exchanged quiet words with him, words a mother knows to say. Her presence had calmed Ruth Ann more than any doctor could.

When he left, Pepper followed him, saying he would see the doctor out. The room came alive with conversation, the

Barneses urging Della and the young women to settle in the guest rooms and Mr. Barnes promising to send Peter help in Dickens, although he knew Della's brother, Preston Frazier, would see to it the Teller home and livestock were tended to. Beulah said something about everything being under control there.

Ruth Ann slipped from her chair and through the door without anyone noticing. She had another conversation to see about. One where she asked the questions and got answers.

She went quietly down the wide staircase. The ceiling of the entrance hall rose two stories with a glass chandelier to welcome guests into one of the finest homes in Indian Territory. Its red carpeted floors and mahogany wood trim made a statement about the family: they had money and weren't bothered showing it with plantation-style living, a heritage Mr. Barnes brought from the Old South.

Pepper Barnes closed the front door behind the doctor. Ruth Ann waited at the bottom of the long curving staircase. Pepper was preoccupied enough with his own thoughts he missed seeing her when he moved down the hallway past the parlor door. Ruth Ann cleared her throat and he halted.

"Ruth Ann. I thought you were still upstairs."

She slowly shook her head and came off the last step. Pepper seemed to be studying her. Maybe to figure out what she wanted. Maybe to figure out what he thought about how she looked. Beulah had sponged off Ruth Ann's face while she and Della sat vigilantly over Matthew, but Beulah had been unable to wash her hair, so she fixed it in a low, matted bun. Hardly attractive for a young woman with prospects, but that wasn't the reason Ruth Ann had followed Pepper Barnes down the stairs.

She decided on the most direct question and hoped it caused the flood of answers she needed. "Who shot Matthew?"

Pepper hesitated. Ruth Ann suspected he knew a lot more than he wanted to say, and he wasn't sure how much to tell her. How much was appropriate to tell a lady, even one who'd been through the things Ruth Ann had.

He glanced up the stairs as though to make sure no other surprises were coming down, then he motioned toward the parlor. "Let's talk in private. There are things you need to know."

Ruth Ann crossed the space between them and entered the large parlor. The last time she'd been in this room, there had been a hundred men outside, circling the mansion and shooting it to pieces. People had been wounded and Ruth Ann questioned if she would make it out alive. Bullets had flown around her, but Matthew was at her side, a calm presence.

Matthew wasn't around to look after her now.

It was impossible to stand still and impossible to sit. Ruth Ann picked an area near the fireplace to pace. When Pepper pulled the parlor's pocket doors closed, her heartbeat quickened. It was inappropriate for her to be alone with a young man like this, but Ruth Ann put that aside. She was a reporter who needed information to write a story. She had to keep that in mind to do right by Matthew.

Pepper didn't seem the least concerned with the situation. He moved to the tray always present in the room with its crystal water pitcher. He poured two glasses, but instead of offering one to Ruth Ann, he set it on the new tea table. The former table had been smashed in the fight between Pepper and Matthew during the mansion shootout.

If Pepper thought Ruth Ann couldn't hold a glass of water, he was right. She clenched her trembling hands. Pepper didn't move and the room was awkwardly quiet.

He finally broke the silence. "I don't know."

Ruth Ann frowned.

"I mean, I don't know who shot Matthew. It could have been any number of people. He's made a lot of enemies."

"But you have a theory. Say it."

Pepper's demeanor shifted. He no longer regarded her as a young woman nor an old friend, but an equal. He looked her square in the eyes and drew out his words. "I have a pretty good idea who did it."

Ruth Ann stilled. She reminded herself this could be one of the most important discussions of her life.

But her impatience won out. "Well? Who?"

"The same man who killed Will Hocks an hour before you were ambushed."

That did it. Ruth Ann melted into the nearest chair, and Pepper offered her the glass of water. There was no way to hide her trembling hands as she took the glass and drank slowly.

Pepper drew a cushioned footstool close and sat. "Daddy didn't think we should tell y'all too soon."

"Mr. Hocks, your foreman is…dead? We were on our way to talk to him…" Ruth Ann halted. There she went again. Matthew lying on his sickbed, and she couldn't keep his investigation a secret.

Pepper nodded. "I figured. No other reason for you to have been on that road."

"Why were you on it?"

Pepper hesitated again. "I had business at the sawmill. I headed out there before dawn."

"Where was Mr. Hocks when he was…shot?" Ruth Ann stumbled over the words, trying to maintain distance from the fact she had known Hocks.

Pepper put one hand on his knee, the other on his hip. He shook his head. "He was in his office. One of the mill men found him that morning, not long before I got there. Seems nobody heard the shot over the saws. No one who will say anything."

Ruth Ann's mind raced to the memory of the tiny room with its stacks of records. "Was anything missing in his office?"

He gave her a look she'd earned. Who knew what had been in that messy space? Pepper wouldn't have had time to sort through looking for important papers.

Ruth Ann sighed. "Why were you coming up the road right when…when…"

She tried to form her thoughts faster than her words, but it wasn't easy with Pepper so close to her.

To her surprise, he chuckled. "You ask a lot of questions, Ruth Ann. You spend too much time with that brother of yours."

As if remembering the situation, Pepper winced but didn't apologize. He never apologized. "To answer your question, I was riding hard to Kosoma to get the sheriff there. I heard the gunshot come from the outcrop. I don't think the shooter knew I was coming down the road. I veered into the woods and heard him coming down a trail. He was riding a big paint pony. I could see his face, or rather, I couldn't. It was masked, so I figured he was an outlaw ambushing someone. I took a shot and hit him in the leg. He jerked around and fired off a couple at me before hightailing back up the trail. I started after him, but caught sight of the road, and a skirt…"

Pepper flushed. "That is, I saw whoever he shot at included a woman, so I came down to help. Didn't plan on her chunking rocks at my head."

He smiled but didn't lift his gaze to Ruth Ann. "I figured he was a bandit, but when I realized who he'd been after, well, I say it was a planned ambush, and a good likelihood of it being the same man who murdered our foreman."

"But why…who would want both of them…that is, who would…"

"Who would want both Matthew and Hocks dead? Could have something to do with the Carney trial. Or the elections. Or both. Plenty of people didn't like Hocks testifying against Carney. Carney has friends, same kind that would like to put the *Choctaw Tribune* out of business."

Ruth Ann knew Pepper didn't believe his own suggestion. There was something hidden behind his averted gaze. He was giving her a rabbit trail to chase down.

Well, she was no rabbit. "What if it had something to do with Mr. Hocks' past? He had his own secrets—"

"Don't pry." Pepper's tone was sharp. If Mr. Hocks had

secrets, Pepper knew them. Beyond that, he might be part of them.

Ruth Ann could yell, insist Pepper tell her everything that might help her find the killer. Or she could...

She softened her voice. "I didn't mean to upset you, Pepper. I just really need to know who tried to kill my brother."

She sniffed and fished a handkerchief from her pocket. It wasn't an act. The thought of Matthew's ashen face and the blood soaking his shirt made her want to sob. But she had to walk a fine line of pretending to plead with Pepper, and maintaining enough composure to form her questions.

The first part of her plan worked too well. Pepper slid closer to her from his seat on the footstool and tipped her chin up. It didn't help her composure that Pepper Barnes was one of the most amiable young men in the Choctaw Nation.

"Hey, don't cry. Matt's going to be all right. He's too stubborn to let one bullet stop him. Before you know it, he'll be writing the story of his own shooting."

This made Ruth Ann smile a little, but Pepper was too close. She stood and moved to the fireplace again. She studied the finely carved surface of the mantel. "I suppose I'm just thinking about what will happen then. Until the shooter is caught, we'll always be afraid of him coming back."

Pepper followed her to the fireplace. "Whoever he is, he's running scared now. He killed a white man. That will bring in the U.S. marshals and he knows that. He'll steer clear for now. There'll be time to worry about the rest later."

To Ruth Ann's dismay, Pepper put both hands on her shoulders and turned her to face him. To be very close to him. Surely he couldn't be thinking of...

The pocket doors slid open with a thud, followed by Beulah's loud call, "Ruth Ann! Oh, there you are. You frightened me. I could not find you."

Pepper dropped his hands and took a good step back. Beulah ignored him as she moved into the room, filling it with her voice. "If you are well enough to roam the house, you are well enough for me to retire you for a long sleep. Now come!"

Beulah gave a brisk nod in Pepper's direction before linking arms with Ruth Ann and sweeping her from the room. Ruth Ann took a deep breath.

I'm sure Matthew never had these kinds of problems as a reporter.

CHAPTER SIXTEEN

WHEN BEULAH SLAMMED THE DOOR to the second guest room behind them, Ruth Ann knew she wasn't about to finally rest.

Beulah leaned against the door as though prepared to guard it with her life. "Praise our God, I rescued you in time! How did you allow yourself to become trapped?"

Ruth Ann's cheeks reddened and she turned away from Beulah's stare. She went to the bed situated along the far wall, its plush comforter inviting her to turn it down and bury herself. But she plopped on it instead, still not meeting Beulah's stare. "I wouldn't have let him, Beulah. Pepper...goodness, I've known him my whole life. I—"

"We must move all of you to safety!"

Ruth Ann giggled, the kind when she was beyond exhaustion and tears. "My dear friend, you make it sound like I'm in mortal danger. I think I can avoid Pepper for a few days."

Beulah dropped on the bed next to Ruth Ann. It jolted them both, and a pin fell from Ruth Ann's bun. Half her hair tumbled around her shoulders.

Beulah sighed and twisted Ruth Ann's hair back into a

harsh bun. "Ruth, it is far worse than you realize. Have you not considered that young Pepper Barnes is the one who shot your brother?"

Ruth Ann jerked away from Beulah and faced her, mouth dropping open. "What on earth...Pepper saved our lives! Why would you think such a thing?"

Beulah rolled her eyes like Ruth Ann had asked a childish question. "The rescue may well have been from a guilty conscience. The shooting was meant to frighten you from your wits and prevent you from discovering the truth about the Barnes family."

"What truth?"

Beulah's eyes flashed with suspicion. "I do not know yet, but I am certain this family has secrets. They provoke fights. The father told me incidents that made me wonder if they join fists rather than hands for prayer around the dinner table."

Ruth Ann giggled again, though not the least bit amused. "The Barnes family would never hurt us."

"You cannot be sure!"

Beulah leaped to her feet and rushed to a travel bag that sat beside the dresser in the room. She dug to the bottom of the bag and pulled out a thin yellow and orange book. She brought it over and fanned the pages under Ruth Ann's nose. "There was such a story in one of these I read, a man murdered in his sleep by his trusted butler of twenty years. Betrayals are things of the real world, Ruth. You should—"

"Beulah Levitt!" Ruth Ann snatched the book and stared at the cover. "This is a Pinkerton detective novel! It's filled with...well, my mother wouldn't approve! Proper young women don't read this sort of thing."

Beulah rolled her eyes. "Oh, Ruth, we read about far worse things in your own newspaper. We learn many valuable things from novels, including the possibility that our closest associates might be our worst enemies."

"Well, that explains everything. You've been reading too much."

She handed the book to Beulah, but Beulah pushed it

back and lifted her chin.

"Read it, and see if you can sleep a night under the same roof as the man who may have shot your brother and is now trying to lure you to a place where he may get you too."

Beulah went to the door. "Sleep here. I am going right across the hall to your mother and brother, and you may be sure I will keep watch over the Teller family until we find a safe place for you." Beulah closed the door behind her.

Ruth Ann chuckled and set the book on the nightstand. Its colorful cover drew her attention to the title: *Pinkerton Detectives Series: Detective Against Detective or, A Great Conspiracy.* How ridiculous for Beulah to read the book and then let it overtake her good sense!

Simply ridiculous.

Ruth Ann sighed and began unbuttoning her shoes. Nothing was simple in the world, especially not in her world. As a reporter and as a sister, she had to consider everything. Pepper Barnes was hiding something. Was it evil, or merely knowledge he wanted to keep under wraps?

A few years back he'd been seeing a white girl down by the Red River, something his parents wouldn't approve of. They had designs on him marrying well and within the tribe. Ruth Ann found herself tangled in the story when rumors started that Pepper was down courting her at Uncle Preston's.

But this story was more than an unapproved relationship. Pepper had revealed a few things, but he was still holding back.

Which brought her reluctantly to Beulah's theory, at least in part. Was Pepper somehow involved in the shootings and wanted to make up for that now? Why did he really think Hocks was killed?

Somewhere among these questions, Ruth Ann fell back against the bed covers, one shoe still on, and fell asleep.

◆ ◆ ◆

It was the next night before Matthew opened his eyes.

Ruth Ann sat vigilant after everyone had retired for bed. She started to bolt from her chair to fetch her mama, but she halted, wondering how long the moment would last. Matthew's dark eyes looked confused as they squinted in the dim light.

Ruth Ann leaned over him and slowly turned up the kerosene lamp on the table by his bed. "*Halito*. And welcome back."

Matthew blinked. He murmured something and licked his dry lips. Ruth Ann poured a glass of water from the tray next to the lamp. She lifted his head so he could drink without choking.

Then his eyes closed and Ruth Ann was afraid he'd pass out again. She set the glass aside and gently poked his shoulder with a trembling finger. "Hey. You've been asleep long enough. Mama will want…"

A soft snore answered her. Ruth Ann sighed and settled back into the leather chair. She picked up the book she'd been reading. Only under the cover of darkness would she dare read the Pinkerton detective novel Beulah had given her. It had a fair share of crime and violence, but being at Matthew's bedside reminded her she lived with those. She might as well know how things were handled in the rest of the world. It might help her in her own.

A few hours later, Ruth Ann felt a tickle on her knee. She jumped, knocking the book from her limp hands. Matthew winced and withdrew his hand.

"Little *luksi*. Falling asleep on the job?"

His scratchy voice rubbed her ears like sandpaper against raw skin, but it was a good kind of pain. It meant they were both alive.

Ruth Ann held her brother's hand and started crying. "I thought you were dead."

Matthew's gaze roamed the dark room. He blinked several times.

"Oh. Am I laid out for my funeral?"

Ruth Ann gasped. "No! No, I meant back on the timber road. I thought…"

His twinkling eyes settled on her.

Since punching his wounded shoulder might cause it to start bleeding again, Ruth Ann settled for a little jerk on his hand. "Stop it. No, don't stop. Tease all you want. I need to know you're good and alive."

"At least the latter." Matthew's tired voice dropped to a whisper. "Where are we?"

"The Barnes mansion. Pepper saved us both…"

At the confused look on Matthew's face, Ruth Ann shook her head. "Don't ask all those questions you've already managed to think up. Just be grateful to be alive. I'm going to fetch Mama. Save your energy for her, then you need to go back to sleep."

She pulled away from his protest. Already, he wanted to get as many answers as he could. If Ruth Ann didn't hurry back with Della, they might find him crawling from bed, ready to mount up and hunt down clues to the man who'd shot him.

Stubborn Choctaw. Stubborn, alive Choctaw.

◆ ◆ ◆

The next morning, a crowd gathered in Matthew's room. Mrs. Barnes was everywhere, serving him a soupy breakfast he hardly touched, and constantly admonishing the others to respect the sick room. Mr. Barnes made jokes. Pepper Barnes leaned against the closed door of the room, arms folded over his chest, one boot crossed over the other as he reclined. Ruth Ann avoided meeting his eyes. Beulah watched the Barnes family like they were circling vultures.

Della sat on Matthew's other side and studied her son's face. She could discern his true condition, not just what Dr. Caldwell said that morning about him being well on the mend, though there was still the danger of infection.

Matthew looked uncomfortable with all the attention. He also looked worn out, but ready to start asking questions. He nodded at Pepper. "I understand I owe you a debt of gratitude." His voice was still hoarse and groggy.

Pepper pushed away from the door and moved closer to the foot of the bed. He leaned against it, arms still folded. "I was in the right place at the right time."

Ruth Ann felt him glance at her, but she kept her eyes on Matthew. Her brother was propped up on pillows, which made it easier for him to see everyone.

Della put a glass of cold water to his lips. He took a sip and cleared his throat. "It was good timing. I've been wondering how that worked exactly. Thought you would be on the train to Springstown, not the road coming from the sawmill."

Ruth Ann wished she could poke Matthew without everyone in the room seeing it. She hadn't told him anything the night before. After their mother had a few moments with him, he'd drifted to sleep. He didn't know all Ruth Ann did, and now he was picking an argument with Pepper. Was it instinct? Could there be a thread of truth in Beulah's accusation?

Pepper shrugged. "Your sister will give you all the details to write an article."

His distant tone told Ruth Ann that whatever closeness he'd felt with the Teller siblings—or her—had evaporated with the morning sun. It was back to a cordial but cool relationship.

Beulah chose to break her silence. Her voice was stiff. "We should arrange to have the Tellers moved home. I am certain they do not wish to impose any longer."

"Nonsense!" Mrs. Barnes went to the side table and gathered the leftovers from the refreshments she'd served. "They'll do no such thing. Matthew is far too ill to be moved anytime soon. Besides, Dr. Caldwell knows his condition, and Matthew needs to be under his care until he's made a full recovery. We have plenty of room—"

Beulah interrupted. "I believe it is best for them to be home and close to family. Dr. Anderson in Dickens is capable of caring for Matthew."

Ruth Ann rose and cleared her throat, looking between the two ladies. "I'm sure we can decide what we need to do when the time comes."

Everyone turned to her as though expecting Ruth Ann to give a speech. Maybe she needed to. "*Yakoke*. Thank you all for everything. God has seen fit to surround us with wonderful people and we are eternally grateful."

"*Ome.*" Della had risen as well, and looked around the room. Her posture said more than all of Ruth Ann's words. They were grateful, but it was time for the Teller family to be alone.

When the door closed behind the last visitor, Matthew laid his head heavy on the stack of pillows, eyes closed. "*Yakoke*, Mama. Annie."

Della motioned for Ruth Ann to lift Matthew's head while she pulled the extra pillows away so he could lie comfortably.

But Matthew wouldn't be still. His eyes popped open and he tried to turn toward Ruth Ann. He winced and Della put a mother's hand on his good shoulder and held him still.

"All right, I won't move." Matthew looked between them. "But tell me what happened. Everything."

Ruth Ann pulled the leather chair close and sat down, eye level with her brother. "What do you remember?"

"Getting shot."

Ruth Ann puckered her lips. Della shook her head and settled in her chair on the other side of the bed.

Ruth Ann summarized what had happened, including what Pepper told her though she avoided details about their private conversation. She'd tell Matthew about that later. Maybe.

Matthew was shocked about Hocks' death, curious about Takba's strange appearance, and suspicious of Pepper's theories about the shooting. Ruth Ann could tell he was gathering the information in a certain place in his mind: adding and subtracting facts, imagining the possibilities, forming a hypothesis. All to create the story of what happened, along with his own ideas. Ruth Ann longed to know what those ideas were, but by the time she'd finished explaining what she knew, Matthew's eyes had blinked one too many times.

Della rose and tucked the blanket under his chin and put her fingers over his lips before he could ask another question.

He accepted this with a sigh. "*Ome*," he murmured before drifting off to sleep.

CHAPTER SEVENTEEN

MORE VISITORS CAME ON THE afternoon train. Uncle Preston and Peter arrived at the mansion while Ruth Ann paced on the front porch, thinking. Uncle Solomon, the former slave who was now foreman of the Barnes horse breeding operation, drove her relatives up in a buggy.

He called to Ruth Ann, "Look who I found loiterin' around the depot. Figured I'd bring 'em here before the sheriff threw this little one in jail. A real troublemaker, this young one!"

While he spoke, she hurried down the wide porch steps and jumped off the last one. Uncle Preston was already out of the buggy and caught Ruth Ann in his arms. He swung her around and she cried.

But Peter tickled her. "Don't believe a word that old man says. He's jealous of my enterprising ways."

Ruth Ann elbowed Peter then hugged him. "You rascal, who's minding the shop?"

"Mr. Levitt, of course."

"But the telegraph—"

"Good grief, Annie, you worry about everything! I had one of my line buddies come operate the wire for the day."

Uncle Solomon caught Peter by the nape of the neck and asked Preston, "Should I throw this little one back? Not enough meat on his bones to cook."

"If you want."

Uncle Preston put an arm around Ruth Ann's shoulders and led her toward the steps while Peter howled behind them. Her uncle spoke quietly. "Is everything all right?"

"Matthew is doing better, but still very weak. He almost...almost didn't make it, Uncle Preston. I'm so glad you're here." She leaned her head against his shoulder when they paused at the door.

He turned Ruth Ann to face him. "I mean, is everything all right?"

She frowned, confused. He shook his head. "Robert Barnes sent me several telegrams. I was assured all was being taken care of, and I turned to managing your affairs in Dickens. But this morning, I received a wire from your young friend, and she said it was urgent I come and take care of my family. She indicated this was not a safe place..."

Ruth Ann's face must have shown her consternation. Beulah had the most infuriating way of poking her nose in other people's business. She meant well, and often it helped, like when the newspaper office burned down. The Levitts helped them overcome the tragedy by leasing the large building they now had, and subleasing to the *Choctaw Tribune*.

But sometimes in her zeal, Beulah went too far.

"Don't worry, Uncle Preston. Beulah is just concerned like we all are. But I'm very glad you came. I know it's a busy season on the farm with the harvest."

Uncle Preston pulled her into a strong hug. Ruth Ann missed those kinds of hugs, an enveloping one that told her everything would be all right. The kind of hug her father would give her. "No season is too busy when family needs help. *Chi hullo li.*"

Someone snatched two pins from Ruth Ann's bun, causing her hair to fall. She yelped and tried to catch it, then gave up and swung a fist at Peter, which he easily dodged.

"Couldn't Uncle Solomon hold on to you?"

"That the thanks I get after slaving over your businesses and house day and night all by my lonesome while you're loafing at this fine place?"

"All by yourself, eh?"

Peter gave his father a sheepish look and handed the hairpins to Ruth Ann just as the front door opened. She turned, expecting to see Beulah greet their rescuers. Instead, she found herself once again standing close to Pepper Barnes.

Her relatives greeted him casually. Ruth Ann tried to hide behind them, desperately working to get her hair back in place. She quit and let it flow around her shoulders as they entered the mansion.

Peter whispered to her, "Don't worry, cousin. Men like to see women with their hair down once in awhile."

It was all Ruth Ann could do to maintain her ladylike composure. But Pepper Barnes conversed with Uncle Preston. He didn't glance her way at all.

◆ ◆ ◆

In Dickens that evening, Lance Fuller paced a rut in the carpet near his Uncle Thaddeus' fireplace. The man should have been home before now. He'd been gone three days without word. Aunt Susan was hysterical. Her husband had said he was going off on business and would return shortly.

All fine and good, except Thaddeus hadn't stayed in contact, and two people connected with his name had been shot—Will Hocks and Matthew Teller. One was dead. The other, who knew? Lance had forced himself to stay at the school, maintaining his front as a teacher instead of catching a train to see Ruth Ann and her brother.

Beulah had given him a dramatic account before she departed on the train, and had kindly sent him a wire this afternoon with word of Matthew Teller's recovery. But this did nothing to alleviate Susan's fears that her husband might never return home. In fact, she was sure of it, which would leave her a destitute widow with no one to care for her.

Lance had quietly requested Mabel to put his aunt to bed early, leaving him alone with his thoughts while he paced.

Those thoughts were interrupted by feet stamping on the porch outside and a key turning in the lock.

He strode to the entryway in time to watch the door swing open and Thaddeus Warren stomp through.

Lance didn't conceal his anger. "Where have you been?"

"Taking care of business." The tone was casual for the moody man.

"Do you know about the two killings?"

This startled Thaddeus. "Two? Only Will Hocks is dead. Matthew Teller is..." The man stopped and settled his blazing eyes on Lance. "Shootings happen all the time here, a country run by heathen Indians. That will change soon."

Thaddeus pushed past Lance into the parlor and halted at the fireplace. He stoked the dying flames.

Lance stayed on his heels. "What do you know about it? Someone tried to kill a newspaper reporter, not a politician, not someone siding with Progressives or Nationals. Not even—"

"You seem to know a lot for not knowing anything." His uncle straightened to look Lance in the eye. "Matthew Teller got what he deserved. Maybe it'll teach him not to poke his nose in other people's business. If not, we'll see to it next time."

A cold sensation flowed through Lance's blood. "My stars, Thaddeus, did you have Matthew Teller shot?"

A pitiful gasp came from the parlor doorway. Susan Warren whimpered and covered her lips. "No," she moaned. "Please no..."

Thaddeus glared at Lance. "See what you've done? Upset the missus. You haven't done me a lick of good since you got here. Now get out of my sight!"

Lance started to fire a retort. But he held it in check like the coward he was. He clenched his fists and turned like a soldier whose commanding officer had just ordered him on a suicide mission. He brushed past Susan, the withering woman who would always be loyal to her murderous husband.

When Lance had come to Indian Territory, his only thought was an escape, a haven where he could hide from his past failings and debts. He hadn't considered the cost of handing over all the blackmail material his uncle could want about his troubles in the East. Thomas Warren hadn't cared about anyone but himself. But Lance Fuller was a schoolteacher whose life had been touched by a classroom full of eager minds, and a pair of young ladies who appreciated his efforts. There was a whole world of possibilities in this rugged land. If only he could find a way to belong, a right to be here. A way to do what was right.

Maybe a courtship with Ruth Ann Teller was the way after all. Wouldn't that be ironic?

◆ ◆ ◆

The following dawn brought yet another visitor to the mansion. Mrs. Barnes had informed them a U.S. marshal was coming to question Matthew. The county sheriff, a Choctaw, had come by before Matthew regained consciousness and asked questions. Ruth Ann couldn't tell him much, but the sheriff and Pepper had a good long talk in private.

Della sat by Matthew's bed after the three of them finished breakfast in his room, enjoying the private family time. Della read aloud from the book of Proverbs.

He that hath knowledge spareth his words: and a man of understanding is of an excellent spirit.

Even a fool, when he holdeth his peace, is counted wise: and he that shutteth his lips is esteemed a man of understanding.

A stir outside drew Ruth Ann to the window. She watched a man riding up on a big sorrel with a white blaze on its face. "Looks like the marshal is here."

A few minutes later, a tall black man tapped on the open door before entering. "Morning, folks. My name's Bass Reeves, deputy U.S. marshal outta Fort Smith. I'm here to talk to Matthew Teller. You him?"

Matthew nodded while Ruth Ann stared. The famous lawman Bass Reeves? Why, he had dragged more outlaws from Indian Territory to face Judge Isaac Parker's court than any other U.S. marshal. But shouldn't Bass Reeves be retired? His reputation was older than she was!

While she stood slack-jawed, Matthew introduced Della, and then Ruth Ann with a laugh. "You'll have to forgive my little sister. She's been reading a detective novel and it's gone to her head."

Heat rushed to Ruth Ann's face. How did Matthew know about the book? But she collected herself and cleared her throat. "It's not that, sir, it's your reputation. It's said you're one of the finest lawman ever to cross into Indian Territory. I want to thank you for the work you've done to make our Territory safer."

Bass Reeves chuckled and pushed his wide-brimmed hat up to reveal his shiny forehead and the flecks of white in his dark sideburns. "Just doin' my job, ma'am. I ain't investigatin' your brother's shooting since he's Choctaw, but I heard there might be a connection with the shooting of a white man, Will Hocks. Anythin' you all can tell me would help."

Matthew motioned to Ruth Ann. "My sister knows more than I do. I was out cold."

Bass Reeves set his eyes on her. "All right, I'll start with you, Miss Teller. What happened?"

Ruth Ann's stomach fluttered. It was one thing to ask questions. It was quite another to answer them. No wonder people looked nervous when Matthew came around.

And it was hard to talk about him getting shot, especially with their mama sitting there. But she made it through by observing Bass Reeves. He was muscular but stood easy, an obviously practiced patience with witness interviews. That must be far easier than arresting a desperado who would love to take the lawman's badge for a trophy.

Marshal Reeves was dressed like most frontier men: worn slacks, dusty shirt, and a brown leather vest. His jacket was probably tied down to his saddle on the warm day. His six-guns set him apart more than anything. He wore two Colts, handle butts forward for a fast draw. The guns might give him away as a lawman, if anyone he tracked down was privileged to see those guns before he saw them. According to legend, that rarely happened.

Bass Reeves had encountered notorious outlaws and gangs with little backup other than an Indian scout he employed in his earlier years. It was easier for a black marshal to hunt down white outlaws since the Indian tribes tended to trust them over white intruders. Bass Reeves was the stuff of legends.

Here he stood before Ruth Ann as though the only thing on his mind was catching the next killer.

The marshal turned his attention to Matthew. "What can you tell me about this Hocks fellow? He have enemies, anyone who wanted him dead?"

Matthew exchanged a look with Ruth Ann. He already knew what he wanted to say. He wanted her to say nothing. Ruth Ann bit her lip, aware Marshal Reeves still had an eye on her.

Matthew spoke slowly. "Could be, marshal. I'm the editor of the *Choctaw Tribune* and I'm currently investigating a story that might involve Hocks."

Bass Reeves nodded. "I've heard about your newspaper, had it read to me. I like the way you leave out all the hogwash others like to fill pages with."

Ruth Ann felt a tingle of pride, though she kept her hands folded modestly in front of her and her mouth shut. She and Matthew could talk later about the power of the press.

Matthew accepted the compliment with a quick nod. "However, I'm not prepared to reveal my findings. I want Hocks' killer caught, but I don't have any hard evidence. Anything I tell you would jeopardize both investigations. I'll let you know if I come across anything helpful."

Ruth Ann gaped at him. Leave it to her brother to treat a

famous lawman just like…well, like he would anyone else. Matthew showed the respect due, but he managed to keep his awe in check better than Ruth Ann. His plan to interview Buffalo Bill Cody at the World's Fair was something Ruth Ann would never…

The World's Fair! She'd forgotten all about it, and it would end in a few weeks. Oh well. It had been a nice dream.

Marshal Reeves jolted her back to the present. "I can respect that, and I have other leads to track down. I have a feelin' we're on the same trail. Could be we'll cross paths at the killer."

He tipped his hat with a slight bow to the women. He backed out the door and left.

One of the most famous lawmen in history, there and gone like it was merely another stop on a long road. Which, for Bass Reeves, that was all it was.

Ruth Ann plopped in the leather chair. "Matthew! That was Marshal Bass Reeves!"

"So he said."

"Matt!" Ruth Ann pounded the chair with both fists to keep from injuring her brother. Matthew and Della chuckled, but Ruth Ann was just getting started.

"Marshal Bass Reeves. He's arrested hundreds, if not thousands, of outlaws in Indian Territory. It's said he's Judge Parker's favorite marshal. Do you know he's hardly ever been wounded in all the shootouts he's been in? Not only that, he's killed less than a dozen men. Most he hauled in were wanted dead or alive. He—"

Matthew threw a pillow at her which caused him to wince, though he tried to hide it. "I know Bass Reeves' record better than you, little *luksi*. I appreciate who he is, that's why I couldn't tell him my suspicions. It might lead him to the shooter and finish any chance I have of getting Mayor Warren."

She jumped to her feet, eyes wide. Della stood and closed the door.

Matthew nodded. "*Yakoke*, Mama. This needs to stay in

the family."

Ruth Ann sputtered. "You think it was Mayor Warren who shot you? But how—"

Matthew waved his hand and tried to sit up. He gasped and stilled. "Stop jumping around, Annie. You didn't hear what I said. I think Marshal Reeves is already on the trail of the killer, and he'll catch him, but I've got to unravel the rest first. Grab some paper. I need you to write a letter to Sam Mishaya."

Ruth Ann frowned. Sam Mishaya wasn't an important sort of man, not influential. And judging from his insults to Mr. Barnes at the Council House, he was a troublemaker. What keys could he hold?

Matthew sank deep in the pillows, hand over his wound. Della went back to his side and brushed his hand away. She peeked under the bandage and frowned.

Ruth Ann moved closer. "What is it, Mama?"

The skin around the stitches was an angry red and black, and white puss spurted out. Ruth Ann swallowed. Matthew closed his eyes, all his energy and fight gone.

Della murmured, "Send for the doctor."

CHAPTER EIGHTEEN

"HOLD STILL!" FRANK SCREAMED in Cub Wassom's ear. He pinned the man to the hard ground again. Cub swung a fist into Frank's temple, knocking him to the side. Frank rolled and grabbed his shoulders when the young man tried to stand. Cub howled and thrashed, then stumbled and fell, breathing heavy.

He gripped his bleeding leg and gritted his teeth. "I'll kill him. He's a walking dead man, that Pepper Barnes."

Frank swiped a sleeve over his own sweaty forehead. Ever since he'd been shot, Cub was meaner than a mother bear robbed of her cubs. Maybe that was how he'd gotten his nickname, Cub. His own mother must have had a time raising him. If a man like Cub Wassom ever had a mother. It was hard to imagine.

Frank had to get the young outlaw still enough to tend his leg again or he'd die for sure. It had already been two days, but every time Frank bandaged the wound, Cub would ride hard or thrash from fever and start it bleeding again.

When Cub went limp from fatigue, Frank dragged him to a tree and propped him against it. He set to work on the bloody leg while Cub babbled.

"If my mama was here, she'd fix me right up. But we'll make it down to Dickens in no time. I'll get my gal and my boy, blow that Matthew Teller's head off, and then we'll go north and meet with Lester. Maybe even stay awhile at Holder's fort. You know about it, right? Up by Wilburton. Holder was the smartest man I knew, he taught me everything, until he got old and wanted a life without dodging bullets. Fool! Look at this money we got!"

Cub swung his arm as if searching for the saddlebags filled with the cash they'd been paid to shoot two men. Frank's aim had been the deadly one this time. Cub's quarry was still alive, and Cub had a bullet in his own leg.

Frank feared his partner would ask to see the money, forgetting they'd buried it before the shootings. They'd pick it up later, after the job in Dickens. If they made it there. Cub was a fool to think he'd be able to change directions and ride all the way to Dickens after the two had already gone several miles north. Frank just had to get Cub bandaged up, rested, and then make sensible plans.

Cub's head lolled to one side, and Frank wondered if he'd finally gone to sleep. That would make things easier. He couldn't handle Cub when he was in his right mind. He sure couldn't stay alive long around him in this mad condition.

But Cub hadn't abandoned Frank when he was about to get gunned down by the Lighthorse. Frank wouldn't abandon him now.

As Frank tightened the bandage on Cub's leg, a smile crossed the outlaw's lips, his eyes still closed.

"You wait and see, we may make us some more money. That little Teller gal will try to run the newspaper. I know that family, stubborn as they come. But it won't be the first time I've had to take care of a woman like that."

♦♦♦

Go home.
Ruth Ann had no logical explanation for the thought. It

wasn't a wise thing to do. Yet the thought whispered to her through the day and into the night after the doctor gave the grim news: the wound was infected. Fever overcame Matthew, and he grew more listless than Ruth Ann had seen him.

Go home.

The Barneses continued their vigilance, making the Teller family comfortable. Beulah returned to Dickens with no more accusations. She promised to keep the shop running, that all would be as it should when they returned.

Go home.

The mansion was the best place for Matthew. The safest, the warmest, the most immediate care. Why, then, was Ruth Ann planning to urge her mother to move Matthew first thing in the morning? No matter how unreasonable, it felt like everything depended on it.

It was time to go home.

This was confirmed when she approached her mother at Matthew's side the next morning and Della simply nodded. The consent came so easily, Ruth Ann rushed to fill in the details. "I'll ask Mr. Barnes for a buggy. Or maybe a wagon would be better."

She glanced at Matthew's face. His skin had paled drastically and sweat glistened on his still features. "I should wire Uncle Preston to meet us at the train in Dickens. I guess we can fix up the sofa, but—"

"We are going home."

Ruth Ann cocked her head at her mother, who was staring deep into her eyes. "That's what I'm talking about, Mama. What…" Her voice trailed.

Della had to explain. "We are going home to Preston's farm. That is where we need to be."

Ruth Ann wanted to protest. Then a cold shiver went through her, like when she'd knelt by Matthew on the road while his life's blood bled out and Takba told her to hold his head.

"Mama…you don't think…you're not getting ready in case…"

She couldn't finish. It didn't matter how grim the doctor's report had been. Matthew was alive. He would stay alive a good long while. Long enough to publish the next edition of the *Choctaw Tribune* and ten thousand after that. Long enough to marry and raise a family and be there until Ruth Ann found her own path in life.

"We are going home. God knows." Della began packing what few things she'd brought from Dickens.

Ruth Ann forced away objections and left the room to find Mr. Barnes. It would be hard to communicate their plan to him. After tossing and turning all night, wrestling with emotions and logic and plain common sense, she didn't have much strength left to put on a front with anyone. But Mr. Barnes would understand. He'd been there when her father's and brother's remains had been returned to the family.

Dr. Caldwell threw a fit when he learned their plans. He warned the trip could well kill the young man. He was reluctant to admit death still lingered close even in the seclusion of the Barnes home, but he remained adamant in his disapproval. Della took his rants in stride, never halting from preparing her son for the move.

Mr. Barnes made arrangements for the train ride, securing a passenger car just for them. He and Uncle Solomon rigged a hammock across the aisle, the swinging easy on a wounded body during the hard jerks of the train.

Matthew lay in the hammock. He drifted in and out of consciousness. When he was conscious, he protested about not being in the newspaper office. He murmured about deadlines and conspiracies until Ruth Ann feared what he might say and whom he might say it in front of. But that was the least of their concerns.

The train ride was a challenge with its constant jerking, but mercifully, it was only an hour long. The most difficult part of the journey would be the nine-mile wagon ride to Uncle Preston's farm. They would try to make it easier by rigging the hammock in the wagon bed.

At the Dickens depot was the usual gathering of cowboys, businessmen, families and the ever-present ladies-in-waiting hovering around the platform. Ruth Ann had warned Peter to tell no one except the Levitts of their coming. This would keep curious onlookers from bothering the family while they quietly moved Matthew to the wagon.

When the train halted, Mr. Barnes guarded the door nearest them. He'd instructed the conductor to allow the other passengers to disembark and load before holding the train an extra few minutes for them to make the move. Ruth Ann could see from the window that Uncle Preston and Peter waited just off the platform in their wagon. The Levitts stood nearby, not drawing attention, but keeping a close eye on the train.

Ruth Ann stayed out of the way while Mr. Barnes and Uncle Solomon lifted the hammock with Matthew in it. They maneuvered through the door. She stood numb, unable to help other than to gather her mother's small bag. At the steps of the passenger car, Uncle Preston and Peter waited to help with the offloading under Della's supervision.

Someone shouted and set loose excitement around them.

"Hey! Isn't that Matthew Teller?"

"Why, he's dead! The family must be bringing him for burial."

A respectful hush fell over the crowd, but only for a moment. Someone scoffed, "Dirty Buzzard shot him. We need to run them back into the hills they flew out of!"

"You think you know! It was a Polecat Progressive who couldn't take his lickin'—"

"Those election results won't stand no more than you!" The sharp crack of a fist connecting with a jawbone sounded. Ladies on the platform screamed and scrambled away.

Ruth Ann kept a steady focus on the transporting process. But when the platform erupted in one huge fistfight, she lost sight of her mission.

Caught in the fray, she was jostled away from where Peter helped Della into the wagon. Beulah called to her, but Ruth Ann was busy ducking beneath swinging fists. She stumbled into a high stack of crates and hoped she could find refuge there, but instead was pinned against the stack by two men with their hands around each other's throats.

Ruth Ann yelped. Someone grabbed her arm and pulled her from under the men. She was pressed close to her rescuer's side. His coat smelled like books.

For a blessed moment, she imagined she was wrapped in Matthew's arms and needn't worry over anyone, not even herself. But the moment passed. She was thrust inside the quiet depot where other ladies had taken refuge. Their wide-eyed expressions caused Ruth Ann to straighten and pull away from the man who held her. Lance Fuller.

"Are you all right, Ruth Ann?"

"I suppose…yes. But I should…" Her gaze drifted out the large window to watch the fight. She needed to get back to her family. She ignored the whispers behind her, and met the concerned gaze of Lance Fuller.

She asked stiffly, "Shouldn't you be in school with your students?"

Lance slowly lowered his hand from where he'd held her arm. He spoke with kindness. "Today is Saturday."

Ruth Ann blushed. "I—I'm sorry, I just…"

"You're just exhausted beyond all reason and this is the worst possible welcome home you could imagine, and all you want is to get home and be away from everyone except those who care for you."

Ruth Ann lifted her head and tried to smile. "That's what I was going to say."

The door behind her banged open, letting in the violent sounds of the fight. It also let in a scuffed-looking Peter, who slammed the door and marched up to her.

"I had to kick a few shins to get over here. Best wait until it dies down before we go out."

Peter shot Lance Fuller an accusing look. Lance nodded

toward the other side of the depot. "We can go out the back way, through the freight office."

Ruth Ann had never been in that office adjacent to the depot. She was glad Peter was with them as Lance Fuller opened the door. She was especially glad her cousin was close when the large room that was filled with workers included Mayor Warren and Sheriff Banny in a discussion.

Startled, they glared at the trio trying to pass through. Ruth Ann caught the growl in Lance Fuller's voice when he said, "Sheriff, there's a fight on the platform you might be interested in."

"That so?" Banny hooked his thumb over the hammer of his tied down six-shooter.

Ruth Ann lost her breath. Images of all the times Banny had threatened them—had threatened Matthew—overwhelmed her.

Peter smarted off next. "That's so, or else someone will take that tin star off your chest and pin it on themselves."

Her knees buckled and Lance Fuller caught her around the shoulders and held her close again. "If you *gentlemen* will step aside, we need to get this lady to her family."

Mayor Warren pressed his lips together and didn't move. Banny took his hat off and stepped to one side. He made a sweeping gesture toward the side door that opened onto the freight platform. "By all means."

The sunlight outside made Ruth Ann dizzy. The fight had faded to the background, though more people rushed through the street toward the depot, anxious not to miss any excitement. Dust hazed the air. Uncle Preston's wagon appeared in the roadway that cut through the empty lot beside the freight office. The wagon halted with her family's surprised faces looking at them.

Ruth Ann politely disentangled herself from Lance Fuller. "Thank you for helping, Mr. Fuller." She wanted to say more, but she was without words.

He and Peter helped her into the wagon bed next to Della and the unconscious Matthew. A blanket stretched from the side of the wagon to the back of the spring seat shaded his hammock and tight face.

Della nodded to Lance Fuller as he left. Then she took Ruth Ann's hand in her warm one, and she felt a weeping time come over her. Her mama said, "We are going home."

Behind them, the train puffed away from the depot, its whistle a final amen.

◆ ◆ ◆

Home had changed from when Ruth Ann was a child. Oh, it was the same majestic log house on the hill above one of the largest lakes in the territory, the same dirt road, the same faces of family. But it wasn't the same. The house was no longer fresh and new. Now, it was planted deep in the soil, as though it already knew what the world had to offer and would remain unmoved always. The road, too, cut deeper from its last grading, the usual bends in different places to accommodate the growing trees along its path. But the faces of family had changed the most.

Gone were her cousins' naive expressions from when life was one big summer evening of jumping in the lake, catching fireflies. Telling stories of love and betrayal and the ancient past around fires. The cousins had lived these things beyond the shelter of youth. Many now had their own offspring and were learning that their parents had indeed been right in their upbringing.

Even with the harsh realities of life, the joy on Uncle Preston's ranch overwhelmed Ruth Ann when the wagon rolled to a stop. Cousins and in-laws, their children, and farm-hands converged on the wagon. She was sure they would carry her if they thought it would relieve even an ounce of her pain.

"Welcome home!"

"We prayed every morning and evening for all of you."

"Rooms are ready, you each have your own."

A tiny voice squeaked, "They put all us boys in one room together—"

A girl's voice rose over the words. "It was awful! All night Aunt May had to shush them."

Ruth Ann was whisked off the back of the wagon. She stood back to observe the faces. There was the promise they would weather another storm together. They were more ready than ever.

Then Ruth Ann caught sight of the aged face on the porch. She flew up the steps and into the Grandmother's arms. A good and safe place to rest.

They were home.

CHAPTER NINETEEN

THE FAMILY ERUPTED WITH joy when Matthew's fever broke. Faith and love filled Uncle Preston's home. Ruth Ann no longer needed to be strong for her immediate family now that they were surrounded by an abundance of strength. How good to simply rest in it.

There was a world of need beyond the serenity of home, but Ruth Ann had no intention of reentering the world anytime soon. What she'd been through the past week, the past year, had earned her seclusion.

Matthew had other ideas. No sooner had he opened one eye than he was telling her what to do. "Annie, you need to pack. You and Beulah get yourselves to the World's Fair."

Ruth Ann was alone in the room with her brother and she was prepared to scold him. But his aged face and sagging left side of his lip kept her in check. "You're delirious. I'm not leaving you and Mama right in the middle of—"

"I'm thinking of the *Choctaw Tribune.*"

His hand slipped beneath the covers and he slowly pulled out a folded newspaper. The *Dickens Herald.* Ruth Ann gasped at the sight of it. Matthew had asked for news on what their rival paper printed about the shooting, but the family agreed to bar such requests until he was stronger. Even Ruth Ann hadn't seen the latest edition. She snatched it and flipped it open. "Did Peter…"

She read the headline and cried.

MATTHEW TELLER DEAD;
CHOCTAW TRIBUNE NO MORE

"We have to get busy, or there's no saving the newspaper from this. Maxwell's lies will spread over the territory faster than truth can keep up, and we won't have a subscriber or advertiser left." Matthew's words were so weak, Ruth Ann held her breath to hear them. "Shut it down, Annie, and go to the fair. Interview Buffalo Bill and get front page stories that will sell all over Indian Territory, all the way to New York. We need to report on Choctaws doing something besides shooting each other up. The U.S. government is watching us. You know there's nothing more powerful than the press when you have God Almighty on your side."

Ruth Ann stared at him. Her brother was serious. Worse, he was right. He always had to be right!

"I can't leave Mama."

"She has plenty who will look after her here. And you're a grown woman now. You can do it."

Ruth Ann wanted to read the truth in his eyes, whether he was trying to force her to do this on her own to make her realize she could. Or did he want to get her out of harm's way? He knew she would return to town with only Peter to look after her while she wrote one controversial story after another to keep the *Choctaw Tribune* alive. Keep Matthew alive.

But she couldn't study his eyes. He had closed them, as if he'd spoken his final words and it was up to her to honor them.

A hundred questions floated in her mind, dozens of arguments. But they had to be saved for later.

Ruth Ann tucked the blanket around Matthew's chest wound. She whispered, "Keep fighting, brother. We have to keep fighting."

She knew he would. She wasn't so confident about herself.

◆ ◆ ◆

Visitors arrived the next morning while Ruth Ann lounged in the great room. Her cousin-in-law, Melinda, had insisted she not help with the breakfast dishes.

Ruth Ann heard the sound of a buggy and greetings called from a young second cousin in the front yard. She tossed aside the book she'd been reading and went to the window.

Mr. Levitt and Beulah were disembarking from a buggy with the assistance of Lance Fuller. Ruth Ann groaned. The Levitts were welcome. But why had Lance Fuller come?

She wasn't dressed for visitors. But she was too tired to worry about the simple gray work dress Melinda had loaned her, and her hair tied back with a faded blue ribbon she'd found in a dresser.

Ruth Ann opened the front door and greeted the guests somewhat cheerfully. But Beulah had enough energy for them both.

She wrapped Ruth Ann in a tight hug. "I hope we are not disturbing you and your family, but we wanted to see for ourselves that all is well. Peter carried the news of your brother's recovery. How we rejoiced! We brought cheese and bread for your own recovery. And your dear mama. How is she?"

While Beulah talked, Ruth Ann stepped to one side to allow the men in, both carrying baskets with food. She tried not to meet Lance Fuller's eyes, but he seemed to have something on his mind anyway. Mr. Levitt kissed her forehead and her heart ached for her daddy.

Ruth Ann knew the bread and cheese were no ordinary offerings. The bread was a special recipe handed down for generations in the Levitt family, and the cheese was shipped in from New York.

These things brought a genuine smile to her lips. "*Yakoke*. Please, come in. I don't think you've met most of the family."

While Ruth Ann's family faithfully attended church, the Levitts weren't a part of the congregation, though they often joined the picnic afterwards. But with Uncle Preston's crew flocking among the dozens of other families, it was impossible to introduce anyone to everyone.

Ruth Ann spent the next half-hour showing the guests around. They ended in the kitchen where they sampled the best in the home. During the chatter and exchange of cultural foods, she made a quiet exit. Being hostess drained what little strength she had for the day.

The back porch was empty and the place to regain her peace of mind. Ruth Ann settled in one of the rocking chairs that lined the wraparound porch. The porch also held rough-cut log benches and wood chairs. This was a favorite gathering place for the family or during a community event like hog butchering or all night hymn singings. Down the steps from the porch was a huge fire ring with a spit for roasting meat for a mass of people.

Laughter. Always laughter. And singing. And storytelling. And more laughter.

Ruth Ann settled deep in the rocker and pushed off with one foot. She never wanted to take the view for granted. The glistening lake spread out beyond the fire pit, stretching around the bend and out of sight. Across the lake was a hearty stand of pines where more log houses stood for family, ranch hands and tenant farmers. Beyond the pines, six hundred acres of crops grew. There were numerous cattle pastures and the ranch had its own gristmill. The Red River lay two miles south.

It was a grand operation. One Matthew had felt led to leave and start a newspaper in the booming, though likely illegal, town of Dickens.

Ruth Ann sighed, thinking of the times she'd longed to come back here, longed to return to the last home she'd shared with her daddy and mama, Philip and Matthew. Their cabin had stood in those pines across the lake, though she had roamed over all the ranch—riding horses, canoeing across the lake for supper at the big house. Her duties included helping with the milk cows early every morning—milking, separating and serving fresh milk for the flood of people that came in for breakfast. Afterwards, there was always more work. Mending, sweeping porches, hanging wash.

Though chores took up the better part of the day, Ruth Ann still had time to explore the world. At least this world. She'd never thought she'd need to know so much beyond this safe place. How frightened she would have been if she'd known the changes yet to come. Her daddy and Philip were buried here.

Ruth Ann felt the presence before hearing a sound. The Grandmother shuffled around the east side of the wraparound porch, looking ancient in the light of a fresh morning. She moved slower these days, and Ruth Ann knew she'd missed a transition in her full-blood grandmother's life. The Grandmother's once raven black hair grew out white now. But Pokni was as hearty as ever, carrying a mending basket in one crooked hand and her treasured sewing box in the other.

Ruth Ann quickly rose from her seat and took the mending basket. The Grandmother nodded and sat in the large rocker near the door. It was Pokni's rocker and no one else ever sat in it whether she was present or not. This was an unspoken ordinance in the family. They asked any unknowing guest to vacate the rocker.

Pokni settled in her rocker, its hardwood fitting every curve of her body. It was as though her body had molded over the years to fit it. Or maybe the rocker had molded to fit her.

The Grandmother motioned for the mending basket to be set next to her rocker. "*Yakoke*, little *luksi*."

A sting pricked Ruth Ann's heart. Matthew used that nickname for her. Maybe that was why the Grandmother had used it. She pulled a rocker close to Pokni's.

They settled in beside one another. The Grandmother doled out work as she always had—Ruth Ann the pupil, the Grandmother teaching a larger lesson than simply patching a tear.

For Ruth Ann, the lesson was usually one in patience. She didn't think it would be that today. She was content with the thought of sitting next to the Grandmother all day, all night, sewing without a word spoken.

But that feeling didn't last long. She began asking questions. "Pokni, do you know a woman named Takba? I think she lives on a white tenant farm, but I'm not sure."

The Grandmother continued her steady rocking, eyes on her work. It amazed Ruth Ann how well the Grandmother could still see.

And Moses was an hundred and twenty years old when he died: his eye was not dim, nor his natural force abated.

That was the Grandmother.

How well she saw with her heart and discerned with her spirit, which was why Ruth Ann asked a question that might take all day to sort through. But she hoped in the end, Pokni would help her find answers.

A few minutes passed before the Grandmother answered with a question. "What do you know of her?"

Ruth Ann continued to mend the tear in a shirt the Grandmother had given her. "She healed my shoulder when I was in a buggy accident. She showed up near Finley and saved Matthew's life, then disappeared. I never got to thank her."

"Did she want thanks?"

"No."

"Then accept the gift."

"I understand. I just…I guess I'm wondering…"

The Grandmother chuckled, and her face wrinkles cascaded and drew up in harmony with her smile. "You are curious. But you don't ask the questions you want answers to."

Ruth Ann dropped her hands to her lap, suddenly tired. She chewed her lower lip. "All right. I want to know who she is, how she heals, and what she knows about our family. It was almost as though…as though she knew Matthew would be shot."

The words tumbled out. Ruth Ann's mind raced. Of course! The Choctaw woman Takba knew. She *knew!*

Ruth Ann jumped up and dropped the shirt in the basket with the needle stuck in it. "She knows, Pokni! She knows who shot Matthew. I have to find her!"

She went to the edge of the porch with every intention of running down the steps, saddling a horse, riding hard for the tenant shanty and…

And what? Ruth Ann turned back and paced to the other end of the porch. She couldn't go alone. Especially if the shooter was still around, despite Bass Reeves being on his trail.

But if he was around, he might be looking to kill the one person who knew what he'd done: Takba.

Ruth Ann marched to the porch steps, determined.

But what could she do to stop a murder? What if she were killed? What would her mama do then?

Ruth Ann halted her flight. The Grandmother watched her.

Exhausted, she plopped at the Grandmother's feet and laid her head on Pokni's lap. She lay still and received comfort from the Grandmother's crooked fingers stroking her hair. The Grandmother began to sing. The lyrics wove around Ruth Ann's heart.

O to grace how great a debtor
daily I'm constrained to be.
Let thy goodness, like a fetter,
bind my wandering heart to thee.
Prone to wander, Lord, I feel it,
prone to leave the God I love…
Here's my heart, O take and seal it,
seal it for thy courts above.

It was all Ruth Ann needed. In fact, she was nearly asleep

when the back door opened and boots scraped across the porch. She didn't care who it was. Anyone in the family would trade places with her.

But it wasn't a relative's voice that sounded startled. "Oh, I'm sorry."

The boots scraped again as though leaving, but the Grandmother said, "Stay."

When Ruth Ann placed the voice with a face, she jerked to her feet. "Mr. Fuller."

She retied the loose ribbon in her hair, and at the same time, tried to nod to the Grandmother.

"Pokni, this is Mr. Fuller, the…" She caught herself before saying *white*. "…the new schoolteacher in Dickens."

Ruth Ann dropped her hands, having no idea how her hair looked. "This is Pokni. My grandmother. That is, Mrs. Frazier."

Lance Fuller stood awkwardly near the back door after realizing the tender moment he'd intruded on. But then he looked at ease. He stepped toward them with a smile for Pokni. His greeting was, well, gracious.

"It's a pleasure to meet you, Mrs. Frazier."

The Grandmother nodded and accepted his offered hand. He took hers lightly because of her frail look. If only he knew.

He lifted his eyes to Ruth Ann. "I couldn't eat another bite of the food they kept dishing out. The Levitts are upstairs visiting your mother and brother. I didn't want to crowd in."

He hesitated as though wondering if he were really welcome at the ranch, or if everyone laughed behind his back.

Ruth Ann looked to the Grandmother, who motioned to the rocker across the porch from them. "You made a good decision. My grandson is weak. He needs rest."

Even a stranger couldn't miss her genuine tone. Lance Fuller relaxed his shoulders and took a seat in the rocker across from them. Ruth Ann wished he wasn't framed by the lovely lake view.

"I didn't thank you for…for meeting us at the depot."

Her face warmed as she recalled what happened, him pulling her close, and then the encounter with the mayor and sheriff. She didn't want to talk about it with Pokni until they were alone again. Actually, she never wanted to talk about it.

Lance Fuller seemed to understand her lack of detail. Ruth Ann was certain that wasn't a good thing—he knew her too well. "I'm glad I was there. That is, it was good to see all of you. I wish I could have come up to Springstown, but school was in session all week. The students kept asking after your family; in fact, I had to talk with them quite a bit. They were concerned about your safety, Miss Ruth Ann. You know how gossip goes."

How well she knew. Christopher Maxwell's outlandish article in the *Dickens Herald* probably frightened the children. She imagined all the stories in town that Matthew was dead. Instead of grieving friends, she envisioned vultures circling the print shop and even their house. She reminded herself that the Levitts and Peter would keep things safe until the Teller family returned.

But would they return? If Matthew was right and the survival of the *Choctaw Tribune* depended on her, all was lost.

Ruth Ann shook away her fears and tried to remember the rules of polite conversation. "Thank you for reassuring the children. They do have vivid imaginations." *And lying newspapers read by gossiping parents.*

Lance Fuller leaned forward, elbows on his knees, and studied his hands. "I've decided to give them an early release for fall. Already half the students are being held at home for harvest, and they've all earned a break from their studies. I'm leaving for a visit to Chicago in two days." He kept his eyes down as though waiting for reaction to his announcement.

Ruth Ann didn't know how to respond. Was he hoping she would object? To ask if it was really a good idea to release school two weeks earlier than planned? Instead, what came out of her mouth shocked her more than him. "I see. Perhaps Beulah and I can make arrangements to travel with you."

His head came up. The Grandmother lowered her sewing

to her lap.

Ruth Ann winced. The last thing she needed was to be beholding to Lance Fuller again! "That is, well, you know we'd already planned a trip and we spoke of traveling together, with Matthew. He told me he wants me to go to the fair and do the interview he'd planned. He can't possibly make a trip anytime soon, and Peter has to stay with the newspaper and the telegraph. It, well…two young ladies shouldn't make a long trip to a city like Chicago…alone."

Ruth Ann took a deep breath to slow her thoughts. How could she have gotten in this predicament? "None of my relatives can make the trip this time of year, and Mr. Levitt's health is still frail. But I shouldn't have—"

"It would be my pleasure to escort you and Miss Beulah to Chicago."

Ruth Ann clenched her fidgeting hands and turned to the Grandmother, expecting her to disapprove.

Pokni didn't lift her eyes from her work. "Ask your mama and uncle."

That would do it. They would never agree to the trip or the escort and that would be the end of it. Ruth Ann would not be forced to make a trip to the World's Fair. She could remain here forever, safe at home.

It wasn't meant to be. Her mama and uncle said yes.

CHAPTER TWENTY

FOR THE NEXT TWO DAYS Ruth Ann lived outside herself, observing the preparations. She saw herself return to town with the Levitts and Lance Fuller and enter the empty box house by the railroad tracks. It might have felt like home if Ruth Ann had the presence of mind to feel anything. Time passed in a blur: packing, instructing Peter on taking care of things, final dinner and goodbyes at the big house on the ranch, Lance Fuller hauling her steamer trunk to the depot.

She wanted to stay by Matthew's side despite him reminding her how important it was to get front page stories the newspaper needed. He gave her the name of the man who could get her an interview with Buffalo Bill, Mr. Grady Lewis. She had to do it, no matter how afraid she was.

"And ride the Ferris Wheel first. After that, you'll be able to do anything."

Matthew's eyes had twinkled, but she made no such promise. Heights terrified her.

On the platform at the depot, Ruth Ann's senses came back and she nearly cried. She turned to Beulah—who was bursting with excitement—and opened her mouth to say she would not make this trip.

But Ruth Ann caught sight of Mayor Warren elbowing his way through the crowded depot.

Surely he'd come to say a final farewell to Lance Fuller. But no. He headed straight for her, his face hard set against her. In one hand he carried a black satchel, ridiculously small looking when he pulled it close to his round belly as he maneuvered across the crowded platform.

Mayor Warren stopped in front of Ruth Ann. It was a strain, but she managed to look him in the eyes without taking a step back. "Good afternoon, sir. Have you come to see us off?"

With no pretended politeness, he barked, "I have papers for you to sign."

"Oh?" The squeaky word sounded dumb to her, but Ruth Ann had nothing else to say.

Beulah stepped in. "She will sign nothing. We are on our way to Chicago, and I would like you not to be around for our departure."

The mayor ignored her. He flipped open the satchel and used his paunch to balance it on while he withdrew a sheaf of papers.

"Miss Teller, your business will be worthless when you return, if you return. You will sign your entity over to me now. The generous compensation will cover your debts."

The mayor shoved papers into her hand, but she sorted through the meaning behind his words. *If* she returned? Did he think the lure of a city would draw her away from her people? Or was there a threat beneath his words?

Lance Fuller and Mr. Levitt, who had been arranging the luggage for loading, joined them. Ruth Ann skimmed the document the man had shoved under her nose. Generous compensation? The amount wasn't even enough to repay Uncle Preston and the Levitts for their help in starting the *Choctaw Tribune*. They knew what *generous* meant.

"Matthew is still alive, sir, and he has no intention of selling." Ruth Ann felt foolish stating the obvious. But what else could she say?

The train whistled, alerting Dickens of its approach. Mayor Warren tapped the papers. "If you try to restart the paper, it'll be a disaster. This is your only chance to salvage anything. You hear? *Worthless* when you return!"

While Ruth Ann stared at the mayor, Mr. Levitt carefully took the papers and the satchel from his white-knuckled grip. The much smaller man returned the papers to the satchel and closed it slowly. He placed it in the mayor's open hands.

"You may discuss your offer when she returns. You will get a much better deal then."

Mayor Warren glared at the Jewish man. "You! You're the one who tricked me into that lease with the subleasing clause. You are despicable. I should throw you all into the street. This is *my* town—"

A squeal blended with the last whistle the train gave as it rolled into the station. Ruth Ann looked past the mayor, surprised to see Susan Warren. She looked more disheveled than ever, hair in a lopsided bun, a large coat thrown over— whatever it was she had underneath. Ruth Ann had a horrible suspicion it was only the woman's robe, judging from the trim peeking out from under the large coat, a coat much too heavy for the warm October afternoon. Worst of all, a bruise was visible on her cheek despite the abundant powder dusted across her drawn face.

Mrs. Warren stumbled to a stop by her husband's side. She ignored the shocked glances from other people on the platform. This had turned into quite a scene.

Mrs. Warren gulped air and grabbed Ruth Ann's arms. "Oh, tell me you signed the papers. You must! There is nothing in Dickens for any of your people. Accept the inevitable! Don't you realize—"

"Susan!" Mayor Warren's tone held a viciousness Ruth Ann didn't want to comprehend.

But his wife understood. She pulled her head down into the high collar of the coat, her face and red eyes hidden by its shadows.

Mayor Warren's head trembled as though he kept himself

from punching something. Or someone. "I told you I would handle this, Mrs. Warren." He jerked a thumb over his shoulder. "Go home."

Whimpering, the woman started to turn away. Ruth Ann stepped forward and wrapped her arms around the robust woman, barely able to embrace her in a full hug. She whispered, "I pray for you. God knows."

Mrs. Warren stiffened at Ruth Ann's touch, then went as limp as a baby, before finally returning the embrace with breathtaking fierceness. Then she jerked away and ran—as well as she could for her age and size—from Ruth Ann.

The train had come to a stop, passengers disembarked and others loaded onto the northbound Frisco. Ruth Ann turned but an ample waist blocked her way. "You *will* regret this day, you heathen savage."

Then Mayor Warren was gone, but she couldn't see for the sudden tears in her eyes. She couldn't understand them, couldn't think where she had been going before the mayor's interruption.

A hand on her elbow guided her toward the train, though she had a sense she should resist. She didn't want to go, didn't want to make this trip into the unknown. Yet there were the steps of the train, and a feeling overcame her. She needed to go. It was right.

The hand released her—only then did she realize it had been Lance Fuller's—and Mr. Levitt embraced both her and Beulah in a final hug, quite a feat for the small man. He put his hands on their heads and murmured a few words in Hebrew, and then, "God go with you, my daughters."

With this prayer, Ruth Ann boarded the train with her traveling companions to search out a world she couldn't imagine.

CHAPTER TWENTY-ONE

TWO DAYS OF TRAVEL INCLUDED changing trains at St. Louis, Missouri, to board a luxurious Pullman sleeping car. But when that train pulled up to the Union Depot in Chicago, Illinois, Ruth Ann was wholly unprepared. During the trip, she'd done little other than watch the countryside change, and she hadn't truly engaged in that, or Lance Fuller's and Beulah's attempts to draw her into conversation. They gave up and left her with her own thoughts.

But arriving in Chicago ended Ruth Ann's solitude and launched her into what promised to be an exciting adventure. If only she could feel excitement. She stood slowly and followed Lance Fuller and Beulah out of the passenger car.

When Ruth Ann stepped onto the crowded platform, the noxious fumes of garbage and a cattle car took away her breath. And when had it grown cloudy? The sky above the city was a hazy gray like a tombstone.

But this depot wasn't a cemetery. Not even the depot in Paris, Texas, compared to the activity here. Ruth Ann stayed by Beulah's side as they entered the massive station. She couldn't help how her spirits lifted. Her curious nature awoke.

Under the cavern-like ceiling, hundreds of people greeted one another, said farewell, laughed, cried. Ruth Ann wanted to memorize it all so she could describe it to her family. Matthew would scold her if she didn't write a load of details in her articles.

The thought of home and family and tragedies made Ruth Ann dizzy, but she forced herself to look forward, on to what she could accomplish for the *Choctaw Tribune*. Come what may, there was nothing more powerful than the press except God Almighty. And He was with her in Chicago.

Lance Fuller left to locate their trunks. Beulah guided Ruth Ann to a less hectic area near a row of hard-backed benches. Ruth Ann turned in a circle. "Oh, Beulah. It's all so big!"

Beulah laughed. Ruth Ann knew her friend had lived in New York a few years. A big city was nothing she couldn't conquer. She was probably just grateful Ruth Ann was aware enough to be in awe. "My friend, wait until we are in the streets. On and on and on! You will not be able to see the tops of buildings from the carriage. They even had to coin a new word for these buildings—skyscraper. I have not been in Chicago, but if it is at all like New York, what a fabulous time we will have!"

Beulah looped her arm through Ruth Ann's and hugged her close. "I am so glad we are here. All is well. What is it your family says? God knows."

Ruth Ann gave her tall friend a sincere smile. "I'm glad too."

A shriek sounded across the way from the benches. "Beulah! Beulah Levitt, it is you!"

Bouncing toward them—yes, bouncing—was a young woman with dark hair piled atop her head under a frilly hat. Curled bangs framed her face and her chocolate brown eyes. She wore a pale yellow skirt and jacket with a braided trim. This well-bred young woman must be Edith Zadok.

Ruth Ann ducked behind Beulah when her friend released her arm to embrace the young woman. They hugged and laughed and chattered so quickly Ruth Ann couldn't make out a thing they said.

Lance Fuller rejoined them and stood close to her. He leaned closer still. "I thought Beulah spoke fast in English. In Russian, they should be caught up on the last eight years in about that many seconds."

Russian. Of course. Ruth Ann felt stupid for not remembering the Zadoks were Russian and that the Levitts had met them crossing over from their homeland. And they'd lived together in a Jewish colony in Kansas.

On the trip to Chicago, Beulah had explained that the Zadoks moved away several years before the colony dispersed because of drought. With the drought, the Levitts migrated to Indian Territory. When another family went to Chicago, they told the Zadoks the Levitts had gone south, and Edith Zadok tracked down the old friends.

Ruth Ann tried to remember all these things before Beulah turned to her. Edith Zadok bounced over and embraced Ruth Ann. She shook Lance Fuller's hand. "You are Matthew and Ruth Ann Teller, yes? You will love Chicago."

Ruth Ann politely returned the greeting. But her mind was blank.

Beulah swept in. "Oh, I did not have a chance to write. This is Lance Fuller, a schoolteacher in Dickens, and he agreed to be our escort for the trip. You see, Matthew Teller was not able to come." She hesitated and glanced at Ruth Ann.

Ruth Ann nodded, hoping her appreciation showed in her eyes. She would rather the Zadoks didn't know all that had happened. The less they knew, the less Ruth Ann would have to explain.

She followed in the wake of Beulah and Edith as they navigated through the depot toward the open doors on the far side. Ruth Ann glanced back. Could she call the stop at Dickens a "depot" anymore?

On the platform outside, porters helped load fine carriages that lined the jammed streets. Ruth Ann knew streetcars operated throughout the city, and she was looking forward to riding one.

Edith went to a tall man standing next to an enclosed carriage—complete with driver and matched sorrel horses—and linked arms with him. With a subdued smile, Edith said, "This is my beau, Abraham Pilzer. He graciously offered to see us home."

Beulah introduced their party. Ruth Ann took in the details of the carriage and the man. Everything about him spoke of wealth obtained with ease. She wondered how a Russian Jewish immigrant had caught his eye, but then she assumed he must be Jewish as well. His accent was thick on the few words he spoke in greeting. There was nothing cheerful about him, nothing to match the bouncy Edith Zadok.

Ruth Ann noted how reserved Edith became in his presence, which was an understandable posture to have with her beau. But Ruth Ann's mother had cautioned her to be the same kind of person no matter who she was with. Della helped her understand that nothing cheapened the value of a person like falseness.

Lance Fuller oversaw the trunks being loaded by a porter and the driver while Mr. Pilzer helped the ladies enter the large enclosed carriage. The scent of the leather seats was a relief from the stench of nearby factories.

The three ladies settled on one side—Edith insisted on sitting in the middle so the newcomers would have window seats—while the gentlemen took the other side.

Yes, gentlemen was the right word. Abraham Pilzer certainly was one, and Lance Fuller had fallen comfortably into the role like he'd been raised in it. Of course, he had, according to the article Matthew found. Lance Fuller was well-trained and at home in this environment. It was in Indian Territory that he stuck out. Coming from a big city, he must have felt completely out of place.

Ruth Ann felt ashamed when she recalled his first attempts at the schoolhouse. She should have been more under-standing. Now that their roles were reversed, she hoped he would show her grace.

Seated in the carriage, with her frontier traveling clothes and modest hairdo, Ruth Ann was out of place next to Edith, and even Beulah, who naturally fit into any situation.

Edith and Beulah chatted continuously, Beulah asking questions and Edith answering, their words overlapping and sometimes slipping into Russian. Abraham Pilzer, seated across from Beulah, kept his eyes out the window, lips in a thin line. He occasionally made a quiet comment to Lance Fuller, who was seated across from Ruth Ann. His nearness made her keep her attention out the window as Edith rattled off street names.

Back home, people needed to pay attention to the roads and trails they traveled, to go slowly enough to make sure they remembered the way home. But in this vast city, Ruth Ann knew she'd be hopelessly lost if she became separated from her party. She might as well be in a foreign country. But at least here they spoke English. Well, mostly.

The street was snarled in an ugly traffic jam and the car-riage stopped. Edith sighed. "So much traffic in this part of the city! People are too impatient and accidents happen, which cause more delays. Oh well. Do you see that building on the left? That is where my father and Abraham are partners in one of the largest banks in the country."

Ruth Ann craned her neck to see out the closed window. Beulah was right, she couldn't see the top of the building. It scraped the sky.

For the next half-hour while they were stuck in the jam, Edith extolled the benefits of living in Chicago and how for-tunate her family was to have moved there. Opportunities were endless for enterprising men, immigrant or not. Factories exploded with businesses to fill the needs of the country. With the World's Fair, many had made a fortune with short-term contracts and then used the money to reinvest in their busi-nesses, which could put them among the elite in the country.

The society life, Edith went on, was exceptional, with some of the finest old families in the country. She'd been fortunate when Mrs. Pilzer took her under her wing and introduced Edith at the many social occasions. It was through this relationship her courtship with the woman's son, Abraham Pilzer, formed.

Here, Edith paused and gazed at her suitor, but he was in a conversation with Lance Fuller. The two were intently discussing the stock market crash last spring, a crash that had devastated many businesses. Mr. Pilzer explained how the leaders of their bank used their wiles to avert disaster. Lance Fuller seemed especially interested in this part until he realized three ladies were listening.

He cleared his throat and smiled. "My apologies, this is a dull way to spend a carriage ride. Perhaps Mr. Pilzer and Miss Zadok could tell us the highlights of the fair."

And so the conversation shifted, but Ruth Ann still found her attention drifting in and out. She had her own plans to make. She needed to contact Mr. Grady Lewis and work up the courage to interview Buffalo Bill Cody.

At a lull in the conversation, Ruth Ann spoke for the first time. "Edith, have you been to the Wild West Show? I understand it's next to the fair."

Edith crinkled her nose. "I had quite enough of the Wild West in Kansas, and I have no desire to see the spectacle of Bill Cody's savages and such on display. Why would someone waste time at that show when there is the White City to enjoy? Ruth, you will love the Court of Honor and the canals. We will go early in the morning and spend the day! Mr. Pilzer made arrangements with his work and will accompany us. Mr. Fuller, too, of course." She batted her eyelashes as she looked between Ruth Ann and him.

Ruth Ann turned her attention to the traffic jam that was finally cleared. One word continued to ring in her mind. *Savages.* How much had Beulah told Edith about the Tellers? Did the Zadoks know they were hosting an Indian? Would it matter?

Ruth Ann leaned her warm forehead close to the cool glass window. She wished they had taken a streetcar.

◆ ◆ ◆

When Edith said they were almost to her home, Ruth Ann was confused. They were still in the city, with five-story buildings that lined the brick streets. No neighborhoods were in sight. Then it dawned on her that these buildings housed people. Some of them *were* homes.

The carriage came to a halt and she stared at a grand apartment building.

"Here we are!" Edith sounded cheerful, but she was turned the other direction. Ruth Ann realized she'd been looking the wrong way. She was the last one out of the carriage and the last to gaze up, up, up at Edith's home.

Ruth Ann pinched her lips together to keep her jaw from dropping at the sight of the elegant home. It was four stories high and included a carriage house and immaculate yard with a long walkway that split at the steps. She wondered if the other path led to a side door she could use.

Beulah voiced enough enthusiasm for all of them. "Oh, Edith, how lovely! The purple trim is divine. I know your mother must love it here."

"Oh yes." Edith took Mr. Pilzer's offered arm and led the way to the front door. Two men in uniforms scurried around the carriage to make sure none of the passengers were carrying anything.

With Beulah stuck to Edith's side, Ruth Ann had little choice but to accept Lance Fuller's arm. They fell in behind the long strides of Mr. Pilzer.

Lance Fuller dropped his formal gentleman's air and whistled low. "I wasn't informed Beulah's friends were among the upper crust of Chicago. Her beau is one of the young geniuses in the financial world. Talk about wealth. This is a fine connection you've made, in case you didn't realize it."

Ruth Ann frowned, partly because Lance Fuller was

treating her like a confidant, partly because she had no interest in viewing Beulah's friends as "connections."

But try as she might, she couldn't fault his observations. Matthew was always making connections that proved invaluable to the *Choctaw Tribune*. Why shouldn't Ruth Ann look at this opportunity in that light?

Once inside, she had to gulp again. The foyer at the Barnes mansion always delighted her with its high ceiling and chandelier. It was perhaps half the size of this wide foyer that boasted three gas chandeliers to light the area with its many doors and sweeping staircase leading to the next floor. A maid took their hats and wraps. A second maid swung the massive door closed behind them.

The first maid explained that Mr. and Mrs. Zadok were out on social calls. They had hoped to greet the guests, but the traffic delays caused them to miss one another.

The guests bid Mr. Pilzer goodbye and a third maid showed the guests their rooms on the second floor.

In her room, Ruth Ann's luggage and a tea cart of refreshments greeted her. Alone at last, she collapsed on the bed and nuzzled her head into the pillows. She didn't care how mussed her hair became. It wasn't in good shape anyway. She wanted to sleep and then do what she'd come to do and go home and publish the next edition of the *Choctaw Tribune*...

A soft tap on the door startled her. It was too timid for Beulah.

Ruth Ann bolted to her feet and fumbled with her hair. "Who is it?"

"Augustine, miss. The upstairs maid."

She cracked the door open and stared into the soft green eyes of a girl in a stiff gray uniform and huge white apron that engulfed her. At least, her eyes seemed soft and green. They were looking down, somewhere below Ruth Ann's chin.

She kept the door mostly closed. "Oh, yes, hello. Can I help you?"

The girl's lips twitched almost into a smile, but her gaze stayed down. "I'm here to help you unpack, miss. I will take care of all your needs while you're here. May I come in?"

"Oh." Ruth Ann felt stupid. Why would a maid come to help her? How many maids were in this home? This was the fourth one she'd seen in ten minutes. "Um, thank you, but I can manage. I'm really tired and will probably lie down and sleep awhile if that's alright."

Augustine curtsied. "Very well, miss. I'll come back at five to help you dress for dinner."

Ruth Ann stared at her. "Oh no, that won't be necessary. I can dress myself."

A tiny smile made it to Augustine's lips. "I will return at five, nonetheless."

The maid never lifted her eyes, but Ruth Ann still felt she was being looked down on.

CHAPTER TWENTY-TWO

THE ZADOK FAMILY BETTER FIT the mold of what most expected Jewish people to look like—the distinct nose, dark hair. Not at all like the blonde Levitts Ruth Ann had grown accustomed to. That wasn't the only difference.

The Zadoks had adapted well to high society since their early days as immigrants to America. After leaving the Kansas colony, they made connections in Chicago within the German Jewish community. That paved the way to lucrative work for Mr. Zadok. His two sons worked at the bank as well, though they were now branching out in their own ventures.

The oldest son was in Europe working on an enterprise he had launched in international trade. The younger son had partnered with a man who had won a contract to sell sodas at the World's Fair, a man named Simon…something.

That was Ruth Ann's great struggle at the formal dining room table beyond knowing which fork to use. Her head ached from trying to keep track of names and businesses and society topics. And she was far underdressed even in her finest. It paled compared to Edith's puffed sleeved emerald satin that glistened. Edith had attended finishing school, but Mrs. Zadok wasn't as relaxed in her wealthy hostess role as someone who'd been born into wealth. But they both played their parts with grace.

Beulah carried herself with enough confidence to overcome less expensive clothing and a lack of formal training. And Lance Fuller blended right in. The Zadoks and Mr. Pilzer spoke a language he understood.

The dreaded moment came when Mrs. Zadok attempted to include Ruth Ann in the conversation. "What a lovely shade of skin, Miss Teller, is it from an Italian heritage?" Without waiting for confirmation, Mrs. Zadok went to the next topic. "Do give us an account of your home. It must be a fascinating place to live."

Ruth Ann took a deep breath. *Lord, give me wisdom.*

"Actually, perhaps you would like to hear about it from Mr. Fuller's perspective. I've lived there all my life, and I'm sure his view would be far more interesting."

It was either the most gracious or the most stupid thing she could have said. She sipped water from one of the two crystal goblets by her plate.

She needn't have worried. Lance Fuller moved in and riveted his audience with breathtaking descriptions of the landscape in Indian Territory and the colorful characters that dotted it. Even Ruth Ann was drawn in, amazed by his observations of her homelands. She kept her reporter's perspective though, and wondered if the descriptions were truly how he saw things or if he wanted to impress these new connections. Or her.

Mrs. Zadok asked about the Indian population but her question went unanswered when a newcomer disrupted the room. He entered with a bounce, relating him to Edith in Ruth Ann's mind.

He greeted them all in general, and kissed Mrs. Zadok's forehead. "Forgive my tardiness, Mother. It will not happen again."

She patted his cheek. "So you say every time. I suppose I will give you a proper introduction anyway. This is our youngest son, Isaac. This is Miss Ruth Ann Teller and Mr. Lance

Fuller, her traveling companion. And you remember Beulah Levitt from Kansas."

It might as well have been the Fourth of July for the fireworks that exploded between the young man and Beulah. Ruth Ann greeted him but kept watch on her friend seated beside her. Was that hate or love in her eyes? Whichever, it was an unmasked passion.

"Isaac." Beulah gave a quick nod. He returned it before taking his seat. He didn't look her way after that.

Edith and Mrs. Zadok started the conversation again with their trained way of keeping it rounding the table.

But thankfully, questions about Indians or memories from Kansas were left alone.

◆◆◆

It was past midnight when Ruth Ann snuck from her room, robe wrapped securely over her nightgown. She tapped on Beulah's door before letting herself in the dark room.

A soft laugh came from the bed. "Do come in, Ruth. I am not asleep either." Beulah turned up the gas lamp on the nightstand, its hissing loud in the night.

Ruth Ann ran to the bed and hopped onto the middle of it. The four poster bed was feather soft like the one in Ruth Ann's room, covered with a lush gold bedspread and a half dozen embroidered pillows.

Beulah grabbed Ruth Ann's hands. "Is this not an exciting place? I know I will not sleep at all. Tomorrow we will see the White City—the World's Fair!"

Ruth Ann sighed and squeezed her friend's hands in return. "I do appreciate you bringing me along, Beulah. Please don't think I'm ungrateful, but I can hardly wait to get on the first train home."

Beulah laughed. "My dear Ruth, you need not let them bother you. We are grateful for their hospitality, but do not be intimidated. The Zadoks are a fine family, and they have found a fine place in society. I do not envy them, neither am I uncomfortable around them. Circumstances have changed but they are still the same people I hoed a garden next to on the farm colony in Kansas."

Ruth Ann leaned toward her friend. She suddenly felt giddy—the tables had been turned. "Has Isaac Zadok changed much? He's certainly an amiable young man—" She halted at the icy look in Beulah's eyes.

"You will not speak of him. He may keep to his own business as well while we are here."

Ruth Ann cocked her eyebrow, but decided not to back down. "What happened between you two? It looked like there was a lot he wanted to say but, well, anyone could tell from the look on your face there was no room for discussion."

Beulah's expression melted. "Was it so obvious?"

"I'm afraid so. I don't know what happened between you two, but everyone will have the same question on their minds."

Beulah regained her posture. "Let them all wonder. It is not for them to know."

"Me either?" Ruth Ann dipped her head in a plea.

Beulah sighed. "I have shared some of the hardest memories of my heart with you, Ruth. Someday, someday I will tell you what kind of memory Isaac Zadok holds."

♦♦♦

Before they departed for the fair the next morning, Ruth Ann found she had plenty of time to write letters home. Despite the late night, she was up at her usual time, only to discover that in the city "early in the morning" was not at all early by her standards.

She composed letters to her family and then a note to Matthew's connection, Mr. Grady Lewis. She perused the *Rand, McNally & Co. Handbook to the World's Columbian Exposition* Edith had given her, though Ruth Ann didn't want to spoil her first impressions with someone else's point of view. She needed to write a fresh perspective on the fair, not a repeated one. Still, the section about the Manufactures and Liberal Arts building caught her attention. It was described as an indoor city of "gilded domes and glittering minarets, mosques, palaces, kiosks, and brilliant pavilions." Would they have time to see it all?

Putting aside the handbook, Ruth Ann still had too much time to look through her limited selection of clothing. What did one wear to a World's Fair?

A soft tap sounded at the door. She had sent the maid away twice yesterday, but perhaps this was the answer to her dilemma. Surely Augustine had been to the fair and could help her "dress."

"Come in."

The door opened slowly and Augustine appeared, eyes down, a bundle of clothes draped over her arm. She closed the door and went to hang the outfits in the wardrobe. "Miss Zadok sent these in hopes you would find something you approve of. She says it will be a long day and a bit cool, and she wasn't sure if you had something suitable."

Though the message was polite, it was a way of saying Ruth Ann's clothing was unacceptable in high society. A spark of rebellion flared up in her and she almost selected her dusty traveling outfit just for spite. But she doused the spark, ashamed of herself. The Zadoks had kindly funded this trip, their only complaint was that the guests could only stay a week. They were buying the tickets to the World's Fair. Ruth Ann would show her gratitude by wearing one of Edith's outfits.

Once she began looking through her choices, Ruth Ann had no regret over her decision. The outfits were spectacular and practically new. Had Edith even worn them?

The ruby red with black trim and puff sleeves Ruth Ann chose was nearly a perfect fit. She was too busy admiring it in the full length mirror to mind Augustine tucking and pinning with expert movements. She even let the maid do her hair.

"Augustine, what's your favorite part of the fair? I want to see the best places to tell my family."

The maid fumbled the knot she was creating, but quickly got it back in place. Ruth Ann tried to meet Augustine's gaze in the mirror where Ruth Ann sat in front of the vanity, but the maid remained intent on her work. "I only went to the fair one afternoon, miss. It was nice."

Ruth Ann couldn't help her disappointment at Augustine's lackluster tone. "Only one day? You didn't want to go back and see more? It's going to close soon."

Augustine went to work on the strands of hair she left loose from the knot. "The Zadoks gave their employees fare and an afternoon off. Sure and it was very kind of them."

Augustine seemed more relaxed now, and Ruth Ann detected a slight accent. Irish.

"Well, my friends and I will be here a week. You could go with us one day. Maybe by then, I can show you my favorite places…"

Ruth Ann stopped when Augustine's eyes briefly met hers in the mirror. First the maid looked shocked, then amused before she went back to work on the bangs. "You are a strange miss. You've never been in so fine a house as this, have you now?"

Again, Ruth Ann felt she was being looked down upon, but she brushed the annoyance aside. At least Augustine was being herself. That was a comfort in this world of frills.

CHAPTER TWENTY-THREE

RUTH ANN'S HOPE OF RIDING a streetcar was delayed again. Abraham Pilzer and his carriage waited outside the Zadok home after breakfast. The group loaded and sat in the same places. The conversation was easy among the sophisticated and confident, leaving Ruth Ann out.

But that suited her fine. She wanted to take in all of Chicago she could from the window. There were so many details to commit to memory. Ruth Ann carried a small tablet to jot notes of the tarnished sky, skyscrapers, smells of the big city. She should have brought Matthew's camera to take photographs, but she didn't trust herself with it. She'd break it or see it stolen. Already, she'd been warned to stay with the group and to keep her reticule close. Pickpockets and thieves roved the fair. It was easy to take advantage of awe-struck tourists.

Ruth Ann thought Isaac Zadok would join their party, but at breakfast he had announced business he needed to take care of, though he hoped to join them at the fair later in the week. She couldn't tell if it was consternation or relief on Beulah's face. It was gone in a blink.

Ruth Ann expected to arrive at the main entrance to the

fair, but the carriage rumbled into a harbor and stopped. There were three steamships anchored in the calm water. She didn't see any sign of the fair. But she was determined to not constantly ask questions and cause her ignorance to embarrass anyone. She touched the borrowed hat to make sure it was pinned in place.

Lance Fuller assisted her from the carriage. "Pilzer, is this the steamship I've heard about? It takes us around the harbor to the fair's entrance by the concert hall?"

With so much detail, Ruth Ann realized he knew the answers. He had asked for her benefit. She wished she could express her gratitude, but she didn't want to encourage him the wrong way one bit.

Mr. Pilzer gave a curt nod as Edith took her place on his arm. "This steamship will take us to the Peristyle Water Gate entrance."

Ruth Ann accepted Lance Fuller's arm and suddenly realized Beulah had no real escort. Her friend was well able to get along on her own, but when he offered his other arm to her, Beulah took it with a laugh that made everything all right.

They boarded the steamship and drifted to the front, though it took awhile to get there because of the introductions to acquaintances of Edith and her suitor. With all the people Ruth Ann shook hands with, she didn't feel a firm grip or see a genuine expression. It reminded her of how Lance Fuller was sometimes. Maybe it was just their culture.

Experiencing cultures was something she'd come to the World's Fair to do. There were over forty cultures represented from around the world.

But Ruth Ann decided to keep her own hidden for now. With the fine dress she wore, hat, gloves and reticule, and Augustine's work making her hair into the latest style, she was safely tucked behind a mask. Only her tablet was out of place, but it was too large for her reticule. She'd have to carry it. Hopefully, it wouldn't mark her as an out-of-towner.

But Ruth Ann knew she would not be noticed today. After the forty-five minute ride on the breezy harbor, the sight before her should capture anyone's attention and imagination. She separated from the group and moved to the steamship's bow to soak in the moment.

The White City it was called. The Columbian Exhibition. The Chicago World's Fair.

She was truly here, staring at the thousands of people and dozens of cultures on the six hundred acres that held two hundred buildings, a midway, and parks.

Ruth Ann started to comment and realized no one was beside her. The view was breathtaking, but not nearly as much as the sudden loneliness in her heart. Matthew should be here. He would truly appreciate the sight in the most practical yet vibrant way. Ruth Ann could only stare and never do the experience justice with words. How she missed her brother!

A cold wind bit her cheek and she blamed the harbor for the moisture on her skin. The wind made her eyes water, that was all. She would be brave today. *God, help me be as alive as I can be in this place.*

"Something else, isn't it?" Lance Fuller appeared next to her. He pointed to the various eye-popping structures. "The Manufactures and Liberal Arts Building, the largest building in the world. It's said to be three times the size of St. Peter's Basilica in Rome. There, the Peristyle Water Gate separates the Grand Basin and Lake Michigan. The Agriculture Building…" He halted.

Ruth Ann hurried to dab away the wetness on her cheeks with her gloved hand. Sniffing, she pulled a pencil from her reticule and began scratching notes to try and capture some of the beauty. "Quite something."

He touched her hand, stilling the pencil. "It'll be all right, Ruth Ann. Everything will, I promise."

What was he promising now? Why? Ruth Ann withdrew her hand and breathed deeply. She smiled. "Of course. This is a thrilling day! I can't wait to see it all."

Ruth Ann craned her neck to take in all she could as they approached the entrance. The enormous Manufactures and Liberal Arts Building with its uniform Corinthian arcade that

ran in a continuous sweep for the entire length of the building, interrupted only by the triumphal arch motifs of the cen-
tral and end entrance pavilions. The incredible moving sidewalk on the long pier that led to the Grecian influenced
Peristyle Gate with its white columns and statues riding atop
the ornate structure. The Agriculture Building with its white
statues of horses, cattle, and Greek symbols.

This was just the beginning.

Ruth Ann lowered her tablet. Sometimes one needed to
be in the moment, not writing about it. This moment was a
time to set aside all thoughts and just be.

◆◆◆

The moving sidewalk was a little frightening at first, but
turned out fun. It moved smoothly, giving Ruth Ann a heavenly sense of floating on clouds. It cost five cents a person—
she was embarrassed when Lance Fuller paid for her—and ran
nearly the entire length of the 3,500-foot pier. They had the
choice to stand or walk on the first platform, which traveled at
two miles per hour, or step up on a second parallel platform,
which ran at four miles per hour and had benches. She learned
that at full capacity, the walkway could ferry over 30,000 passengers per hour. Ruth Ann couldn't count how many people
rode it now, but it might make capacity this hour. Edith explained that even more people were visiting with the end coming closer. The mayor had designated a day later this week as
"Chicago Day" and the fair coordinators expected top attendance.

How could there be more than today?

Lance Fuller was Ruth Ann's ally. He made light of anything that overwhelmed her, answered his own questions, and
pointed out sights when the group exited the moving sidewalk. Ruth Ann gave it another look, fascinated. "I wish I had
the camera."

He shook his head. "It wouldn't do you any good. The
fair banned all cameras unless you want to pay a ridiculous

permit fee, or rent the Kodak number 4, aptly dubbed the *Columbus*, from an exclusive contractor. Otherwise, all photography is monopolized by a single photographer hired by the fair."

Ruth Ann frowned. "Doesn't sound like a complete perspective of the fair will be shown to the world that couldn't come."

Lance Fuller shrugged. "This is the builder's city. With all they went through to create this dreamland, they earned the right to do what they want, I suppose."

Edith had kept conversation going with Beulah, but took a breath in time to hear his remarks. "Come now, Mr. Fuller, no business talk today. We are here to enjoy the grand displays of man's finest achievements."

Man's finest achievements? Ruth Ann oddly felt like her brother's newspaper should be on display. She couldn't help smiling.

Edith insisted they wait in line to take a gondola ride on the Grand Basin, a long body of water that stretched between the Peristyle and a gold-topped building at the other end, and surrounded by enormous white buildings. Ruth Ann couldn't imagine waiting for anything. There was so much to see! But she kept her impatience hidden and chatted with Beulah. They managed to keep their girlish squeals between themselves. While waiting in line, the group munched on a new snack called Cracker Jack, introduced at the fair.

Ruth Ann was swept along in a fairytale like none she'd dreamed of. She even let herself enjoy Lance Fuller's company. This wasn't a day for anxiety. The autumn weather was beautiful, the group pleasant, the setting divine. Indian Territory and all the troubles of the *Choctaw Tribune* were far, far away.

CHAPTER TWENTY-FOUR

THE NEXT DAY, RUTH ANN once again found it late in the morning before the group loaded into Mr. Pilzer's carriage and headed for the fair. She kept her nose in the fair handbook, wanting to educate herself as much as possible so she could easily absorb the sights and sounds without trying to memorize facts too. If only she could get a copy of one of the newspapers in town. But what would the high society Zadoks think of a woman reading a newspaper? Certainly, women seemed bolder and freer here in Chicago than other places she'd read about. An article in a Chicago newspaper Matthew subscribed to said there were a great many women's rights movements taking place during the fair. But in society circles like the Zadoks, women were still an ornament for a man's arm. At least, that was what she'd witnessed whenever Edith was in Abraham Pilzer's presence. But it was none of her business. She just didn't want to embarrass her hostess by committing a backwoods error.

The handbook was loaded with fascinating details that made Ruth Ann so very glad to be in Chicago. She would soon have enough glorious stories to fill an entire edition of the *Choctaw Tribune*. Wouldn't she?

Ruth Ann lowered the handbook and glanced out the window at the skyscrapers they passed. What stories did she have? Oh, she could write lovely reports, breathtaking details. But what about stories?

Her thoughts were interrupted with a tinge of disappointment when they arrived at the same harbor. She'd hoped they would enter through one of the other entrances to give her a different perspective. Besides, the steamboat ride took entirely too long when the whole world awaited.

But Ruth Ann patiently stayed with the group who was making this time at the Columbian Exposition possible. She wondered how Edith would react when Mr. Grady Lewis answered her request and Ruth Ann went off to see Buffalo Bill.

On the steamboat, they were joined by associates of Mr. Pilzer. When she learned the gentlemen and their wives would be joining them for the day, Ruth Ann was relieved. She wouldn't feel so obligated to constantly engage in the group chit-chat. She could observe strangers around her, get the stories Matthew wanted. Maybe she'd stumble across a second front page story besides Bill Cody's.

Ruth Ann needn't worry about Lance Fuller much either. During the carriage and now steamboat ride, he was preoccupied with his own thoughts and only occasionally remembered to smile politely and make conversation. He looked around as though expecting to see someone he knew. If Ruth Ann watched closely, she could detect apprehension in his features, like when he taught school the first day. If she looked even closer, she might guess it was fear rather than apprehension. But Ruth Ann made it a point not to look closely at Lance Fuller.

The White City under the morning light took her breath away. The group was standing in a relaxed circle at the bow and Ruth Ann nudged Beulah. With a smooth glide, Beulah covered their slipping away to the rail.

A cool October breeze snapped across the water and Ruth Ann's face, but she smiled. "I wish Mama and Matthew and Peter and everyone were here. They would love this."

Beulah threaded her arm through Ruth Ann's and hugged it. "But you are here for them. That was their desire."

Ruth Ann leaned her head against her friend's shoulder, though she quickly straightened with a girlish giggle. "Sorry, I didn't mean to give you a mouthful of feathers."

She wasn't used to wearing such elaborate hats or the extravagant emerald hue of the dress she wore.

"Nonsense. Feather me all you want. We are in a dream anyway."

True. The domed Manufactures and Liberal Arts Building, the largest building in the world, couldn't be anywhere but in a dream.

The group disembarked and Ruth Ann checked her impatience as they rode the moving walkway. She wanted to walk on it the way some people did, but the rest of the group was too busy chatting to notice how slowly they moved while they stood and talked. The group had grown to a dozen, allowing Ruth Ann to settle into her own thoughts. Lance Fuller was still looking over his shoulder.

When they disembarked from the moving walkway, Edith and Abraham Pilzer led the way—away from the Manufactures building Ruth Ann hoped to go inside. Yesterday, they had strolled the paths and admired the stunning landscape, but hadn't been in any exhibits. She moved to Edith's side and asked quietly, "What are we seeing today?"

Edith smiled the way she did in her beau's presence—elegant, but stiff. "Why, there is no agenda when we come to the fair, Ruth Ann. We will simply stroll the paths. This area was once a veritable swamp known as Jackson Park, but see how it has been transformed. You cannot appreciate the beauty if you are in a hurry."

"Oh, I'm not in a hurry, it's just..." Ruth Ann fell silent. The more she talked among the refined, the more she sounded like a hick to her own ears. Besides, Edith was gazing up in her beau's face. Ruth Ann wondered if they had fallen in love here at the fair. It had a sweeping effect if people didn't have their feet firmly planted. But she wasn't sure it was love between Edith and Abraham Pilzer.

Ruth Ann drifted to the back of the group. She understood the importance of not rushing, but this was tedious. The whole world at her fingertips and her companions were crawling along like turtles. Would the entire week be like this?

The gravel path caused most everyone to separate into couples and the pace slowed even more for quiet remarks between them. Lance Fuller seemed to realize he was supposed to be Ruth Ann and Beulah's escort. He came up from where he'd been lingering further and further behind. "Pardon me, ladies, but I have something I need to do. I'll catch up with you this afternoon."

He disappeared in the crowd behind them.

Beulah didn't hesitate. She called ahead, "Edith, we are going with Mr. Fuller. We will join you again soon!"

Ruth Ann halted in surprise. The rest of the group was large enough that no one paid Beulah's unladylike shout any mind. But Ruth Ann minded. "Beulah, we can't go off with Mr. Fuller. We don't even know where…"

Beulah was already off. "Then we should hurry, should we not?"

When Ruth Ann caught up with her by slipping and sliding over the gravel in shoes too large for her, Beulah continued. "Come now. You do not want to spend the day with that boring group, do you? This is the World's Fair! I have a feeling Lance will lead us to much more excitement than love birds who cannot even see the path they walk."

"But what if we get lost?"

"All the more fun. Think of the stories we will be able to tell."

By now they were in the thick of the crowd. Beulah had an advantage with her height and confident stride. Ruth Ann tried to keep up. She wasn't frightened—much. She'd read about Columbian Guards hired to watch over fairgoers and provide help, but there were still reports of thieves and pickpockets that roamed the area. Not to mention how easy it seemed for people to disappear in a city as vast as Chicago.

Ruth Ann held her reticule close. Uncle Preston had given her enough money to see that she was taken care of on the trip, and also an extra train ticket home just in case. She'd stowed most of the money and the train ticket in her luggage back at the Zadoks, but she still could be taken as a wealthy target in Edith's fine clothes. Beulah also wore a borrowed dress from the Zadok's ample supply. The brilliant blue made it easier for Ruth Ann to keep an eye on her friend in the crowd.

"There!" Beulah raised up on tiptoe. "I believe I saw him going into the Manufactures building."

Beulah led the way to the grand building while Ruth Ann struggled to keep her balance at the enormity of it. Near the entrance, she could no longer see both ends of the building. It gave an eerie impression of stretching into eternity. Or at least into the twentieth century.

They entered with a crowd and Ruth Ann knew they would never find Lance Fuller in the mass of exhibits and people. An indoor city just as the handbook described.

She held on to her pinned hat to look up, up at the intricate bracing holding back the steel and glass sky. Dangling in midair were five gigantic electric chandeliers. The handbook had said they were seventy-five feet in diameter. Ruth Ann was so overwhelmed by the enormous dome she couldn't decide if the chandeliers looked larger or smaller in real life.

In the center of the building stood a clock tower, its seven foot face giving the time in days, hours, minutes and seconds. Even though the tower rose a staggering one hundred and twenty feet, the glass ceiling still stood over one hundred feet above it. Arches at the clock base allowed circulation of visitors underneath.

A familiar laugh enabled Ruth Ann to breathe again. Beulah tugged on her arm. "I saw our Lance getting on an elevator. I understand there is a promenade on top of the building."

Elevator? They were going to the top of *this* building? Impossibly terrifying. But Ruth Ann couldn't sort through her emotions of fear and excitement as Beulah dragged her through the street-like center aisle, known as Columbian Avenue, and past the thousands of exhibits they'd never have time to explore. Gobelin tapestries at the French pavilion. American companies showing off their wares—toys, weapons, canes, trunks, and a large display of burial hardware. How morbid. Yet the reminder of man's mortality was a needed one in this fantasy.

They neared the tower elevators, and Ruth Ann trembled. "Are...are you sure he went..." She couldn't finish.

The elevator was shocking, nothing more than a long platform with a fence around it, leaving the view wide open for the two hundred foot ascent.

Beulah fumbled with her reticule and withdrew coins. Ruth Ann realized the elevator cost extra. "Beulah, we can't afford..."

The elevator gate was opened by its uniformed operator and Beulah handed over their fee and pulled her on with the other passengers. Ruth Ann tried to breathe evenly and not to think of what lay ahead. Or rather, above. She regretted her earlier thoughts of wanting to rush through to see everything. The strolling group on the paths certainly wouldn't dash through the largest building in the world and ride one of its elevators to the top. Of course, they also didn't feel the mind-tingling excitement coursing through Ruth Ann.

That was replaced with sheer terror when the elevator began its rapid ascent. To her horror, rather than them rising, the dizzying view of the thousands of exhibits dropped away below.

At the top, Ruth Ann clutched her midsection, feeling faint. A narrow stairway led over the open space to the platform and doors above. If Beulah hadn't been attached to her arm, Ruth Ann would have crumpled to the floor. All the way to the floor two hundred feet below.

"Look, Ruth! You can see all the exhibits from here! What a story you can write."

But Ruth Ann refused to look down, not even for the

Choctaw Tribune's sake. Beulah had to support her going up the steps. Once outside in the cool autumn sunlight, Ruth Ann leaned against the wall next to the door. She closed her eyes and trembled. She was afraid of vomiting and embarrassing everyone.

"Ruth? Ruth Ann?"

Ruth Ann cracked her eyes open, and her attention was drawn to the view from the promenade.

The blue sky was blinding. She blinked and realized she wasn't looking at only sky. The lake they'd sailed in on the steamboat lay in front of her, Lake Michigan. How different the view from atop the building than from the lake! Ruth Ann glanced out the corner of her eyes to the left, then to the right. The bulk of the fair lay on the other side. Did she dare look? How many ladies had fainted at the sight of the panoramic view of the fair? Ruth Ann breathed carefully. She didn't want to be the first one.

"I—I'm all right. That ride was a bit nauseating, wasn't it?"

Beulah grinned. "I found it exhilarating. But no matter. You remain here and calm yourself while I look for Mr. Fuller." She patted Ruth Ann's arm as though calming a frightened child, then she turned away to begin her search at the north end of the crowded promenade.

Ruth Ann stood still until the thought occurred to her that the only way down was to ride the elevator again! Flush and close to swooning, she edged along the wall she'd been leaning against, away from the elevator entrance, looking for another sight besides the great lake. She moved around the corner.

She halted when she caught sight of Lance Fuller. Or rather his back, his shoulder leaned against the same wall holding her up, only he stood a dozen feet away.

The last thing she needed was his sympathy. She started to ease back the way she'd come but halted at the gruff words of the man Lance Fuller was speaking to.

"Maybe you'd like to jump off a ledge yourself. Cleaner

than stepping in front of a train."

Ruth Ann froze. What a horrible thing to say! She couldn't hear Lance Fuller's reply, but the man responded with, "This isn't over yet. You have it good in Indian Territory. Sink your roots deep."

This time, Ruth Ann thought she heard Lance Fuller mention money.

"Yeah, yeah, you'll have what you need in that account we set up. But take my advice—stick with what you have going. There's nothing here for you."

Ruth Ann sensed the conversation coming to an end. She quickly slipped back around the corner. It was harder to breathe now than when she stepped off the elevator. She leaned against the wall.

"Miss Ruth Ann, what are you doing here? Where are the others?"

Lance Fuller was at her side. Had he seen her eavesdropping? He acted off-balance, as though unsure whether to play the part of a charming gentleman or just be himself. Who was Lance Fuller exactly? Why had he been meeting with a brutish sounding man atop the Manufactures and Liberal Arts Building?

"I—we…that is, Beulah thought we'd go with you to see the sights rather than stay with the group." She knew her face was flushed and she couldn't meet his eyes.

Lance Fuller glanced behind him, then relaxed and took her elbow. "The elevator ride was pretty jarring, wasn't it? How about a nice, steady view to calm your nerves?"

Ruth Ann was too weak to protest, though she looked around to see if she could spot the man he'd been talking with. But she hadn't gotten a good look at his face.

It didn't matter. The view from the south side of the promenade was brilliant. The White City, as it was called with its uniform Beaux-Arts style structures all painted in white, shone magnificently in the late morning sun. The Grand Basin stretched through the Court of Honor with the enormous Statue of the Republic and Peristyle at the end closest to them while the gold-domed Administration Building guarded the other end. The Wooded Island, lagoons, over two hundred structures. Ruth Ann could see it all from here.

She shook her head, thankful it was no longer spinning. "To think, this was a swamp two years ago."

"And that's what it will be again soon."

Ruth Ann turned to Lance Fuller, aghast. "What do you mean?"

He swept his arm around to indicate the whole six hundred acres. "All of this was meant to be temporary. The buildings, everything, will be destroyed when the fair ends. Most want it to happen quickly rather than with a slow, miserable fade. It was never meant to last." His voice dropped to a whisper on the breeze. "Sometimes I wonder what is."

When Ruth Ann couldn't reply, he continued. "Maybe it's better that way, to go out with a bang at the end of a dream rather than try in vain to keep it alive a little longer. That damages its legacy, turning it into a dismal failure rather than a glorious memory. The men who built this dreamland accomplished the impossible, and showed who was made of good mettle and who was not." He sighed. "This fair served its purpose well, and when that purpose is complete, its life will be also."

Ruth Ann thought of all the inventions here, from the Cracker Jack snack to Mr. Ferris' wheel, and she wondered if those things would make it into the twentieth century. Would ending the dreamland fast be the best thing to keep its spirit alive?

What of the *Choctaw Tribune*? Was it better for it to go out with a bang than spiral into miserable failure?

Lance Fuller finally looked at her and quickly offered a handkerchief. "I'm sorry, I didn't mean to upset you. We're here to enjoy this place, not think about it ending. We'll be long gone before then anyway."

Ruth Ann sniffed and dabbed her eyes. She stared at the triumph before her. It reminded her of Matthew and his dream.

Beulah found them and Lance Fuller suggested they spend the rest of the day in the building below viewing the displays of great nations—the United States, Germany, Great Britain, France, Austria, Italy, and more. They would dine in the French restaurant and have a wonderful time.

Ruth Ann recalled the mention of money in the odd conversation she'd overheard. Since they were separated from their sponsors, who would pay for this day?

CHAPTER TWENTY-FIVE

THAT EVENING, AFTER LANCE FULLER managed to
cover the expensive food at the fair, Edith Zadok scolded
them for wandering off then announced they wouldn't attend
the fair the next day. They had social calls to make. But Beulah came to the rescue and convinced Edith the three from
Indian Territory needed to see more of the fair before time
ran out, and they could make out fine on their own. Edith
reluctantly agreed.

Tired as she was becoming, Ruth Ann urged Beulah and
Lance Fuller to leave early enough to make the fair when it
opened at eight the next morning.

With Lance Fuller as escort, they headed off in the
Zadok's carriage to a train station that would take them the
way most visitors of the fair went—by elevated railway.

Wait. *Elevated?*

After the Zadok's driver let them off under the station,
Ruth Ann, Beulah and Lance Fuller climbed metal stairs along
with dozens of others who were going up. The rattle on the
rails above Ruth Ann made the structure tremble. She forced
herself to watch the people in front of her and nothing else.

On the train, they rode above the city and curved around

toward the fair. Ruth Ann was glad she braved looking out the window in time to catch a glimpse of her primary target for this trip. Below, just outside the fair, was Buffalo Bill's Wild West and Congress of Rough Riders of the World. But she still hadn't heard from Matthew's contact to gain her a private interview with Buffalo Bill, and time was running out.

They passed over the fair's fence and descended to the railroad station near the Transportation Building.

Lance Fuller must have gotten more money—he paid their fifty cent admission and they were ready for another breathtaking day.

It started in the Transportation Building to see the wide array of locomotives, carriages, even a steamship replica outside. Mechanical mannequins on a raised platform contraption peddled English bicycles continuously in place. Beulah was convinced they should get bicycles to take home.

The day moved far too quickly from there—the Horticulture Building with its five domes and exotic plants from around the world; in the Mines and Mining Building were diamonds, silver, copper and a golden castle from Mexico; phenomenal feats in the Electricity Building; incredible aquariums holding thousands of underwater species in the Fisheries Building.

The only instance time slowed was when Lance Fuller bought Ruth Ann a souvenir coin purse made with mother-of-pearl on a brass frame and a red velvet interior. Painted on it was a soft image of explorer ships and an endless ocean. She would have flatly refused such a gift except he also bought Beulah an ivory fan. And Ruth Ann truly admired the fine little coin purse. But she stopped making a fuss over things that caught her eye, like the Remington and Underwood typewriters. She'd love to take one home to Matthew.

By afternoon, Ruth Ann was exhausted. Even Beulah slowed. Lance Fuller suggested they return to the Zadoks and retire early to prepare for another full day of exploring the Administration Building, state and foreign buildings, the Machinery Hall, the Fine Arts Palace. So much more to see. No wonder it was said it took two weeks to sufficiently cover the fair. They had to do it in one.

While she wrote letters home after dinner that evening, Ruth Ann knew she needed to do more than see the World's Fair. She needed stories, fantastic stories of what other visitors had experienced. Tomorrow, she would find some.

But Ruth Ann overslept and awoke to find the Zadok's had social obligations for the day, and Lance Fuller was nowhere to be found. She felt a twinge of panic. Time was running out to get the stories she needed for the *Tribune*.

Beulah was undeterred when they met in Ruth Ann's room to plan their fourth day at the fair. "We will simply go on our own."

Ruth Ann gulped. "We can't…do you think we could?"

"Yes, and furthermore, we will wear our own clothes!"

In the most comfortable clothes, shoes and hat Ruth Ann had worn all week, the two ladies from Indian Territory set out on the streets of Chicago. And promptly got lost.

It took directions from three policemen to get them to the correct elevated train station. Ruth Ann longed for another way to go, but according to one guidebook, there were only three common entrances to the fair—by boat, by elevated rail or through the ground level Midway Plaisance. The elevated train would have to do.

In spite of this being her fourth visit, Ruth Ann felt lost when they went through the train station and entered the fair. She'd brought enough money to take care of a few things, but she and Beulah would take turns carrying the hamper of sandwiches. Ruth Ann was tired of cringing over the exorbitant food prices no one else seemed to notice.

Once they were standing in front of the gold-domed Administration Building, Beulah asked, "Where shall we go first?"

Before Ruth Ann recovered from the surprise of having to make a decision on their direction, Beulah answered herself. "We have not seen the Woman's Building yet."

They looked at the map and started off, past the Admin-

istration Building and to the Court of Honor with its Grand
Basin and the Manufactures and Liberal Arts Building in the
distance to the left, and the Peristyle Gate straight ahead with
glimpses of Lake Michigan between its stately white columns.
When they entered the Court of Honor, with its gleaming
white buildings, their pace naturally slowed. There was an unspoken rule that no one hurry through the area, nor speak too
loudly. There was a respectful hush among the strolling couples in awe of the beauty. The fair wasn't crowded this early in
the day.

When they nearly reached the end of the basin, Ruth Ann
halted and gazed at the enormous Agriculture Building. She
frowned. "I believe we came the wrong way. I thought the
Woman's Building was next to this, but we're almost to the
Peristyle and the lake."

A quiet laugh drew Ruth Ann's attention behind her. She
turned and was greeted by a woman in a reserved navy blue
dress who held a small brown valise as though she planned to
attend a business meeting rather than the fair. "You're looking
for the Woman's Building? It's at a diagonal from here, quite a
ways away."

Beulah laughed and introduced herself and Ruth Ann. "I
am afraid neither I nor my friend are very good at directions.
But it is just as well. You can find so much when you are
lost."

The young woman laughed again and shook their hands.
"I'm Amelia Grace Longstead. I have no immediate plans, I
could walk you to the Woman's Building."

Ruth Ann noted the woman was alone, without an escort
or a group. Alone in Chicago, at the World's Fair! What an
interesting story. "We appreciate it." As they strolled away
from the basin, Ruth Ann asked, "Do you live in Chicago?"

"I've lived here all my life. I watched the fair being built."

"How exciting! Did you expect it to be so grand?"

"If I hadn't known the reputations of the men behind it,
I wouldn't have. Even knowing them, with all the setbacks
and economic disasters the country has seen this past year, I

wouldn't have dreamed it would become real. But tell me, where are you ladies from? How long will you be in Chicago?"

Ruth Ann quickly answered with little detail. She had so many more questions to ask to get a story. Thankfully, Beulah walked along quietly, admiring the landscape and lagoons. She seemed to sense Ruth Ann's purpose. "Miss Longstead, what about this economic collapse? How has it affected Chicago? Do you think more people would have attended the fair otherwise?"

"Perhaps in the beginning, but as word spread, people came just for the hope the fair represented. The Chicago World's Fair has become essential to the well-being of our nation."

Spoken like a true Chicago citizen. Ruth Ann smiled and started to ask another question, but Amelia Grace Longstead beat her to it. "Has the fair met your expectations, Miss Teller?"

"Met and exceeded them. But what about..." Ruth Ann had so many thoughts running through her mind, she was afraid she'd forget what Amelia said. She halted and withdrew her tablet from the hamper. "Pardon me, but may I quote what you said about the fair being essential to the nation? I write stories for my brother's newspaper."

Amelia Grace Longstead had smiled when the tablet appeared, but now she giggled. "I see! Here I thought what a good story I had for the day with visitors from Indian Territory." With practiced movements, Miss Longstead opened her valise and withdrew a well-used tablet. "I write a daily column about the fair for the *Chicago Tribune.*"

After the three of them shared a good laugh, Ruth Ann said, "That's what I'm here for today. Stories. I need many to take home for the paper."

"And what is the name of your brother's newspaper?"

Ruth Ann hesitated, wondering what preconceived notions Amelia Grace Longstead had about Indians. "The *Choctaw Tribune.*" To her dismay, Miss Longstead laughed again.

"What a coincidence that two female reporters would

meet at the fair, writing for newspapers with very nearly the same name."

Ruth Ann smiled, relieved. "A coincidence indeed. I'm very happy we made your acquaintance, Miss Longstead."

"Call me Amelia Grace. I think the three of us just might spend the day together."

And they did. Not only did Amelia Grace show them the Woman's Building and give its history and guide them through the many achievements featured inside, she took them on a tour to see hidden treasures sometimes overlooked at the fair. Aside from the men who built it, she seemed to know more about the fair than even the Columbian Guards. On one of the wide, arched bridges, they encountered a guard trying to give directions to a lady demanding to know which building the pope was in.

The guard stared at her. "The pope? The pope is not here."

The older woman, bent crooked at the waist, waved her closed parasol like she might batter him with it. "Where is he then, young man?"

"I don't know."

"You've lost the pope! Why you—"

Amelia Grace strolled up to the lady. "The pope is currently in Italy, I believe."

The woman swung around with her parasol, glared at Amelia Grace and waved her free hand. "And where is that, young lady?"

"In Europe."

The woman sighed, exasperated. "And where is that?" She pointed at the buildings across the lagoon. "In there? Or in that one?"

Amelia kept a kind smile. "You might find what you're looking for in the Manufactures and Liberal Arts Building. Take a left and another left and follow that walk around to the right. You can't miss it."

Ruth Ann pressed her lips together to suppress a giggle. Beulah pretended to dig around in the hamper, hiding her smile. No one could miss the largest building in the world. The woman would indeed find Italy there, and all of Europe, if not the pope.

When they continued on into the state and foreign buildings section of the fair, Amelia Grace glanced at Ruth Ann as if suddenly realizing something. "Have you been to the ethnography exhibits near the Anthropology Building? It's on the complete opposite side from where we are, near the Peristyle and the South Pond, but you might want to see it before you leave Chicago. You being from Indian Territory, I'd be interested to know what you think of the native villages on display. There is a building-sized replica of an ancient cliff dwelling, and Indians who live in wigwams and paddle the lagoons in birchbark canoes to show their culture. Some people feel the fair makes too much of putting ethnicities on display. What do you think of this?"

Ruth Ann said the first thing that came to mind, which wasn't much. "I suppose I'd have to see for myself." In truth, she wasn't sure if the ethnography area needed to go at the top or bottom of her list of things to see. The ethnography area sounded fascinating and degrading at the same time. How would she feel about putting her family and culture on display? Though for them, that would mean setting up a print shop and things being in constant suspense over political issues. Her family might be as entertaining as a circus. Or a Wild West show.

Which reminded her...she had to do the interview with Buffalo Bill, but she wasn't sure she was ready to make up her mind about his show either.

In the state and foreign buildings area, Ruth Ann saw the most disturbing sight yet at the fair. The Krupp Pavilion showed off heavy German guns, the most fearful being Fritz Krupp's "pet monster." The barrel was as long as two railroad cars, and the gun was said to weigh 250,000 pounds. Ruth Ann fervently hoped no country ever faced a war with Germany.

During the exhausting walk through the state and foreign

buildings, the ladies splurged on chocolates and root beer from one of the Hires Root Beer Oases. It took both Amelia Grace and Beulah to convince Ruth Ann it did not contain alcohol like Choc Beer! But the taste was like the sassafras tea she'd grown up drinking, only this was carbonated.

Amelia Grace shared intriguing stories about fair visitors. Beulah's favorite was of two cousins who rode bicycles from Nome, North Dakota, to see the fair, and Ruth Ann's favorite was of a woman who walked 1300 miles along railroad tracks to reach the fair. All the way from Galveston, Texas! And Ruth Ann thought she'd come a long way for this.

They had three days left to see it all.

CHAPTER TWENTY-SIX

THE NEXT MORNING, THE LARGEST group yet—including three of Edith's friends and their beaus—left the Zadok home in their carriage and Mr. Pilzer's, though Isaac Zadok still did not join them. They departed at a decent hour for the fifth day at the World's Fair. After rushing around the past few days, Ruth Ann was glad to be with the group who would meander at a leisurely pace. But Edith admonished her to stay close this time. The attendance was expected to set a record. The mayor had designated this as Chicago Day at the fair and it seemed every citizen of the city planned to attend.

Ruth Ann hoped to see Amelia Grace Longstead. But once they arrived by boat in front of the Peristyle and she saw the amount of people already in the Court of Honor, she doubted she would see the young female reporter again. At least she and Amelia Grace had exchanged addresses so they could correspond by mail.

Lance Fuller had given no explanation for his absence the day before, and Ruth Ann was too occupied to wonder where he'd been. He was attentive to her all morning in the stifling crowd. Ruth Ann wasn't sure which made her more uneasy.

After strolling aimlessly for two hours, the group decided

to have their noon meal on the Wooded Island surrounded by the lagoon. They crossed over one of the arched bridges and Ruth Ann immediately felt at home in the natural foliage away from the towering buildings, roads and stone fountains. Here, the paths were lined with a summer's worth of natural growth, and ducks quacked through the foliage, seeking soft-hearted picnickers. No doubt they'd found hundreds of sympathizers judging by their plump bodies.

At one end of the island stood the Japanese Ho-o-den replica Ruth Ann had seen across the water from the state and foreign buildings area. From here, she could see the pointed dome of the U.S. Government Building across the lagoon. But otherwise, she pretended she was in the country, even though there were a thousand other people picnicking on the large island.

Mr. Pilzer and Lance Fuller purchased food and drinks, and Beulah spread out the blanket they'd brought in a hamper. In spite of the formal air among the society people, Beulah soon had conversation bubbling with genuine excitement about the fair. She challenged falseness wherever she went.

How good it was to see her like this. Ruth Ann recalled last spring when the two had nearly lost their friendship, and since then, there was an undercurrent of tension they chose to ignore. But this trip was binding them together in sisterhood.

Things were going so well Ruth Ann didn't think anything could disrupt the day. But she was the first to see Isaac Zadok coming toward them. He was accompanied by a well-dressed young couple.

The rest of the group spotted them and welcomed the newcomers. Beulah's expression was neutral.

Isaac Zadok did not single her out as he introduced them all cordially, and motioned to the couple with him. "This is Mr. and Mrs. Jozef Walzman. I partnered with Mrs. Walzman's brother, Simon Ostrau, on his contract for selling the soda-water drinks you have."

The Walzmans and Isaac Zadok seated themselves and joined the conversation. Ruth Ann immediately liked the couple. Mr. Walzman was obviously a man of stature; he and a cousin manufactured men's clothing, and he traveled extensively throughout the United States to take samples to faraway places like New Mexico and Texas. He and his wife, Gisella, had been married three years, and she was especially thankful that the World's Fair near their neighborhood had given her husband reason to stay close to home.

Jozef Walzman took an interest in Ruth Ann when he learned she had been born and raised in Indian Territory. "I've been through Indian Territory in my travels. Fascinating country. I could not help wondering, however, where the Indians were?"

Though Beulah looked alarmed, Ruth Ann chuckled. "Oh, we're here and there. You never know where you might see a Choctaw, even at the Chicago World's Fair." They all stared at her.

Oh dear. Ruth Ann kept her gaze on the kind faces of Mr. and Mrs. Walzman. She didn't know what everyone else was thinking, but she remembered the ethnology exhibits Amelia Grace told her about. Would these folks be scandalized if she made a comment here at the Columbian Exposition that it was really the native Americans who discovered the lost Columbus rather than the other way around?

Gisella chimed in. "May I ask what your family does, Miss Teller? Are they farmers, business owners perhaps?"

Ruth Ann had already said too much, why stop now? "Both. My uncle has a large ranch near the Red River. My brother, mother and I moved to Dickens over a year ago for my brother to start his own venture—a newspaper called the *Choctaw Tribune.*"

Edith's eyes widened. She glanced between Ruth Ann and Beulah. "A newspaper? What sort of news is there to report in such a territory?"

Her question was genuine, not condescending, so Ruth Ann chose not to be offended. "Same as anywhere, I suppose. We recently had tribal elections that caused quite a stir." She hesitated. Another mistake.

Beulah seemed to think the topic was wide open now. "You would not believe the adventures the Tellers have. Last winter we visited a family and they were attacked by a rival political party and we were nearly killed! The shooting lasted for hours. And just last week Matthew Teller—"

Lance Fuller cleared his throat and gave Beulah a look loaded with warning. Ruth Ann was frozen. Edith stared at them, shocked.

When Beulah pinched her lips together, Lance Fuller tried to help. "Ruth Ann does fine writing herself. I believe she has an appointment to interview Buffalo Bill Cody..." He faltered when Ruth Ann turned to look at him but she heard Edith's gasp loud and clear.

"Um, Ruth, you do not actually play the role of a...*reporter*, do you?"

Ruth Ann felt like a fine brooch dropped in horse manure. Apparently Edith didn't read Amelia Grace Longstead's daily column. Though women were making great strides in areas such as becoming doctors and reporters, Chicago society women lived in their own circles, going nowhere it seemed. "Yes, I do report important news when I can. Here in Chicago. Witch hunters in the Choctaw Nation. A lynching in Texas."

Silence fell over the group. Then Jozef Walzman snapped his fingers. "I knew the name of your newspaper had a familiar ring. I read a copy on the train, and I do recall an article by a female reporter about the brutal lynching. A well-done story, I would say."

Suddenly lost in his own world, Mr. Walzman grew animated. He set aside his soda and waved his hands. "We need more sanity in this world. There is too much ignorance and not enough justice. I see hatred between races. Indians are still looked on as savages. Blacks are seen as unintelligent beings."

He wiped his mouth with a handkerchief and waved one hand again. "There is a movement among our own people, the Jews, to rise above other minorities and blend with the elite society that excludes other races. I am adamantly opposed to such nonsense. God created only one race—the human race!"

Mr. Walzman's fiery gaze swept the group as though waiting for a challenger. Ruth Ann noticed Edith look down and Mr. Pilzer pin his lips. None of their Jewish society friends moved.

Beulah stared at Mr. Walzman. Her expression changed to one of curiosity. "But how can we preserve our heritage, our identity as Jews in this American culture if we do not align ourselves with the ones who are rising?"

Walzman shook his fist at the world around them that had vanished in the intense conversation. "Look around you, Miss Levitt. The entire world is here! They are sharing ideas, forming new societies, breaking the restricting molds of class and race. And as far as preserving our Jewish identity? Have you not heard of Hannah Solomon? Right here at the fair, she formed the National Council of Jewish Women. And some of the most powerful Jewish leaders are here, discussing, arguing, fighting over new ideas that could unify Jews around the world."

Walzman paused to take a deep breath, but when no one was brave enough to even sigh, he went on. "It is time. A new era. Those who lead it will be in turmoil, but in their wake, we may all live better lives. For us Jews, they should be lives that honor our God."

Face still red, Jozef Walzman took a long drink of his soda. His wife chuckled and lightly clapped her hands. "My husband, the world changer."

There was no mockery in her tone, only admiration so deep it made Ruth Ann's heart ache. How good to have met this young couple.

As though wanting to relieve the awkward atmosphere in the group, Isaac Zadok swept his arm toward the activity around them. "Come on, all of you. Like Walzman said, there is a whole world we need to be a part of."

The last part he said with a quick glance at Beulah, but Ruth Ann could tell her friend was miles away. So far away, she was likely back in Indian Territory, reminiscing about a similar argument that had nearly ended a friendship.

The Walzmans excused themselves, saying they had a group they were to join for the afternoon.

Ruth Ann's party said they would go to the Machinery Hall next, but she lagged back and made her decision almost too late. She turned and hurried through the crowd. When she caught up with the Walzmans, they were conversing with a young man. "Oh, I'm sorry. I didn't mean to interrupt."

Jozef Walzman waved off her apology. "Not at all. Please meet Gisella's brother, Simon Ostrau. The one who does the soda-water, you know."

They laughed, but Ruth Ann hurried to say, "I appreciate what you said, Mr. Walzman. One of the reasons my brother started the *Choctaw Tribune* was to spread truth. There's so much injustice in the world, and no less in Indian Territory."

Mr. Walzman cocked his head. "And you, Miss Teller? What do you believe?"

"The same. It's why I stay in as much trouble as Matthew."

They laughed and Jozef Walzman drew a card from his pocket. "I would like to subscribe to your newspaper, Miss Teller. Please send it and an invoice to that address."

Ruth Ann took it eagerly. "I'll take care of it as soon as I return home." She met his kind eyes with a firm nod. "And thank you again. Please don't stop sharing what you believe in. It makes a difference."

Mr. Walzman sighed and an ancient look crept into his eyes. "My goal in business is to provide for my family and the future, and give the rest away. I'm teaching other business owners to do the same. There are so many needs in the world. I want to try and cure the things that seem wrong."

Gisella wrapped her arm around his. "It shouldn't take you more than a lifetime or two."

With final goodbyes, Ruth Ann left the trio and turned back toward her group. But all she saw were the crowds.

Panic seized her and she clutched her reticule and tablet

close. Which way had the others gone? She recalled Edith's stern warning that morning. She said reports of people gone missing in Chicago had increased with all the world there.

Ruth Ann moved in what she hoped was the right direction, praying with each step. *Lord, show me the way...forgive my foolishness...I deserve to be robbed, killed, but Lord, I don't want to be...*

The Machinery Hall. Yes! She could ask someone the way and she would find her group, and they wouldn't even realize she was missing...

Ruth Ann was almost running when someone grabbed her arm. She shrieked and battered the attacker with her tablet.

"Ruth Ann! Stop!"

She halted, hot enough to faint. She glared at Lance Fuller. "I—you—you shouldn't have grabbed me!"

Lance Fuller straightened his derby hat and shook his head. "Didn't you hear me call? You were going the wrong way, and where did you disappear to? When I got back to the group, you were gone."

Ashamed, Ruth Ann dropped her gaze and tried to form an apology, but she couldn't get past her embarrassment. How could she go from a lovely conversation with a young Jewish couple to battering her escort?

Lance Fuller gently took her arm and guided her back the way she'd come. "Don't worry about it. I know what an adventurous creature you are, and I admire you for it. I'll just have to keep a sharper eye on you!"

Ruth Ann tried to laugh away her tension, but it came out as a silly giggle. One moment, Lance Fuller acted like he was courting her—she had not given him permission to!—then he acted like a medieval guardian charged with protecting her, and then sometimes, he didn't even know she was around.

If only Matthew were here. What was he doing right now?

♦♦♦

After the Machinery Hall, the group decided on an early dinner before dark. Ruth Ann hadn't been at the fair after dark, and she was very glad to be with a large group. There would be a firework display that evening.

They dined at a German food stand, feasting on the best sausage Ruth Ann had ever eaten away from home. Well, the only sausage she'd eaten away from home. But its spicy flavor made her wish she could follow it with grape dumplings.

Isaac Zadok was a superb tour guide. He seemed to know the fair inside and out from his business partnership with Simon Ostrau. He pointed out sights they had missed the past four days.

But when they reached the Mines and Mining Building, Ruth Ann noticed Lance Fuller's bored expression. He frowned at the building. "Why don't we go to the Court of Honor? It's astounding in the daytime, but everyone should see it in the evening at least once. The fireworks will start soon, too."

At the front of the group, Isaac Zadok didn't seem to hear. He led the way into the building.

Lance Fuller tapped Beulah's arm. She'd been staying around the back of the group, either lost in thought or avoiding being close to Isaac Zadok. She turned to him and he spoke quickly.

"Tell the others we're going exploring. We'll meet you all at the Zadok home tonight."

Beulah nodded without seeming to hear, and entered the Mines and Mining Building.

Ruth Ann tried to stay rooted in place, shocked by the exchange, but Lance Fuller pulled her away. She momentarily lost her senses, then regained them and pulled back.

"But we need to stay with the others. What's wrong with—"

"Come on." He tugged on her arm and got her moving again. "There's so many more interesting things at the World's Fair than seeing the Mines and Mining Building again. Don't you want to watch the fireworks, then go to the Midway

Plaisance and ride the Ferris wheel? This group is too stuffy for that. We can enjoy things more on our own."

Ruth Ann set her jaw with the family stubbornness. Ever since they'd arrived, Lance Fuller acted like this was familiar territory. At first, she excused it as his social training, but it was more than that. There was his mysterious meeting on the promenade and his unexplained absence yesterday. It was time to let her suspicions show.

"Mr. Fuller, it's improper for us to traipse around the fair without a chaperone. And how do you know so much about the fair? From a handbook? I thought you hadn't been to Chicago before."

Lance Fuller hesitated, then sighed. He spread his hands in front of him in an apologetic gesture. "You caught me red-handed. I did come here briefly after the opening, but the construction wasn't even finished. I didn't want you to know I'd been and spoil your first impressions by answering a boatload of questions. I wanted it to be fresh and a true wonder. Did I succeed?"

His eyes were sincere, but Ruth Ann's suspicions escalated. Lance Fuller had lied when he said he'd never been to Chicago. What else was he hiding, and why?

Suddenly, this situation turned into a perfect opportunity to be a reporter like Matthew, one who uncovered secrets and untangled stories. This was her chance to learn the dark secrets of...well, who knew what? It wasn't completely proper, but didn't Amelia Grace Longstead roam the fair alone?

Ruth Ann calmed her pulsing heart. "The fair has been more than I ever imagined, thank you. And I would love to see the Court of Honor at night, and the fireworks. And ride Mr. Ferris' wheel, and see what else you discovered when you were here before."

"Perfect." Lance Fuller took her hand and tugged it through the crook of his arm. He led Ruth Ann away from the Mines and Mining Building.

Here she was, alone with a man she hardly knew in the middle of hundreds of thousands of people from all over the world, a man who was friends with their enemy, who was hiding something about his past.

This was a perfect opportunity, all right. But for which one of them?

CHAPTER TWENTY-SEVEN

THE COURT OF HONOR WAS impressive during the day. But at evening, it was stunning. Isaac Zadok had given them a lesson about Mr. Tesla's electricity running the fair, including all the marvelous lights. The inventor had beaten out a bid by a man named Edison.

But all those facts could never have prepared Ruth Ann for this sight.

She stood near the fountain statue of Columbus' ship before the Grand Basin and the Court of Honor, unable to breathe. Electric lights trimmed the white buildings with illumination from one end to the other, their glow double as they reflected off the water in the wide pool. The gold Statue of the Republic at the other end seemed positioned to offer grounding for those who were swept off their feet by the beauty.

Lance Fuller offered Ruth Ann a white handkerchief. She took it, embarrassed by her tears. Wasn't this the third time he'd caught her crying at the fair? But he smiled gently. "You are quite a lady, Ruth Ann Teller."

She tried to laugh, but coughed instead. "For an Indian, you mean."

"No." He shook his head and lifted his hand as though to take hers, but stopped. "I mean for you. The young women I've known are phony inside and out. They're only interested in landing the right man to give them the status and wealth they and their family want in society. I know you'd be just as happy to live your life without all that."

Ruth Ann watched the gondolas in the Grand Basin. They glided along with couples lost in their own world.

"I'm happy wherever God puts me."

"Are you?"

There was doubt in his voice, and Ruth Ann risked a look into his face, but he was staring at the lights.

She thought about his response, and took a chance. "Aren't you? Happy with the calling God has put on your life?"

"I suppose I haven't given Him much consideration."

"Oh."

Ruth Ann didn't know what else to say. Lance Fuller went to church like most people around Dickens. But so did many people who didn't live Christ in their daily lives. How could someone claim to be a Christian without the evidence in their life?

And so it was, that Lance Fuller likely was not. That caused any thought of a courtship not only to leave Ruth Ann's mind, but also put it back in the right place. She really didn't know him at all. "Mr. Fuller, I think we should find the others now."

He jerked as though coming out of a daydream. "Not yet." His eyes gleamed with mischief. "You haven't ridden the Ferris Wheel."

Fireworks exploded over Lake Michigan.

◆◆◆

A long walk across the fairgrounds later, they arrived at the Midway Plaisance. Music, sharp smells, colors, shocking displays. Whole villages, along with their inhabitants, had been imported from Algeria, Dahomey, and others, and there was the Street of Cairo with camels and over two hundred Egyptians.

Ruth Ann gasped when she saw the Ferris Wheel. It was said to rival the height and steelwork of the Eiffel Tower, erected at the World's Fair in Paris a few years before, but she had never seen that either. Perhaps it could have prepared her for this.

The wheel was enormous not only in height, but width. It carried three dozen enclosed cars the size of Pullmans. They swung precariously in the air high above the ground as the spindly wheel slowly turned.

A hand steadied Ruth Ann. She realized she had leaned so far back trying to watch the bizarre contraption, she'd nearly fallen over. Lance Fuller leaned close to be heard above the noise of the Midway.

"Something else, isn't it? I didn't ride before because it wasn't operating yet. We'll experience this together."

The line moved forward and Ruth Ann numbly followed as a car emptied, and another forty people boarded. The wheel turned again and the car swung. Some people inside gasped. Apparently it was their first time as well. Though the cars were fully enclosed and had metal grates over the windows, Ruth Ann felt faint thinking about the elevator in the Manufactures and Liberal Arts Building. She'd forgotten Matthew's admonishment to ride the wheel so she'd have the courage to do anything after that.

Near the gate where tickets for the wheel were sold, Lance Fuller reached into his trouser pocket for money. But Ruth Ann took a step back and bumped into the couple behind them.

"I can't. I mean, I…" She gazed up at the enormous wheel again and closed her eyes against a wave of nausea.

Lance Fuller gripped her elbow and led her away from the line. They stood close to a food vendor, the exotic smells increasing Ruth Ann's nausea.

"I'm sorry, I suppose I'm afraid of heights…" She accepted the cup of water he offered. "I really would like to go back to the house now. It's been a long day."

"Of course." He sounded understanding and Ruth Ann didn't feel so humiliated.

They left the Midway and were soon at the ground level entrance Ruth Ann hadn't wanted to use before. "But what about the others? Should we try to meet them at the Peristyle?"

Lance Fuller kept close to her side as the crowd pressed through the gate. "I'm sure they've left by now. We'll take the elevated railroad and then a streetcar back to the Zadok home. It'll be faster than going the way we came in, and we won't have to flag down a hack."

Ruth Ann was too tired to worry about how they would get home. She didn't know exactly what time it was, but it was far later than she usually stayed up. She reluctantly climbed the steps to the elevated railroad station with Lance Fuller. It was darker than the Midway without so many electric lights. After waiting in a long line on the busy platform, they boarded.

The train continually stopped and started with a jerk. The conductor called out stop names. He may as well have shouted in one of the foreign languages at the fair.

Ruth Ann had no idea how to navigate this city. She'd memorized the Zadok address, but how would a lone woman make it safely there? If she were to become separated again...

"This is our stop." Lance Fuller nudged her off the train and guided her down the stairs. They boarded a streetcar, ground level to Ruth Ann's relief.

A week ago, the thought of riding an electric streetcar would have thrilled her, but after the excitement of the fair, a streetcar was simply a means of transportation. And right then, Ruth Ann was anxious to be transported home.

They stood in the crowded aisle, the seats full. Lance Fuller showed her how to hold onto the looped leather handles hanging from the ceiling. The car jerked into motion. Ruth Ann held on for dear life.

At their stop, she disembarked to streets lit by gaslights.

There were fewer people around than she'd been accustomed to since arriving in Chicago. But this did not look like the Zadoks' neighborhood. The streets were piled high with garbage and debris.

Lance Fuller threaded her hand through his arm again. "It's a few blocks over. This is the fastest way, and I have a feeling the Zadoks are ready to jail me for having you out so late already."

Ruth Ann tried to stay calm. She had no choice but to trust him.

A raw odor struck her and she put the handkerchief he'd given her earlier under her nose. The material fluttered around her dry lips when she tried to breathe. She halted at a lumpy form near a drain. When she realized what it was, she drew back. A dead dog lay among the garbage in the street.

Lance Fuller grimaced and guided her around it. "Sorry, we shouldn't have taken this route. Though unfortunately, this isn't the worst Chicago has to offer."

There were fewer and fewer pedestrians on the street as they went until they finally turned a corner to reveal no one. Lance Fuller stiffened beside her, making Ruth Ann jump.

He stared at shadows, and she frowned in confusion. But then the shadows took the form of two men. They were hardly dressed as gentlemen. That was all Ruth Ann noted before they sprang forward.

Lance Fuller pushed her to the side and she stumbled on the steps of a building. She twisted around to see a man leap toward her, a knife blade glinting in the moonlight. She screamed.

The man never reached her. Grabbed from behind, he was pulled back and received a blow to his jaw. But he recovered and charged Lance Fuller only to be dodged. Lance Fuller landed two quick blows that sent the man sprawling next to his partner on the brick street.

Ruth Ann scrambled to her feet, tangled in her skirts and dizzy. Lance Fuller caught her in his arms.

"Are you all right, Ruth Ann?"

She pulled away and nodded. "Yes...yes, oh thank you." She looked behind him, and her eyes widened at the sight of the two men laid out flat on their backs. "How did you..."

"Three years on the college boxing team."

People began to crowd around the sight. Ruth Ann chuckled nervously. "Well, that explains everything."

CHAPTER TWENTY-EIGHT

IT WAS QUIET IN THE conservatory the next morning. Ruth Ann discovered the garden-like room when she explored the first floor of the Zadok home before most of the household was awake. Only a few servants stirred, and they left her alone.

This room let in the first rays of the sun that could penetrate the lingering coal-smoke of Chicago. The rays were enough to ease the chill surrounding the green plants and flowers that bloomed along a man-made path. Ruth Ann walked this path, following the sun's rays. She arrived near the entrance again and settled on one of the cushioned sofas with a writing table to one side.

She picked up a pencil and stationery paper, not sure what she was going to write or to whom. How could she tell her mama and uncle everything with mere words on a piece of paper? But then, wasn't that all the *Choctaw Tribune* was?

Her thoughts jumbled together. The late night at the fair with Lance Fuller. The report of over seven hundred thousand people attending the fair for Chicago Day. The attack on the dark streets. The shocked faces when they'd arrived at the

Zadoks. Edith nearly fainted at the sight of them, and when they told the story of the fight, she did faint. Mr. Pilzer was close enough to catch her.

The whole household was in an uproar, but Beulah had whisked Ruth Ann away and secured them in her room before demanding every detail.

Now Ruth Ann sighed, sketching a rose in the corner of the stationery paper. She had no idea how the Zadok family would act at the breakfast table. Hopefully they would pretend the day before had been perfectly normal for the World's Fair in Chicago.

She thought about the notes she'd taken of the fair, but nothing was front page worthy back home. Even the attack didn't compare to the daily fights and regular killings in Indian Territory.

Her mind drifted to the shootings and Bass Reeves' hunt. Had the marshal caught the shooter? Was Matthew, even in his weak state, working to uncover the larger scheme?

Ruth Ann felt utterly useless this far from home. While she thoroughly appreciated the opportunity to attend the fair, she felt guilty for not securing much material for the *Choctaw Tribune*.

But that wasn't truly why her family had sent her here, was it? They wanted her to be safe, and to enjoy some of her youth away from constant battles.

She hadn't managed that, either.

If only Grady Lewis would answer her note about an audience with Buffalo Bill Cody. That would make this entire trip worthwhile and save the *Choctaw Tribune* from Maxwell's vicious propaganda.

Voices jolted Ruth Ann from her scribbling. She disentangled her feet from where she'd made herself too comfortable curled on the sofa, and stood just in time.

In deep conversation, Isaac Zadok and Simon Ostrau strolled through the double doors into the conservatory. They halted when they saw Ruth Ann and greeted her pleasantly.

She gathered the stationery paper and her tablet. "I'm

sorry, I didn't think anyone would need this room so early…"

Isaac waved off her words. "Not at all. We had a few business matters to discuss before breakfast, but that is not important. How are you this morning, Miss Teller? I hope your experience last night will not be your lasting impression of Chicago."

Ruth Ann's side ached from her collision with the stairs, but she was almost grateful for the incident. It gave people something to talk about besides her and Lance Fuller being at the fair without a chaperone.

"Oh, I'm well. And after seeing the Court of Honor and so many other sights, the incident won't be the first story I tell when I get home."

She smiled and eased toward the door. She didn't feel comfortable chatting with two young Chicago businessmen.

But Simon Ostrau lifted a finger in question. "Who was that young man with your party yesterday? He seemed familiar."

Ruth Ann caught her breath. Did this man know Lance Fuller? "You've probably met him in your social circles. Lance Fuller. He's from New York."

Simon Ostrau raised one eyebrow. "Lance Fuller of Harvard, the son of Richmond Fuller? Impossible. He's in Europe."

The facts fit except the part about Europe. Ruth Ann's stomach dropped to her toes.

Isaac Zadok took an immediate interest. "Are you certain? It must be two different Lance Fullers then."

But Simon Ostrau snapped his fingers. "I recall the other fellow now, I saw him at the stock exchange. Seemed he was in some kind of trouble, but I never met him face-to-face."

Ruth Ann licked her lips. "Do you recall his name?"

Simon Ostrau rubbed his chin. "No, but it was certainly not Lance Fuller. Mr. Fuller and I are acquaintances through business affairs. I have worked with his father on projects. After graduation, Lance Fuller took a professor position in Paris. A brilliant young man."

Ruth Ann wondered if her legs would support her for any more revelations.

Isaac Zadok frowned. "If this Mr. Fuller we have here is an imposter…"

In the hall, Augustine passed carrying an armload of linens. Isaac called her to them. Ruth Ann noticed how she kept her eyes down with him as well. "Yes, sir?"

"Do you know where Mr. Fuller is?"

"He left before dawn, as usual."

"As usual?" Isaac Zadok frowned. He looked between Ruth Ann and Simon Ostrau before asking Augustine, "Where does he go?"

Ruth Ann wondered how much more the help knew about the people in the household than the people in the household knew.

The maid shifted her load of linens. "James sees him leave through the servant entrance. He walks toward the streetcar stop, though we couldn't say if that's where he goes or not."

Isaac dismissed her. "It seems things are not what they appear." He looked to Ruth Ann. "How long have you known Mr. Fuller, or whoever he is?"

Her side ached with fervor. She laid her palm over it as if needing to hold it in place. "He came to Dickens not long ago to teach. The mayor knows him…"

Mayor Warren. This was one of his schemes! Goodness, she needed to get home and tell Matthew…

But tell him what? She didn't have the entire story. "Is there a way we could quietly investigate this? Find out who Mr. Fuller really is?"

"We will find out. Leave it to me." Isaac Zadok exchanged a knowing look with Mr. Ostrau, who nodded. "But I cannot allow the man to remain here. I will see that you and Beulah—Miss Levitt—are kept safe and away from that imposter."

"*Yakoke*," Ruth Ann murmured, then louder, "Thank you. But I would like to be a part of the investigation. This will make front page back home."

"I will give you the details after the investigation is complete. We have professionals who will do the job. Please, do not worry and try to enjoy the remainder of your stay."

The young men excused themselves and left.

Ruth Ann collapsed on the sofa. But she wasn't alone long.

Augustine slipped through the door and extended a sealed envelope to Ruth Ann. "This just came for you, miss."

Her posture was informal; she acted differently when she was alone with Ruth Ann. But didn't everyone? Wasn't everyone and everything no more than a false front of their true selves like Lance Fuller?

Suddenly angry, Ruth Ann snatched the envelope and ripped it open. She skimmed the note.

To Miss Teller—

Mr. Lewis sends his deep regret over this miscommunication. He is currently in London until the end of the year, and will not be able to arrange an introduction with Mr. Cody.

Respectfully,
The Office of Grady Lewis

"Any reply, miss?"

Ruth Ann sighed. "No reply, Augustine. No reply."

♦ ♦ ♦

Ruth Ann requested a late breakfast in her room since that wasn't abnormal in Chicago society. But she couldn't dodge Beulah long. Her friend urged her to join a ladies' luncheon hosted by Mrs. Zadok before they went to the fair for the afternoon. With Beulah's excited chatter, Ruth Ann couldn't bring herself to mention Lance Fuller, or whoever he was. Besides, they were trying to keep the investigation quiet.

Who were those investigators anyway? The young Jewish gentlemen seemed as confident in them as Matthew was in

Bass Reeves.

Settled on the sofas and chairs in the Zadok's parlor, the ladies kept pleasant conversation sailing around the room like a well-rehearsed dance. Ruth Ann was content to stay outside the main flow and nibble on a tea cake. But she didn't stay unnoticed for long.

"Miss Teller, do tell us about Indian Territory."

The request came from an older woman who appeared cultured, with her nose in the air. She'd hung the words *Indian Territory* out like a skunk's tail pinched between her thumb and forefinger. She appraised Ruth Ann and Beulah with a critical eye. "How do you survive in such a wilderness with all those Indians?"

Beulah clanked her teacup into its saucer. The genteel voices in the room gasped at the noise. Ruth Ann gratefully allowed Beulah to take command.

"We do quite well, Mrs. Williams. You must be a fighter to survive in Indian Territory—stout in body, mind, and soul. I know people more dedicated to their faith and one another in that wilderness than I've seen here in Chicago, save that man we met at the fair, Mr. Walzman. He spoke his mind despite those who would have us believe our identities and very existence depends on tromping the dignity of other races."

Beulah sucked in a breath and set her gaze on Ruth Ann.

She stared back at her friend, her eyes wide. She blinked and saw tears in Beulah's eyes.

Beulah burst into sobs and Ruth Ann quickly moved to join her on the sofa. The young lady who had been next to Beulah gladly vacated the seat.

Mrs. Williams huffed. "Well, I never!"

Ruth Ann tugged Beulah close. Beulah whispered, "It's true. It's so very true. I was so very, very wrong."

In that moment, Ruth Ann wholly regained her friend. But the sweet moment didn't last. Another woman, with a voice like a hoarse crow, spoke up. "They are from a different world, you know. Take that man who escorted them. I understand, Edith, that your brother is not allowing him to return to this house because of the indecent incident last night."

All the fine ladies in the room gasped. Edith looked pale enough to faint again. Mrs. Zadok fanned her own red face. "Would you care for more lemonade, Mrs. Williams? Cookies, anyone?"

Mrs. Williams shook her head. "Absolutely scandalous. I know they are your guests, Mrs. Zadok, but really. We all have reputations to maintain."

Ruth Ann snapped. "That is not why Lance Fuller was kicked out. That's not his real name. He's an imposter and—"

She halted. Beulah pulled away and stared at her. Ruth Ann couldn't meet her gaze.

Mrs. Williams spoke slowly. "You mean your suitor has been deceiving you?"

Every lady in the room looked at Ruth Ann as though she'd just been stabbed.

Tempting as it was to flee, that hadn't gone well last time. Ruth Ann would exit this room with the kind of dignity her family had shown since the Removal from their homelands.

"I appreciate your concern. However, I've faced worse situations as a reporter for the *Choctaw Tribune*."

She paused to allow the shocked whispers to run their course through the ladies. Edith sagged against her mother.

"*Chahta sia.* I am Choctaw. I came here for the fair experience and to write a front page story based on an interview with Buffalo Bill Cody. However, that will not happen now, and there is no reason for us to stay any longer."

She rose, pulling Beulah up with her. Ruth Ann nodded to Mrs. Zadok and Edith. "We greatly appreciate your hospitality and kindness, but it's time we went home. There's much work to do there."

Arm linked with Beulah's, Ruth Ann led the way out of the parlor and out of the falseness of high society.

Behind her, she heard the shocked whispers.

"I thought Indians dressed in buckskins!"

"Do you think she's secretly a part of the Wild West Show?"

"An Indian? But where are her feathers?"

◆ ◆ ◆

When the soft tap sounded at the door to her room, Ruth Ann assumed it was Augustine with the railroad tickets. She had decided to use the offer of asking the servants for whatever she needed. She'd sent the maid off with money to pass to a butler or driver or whomever to go and purchase tickets for her and Beulah to return home on the next train to St. Louis.

But when Ruth Ann turned from packing and opened the door, Augustine held a white notecard out to her. "From the younger Mr. Zadok, miss."

"Oh. Thank you. And the tickets?"

"He requested I leave them with him, miss."

Ruth Ann sighed. "Very well." On impulse, she reached out and tipped Augustine's chin up so their eyes met briefly. "*Yakoke.* That's *thank you* in the language of my people."

Shock showed in the maid's eyes before she hurried away. She didn't even ask if Ruth Ann wanted to send a reply.

Ruth Ann read the note from Isaac Zadok. He wanted her and Beulah to meet him in the conservatory. He had news.

It took her a full minute to convince Beulah to accompany her. At first, her friend adamantly refused. Then she showed a hint of yielding when Ruth Ann told her what the news might be. But it took threatening to accept another tea invitation to get Beulah moving toward a face-to-face meeting with her old acquaintance, or whatever Isaac Zadok had been to her.

In the conservatory, Isaac Zadok paced in front of a wood bench set further down the sun-speckled path. Beulah trailed behind Ruth Ann, her feelings not masked on her face.

Isaac Zadok looked up but quickly focused on Ruth Ann. "Miss Teller, I have grave news. It seems your Mr. Fuller is indeed an imposter. He even created false credentials for his deception. I am sorry."

Ruth Ann took a deep breath. "Did you uncover his true identity?"

Isaac Zadok withdrew a piece of paper from his pocket and unfolded it. "The private Pinkerton detectives we hired did a thorough job. It seems the man is someone who graduated with the real Lance Fuller. But the investigation revealed the imposter's real name is Thomas Warren."

"Thomas Warren?" Beulah frowned.

But Ruth Ann stuttered, "Thomas *Warren?*"

Beulah gasped when the significance of the name sank in.

Warren. Thomas *Warren.* A relative of Mayor Thaddeus Warren! Ruth Ann dropped onto the hard bench with a thud.

In the background, Beulah raged, her hands illustrating what she would do the next time she saw the imposter who tried to steal her dear friend's heart. The ranting stopped and through her mind as murky as the Chicago skyline, Ruth Ann was aware of the sudden stillness between Beulah and Isaac Zadok.

He broke through first. "I am sorry, Beulah. For Kansas. I never should have tried to find a place in your heart. I knew it was hopeless, but I had a hopeless love for you. I believed going away with my family was best for us both. I never realized until your last letter that I only had to try harder."

Isaac Zadok took Beulah's hand. She let him.

Ruth Ann rose quietly from the bench and tried to slip away, but Beulah hooked her arm though her friend's. "You will not leave, Ruth Ann Teller. The past was long ago. There is another in Isaac's heart now."

Ruth Ann turned back to them, surprised. Isaac Zadok nodded. "I plan to soon be engaged. But it will give me peace to be forgiven first."

Beulah gave a quick nod. "All is past. That is, if you will grant one request."

"It is yours."

Beulah glanced at Ruth Ann and she caught the familiar gleam of mischief. "You will arrange an audience for my friend with one Mr. Buffalo Bill Cody."

♦ ♦ ♦

Under the elevated railroad entrance to the fair, Isaac Zadok had the carriage drop the trio off. But the attention of folks in the street wasn't on the extravagant fair. It was on the huge exhibit set up right across the street from it.

Buffalo Bill's internationally famous Wild West and Congress of Rough Riders of the World had been rejected by the Columbian Exhibition organizers during the planning phase of the fair. Not deterred, the showman set up shop next to the fair. It was said his show nearly ruined the fair when he drew some three million people through the summer. Supposedly, Mr. Ferris' wheel had saved the fair from ruin.

Ruth Ann took in as many details of the Wild West exhibit as she could while keeping up with Isaac Zadok and Beulah. The two were getting along fine, chatting cordially. It was good to see. It helped Ruth Ann keep her mind off a certain other person.

There was plenty to occupy her mind though, as they reached the entrance to the grounds of the twice daily show. The blend of horses, cattle, riders, dust stirring—Ruth Ann felt at home in the environment. But it didn't calm her nerves at the impending meeting with the famed Buffalo Bill Cody. What sort of questions would Matthew have asked?

Buffalo Bill was said to be one of the few white men the great Lakota Sioux Chief, Sitting Bull, had trusted. Cody was also known as a colorful frontiersmen and animated storyteller, a rugged showman like the world had never seen.

How could Ruth Ann even speak to him! What if he laughed at the idea of a female reporter interviewing him? What if his aura overwhelmed her and she made a fool of herself? What if she lost her last chance of a front page story for the *Choctaw Tribune*? Would the newspaper even be there when she returned or had Maxwell and Warren buried it completely? Ruth Ann barred the rampant thoughts and focused on her surroundings.

Isaac Zadok led the way around a massive tent. A small

box wagon sat near the tent's wall, out of place in its lack of color. Perhaps that was the point, to keep from drawing attention to what must be an office.

Isaac knocked on the door, waited and knocked again. Ruth Ann held her breath, wondering if the famed Buffalo Bill himself would open the door.

On the third knock, the door was opened by a grumbling man who gave them a hard look.

"What do you want?" The grizzly-like man wore a worn leather jacket and tattered trousers. His bloodshot eyes made Ruth Ann wonder if he'd been in a deep sleep. Surely this couldn't be…

"Sir, I am Isaac Zadok and I have come to see Mr. Lawson about a meeting with Mr. Cody—"

"Lawson ain't here, neither's Bill. Won't be back 'till next week. It's up to me to run the whole shootin' match until then. If you got business that has to do with the show, I'll invite you in. Otherwise, beat it."

Ruth Ann's knees weakened and she wanted to lean against Beulah, but restrained herself. It wasn't the worst thing that could happen. Well, maybe it was after all the other worst things.

But peace filled Ruth Ann. Some things weren't meant to be. Not in the way she or others thought anyway. It was time to go home, return to the battle. If they had to fight on without the *Choctaw Tribune*, so be it. God would make another way. He always did.

Beulah huffed. "Where is Mr. Cody? It is urgent we find him—"

Ruth Ann touched her friend's arm and shook her head. "It's all right. It's time we went home."

Before long, the young women from Indian Territory departed for the Union Depot, prepared to leave Chicago and its drama far, far behind.

CHAPTER TWENTY-NINE

RUTH ANN FIDGETED AT THE depot, regretting her haste to get there early to ensure no traffic snarl caused them to miss their train. But the traffic had been clear, and they were an hour early. Beulah and Edith Zadok kept themselves occupied in quiet conversation, often slipping into Russian and evidently speaking about deeper subjects than they had up until then.

While they talked, Ruth Ann paced the platform, though she was careful not to stray too far and lose sight of her group in the busy area. Isaac Zadok had accompanied them but he found conversations with one business acquaintance or another. Ruth Ann wondered if any of them were undercover Pinkerton detectives like the ones who'd uncovered the true identity of Lance Fuller. After this experience, she wondered if she should write a detective novel herself. She'd need something to write if the *Tribune* was no longer in business.

Ruth Ann thought about the simple telegram she'd received in response to hers, informing her family she would return early. The response came from Peter, though without any of his playful drama: *Good. We need you.*

A sense of doom had settled over her. What could they

possibly need her for? The family was able to take care of everything. There was nothing she could do in town except explain how she, above all others, had been duped by the new teacher she helped welcome into Dickens.

The hands on the huge clock over the depot office moved and a whistle alerted her that yet another train was entering the station. It was the one they would start their journey home on. Ruth Ann breathed a sigh of relief and turned toward the luggage, but she nearly bumped into a man.

"Oh, pardon me." She had to take a generous step back to see his face. He had a stiff smile, but it was the woman on his arm who spoke up. "You Ruth Ann Teller?"

"Well, yes, but—"

"Good. We caught you in time." The woman sighed.

The train eased its way alongside the platform. The woman handed a sealed note to Ruth Ann. "You need to come with us. Tom said it means life or death for someone close to you."

The train screeched to a halt and porters hustled to load luggage. Ruth Ann opened the note and tried to distance herself from the urgency around her.

Dear Ruth Ann,

Please forgive me. There is so much to explain, but there is no point in it unless you can find a way to forgive me.

I've made an arrangement I hope will begin to prove my intentions will only be in your best interest from this time forward. Please come to the Woman's Building at the fair. You won't have to see me in person. Someone else will make the introductions.

I beg your forgiveness once again and hope to make it possible for you to see me without disgust the next time we meet. If ever.

Yours regretfully, and as I hope you will think of me,
Lance Fuller

Ruth Ann stared at the couple. They were complete strangers, and judging from their common clothing, not the type she would have met in the Zadok's parlor.

"I'm sorry, I can't. This is my train."

The man finally spoke. "It's important, Miss Teller. And I checked the schedule, there's another train this evening." His voice was familiar. Ruth Ann stifled a gasp. This was the man from the top of the Manufactures and Liberal Arts Building!

The woman's eyes were dull, as though uninterested in her task. "It really is important. I've never seen Tom so worked up."

Beulah swept in and latched onto Ruth Ann's arm. "Come, my friend, it is time to say goodbye to our hosts."

Ruth Ann stared at the man. He wasn't as terrible looking as she'd imagined when his gruff voice talked about people killing themselves.

The woman cleared her throat. "Come with us to the Woman's Building. There's someone there you can meet who will get you the story you need to save someone. That's what Tom said, anyway."

Her tone left Ruth Ann wondering if the woman doubted the words of the liar as much as she did.

But in one of those moments to reflect on while sitting in a rocker next to the Grandmother, staring over the calm waters of the lake back home, Ruth Ann found herself nodding.

"All right. I'd like to see what Mr. Fuller—that is, what Tom has up his sleeve this time."

Amid furious objections, Ruth Ann sent Beulah off on the train with their luggage, and Isaac and Edith Zadok on to other social duties. She followed the mysterious couple to the nearest streetcar stop.

This wasn't something to think about. It was simply something to be done.

God knows.

♦♦♦

The Italian Renaissance-style Woman's Building had been designed by a woman, though she was given only one-tenth the pay of a male architect. But that was another story. Up the wide steps, the odd trio entered through the doors beyond three white arches. Ruth Ann was flanked by her mysterious escorts. She didn't know their names. She didn't bother to ask. Since they were friends of the so-called Lance Fuller, who knew if they'd give their real names anyway?

The first time she'd been to this building, Ruth Ann was too engrossed in conversation with Amelia Grace Longstead to pay proper attention to the exhibits that would take a day to explore. The open space showed off two stories with the arch theme continuing, uniform on both floors. The glass ceiling let in ample natural light that shined on the multiple exhibits. Ruth Ann wanted to pause and take in the magnitude of the accomplishments of women around the world, but the lady nudged her.

"We're late."

The man stayed behind them, not seeming appreciative of this place.

They navigated the crowds to reach the far wall. Huge doors opened into a lecture hall. A speech must have just concluded, because droves of women filed out, chattering with excitement.

The woman beside Ruth Ann sighed. "Well, just wait here. Someone will come get you."

With that, her mysterious companions disappeared in the flow of the crowd.

Ruth Ann stood to one side, out of the way of traffic. She picked up bits of conversations around her, but not enough to piece together what the lecture had been.

"She is so charming!"

"Something to tell my grandchildren about some day. Imagine the honor!"

"I don't believe I've heard a more gracious speaker."

When the flood became a trickle, Ruth Ann stepped into the lecture hall, but decided not to venture too far in. If someone was coming for her, she wanted to be found. She had missed her train, ignored Peter's ominous telegram, and was now lost at the World's Fair, and Chicago itself. She was alone in the world. Hopefully there was a good reason.

"Are you Miss Teller?"

Thankful someone knew her name, Ruth Ann turned to find another couple by her. But they were the opposite of the last pair. From the top of his top hat, to her elegant black boots peeking from beneath her fine satin skirt, the couple was beyond the sophistication Ruth Ann had witnessed even in the Zadok's parlor.

Tired and anxious, Ruth Ann chose to be frank. "Yes. And you are?"

The gentleman smiled, a proper way of concealing his amusement at her ignorance. "A pleasure, Miss Teller. I can see the son of my old friend neglected to inform you we would meet you here. I am Senator Blake of New York. My wife, Mrs. Blake."

Ruth Ann acknowledged Mrs. Blake's stiff nod. A U.S. Senator and his wife? She simply had to smile and embrace the bizarre. "A pleasure. I'm sorry, I had no idea what to expect when I came here. The message I received was somewhat cryptic."

The senator nodded and led the way toward the front of the room. "This way, please, Miss Teller. The First Lady will have a moment after her current conversation. But only a moment. I know you will respect Mrs. Cleveland's time. As you can imagine, she is bombarded with reporters when in public."

Reporters. Mrs. Cleveland. The First Lady.

Ruth Ann processed the information backwards and was breathless by the time they reached the podium.

A cluster of finely dressed women surrounded the most beautiful of them all. She was a few inches taller than the other ladies, accentuated by hair swept up in a puffed bun with curled bangs done well enough to set a new trend. Still shy of thirty, she had a youthful yet motherly appearance. Which would be the case after the birth of her second child while entering into her second tenure as First Lady of the United States of America. Mrs. Frances Clara Cleveland.

President Grover Cleveland's wife.

Ruth Ann held back as far as she could in her traveling clothes from Indian Territory and her hands trembling.

Several of the women greeted the senator and his wife. The First Lady turned to them with a radiant smile that made Ruth Ann want to cry. Where was her courage?

Mrs. Blake made the introductions. "Frances, this is Miss Ruth Ann Teller, a reporter from a little newspaper in Indian Territory. She wanted to ask you a few questions."

Mrs. Cleveland nodded, comfortable in her role. "Of course. What did you think of the lecture, Miss Teller?"

There were no words. It would be best for Ruth Ann to turn and flee.

You aren't capable. You'll ruin everything.

In response to the harsh words, another voice—oh so warm and familiar—whispered, *That's my Ruth Ann. That's my girl.*

Her daddy. He was strong for her when she had no strength. Like when she knelt on the road beside her bleeding brother.

Yes. She'd faced worse moments than this.

"It's a pleasure to meet you, Mrs. Cleveland. I'm sorry, but I wasn't in time for the lecture. However, I do have a few questions."

Not overthinking her words, Ruth Ann managed intelligent questions about women's position in society, and the First Lady's thoughts on the World Fair's impact on America. She even calmly withdrew her tablet and took good notes.

The other women took in the exchange with interest, and often nodded in agreement. One lady entered the conversation. "Where did you say you were from, Miss Teller? What newspaper?"

Ruth Ann contemplated the woman's fine appearance, wondering if she were the wife of a senator as well. "I'm from Dickens, a small town in Indian Territory. My brother publishes a newspaper called the *Choctaw Tribune*."

"Fascinating."

"There are so many cultures here."

"You are a fine representative."

But it was Mrs. Cleveland's gentle smile that captured Ruth Ann's heart. "Your readers might be interested to know that when I was growing up, I was told I was related to the former Choctaw Chief Peter Pitchlynn. I've never been able to trace the bloodlines, but it's fascinating to meet someone from the Choctaw people."

Ruth Ann's knees dipped like they'd been whacked from behind but she stayed steady on her feet. "I'm sure our readers will find your story fascinating indeed."

Readers like her mama. The Grandmother. Uncle Preston, Peter, the Barneses. The Levitts. Jozef Walzman. Mrs. Warren.

All races.

The time with the First Lady ended too quickly, though it had been much longer than a moment. Ruth Ann tried to think of a gracious way to express her appreciation, but there wasn't a way.

She inclined her head toward Mrs. Cleveland. "*Yakoke.* Thank you for taking time to answer my questions."

The First Lady gave Ruth Ann another radiant smile. "A true pleasure, Miss Teller. Do come and visit if you are ever in Washington. I will be there another four years!"

She laughed in a genteel manner and offered Ruth Ann a crisp white card before sweeping away with her companions. Ruth Ann was left alone in the large lecture hall of the Woman's Building at the Chicago World's Fair.

But she wasn't afraid.

With a contented sigh, she turned to leave the room but halted. A familiar form stood near the doors, waiting for her. How long had he been there?

Taking another deep breath, Ruth Ann moved confidently across the distance between them. She tried to form an appropriate comment. Should she thank him for arranging the meeting? Demand he tell everything about his past? Call on the Pinkerton detectives?

By the time she stopped in front of him, Ruth Ann was tired again and had little to say. "You lied to us."

Lance Fuller—Thomas Warren—nodded. "I did."

They stared at each other. Finally, he continued. "The next train leaves at 6. I came to escort you home, if I may."

Ruth Ann glanced at the tablet she clutched and thought about its sporadic notes. Traveling to Chicago. Vague descriptions of the city and its people. Smatterings about the Columbian Exposition. Quotes from an interview with the First Lady of the United States.

At the last one, Ruth Ann lifted her chin. She had one more story to get, a final fear to overcome before she went home. "You may. But first, I want to ride the Ferris Wheel."

sure why she asked the question, but she had plenty more if he would be honest with her. She had no way of knowing.

He answered, quietly, though there was little danger of anyone hearing their conversation as the forty other people in the car chattered. "I spent last winter here. The couple you met, they're sort of friends of mine. They let me stay with them while I...I tried to regain position after leaving Washington, D.C. The building of the fair offered opportunities to make a fortune. But I'm not good at that."

The wheel moved again, taking them higher. Ruth Ann gazed at the intricate steelwork of the wheel and realized everything was dropping away like on the elevator. She must have lost her balance, because Lance Fuller held her arm to steady her until the car stopped again. "I went to New York before the stock market crash, hoping to connect with an old banker friend of my father's. He gave me a huge loan, but I lost it all in the crash. I didn't know how to face him, and took out more loans to try to pay him back. But he shot himself the next week."

The wheel started, and Ruth Ann gripped the window seal. She remembered the conversation she'd overheard on the promenade of the Manufactures and Liberal Arts Building. She whispered, "How terrible." Had Lance Fuller contemplated suicide that day?

"I had other debts, and the loan sharks chasing me in New York trying to blackmail me into doing their dirty work. I came back to Chicago, but all the opportunity at the fair was over. Still, I didn't have anywhere else to hide. This is where Mayor Warren...my Uncle Thaddeus found me."

The wheel turned and stopped. They were at the very top of the two hundred foot wheel. Ruth Ann could see all of the glorious fair and across to Lake Michigan. She turned her head and saw Chicago too.

"He and my father were never close. As you might have guessed, Thaddeus Warren is a blowhard who craves power but wouldn't know what to do if it slapped him in the face, which it has. And unfortunately, it influenced me. I just need-

CHAPTER THIRTY

CAMEL RIDES ON THE STREET of Cairo. Music [
Military Band in the German Village. Barkers trying to
visitors into their shows. Ruth Ann was relieved wher
strolled through the Javan settlement. The Javanese v
tranquil representation of their Indonesian island, Java.
sat in the doorways of their thatched roof dwelling
played instruments. Ruth Ann wondered if they were as
to go home as she was. But the Ferris Wheel towered ah

She and Lance Fuller—she couldn't think of him a
one else here at the fair—hadn't spoken during the shor
from the Woman's Building to the Midway Plaisance.
they arrived at the wheel, she bought her own ticket |
waiting in line. Soon, they mounted the wooden step:
wheel had just finished a full revolution and Ruth Ann e
the first car being loaded for the next ride. It would tak
for the wheel to fill to its capacity of over two thousan
ple. She moved to stand at the front of the car near th
window. The wheel moved and the car swayed gently.
Fuller stood at her side as the car swept slowly up
stopping again while the next car was loaded.

"Why were you in Chicago before?" Ruth Ann

ed a safe place to start over. There were bad financial reports across the country, and stories of men I'd known when I was a boy committing suicide. Thaddeus' plan sounded devious but good at the time. I could go to Indian Territory and get a fresh start, teach school, marry a…"

The wheel turned. The fair and lake disappeared from view.

"I didn't want to hurt anyone. I didn't want Indian land. I just wanted to get away. When Beulah invited me to Chicago, I figured it would be a good cover to check on things with my previous associates. When Isaac Zadok sent the Pinkertons to investigate me, I thought I'd land in jail. But I haven't committed any crimes, at least not in the States. The forged papers in Indian Territory Thaddeus did and…well, the Pinkertons didn't have anything to hold me for. They knew it was best for me to just go back to I.T. and keep using the name Lance Fuller. It's not safe to be Thomas Warren anymore. That's fine with me. I didn't like him."

The car swung and kept moving. The wheel was loaded and ready for its nine-minute nonstop revolution. The sensation of gliding in an arc through the air was marvelous. Ruth Ann found that if she stared straight ahead, things didn't drop away. Instead, she floated on clouds.

Everyone seemed in awe. Conversations quieted. Then a young man stepped away from the lady he'd been standing with and knelt on one knee. He took her hand and proposed. The young lady cried and nodded while the entire car applauded.

Lance Fuller looked down with a sad smile. Ruth Ann knew he was thinking of someone he'd met not long ago.

The car began its descent and Ruth Ann felt disconnected from the world. She'd done it. She'd ridden the Ferris Wheel! Just like Matthew had wanted her to. Her journey was complete.

Matthew. She shuddered when she remembered the gunshot, the blood. And Will Hocks was dead. Why both of them? Who had done it?

Cold horror sank into her. Mayor Warren. She had told the man how Will Hocks had given away secrets to Matthew, and Warren knew Matthew would put the pieces together. It was her fault Mayor Warren knew anything, and he had hired men to kill Matthew and Will Hocks. It was her fault.

"Ruth Ann!" Lance Fuller shook her shoulder.

She stared at him. "It was your uncle, wasn't it? He had my brother and Will Hocks shot because I told Thaddeus Warren everything. It's my fault..." She bowed her head.

"Ruth Ann, listen to me. I've done an investigation of my own. There's another man involved and believe me, it goes much deeper than Thaddeus' marriage to the Choctaw woman. I believe there's a tribal member in this whole thing even deeper than Thaddeus, something Will Hocks was involved in. I'm sure Pepper Barnes knows something about it. He made inquiries about a Choctaw with investment connections here in Chicago. I think..."

Ruth Ann couldn't look up. The wheel halted. It was time to get off.

He gently took her arm. "Everything will be all right. I'll find the truth, no matter what."

The journey home was a quiet one, though not painfully so. Lance Fuller said little until they entered Indian Territory the next day, and the Tushkahomma stop. That town had Ruth Ann remembering plenty—the tribal elections, Mr. Barnes' timber operation, Mr. Hocks' murder, Matthew shot. Ruth Ann shuddered and wasn't at all displeased when her escort finally broke the silence.

"I was born and raised in Washington, D.C."

Ruth Ann gave a nod of acknowledgment, not surprised he'd finally chosen to speak. They'd reach Dickens in a few hours.

"My father was a United States senator, and he wanted me to follow in his footsteps. When he died suddenly of a heart attack, I decided to determine my own destiny in life." He paused. "I would have been better off being my father."

The train lurched and got under way again. The Springstown stop was next.

It didn't take long for Ruth Ann to realize Lance Fuller was waiting for a response, permission to go on with his life story. If she didn't give it, he would say nothing else about it, perhaps ever again. And she would never know who he truly was.

"How old were you? When your father passed?"

A pause. "Seventeen."

"I was fourteen."

"Pardon?"

Ruth Ann turned from gazing out the window and met his eyes where he sat across from her. How long had it been since he'd slept? Beulah's Pinkerton novel said those with a guilty conscious never slept well, but Ruth Ann knew this went deeper.

"I was fourteen years old when my father and oldest brother were killed by outlaws."

Lance Fuller looked stricken. "I had no idea…I mean, I knew your father was no longer alive, but I didn't realize…"

A respectful silence fell between them. Ruth Ann wasn't in a hurry, but she finally asked, "So you chose finance instead of politics?"

Lance Fuller gave a scornful laugh. "Unfortunately. I had as much aptitude for that as a mule in a horse race." He studied his hands. "I went to college and charmed my way to a degree, but most knew I wouldn't amount to much since I no longer had my father's backing. I met influential people, but only the unscrupulous took an interest in me. And my inheritance. Wasn't long before I'd been swindled out of everything. I got involved in more worthless ventures before going to Chicago."

Ruth Ann studied him. There were so many questions she wanted to ask, but she knew he wouldn't last through them.

She thought of the guilt she'd carried since her realization on the Ferris Wheel. Lance had assured her the shootings weren't her fault. But how could he be sure unless he knew… "Lance…Lance, who shot Matthew?"

He stiffened and a bolt of fear went through Ruth Ann. The question had made him angry. She glanced around at the few passengers in their car. None paid them any mind, but their presence made her feel safer.

But when Lance Fuller answered, Ruth Ann knew the anger wasn't directed at her. "I think we both know who hired it done. I don't have the proof yet, but I will."

He sighed, shifting his personality. He looked like he did when he'd first gotten off the train in Dickens. Gracious and confident. And a thousand miles away. "I didn't expect you to be like you are. I mean, Susan had said you were a nice young lady, that I would enjoy courting you, but she really had no grasp on the depth of your heart. It's been good to know you. I wish things had been different."

They rode in silence awhile, then the train engine whistled, signaling the coming stop at Springstown. Lance Fuller picked up his hat and bag from the seat next to him. "This is where I get off. You're almost home."

"But—"

He shook his head. "I don't belong there. I'm no school-teacher. I'm not even a man. Maybe someday I can come back when I'm good enough to fit in. You're good people."

The train slowed and he started to stand. Ruth Ann stopped him with a hand on his arm, a flood of words rushing through her mind, but she settled on the most important thought. What her daddy would have said. "God knows, Lance Fuller."

He gave her an indulgent smile. "I'm afraid I'm too dis-connected for Him to know who I am."

"You're wrong." Ruth Ann's voice softened. "You seem to think there's something special about me. There is. His name is Jesus Christ, the One who loves and forgives and makes me whole. That's my goodness, Lance Fuller. It's His goodness. You think on it." Not certain what else to do, Ruth Ann pulled back and dropped her eyes.

She listened to the rustle of his suit as Lance Fuller stood. Listened to the scuffing of his boots down the aisle as he left the car. She didn't look up until the train whistled and started to pull away from the depot. She raised her head enough to catch sight of the emptying platform. Lance Fuller stood alone, staring at her. While she was grateful she had no feelings for the young man, she didn't want him to disappear forever.

She lifted one hand in farewell. He returned it.

"*Chi pisa la chike*, Lance Fuller," she whispered to the glass window. "I will see you again."

CHAPTER THIRTY-ONE

FRANK BEAN DRAGGED THE SADDLE off his sweaty mount with a grunt. It had been a hard ride and he'd almost gotten his head blown off the third time he urged Cub Wassom to halt for the night. They'd ridden right through supper, and now it was past midnight. Frank had had enough. Either they were going to stop or Cub would have to shoot him.

Fortunately, they stopped.

The younger outlaw hobbled his horse and yanked the saddle off. He tossed it on the ground and stumbled to lie down next to it. Though Frank had taken care of the gang leader day and night since he'd been shot, Cub Wassom showed no thanks to anyone, anytime, for any reason. Frank didn't care, as long as the money came in like Cub boasted it would, and Cub didn't look down the barrel of a six-gun at him.

Frank dropped his saddle and used it as a pillow. He was too tired to eat, sleep, or think.

Cub jolted upright and whipped his six-gun from his holster still strapped on. He aimed Frank's direction. Frank scrambled for his own gun but when he drew it, he turned in the direction of a rustling noise. He shouted, "Who wants to get shot?"

At first, nothing materialized in the darkness of the woods. Then slowly, Frank made out the form of a man with no face.

He blinked and saw white teeth spread in the shape of a smile beneath a broad hat.

"Didn't mean to scare you boys. 'Bout time you stopped. Thought I was gonna have to track you to dawn."

Cub made noises behind Frank, but he didn't dare take his gaze or his aim off this strange man who stepped into the moonlight close to them. Cub must have managed to get to his feet, though he wouldn't be able to put any weight on his leg. "Who do you think you are?"

"Just someone lookin' for action. Things are gettin' right peaceful up north, so when I heard two of Dan Holder's men were ridin' toward the Red, I figured to follow the trail and see where it led. Heard you might need help with a trouble spot down near Dickens."

Frank chanced a look at Cub, who kept his gun on the stranger. Cub's lips were pinned tight. Frank pushed himself off the hard ground and decided to ask the next question. "You a friend of Holder's or something?"

"Or somethin'. Holder got no friends, 'less you count Lester that yellowed out on you. Yeah, I know about the shootin's, about Matthew Teller. Heard you fellows got good pay for those, and I figured might be more where that came from. I don't miss what I shoot at."

Frank stiffened, feeling the animosity coming from Cub. Neither had said anything about how Cub's aim had been a hair off, leaving the man alive he'd been paid to kill. Frank knew Cub planned to remedy that soon. They'd hide out a day near Dickens before finishing the job and finding a new target with a woman and a baby along. Frank didn't like that idea.

But he did like the idea of having another gun on their side. The U.S. marshals would be tracking them for killing the white man, Will Hocks. More specifically, tracking Frank Bean for killing him.

The stranger stepped closer to them and pushed his hat up his forehead, still smiling when he hooked his thumbs in his gun belt. No wonder Frank hadn't been able to see his face. The stranger was a Negro, a giant of a man, but old. Older than Frank, leastways. But there was something in the easy, confident way he carried himself, the two tied down six-guns with handle butts forward and the smile that spoke of a seasoned veteran. He was good at whatever he'd done to live this long.

Cub must have been thinking along the same lines. He holstered his gun and glanced at Frank. "If you're willin' to ride hard and shoot straight, you can come along. But like you said, Holder's got no friends. Neither do I."

"I got one." The stranger clicked his tongue. A big sorrel with a white blaze on his face trotted up to him. "And he's likely to outlive all of us."

Cub dropped to the ground again and leaned against his saddle. "We ride to the Jessop place tomorrow. You boys better be ready to keep up with me."

◆ ◆ ◆

Some men thought they knew it all. Some knew nothing. Most didn't care. There were a few men though, who would rise above all the clamor and senselessness and make something of themselves. This was Sam Mishaya, and he knew it. No more would he be stomped on. Or worse, ignored, like he had been during the race for the Choctaw senate seat five years ago. No one thought much of him. No one thought of him at all.

Sam crouched on the dirt floor under the table in the dark cabin, his fingers inching just ahead of his knees. He found the leather string under a thin layer of dirt and pulled the iron key on the other end free from its hiding place. Shuffling backward, he pushed himself clear of the table. Almost. He raised up and his head banged the edge of the table. He cursed and scrambled and raised up in time to catch the wax candle as it rolled over the edge. The hot wax molded to his hand and Sam cursed again. He slammed the base of the candle back on the table.

The flame hadn't gone out. Nice to have something go right in this cabin. Few things did, but all that would change soon.

Sam pushed himself to his feet and pulled the metal box sitting on the table close to him. The bandana he'd wrapped around the box before burying it kept the box clean, and the key fit easily in the lock. It clicked and he flipped the lid open. He squinted at the papers in the faint light of the single candle before he located the one he needed among the leases he held from men like Thaddeus Warren, Jake Banny, and Christopher Maxwell.

Sam settled into the only chair in the cabin and carefully copied the lease agreement onto a clean sheet of paper. By the end of the week, he would have another fool white man to help him along the road of being the most successful man in the Choctaw Nation. And for now, no one would know.

Someday, they would. Sam would see to it. They would read shocking headlines about the mixed-blood baron who had leased half the Choctaw Nation communal land to white intruders to build towns, mines, and railroads. He was a shadow behind more than Matthew Teller would ever know. If Teller had been smart enough to put the pieces together at the council grounds, he would have done a lot more than sling Sam around like a rag doll.

Sam finished copying the lease agreement and started to return the papers to the metal box. A bulk under the stack of papers reminded him of the threat he still faced. He lifted the six-shooter from the box and checked to see that it was loaded. Time he took care of the final threat himself.

It was hard to overlook a man who was about to put a bullet between your eyes.

Sam snuffed out the candle and rolled it on the dirt floor of the cabin. He pocketed it and left the cabin under cover of darkness. He had to bury the metal box again, and see to it the Tellers buried the last of their men.

CHAPTER THIRTY-TWO

RUTH ANN WASN'T SURE WHO she expected to welcome her home, but she hadn't expected to see just Peter searching the passengers for her. Not even Beulah was in sight.

Her young cousin gave her a bear hug and shouted in her ear. "What took you so long! We need you here."

Ruth Ann pulled away and wiggled a finger in her ear, an action the Chicago society ladies would find appalling. "I had one final interview. What's wrong? How is Matthew? Where's Mama?"

The questions tumbled out of Ruth Ann while Peter dragged her across the platform, dodging the crowd. "Aunt Della is fixing your welcome home dinner. I'm supposed to fetch you there, but things are falling apart. The newspaper shop is a wreck. Me and Mr. Levitt did our best, but there's only two of us…"

They landed on the boardwalk lining the main street of Dickens. The lack of tall buildings—skyscrapers—was refreshing. It was good to be home in Indian Territory. Ruth Ann took a quick glance at their box house by the railroad depot. It looked worn, but intact.

They weren't headed for there, though. They were going where the emergency always was.

Peter didn't stop rambling. "The telegraph wire has been terrible, busy with unimportant stuff, nothing worth reporting. Town's just as dead. But that's not the worst."

They rounded the corner to turn off Main Street and headed to the office of the *Choctaw Tribune*. Ruth Ann pulled back on Peter's arm, bringing them to a halt. "Things were bad when I left. I can hardly see them being worse."

"They are." Peter nodded, convinced. "Matthew's given up."

♦ ♦ ♦

With the quiet direction of Mr. Levitt in the equally quiet shop, Ruth Ann went out back where she found her brother.

Matthew was seated on the cluster of crates. He came out here to write when he had a particularly hard article and there were too many distractions inside.

But he wasn't writing now. His left arm was in a sling. Head leaned back against the building and his eyes closed, Ruth Ann wondered if her brother—pale, thin, worn down— was asleep. She settled on a crate across from him. It felt right to be close, to catch him if he fell.

He'd finally gotten a haircut.

Eyes still closed, Matthew said, "I hoped you'd be on that train. You should've come back with Beulah. Stubborn Choc- taw."

Ruth Ann couldn't help a small smile. If he was well enough to scold her, he was well enough.

"Speaking of stubborn, what are you doing out of bed?"

Matthew opened his eyes but kept his head leaned against the wood wall, staring at the clear sky of the autumn day. "Guess I figured I needed to do something, to feel something. But it isn't working. It's over."

He sounded worse than when he was near dead. He sounded defeated.

We need you.

Now Ruth Ann understood Peter's message. They could lose more than the *Choctaw Tribune*. In greatest danger was Matthew's tenacious spirit, his dream. His will to fight, to do what was right, to do God's will. All that could be lost in one long sigh.

But what could Ruth Ann do? Doubtless all her family had tried to raise Matthew's spirits.

"It's all right, Annie."

It took Ruth Ann a moment to realize Matthew was looking at her, his eyes dull. She remembered the last time he'd said those words to her. Then, he'd tried to alleviate her guilt. Now he meant something else, yet the same thing. He meant it was all right she hadn't gotten the story with Buffalo Bill Cody. It was all right that all the blood, sweat and tears he'd poured into the newspaper had been for naught. It was all right he'd failed, that it was all over.

But everything wasn't all right. Ruth Ann bristled against defeat. "It might be all right for you. You're sick and need rest, so go back to Uncle Preston's. I have a newspaper to publish with stories from Chicago, things the *Dickens Herald* never dreamed of. You'll never believe who I interviewed!"

"Annie…"

"We'll catch up to Mr. Maxwell's lies and put them in the grave with truth. The *Choctaw Tribune* is alive and well."

"Ruth Ann…"

"And do I have something to tell you about Lance Fuller! Well, I suppose Beulah already told you who he really is, but—"

"Annie." Matthew leaned forward and grabbed her hand. He winced and lost his breath.

Ruth Ann supported him with a hand on his right shoulder. "You should be in bed!"

Matthew tried to smile, but grimaced instead. "Don't try to lay me out for my funeral again."

"I'll bet you snuck out without Mama even knowing. She'll tan your hide when I get you back home."

"Annie."

Ruth Ann finally heard her name and knew what he was about to say. Matthew squeezed her hand tight, so tight it brought tears to her eyes. She was glad for the strength but not the reason. He was telling her to give up.

She kept silent so he could have his say, so she could take him home, so she could make everything right again.

"It's no good. I tried, you tried. We all did, but it's over. Maxwell keeps spreading lies about us and the *Tribune*. We don't have the evidence we need to oust the mayor. He's been circling like a buzzard, waiting for me and the newspaper to die. I don't want to give up. You know I don't..."

Matthew's eyes drifted close and he seemed to have trouble breathing.

Ruth Ann clenched his hand in both of hers. "Then don't. Don't give up, you crazy, stubborn Choctaw. We still have a chance. I know we do." Her own voice sounded too desperate, but she clung to hope.

Matthew shook his head. "Stop, Annie. We know when we're licked. It isn't worth it."

"Not worth it?" Ruth Ann murmured. Was that true?

"Listen to me, little *luksi*. I want you to promise you won't try to publish another edition. We need to move on. There's more to life than pen and ink, you know."

He managed a smile, but Ruth Ann ignored it. She whispered, "Whatever happened to 'there's nothing more powerful than the press, short of God Almighty?'"

"If that's true, and I always believed it was, I guess God Almighty doesn't want us doing this anymore." Matthew squeezed her hand so tight it cut off Ruth Ann's response. "Promise me, Annie."

I see what is wrong with the world and try to fix it. Mr. Walzman's words echoed in Ruth Ann's mind. Jozef Walzman was passionate about his work, his business, and his life, not so he could make more money or become famous, but to make things right in the world. He reminded her of Matthew.

There were so many wrongs, they needed more men and

women with that kind of attitude. Not fewer.

Ruth Ann recalled the Woman's Building filled with the accomplishments of women around the world, even the building itself. They weren't doing it in a way that said they wanted to take men's positions, but it did show women capable and willing to do more than stay in the kitchen, as Mayor Warren had once told her to do.

There were many things Ruth Ann had to tell Matthew, things that would change everything, or at least some things. First, she had to bargain for a compromise.

"One more edition, Matt. Every newspaper has a final edition. Please. Peter will help, and Beulah. You know we can do it."

Once that "one more edition" was done, she'd work on the next, and the next.

Matthew shook his bowed head. He was just tired. He'd be back to himself before long. She had to keep things going until then.

He muttered something under his breath that sounded a whole lot like, "Stubborn, stubborn Choctaw," before gripping Ruth Ann's hand hard and pulling himself to his feet.

She supported Matthew until he found his balance, though he didn't straighten to his full height. He favored his left side where the bullet had ripped through his chest. "Nothing dangerous, understand? Just a few stories of the tea parties in Chicago. That'll do."

"Of course." Ruth Ann smothered the smile that blossomed at the memories.

Seeing practically every new invention in the world, picnicking with the passionate Jozef Walzman, meeting the First Lady of the United States, revealing the true identity of Lance Fuller.

A few tea party stories like the Boston Tea Party and the American Revolution. That was all. Because somewhere along the way of helping her brother fulfill his calling, Ruth Ann had discovered her own.

CHAPTER THIRTY-THREE

PUBLISHING A NEWSPAPER WAS harder than it sounded. Ruth Ann had experience in each part, but attempting to do the entire process herself was a massive undertaking—organizing story material, writing the articles, laying out the design of the newspaper, typesetting in two languages, the actual printing.

Writing. That was the first thing. With a deep breath, Ruth Ann sat herself down as soon as she returned from a visit home for her mama to feed her and give her the strong embrace she needed. She left Peter there to take care of chores and keep Matthew home.

Ruth Ann was alone in the shop with Mr. Levitt home resting. Beulah was out using the Teller's buggy to visit her music pupils, trying to revive the choir for rehearsal before Thanksgiving was upon them. Without a school day to draw them in, the children were harder to round up than stray steers. And who knew when they'd have a school day again?

Ruth Ann jotted a subject across the top of separate sheets of paper. So many stories! The Columbian Exposition and its exotic experiences, the industrial capital of Chicago, the Lance Fuller incident, Mrs. Cleveland. Where to begin?

But something else niggled Ruth Ann's mind. Matthew's primary story, still unfinished. If this was the final edition of the *Choctaw Tribune*, they had to include that. But what was the ending? Who had leased the mayor land to build an illegal town, tearing at the fabric of the Choctaw Nation?

The entire thing would likely unravel if she could answer one question: who shot Matthew? That alone would set Maxwell and his newspaper back on their heels.

Before long, Peter returned and took over the telegraph, thankfully not pestering her. Matthew's low spirits had affected even him.

Ruth Ann scooted her chair away from the makeshift desk and thumbed through the wooden box where Matthew kept newspaper clippings and handwritten notes pertaining to articles he was working on. There wouldn't be anything blatant in here, but perhaps she could piece together clues to get an idea of what his theories were about the mayor.

Half an hour later, she had nothing new.

The bell over the front door rang and Ruth Ann dreaded looking up. She didn't feel like facing anyone, whether it was a sweet little church lady who wanted a notice in the newspaper about a social picnic, or the mayor coming to boot them out of his building. But the telegraph sounder clacked away and she was the only one to serve customers.

Ruth Ann lifted her head reluctantly, then caught her breath in surprise.

"Ruth Ann, I need to talk to you."

She placed her palms on the table and pushed herself up. She managed to smile at Pepper Barnes. "Come into my office."

She motioned to the chair in front of the table, but regretted her half-hearted joke. Pepper Barnes wasn't the kind of young man to favor a woman being in an "office."

But he didn't seem to notice as he dragged the chair to the side of the table so nothing was between them when they sat down. He had his usual confident air, and Ruth Ann tried not to recall the time they were alone in the parlor of the

Barnes mansion.

Pepper let his felt hat dangle loosely between his fingers. "I stopped in to see Matthew, but he was sleeping, so I need you to give me the directions."

Directions? Pepper Barnes was studying her like he had more than directions on his mind. But it wasn't personal. Ruth Ann recognized the commanding manner he had when talking business.

She folded her hands in her lap formally and nodded for Pepper to continue.

He glanced behind him as though to make sure Peter hadn't snuck in. The sounder had gone quiet. "I understand you've been out to the Jessop place before."

Ruth Ann cocked her head. "Do you know them?"

"Let's say I know of them." Pepper turned toward her again. "Was there any sign of a man living there?"

She recalled the eventful visit to the Jessops. Being shot at, the buggy overturning, Lance Fuller with a pocket pistol. A baby's cry.

But there hadn't been any sign of a man, especially considering how run down the place was. The children weren't old enough to keep it up, and the young woman Amarillo couldn't do it all. And the Choctaw woman? Ruth Ann didn't think she lived there, especially since she'd saved Matthew's life on a road up by Springstown, a long way from the Jessop place.

But why did Pepper Barnes want to know? Could he help with a good story? Instead of answering, she decided to ask her own question. "Who do you think is out there?"

Pepper stared at her. His scrutiny made Ruth Ann want to squirm but she resisted and braced herself for what might come. Pepper didn't disappoint.

"The man who shot Hocks and your brothers."

Ruth Ann took a sharp breath. "My...*brothers?* You mean..."

Pepper didn't flinch, didn't let up his hard gaze. "A man who rode with the gang that ambushed your father and Philip four years ago. The same man who did these shootings. He has a baby boy out at that shanty."

Pepper withdrew a tattered newspaper clipping from his coat pocket. He offered it to Ruth Ann, who took it with trembling fingers. She recalled what Lance Fuller said about Pepper Barnes knowing things.

He leaned back. "Found that in Matthew's jacket after the shooting, put pieces together. That's why I'm here."

There was no shame with his admission that he'd rummaged through Matthew's things. Pepper Barnes didn't make a habit of apologizing.

The newspaper clipping was of a train robbery five years ago. A name was circled in the article. Reading the whole story, Ruth Ann found the circled name was of the youngest gang member, a Choctaw named Cub Wassom. The name sounded familiar, but there were so many outlaws in Indian Territory both then and now they were hard to keep up with. Lawmen like Marshal Bass Reeves would never be out of a job.

But why was this outlaw important enough for Matthew to circle his name? Ruth Ann rubbed her temple. If she tried to decipher every note of her brother's, the strain would put her in an early grave.

Ruth Ann reached for her tablet and reticule while she rose to her feet. "I best go out there and see about it."

Pepper stood, his eyebrows scrunched together. "I have my own plan and it doesn't include you."

"I am going, whether with you or not. But I suggest you stay with me. I know something about that place you don't."

Ruth Ann moved around Pepper and headed for the telegraph office. She was determined to find the truth. And having been out to the Jessops before, she knew how to avoid getting shot by young Stephen Austin.

At the doorway of the telegraph office, she gave Peter orders with an authoritative tone that silenced his questions. She gave him strict instructions on what he was to do and not do—tell anyone where she'd gone.

Taking advantage of his dumbfounded state, Ruth Ann left the office. She went straight to the barn behind their box house and saddled her horse, Skyline, and rode out of town without being seen. Pepper Barnes was right behind her on one of his father's fine Choctaw horses. They would make good time. Whether it was hastening to death or not, only God knew.

◆◆◆

It was a dusty ride with the dry spell. But it was good to breathe the fresh air of the country, so far from the factories and overcrowded districts of Chicago.

Ruth Ann kept her horse at a steady trot, eyes and ears alert. Pepper Barnes rode alongside her. Before rounding the corner that had preceded their buggy's wild ride on their last visit, she pulled Skyline to a halt.

"It's just around the bend. But last time, we were shot at from the house. The oldest Jessop boy doesn't like visitors. I guess I know why now."

Pepper turned one way in his saddle, then another, looking up and down. He pointed up to the left. "We'll take cover on that wooded knoll and watch the place, see who's around."

Startled, Ruth Ann realized how easily he took charge. While she'd desperately needed his leadership when Matthew had been shot, she bristled at being ordered around now. But this was no time to protest.

Ruth Ann guided her horse behind Pepper as he made a trail through the thick underbrush. When they'd gone deep enough to conceal their horses, he halted and dismounted. He tied his horse to a low tree branch and withdrew a Winchester from the scabbard on his saddle.

Ruth Ann slid to the ground and tied Skyline next to his horse. She realized Pepper wasn't treating her like a helpless woman after all. He expected her to follow his lead and take care of herself, same as he expected from anyone. It was an attitude people deemed beneficial for someone like Pepper who was destined for tribal politics.

But this was far from a court of law.

They crept through the underbrush of the thick pines that hemmed in pastureland. They topped the knoll. Pepper had been right, this was the perfect spot.

Ruth Ann released her grip on her skirt she'd held close in the underbrush. It was easy to see the shanty down the slope and the road that led up to it. A thin wisp of smoke rose from the chimney. Someone was home.

She squeezed between two pines and parted the branches to get a better look. She corrected her evaluation. There were several people home. Behind the shanty a rope corral held three horses, and saddles littered the area. Ruth Ann was certain the horses hadn't been there before. The Jessops had visitors.

She pulled back and stepped close to Pepper, who surveyed the front yard and the pastureland beyond the house. Though they were a long way from the house, Ruth Ann kept her voice low.

"There are three horses in the back that weren't there before. Do you really think Cub Wassom would come here?"

Pepper moved to where she had been, took a look and came back. "He has a son in that shanty. He's been on the run since the shooting, and he's getting ready to clear out of these parts for good. He'll take the boy."

Everything Pepper said was so certain. With a sad heart, Ruth Ann agreed with him. There was no one to stop the outlaw from taking off with the baby.

No one but her and Pepper.

But what about Amarillo? She didn't seem the kind of young woman who would, well, take up with an outlaw. But Ruth Ann really didn't know her, and her previous visit had been so mysterious she still didn't understand it.

The nearest law enforcement was for Indians only. If this was a white gang, only Cub Wassom would fall under their jurisdiction. No wonder outlaws found refuge in Indian Territory with laws that were almost impossible to enforce.

Pepper rested the barrel of his Winchester in the crook of a branch and took a relaxed stance, his eyes on the shanty. "They know they can't stay here long, but they'll wait until dark to leave. I'll set up along the route they're most likely to take."

Ruth Ann frowned. "What about the baby? You said he came for him."

He glanced at her then away. But she'd seen his eyes long enough to know she'd given him a rare pause, thinking of something he hadn't.

"I'll be careful. Can't rush the house if there are women inside."

Ruth Ann fidgeted. "Maybe I should ride to town for help."

Pepper gave her a patient look. Of course. There was no one in town they could call on. Sheriff Banny would be no help, and Peter was too young and anxious to be involved. This was dangerous business.

Then why am I here? An unarmed woman. Pepper should have sent me back. Why hasn't he?

There were few reasons. Ruth Ann couldn't help but re-call Beulah's accusation of the Barnes family, especially Pepper. What if he was luring her away to do her in?

That was ridiculous. Pepper Barnes might not be her closest friend, but she felt safe with him. Beulah read too many detective books, and romantic ones, too.

Ruth Ann firmly rejected any such notions. Pepper Barnes never had and never would want to court her. And that was just fine with her.

The days growing shorter, it wouldn't be long before dark. But Ruth Ann still settled on a log to rest. She tried hard not to fidget in the quiet that Pepper Barnes seemed comfortable with. He watched the shanty.

It wasn't long before the silence proved too much and Ruth Ann broke it. "I never really thanked you for what you did when Matthew was shot. We'd both be dead if it weren't for you."

Pepper didn't respond, didn't even tilt his head like he was listening.

"You haven't told me how you found out about Cub Wassom. You haven't told me about...about how he was involved in the ambush on my daddy and Philip."

There was silence again, but Pepper finally shrugged one shoulder. "Some things are best left alone. It's enough to know it happened. That's enough to bear."

Again, Ruth Ann sensed Pepper was hiding something, but no longer felt it was something she needed to uncover. Not yet. But it didn't stop her from asking another question. This, she had to know. "Did Mayor Warren hire Cub Wassom to shoot them because he knew Mr. Hocks told Matthew about the mayor's Choctaw wife?"

Pepper glanced at her and shrugged again. "I don't know anything about that. But there's someone else in this with a lot more to lose than your Mayor Warren. Someone is trying to sabotage our timber operation. That's why they went after Hocks. Matthew was close to finding out the name of the man in charge."

He paused, as though making a hard decision. "You deserve to know something with all you've been through. There's a Choctaw who leased the land for the townsite of Dickens. This man is in with Warren and Banny, who are also financing an illegal timber operation. Hocks knew more than he told even me. So there was nothing you could have known about Will Hocks to get him killed."

Ruth Ann finally let herself believe it. One thing she'd learned about Pepper Barnes—he didn't tell the whole truth, but he didn't lie, either.

"When you found out where Cub Wassom was, why didn't you go to the Indian police? Why come yourself?"

Pepper grunted. "Politics."

Ruth Ann knew what that meant. Lack of evidence. The Choctaw chief still in a feud with the Barneses. The Indian agent tired of dealing with Indian outlaws. The fear of Cub Wassom getting away with the murder of the Barneses' foreman, Mr. Hocks.

The last point was most likely the real reason Pepper came after Cub Wassom. Alone.

The thought occurred to her so suddenly, Ruth Ann jumped from the log. "You plan to kill him, don't you? Be the judge, jury, and executioner."

Pepper lowered the Winchester from its prop and turned fully to her. "This man shot your daddy and brother down in cold blood and watched them die. Shot Matthew. What do *you* want me to do?"

Ruth Ann twisted her skirt between her fingers to keep from screaming. "You have no right to…to say something so hurtful. You know I…"

Pepper looked like he might step toward her, but halted and put his Winchester back on the tree branch. "Someone is going to die today. That's how it's done in this territory, how the bad men do it, and how the good men bring justice. You better pray it's the bad men who die today."

Ruth Ann gritted her teeth. Pepper Barnes wasn't treating her like a proper lady, but he wasn't treating her like a child either. She might appreciate that, but right then, she just wanted to chunk another rock at his head.

Pepper shifted and pointed across the way. "They'll take the south road, circle down by the Red and head out that way toward the west. I know a place to get ahead—"

The sound of a horse trotting along the road silenced him. He moved to the edge of the trees and swore under his breath.

Ruth Ann took quick steps to reach his side. She stifled a scream.

A buggy rolled toward the shanty at a good clip. Beulah.

CHAPTER THIRTY-FOUR

RUTH ANN PUSHED THROUGH THE tree branches, lips parted to scream a warning. Pepper clamped a hard hand over her mouth, locked his rifle across her arms, and yanked her back into the woods. She clawed at his hand. Terror seized her. The door of the shanty swung open.

Pepper hissed in her ear. "Quiet. You'll get her killed."

Despite the fear charging through her, Ruth Ann remembered something. Pepper liked Beulah. He wouldn't let her be harmed. This calmed Ruth Ann enough to go limp, and Pepper released her.

Beulah moved the Teller's buggy horse along confidently toward the shanty. Amarillo stepped out the door, her posture stiff. Beulah stopped the buggy near the shanty and climbed down. They exchanged a few words, and she went inside.

Then a man appeared in the doorway, a Winchester in the crook of his arm, one hand on the trigger area. From this distance, he looked to be a white man. He surveyed the road behind the buggy, then his gaze swept toward the woods where Ruth Ann and Pepper hid. He showed no sign of detecting them and, seeming satisfied, closed the door.

Beulah had unwittingly walked into a nest of outlaws.

"Pepper."

Ruth Ann hated the whimpering sound of her voice, but she couldn't help herself. Pepper didn't feign patience with her. "Quiet."

His behavior made her aware of the precious few minutes they had to do exactly the right thing. She didn't have an idea what that was.

Whether he did or not, Pepper acted quickly. He deftly made his way down the knoll through the tree shadows. Ruth Ann realized he expected her to follow. She didn't know what else to do.

Chihowa, protect Beulah. Protect me and Pepper and all of the Jessops. God, help us...

They crept along the woods until the trees ended and nothing but high grass offered cover. Thankfully, there wasn't a window on this side of the shanty. They hurried across the open space and dodged behind a broken down wagon in the back. Pepper halted beside it to catch his breath and take a cautious look at the shanty.

Ruth Ann pressed her hand against her chest, trying to slow her heart. She quieted her breathing in time to hear the metallic click of a gun hammer somewhere close. Very close.

Pepper heard it too and turned back toward her, but his focus was on a hole in the side of the wagon bed. She slowly followed his gaze to see the terrified eyes of Stephen Austin Jessop. He sighted down the barrel of an old Springfield rifle aimed at Pepper's nose.

"Stephen Austin." Ruth Ann couldn't believe how quiet yet authoritative her tone sounded. "You put that gun down. We're here to help."

The boy must have been as scared as her. He gripped the rifle barrel with white knuckles, and his finger pressed against the trigger of the cocked gun. His voice shook. "Don't know this one. He might be one of them."

Ruth Ann shook her head. "No, he's a friend here to help."

When the boy didn't respond, she hissed low but commanding, "Stephen Austin, look at me!"

The boy darted his eyes toward her. She took a breath. "You know I'm Ruth Ann Teller from Dickens. Remember? I'm a friend of Miss Levitt. She's in trouble, and I expect your sister is too. We don't have much time. Now put that gun down."

He studied her hard, and Ruth Ann sensed Pepper's impatience. She prayed he would hold still a moment longer. If he tried to yank the gun away from the boy, it would likely discharge and give them away. Not to mention the bullet might kill him.

Stephen Austin Jessop released the hammer of the gun, lowering the barrel at the same time.

Pepper didn't waste another moment. "How many guns inside?"

Stephen Austin, still crouched in the bed of the wagon, pressed his face close to the hole in the side. "Three men with sidearms and Winchesters, a mean bunch. Sissy made me take the young'uns to the creek to hide and told me not to come back. I've just been waiting for one of them to poke his head out so I can blow it off."

Ruth Ann had no doubt Stephen Austin would do just that. She wanted to take the rifle from him, but she held still, holding on to the wagon for support. Her legs cramped.

Pepper eased to the back of the wagon again. He glanced at the rope corral not far away. He asked over his shoulder, "Who else is inside?"

Stephen Austin frowned. "My sissy, Takba, and Miss Levitt now." Ruth Ann heard the regret in his voice. Beulah would be surprised at the rough concern he showed.

Pepper turned back to the boy and pressed his shoulder against the wagon bed. "You want to help them?"

Stephen Austin eyed him. Ruth Ann didn't blame him for being suspicious. Pepper was clearly not white, and the boy had more than his share of reasons to distrust an Indian. But Stephen Austin nodded, a touch of pride lifting his chin. Pepper didn't treat him like a little boy.

"Slide that gun to Ruth Ann and climb out real quiet. Make a beeline for that rope corral, and when I give the signal, untie the rope and jump out of the way. I'll fire off a few shots to stampede the horses. We'll bring those cowards out in the open."

Stephen Austin shoved his gun through the hole. Ruth Ann grabbed the barrel of the old Springfield and the boy slipped to the back of the wagon and dropped to the ground. He darted across the open area of the yard. Makeshift curtains covered the windows in the back of the shanty but one peek by the outlaws and they would see the boy.

He was fast and soon crouched by the rope corral. Pepper motioned Ruth Ann to his side. She swallowed and moved closer. He whispered, "You only have one shot. Save it until you need it."

Ruth Ann didn't know what he meant, didn't want any shooting to start, but said nothing. She gripped the rifle.

Pepper started to raise his hand to signal Stephen Austin but stopped. He took the Springfield from Ruth Ann, leaned it against the broken wheel of the wagon and drew a Colt .45 from where it had been tucked in his belt. He handed it to her.

"As soon as that rope drops, fire two rounds overhead."

Pepper leaned against the bed of the wagon and braced his Winchester against his shoulder. He raised his hand off the action, ready to signal the boy.

Ruth Ann clutched the Colt, taking slow breaths. She aimed over the corral and cocked the hammer. The horses were anxious, stirring around in their confined area. Closer to them now, she saw how hard they'd been ridden. Dried lather marked where the saddles had been. Only one of the horses appeared cared for. The huge sorrel with a distinct white blaze just like…

"Pepper." Ruth Ann's squeal came too late.

Pepper waved his hand and Stephen Austin untied the rope and dropped the corral fence. He jumped back, expecting the horses to stampede.

Pepper hissed, "Fire!"

Ruth Ann froze.

He raised his Winchester and popped off two rounds before swinging his rifle back to the shanty door that swung open. The white man stepped into the doorway, Winchester in hand as the horses stampeded past him. He fired in Stephen Austin's direction, but he only got off one shot. He was dropped by Pepper's bullet.

Screams sounded inside the shanty. Two more gunshots. Gun smoke drifted through the air and cleared. Silence.

Someone called from the dark doorway. "Who out there?"

Ruth Ann recognized the voice. "It's Ruth Ann Teller, Marshal Reeves! And a friend, Pepper Barnes, from the mansion in Springstown."

The barrel of a Colt showed first before Marshal Reeves stuck his head out the door. Hatless and with no badge visible, he stepped over the body of the man in the doorway. When Ruth Ann and Pepper showed themselves, he lowered his gun.

"Well, I'm glad to see you. Reckon your friend will be, too." He bent and examined the fallen man.

Stephen Austin bounded out of hiding and rushed the doorway. He leaped over the dead man and stumbled inside.

Ruth Ann started to follow, thinking only of Beulah. But Pepper caught her arm, halting her painfully. He addressed the marshal. "What about Cub Wassom?"

Marshal Reeves stood and holstered his Colt, handle butt forward. "Inside, dead as Frank Bean here. You caused enough ruckus for me to get the drop on Cub. Said he'd never be taken alive. Probably the one true thing he ever said."

Ruth Ann looked at Pepper when his grip on her arm tightened. Bitter disappointment showed on his face, but she had no patience for his lost revenge. She handed him his Colt, shook herself free and stepped gingerly around the dead man in the doorway. Inside, she was caught in Beulah's bear hug. Ruth Ann held her friend tight while her gaze went around the dim room. Amarillo, pale and with a black eye, scolded Stephen Austin.

Chairs overturned on the dirt floor. The fire in the cookstove nearly out. And then Ruth Ann saw him.

The Choctaw woman Takba was stretched over him, sobbing. She pounded his chest with her fist. His gun was still in his hand that lay in a pool of blood.

This man, the one who had shot Ruth Ann's brothers and her father.

At least according to what Pepper Barnes said. Who knew anything for sure? Ruth Ann didn't know herself or her feelings in that moment. She hugged Beulah tight.

From the lean-to with its blanket door, a baby cried.

CHAPTER THIRTY-FIVE

PETER SQUIRMED IN HIS chair by the sounder. It was past time to close but he couldn't go to Aunt Della's yet. What was he going to tell the family about Ruth Ann? Matthew would tear him apart if he knew the truth.

It would be easy to make up a story, to say Ruth Ann was working hard on the newspaper, say he would take dinner back to her.

But Peter hadn't storied his way out of trouble in a while. It was boyish and he was practically a man now. That made life more complicated.

Worst of all, he was starving. He could hole up in the newspaper office all night and maybe Matthew wouldn't even come check on them, but Peter couldn't do it on an empty stomach. That left one option.

The Levitts would be sitting down to dinner about now and it would be easier to dodge their questions than family. Maybe Beulah wouldn't be home and Peter could fill up on whatever Mr. Levitt was having. And bring some of their delicious bread back to snack on until Ruth Ann returned.

How long would she be gone? Peter squirmed in the chair again. She'd made him promise not to leave town to come after her. Keeping promises was another pesky thing about being a man.

Well, promises only went so far. If she wasn't back by dark, he was going after her.

But he couldn't do it on an empty stomach.

Locking the front door of the shop, Peter went out the back and walked along the worn path to the Levitt house not far away. The scent of fresh baked bread wafted toward him. He'd soon be set to save the world.

◆◆◆

Matthew lay stretched out on the sofa, arms crossed over his aching chest while he watched his mother pace. Yes, his calm, strong mama was pacing, though she would deny it.

Della moved to the mantel with a dust rag in hand to go over the polished wood a third time while straightening framed photographs and the flute propped at one end. She went to the window and straightened the lace curtain again after taking a quick peek into the growing darkness. Then she went to the kitchen and clattered around before coming back in the front room. Fresh rag in hand, she started on the mantel again.

Yes, his mama was pacing. Matthew leaned his head back on the arm of the sofa and closed his eyes. In the evenings, after a day of excursions and scolding from her, he usually had a headache. Well, at least in the evenings since he'd been shot.

I am for peace: but when I speak, they are for war.

The verse from Psalms floated around him. He was tired of the fighting, the arguments, his mother pacing. Had she always done that when he was gone? Or because it was Ruth Ann out late in a dangerous newspaper office? Della had started pacing when Ruth Ann left for Chicago. Or maybe she had started when he published the first edition of the *Choctaw Tribune*.

Either way was his fault. Della was worrying a rut through the house and through their lives. He wasn't strong enough to bear that or anything else anymore. It was time to quit.

He had prayed. God was silent. Matthew had nearly gotten himself and his sister killed. The answer was clear as a burning bush. He'd failed and it was time to move on. Once he had the strength.

Right then, he only had strength to rise up from the sofa and drop his bare feet to the floor. He reached for the boots he'd left by the chest-table and waited until the dizziness passed before pulling one on.

Della stood over him. "Where are you going?"

Matthew breathed as full as the pain would allow. "Can't let her stay out all night with no one but Peter to help. He'll fall asleep as soon as she has her back turned."

Della sat on the chest in front of him and put both hands on his shoulders. He looked up and deep into her eyes. Tears gathered in them. Matthew winced. He'd caused every tear, every bit of pain. The damage from that bullet was nothing compared to what he'd done to his mother's heart.

"I'll bring her home, Mama."

Her grip on his shoulders tightened. "Have I done right?"

She asked so much in that simple question. Worse, it showed her doubt, and Matthew couldn't stand that. His mama was always sure, always strong. If she questioned her own actions...

"You've done right. Now I will. Don't you worry."

Matthew rested his palm on her cheek but she quickly pulled him into a tight embrace. He gritted his teeth against the pain in his chest. He breathed carefully and hugged her close.

"It's all right, Mama. Shh, it's all right. *Chi hullo li.*"

Della rubbed his back and pulled away. She stood and went into the kitchen.

"Tell her to come home. I have her supper warm. Then I will help her finish her work."

How much his mother could say in a few words. How

encouraging and right she could be.

Matthew stood, hooked his left arm in the sling, and took his hat from the rack beside the door, then hesitated. He watched his mother in the kitchen where she was setting a single place at the table.

She'd given her life for her children. One child dead. Another kept death too close. The last was a young girl who couldn't be looked at the same way as the boys. There were many more dangers for her.

The fraudulent Lance Fuller came to mind. Matthew crushed the brim of his hat. Sometimes Ruth Ann was too kind for her own good.

The train whistle sounded in the distance. Matthew wondered if anyone interesting would get off, but he quickly shook his head. It didn't matter what the news was anymore. He wouldn't be reporting it. Even the case of Mayor Warren held no interest. It was all over.

Matthew donned his hat and went out the door.

It was a short walk across town to the newspaper office. At least it used to be when he could walk straight and breathe normal. But there wasn't anyone about this evening and he could rest heavy against the hitching post by Bates General Store.

The train signaled its farewell and pulled out of the depot a hundred yards behind him.

Matthew pushed off the post and rounded the corner to see the darkened picture windows of the newspaper office and repair shop across the street. He frowned and crossed to the boardwalk in front of the building. The whole shop was dark. He rattled the front door. Locked. He withdrew his key, unlocked the door, and stepped inside. Ruth Ann and Peter must have gone to the Levitts, perhaps to eat. If Beulah had come by, that was explanation enough.

Matthew didn't feel like walking to the little home of the Jewish family. Besides, they would be back any moment. That was, if Ruth Ann expected to get a newspaper out anytime in the next week.

He shook his head with a smile. His sister had a heart the size of Texas, but she was still young. Publishing an edition of the *Choctaw Tribune* was a huge task. She'd need his help. He would give it, but with the reminder of her promise to make it the last edition.

He knew she wanted to please him, make him proud of her and her work. Maybe he never showed how proud he was.

Matthew went to the press and put his hand on the slick handle he'd so often pulled down when printing off the newspaper in two languages. The smell of ink and paper threatened his resolve, but he let it strengthen him instead. They'd had good times but that was in the past.

He moved to his makeshift desk, remembering the fine oak desk he'd made when they started. It had burned in a fire likely set by Jake Banny with the backing of Warren and Maxwell.

So much had been lost that night. But so much gained. From the ashes had risen this fine shop and a bond with the Levitts that made them a strong team. Matthew could never repay Mr. Levitt for his kindness, except to get out of his shop and let them have peace for once.

Suddenly exhausted, Matthew sank into his chair and thumbed through the papers scattered on the desk. A clipping caught his eye. He lit the lamp on the wall but kept it low to prevent another headache. He held the clipping up and caught his breath. This was the article with the circled name, Cub Wassom. A man Matthew had violent dreams about.

Where did Ruth Ann find this? How much did she know...

A whoosh of air went through the room. Matthew had spent enough hours here to know every breath of this building. The back door had just opened. Ruth Ann and Peter must finally be back.

But why so quiet?

Standing quickly, Matthew blew out the wall lamp, casting the room in muted light from the moonlight through the front picture windows.

The door to the storeroom opened and he turned to see the outline of a man there, six-shooter in hand.

Matthew held his breath. There was nothing he could do. If the man was going to shoot, he was going to get shot.

"Matthew Teller?" The voice was familiar but not friendly. "Yeah, thought you'd be in here. Just can't stay away from that printing press no matter what it costs you."

The short man took a step forward and Matthew knew.

"Sam Mishaya."

He had the full story now. "I should have known you were behind all this. I was getting close to the truth about you and Warren, wasn't I? I hope your betrayal bought you a fine place somewhere besides the Choctaw Nation."

Mishaya moved into a beam from the moonlight, showing his grin. He was a spindly man, the reason it had been easy for Matthew to handle him on the Council House lawn. But he was a big enough man with a gun in hand.

"Not for you to worry about now, is it?" Mishaya's lips dropped into a snarl. "You shouldn't have been worried about it to begin with, would have saved us all trouble. Don't know what you were so up in arms for. You'd have done the same, given the opportunity."

Matthew shook his head slowly, needing to think how he could defend himself, but his thoughts were clouded. All he wanted was a full confession.

"I haven't done the same. I wanted what was right for our people. You sold us out, leasing this land to a white man to build a town. I set out to right that, to bring back honor to our blood. Funny, history will remember things you did more than anything I did."

Mishaya sneered. "*Did* is right, Matthew Teller. I should've shot you myself instead of sending Wassom. Too bad you won't be able to write that final story about how the fabric of the Choctaw Nation is about to unravel with smart ones like me pulling the strings. Someone's going to be king in this territory. No reason it can't be me. It sure won't be you."

Mishaya cocked the hammer of his six-shooter, the deadly click reverberating through the quiet room.

The report of the gunshot shook Matthew to the core. He grabbed his chest, rubbing the searing pain there. But there was no blood.

Mishaya took two steps into the room. He held the gun up but it slipped from his fingers. He fell flat on his face.

Matthew stared at the blood spreading over the man's back. But his attention quickly snapped to the figure coming through the storeroom door.

"Are you all right?"

Matthew had no words to say to the fraudulent Lance Fuller, who eyed him before pocketing his derringer and squatting next to Mishaya. He felt for a pulse, then scooped up the dropped six-shooter and stood.

"Just winged him. He'll come to before long."

Matthew said nothing. Lance Fuller suddenly looked sheepish.

"I followed him on the train all the way from the territory line." He waved off further explanation. "Let's just say I did some investigating on my uncle. None of it matters now, I guess."

The mysterious young man looked down at the man he'd shot, then at the gun he held loosely in his hand.

The sound of boots thudded on the sidewalk outside. The clatter jolted Matthew back to his senses. "It matters. It matters a lot."

The front door banged open and Sheriff Banny stomped in. Charlie Simms—the blacksmith—and Mr. Bates, owner of the general store, were behind him. Amid the flurry of questions and accusations, Matthew lowered himself to the edge of the table and rubbed his chest.

His mind was foggy until the appearance of Peter and Mr. Levitt at his side.

"Where is Ruth Ann?" Mr. Levitt asked. Matthew jerked to his feet.

"Isn't she at your house?"

"No, son. Young Peter said she had work she was doing

for the newspaper."

They looked at Peter, who shuffled his feet in a way that sent fury through Matthew. He grabbed a fistful of his cousin's shirt and yanked him close.

"Where is she?"

"I…uh, well, she made me promise…"

Matthew twisted the shirt to tighten the collar around Peter's throat.

"All right, she rode out with Pepper Barnes. She wouldn't say where, just that I was supposed to keep working until she got back."

Pepper Barnes had that newspaper clipping from Matthew's jacket. He knew who had shot Hocks same as Matthew had figured out from reports of Choctaw Lighthorsemen who'd been trailing Cub Wassom and his gang. Pepper had come here to…

Matthew released his cousin. "Pepper Barnes only has blood on his mind, and he won't look after her. I've gotta go after them."

Sheriff Banny boomed, "Everyone calm down and shut up! No one's going anywhere until we straighten this thing out."

An old burn came back into Matthew's gut, the kind of burn he had when writing a critical story. And when it came to protecting his family.

It was a fighting kind of burn, one he thought was doused forever. But he was ready to fight now, whether Banny or Mishaya or Cub Wassom. Or himself. He would fight his own lethargy and guilt. He'd never stop fighting again.

The sound of horses' hooves thundered up the street. Through the picture windows, he caught sight of the riders.

Pepper Barnes and Ruth Ann skidded to a stop. She was off her horse before him and bounded through the open door, her face glowing.

"Matthew! What are you doing out of bed?"

She crushed him in a hug, but pulled back with a gasp.

Her gaze went around the room, eyes wide when she saw Lance Fuller and the sprawled out Sam Mishaya who was coming to.

But Banny inserted himself again, hand on his holstered Colt like he was about to yank it out and start shooting. "All of you settle down! This is my town and I'm going to throw the whole lot of you in jail."

Tucked under Matthew's arm, Ruth Ann jutted her chin out at the sheriff. "You'll have to take that up with Bass Reeves. *Marshal* Bass Reeves. He's right behind us."

She smiled more smugly than Matthew had ever seen. But the smile vanished and she looked ready to cry when she gazed up at him.

"I have a lot to tell you, but you'll get mad."

She buried her face in his shoulder, her tears soaking through his shirt.

The fighting fire in Matthew's gut was still there, but the pain in his chest finally eased.

CHAPTER THIRTY-SIX

SUNDAY MORNING DAWNED AS THE coldest day of the autumn season so far. The air invigorated Matthew with a sense of newness stronger than springtime. It was time to begin again.

But things in the past still needed to be dealt with. In church, he saw Lance Fuller lingering near the back.

After the service, Matthew walked by and gave a jerk of his head, indicating Lance Fuller should follow him. Fuller did, head down like a chain gang prisoner. Most the people in town knew he wasn't who he had claimed to be, though they didn't know his true identity. Matthew moved away from the curious gazes. He strolled up to the fenced cemetery and opened the gate.

Cemeteries were a good place to talk. They served as a reminder that life was brief and people should commit to live it right.

Matthew was restless after being confined in bed following the scrape in the newspaper office. He roamed around the sporadic tombstones with Fuller staying a step behind him. Matthew halted and turned to face him squarely.

"You deceived my sister."

Lance Fuller flushed, his gaze on the nearest tombstone. He probably wondered if Matthew planned to shoot him for defrauding his sister. Matthew crossed his arms over his chest. He'd thought about it.

His quarry shuffled his feet before finally raising his eyes to meet Matthew's.

"I did wrong by her. But I'm moving on as soon as I see Mrs. Warren...my aunt off." Every word stuck in Fuller's mouth like there was tar on his tongue. "Unless...if you want me to court Ruth Ann properly, I'll do that."

Matthew tightened his grip across his chest. "What makes you think you're fit for that?"

Lance Fuller's gaze dropped and so did his shoulders. "I'm not. I assumed it was the honorable thing to do."

"It is. So is taking care of your aunt since her husband hightailed it out of town."

Matthew still found it hard to believe the mayor had snuck off in the middle of the night. Apparently, the man thought his life was in danger, and it probably was. Mishaya had friends who would blame the white man for the trouble, and Jake Banny was a threatening force on either side. Dickens had been a good front for their maneuvers, but their plans to do away with the Barneses' timber operation and gain exclusive contracts through Mishaya had fallen apart.

But that wasn't the issue here.

Matthew braced his legs apart, knowing his stance was intimidating. But he wouldn't stand a chance in a fistfight in his condition. Ruth Ann had told him about the fight with the bandits in Chicago. That was twice now they owed Lance Fuller their lives, unfortunately. That was the only reason Matthew had bothered with this conversation.

"You aren't worthy of courting my sister. No one is. But that's just how a brother thinks."

Fuller drove his hands deep in his pockets against an icy

chill that gusted through the cemetery. The wind carried sounds of laughter from children playing in the churchyard, waiting for food to be served.

The two men stood in silence a time before Lance Fuller raised his head.

"She told me something on the train, something I can't get out of my head, about Jesus and love and forgiveness. I'm not a religious man, but I couldn't help thinking about her. That is, how she and your family are. The whole Choctaw Nation has been done wrong by scoundrels like me for generations. Yet you're still here. Aren't you bitter over the things everyone from presidents to my uncle to me has done to your people?"

The question was too large for a quick answer. Matthew stilled his heart and prayed.

To his credit, Lance Fuller didn't move, didn't stalk off at Matthew's silence, didn't shift his feet in anxiety. He waited.

Matthew dropped his arms, and the cold air chilled the warm spot across his chest. "We forgive, but not by our own strength. We don't faithfully have church just because it's the good thing to do. It's our redemption, what we come back to when we fail. Jesus Christ isn't just a good way; He's the only way."

Fuller brought his gaze up slowly and took his time studying Matthew's face.

"I've never heard anyone except you people talk like it was real. You make it…you make Him sound alive."

Matthew nodded. "He is."

Lance Fuller rubbed the back of his neck and Matthew sensed that part of their conversation was over.

"Now, what about my sister?"

Fuller gulped. "She's a fine young woman. There's something real about her, and when I first came here, it made me feel real too. Scared me because I thought I might fall in love. Only I didn't. But I'm willing to do the honorable thing. It's just…"

Matthew raised one eyebrow. "Yes?"

"Well, she's…I…"

"You're just not interested?"

Lance Fuller looked at the sky. "That sounds pretty foolish."

Matthew sighed. "I'm relieved."

At Fuller's stricken look, he chuckled and offered a handshake. "I like the name Lance Fuller. You should keep it."

Fuller slowly took the offered hand and Matthew gripped hard. "Those children still need a teacher. Think about staying on."

He left Lance Fuller in the cemetery and went back to the congregation and one of the last picnics they would enjoy before cold weather forced them indoors.

Matthew knew Ruth Ann had watched the pair intently from her spot near a sawhorse table. She buttered bread and glanced casually at him.

"Mama made you a plate. She still thinks you should be in bed."

"I probably should."

He snagged the piece of buttered bread from her hand and dodged her playful swat. "Have I mentioned how proud I am of you?"

Ruth Ann jerked back like he'd poked her with a hot iron. She stared at him, then burst into tears.

Women. I'll never understand them.

Matthew put his arm around Ruth Ann and led her away from the staring girls at the table. He tugged her behind one of the wagons. "What did I do now?"

Ruth Ann shook her head and her voice bubbled with giggles. "Nothing, nothing at all. I'm just glad we're all here. Alive. It's good."

"Even with that Lance Fuller around?"

She chewed her lower lip. "He's really not so bad. I think he has a good heart."

"I think so too."

She pulled away, her eyes round like saucers. "Did he ask…did you give him permission to…" She choked and stared at Matthew.

He looked off toward the crowd, trying to remain serious. "Did you want me to?"

Ruth Ann gasped, her hands clenched. "I…well, I forgive him and all but…oh Matthew!"

He let a little smile out. "You're just not interested?"

She shook her head and whispered in her guilty tone that sounded so innocent, "No. Is that foolish?"

Matthew patted her head like their daddy did when she was a little girl. "No, Annie. It's not foolish at all."

After finishing the picnic clean-up, Ruth Ann knew where she needed to go. Mrs. Warren hadn't come to church, making this the first service she had missed to Ruth Ann's knowledge. There was no telling what condition the woman was in after being abandoned by her husband. It was likely no one had been to see her, since most of her supposed friends had merely tolerated her because of her husband's former position.

Lance Fuller was still living at the house, trying to help Mrs. Warren prepare to leave Dickens. While Ruth Ann didn't want to be around the young man just yet, she also knew Mrs. Warren needed help. When she saw him talking to the preacher before the two entered the church, she knew it was time.

Ruth Ann slipped away with a basket of bread after a quiet explanation to her mother. She wove between wagons on the way to the newspaper shop. She sensed someone following and spun on them.

"Peter Frazier, you just go on back. I can take care of this myself."

Peter shuffled from the shadows. "Sorry, Annie, I just don't want you to get into anymore shooting scrapes without me."

She tried to keep her stern expression, but her cousin was endearing at times. "I'll give a holler if I need anything, all right? Now go on and get a third helping of those grape dumplings. You need something to hold you down in this breeze."

Peter smirked but didn't argue. He sprinted back to the picnic.

After Sheriff Banny had disappeared not long after the mayor, Ruth Ann felt much safer in town. She went to the newspaper office, picked up a book she'd left there and tucked it in the bread basket on her arm.

A short while later, Ruth Ann knocked on the front door of the Warren place. She noticed how unkempt the place was, but that was understandable. Her heart had a sudden ache for Mrs. Warren.

Ruth Ann knocked again, knowing the woman must be home. Perhaps in a back room, packing. Was Mabel working today? Likely not, being Sunday.

Still no answer. But Ruth Ann couldn't leave. This was where she was supposed to be, if that meant standing on the porch until sunset.

But Lance Fuller would be back before then. She could wait for him, but that was more mortifying than what she decided to do next.

Carefully, Ruth Ann tried the doorknob. It was unlocked.

Poking her head inside, she called softly, "Mrs. Warren? It's Ruth Ann Teller. May I come in?"

Ruth Ann took the lack of objection as permission. She slipped into the dim house. Not a lamp was lit and the overcast day made Ruth Ann pause in the hallway to let her eyes adjust. She rubbed her arm briskly, surprised at the chill in the air. She crept forward and glanced in the parlor. A fire had been started that morning, but had long since died out. Did Mrs. Warren leave on the train while everyone was at church?

Basket still on her arm, Ruth Ann crept deeper into the cold home. If Mrs. Warren was napping, she didn't want to disturb her. But Ruth Ann simply couldn't leave.

A door at the end of the hall was cracked open and she heard a faint sound. Music.

She pushed the door open and whispered, "Mrs. Warren? May I come in?"

Ruth Ann saw the phonograph first, sitting near the window on its stand before the drawn curtains. A bed came into sight next, along with the woman who lay under the covers.

Ruth Ann started to pull back, but she was drawn into the room instead, drawn closer by the white lips on Mrs. Warren's pale face. The woman must be ill, though Lance Fuller hadn't said anything. Of course, she hadn't actually had a conversation with him that morning.

Her shoes were muffled by the thick burgundy carpet. She halted by the bed and watched the covers rise and fall over the ample form.

Ruth Ann turned to set her basket on the armchair by the bed. In the process, she knocked something from the lampstand. The carpet muffled the sound, but Mrs. Warren fluttered her eyelids.

Clumsy! Ruth Ann set the basket on the floor and lifted the fallen object. It was the figurine, the little lady in the white dress with her pink sash that Mrs. Warren treasured.

She set the porcelain figurine next to an empty medicine bottle on the stand. The doctor must have been there. She turned to meet Mrs. Warren's glassy eyes. The woman moved her lips a few times before words came out.

"I thought...I thought it might be him..."

Ruth Ann settled her hand lightly over where the woman's was under the covers. "I didn't mean to bother you, Mrs. Warren. I just came to see you and bring you a gift before you left. I didn't realize you were ill."

The woman moved her head back and forth and a single tear spilled from her eye. Ruth Ann wiped it away. The poor woman was probably mortified to have anyone see her like this. Mrs. Warren prided herself on looking pristine, though she seldom did.

But this was the worst. Her hair was a mass of tangles against the pillows, her eyes had puffy bags under them, and she smelled as though she hadn't bathed in weeks.

When the woman seemed unable to talk, Ruth Ann turned to her basket and lifted the book out. "This is a copy of *American Notes* by Charles Dickens. I know how much you adore his writing."

That adoration was the reason the mayor had chosen the name of their town. He wanted to please his wife. What had happened since then?

Mrs. Warren closed her eyes and turned her face away. Normally, Ruth Ann would have taken that as a dismissal, but there was nothing normal about the circumstances. She sat in the armchair near the bed and thumbed through to chapter twelve.

"Mrs. Warren, you might enjoy this section. It's when Mr. Dickens met Peter Pitchlynn, a former chief of the Choctaw Nation. Would you like me to read? It helps pass the time when you're ill."

Mrs. Warren kept her face turned away, but her eyes fluttered. That was encouragement to go on, wasn't it?

Ruth Ann cleared her throat and read. "'He spoke English perfectly well, though he had not begun to learn the language, he told me, until he was a young man grown. He had read many books; and Scott's poetry appeared to have left a strong impression on his mind: especially the opening of *The Lady of the Lake,* and the great battle scene in *Marmion,* in which, no doubt from the congeniality of the subjects to his own pursuits and tastes, he had great interest and delight. He appeared to understand correctly all he had read, and whatever fiction had enlisted his sympathy in its belief, had done so keenly and earnestly. I might almost say fiercely. He was dressed in our ordinary everyday costume, which hung about his fine figure loosely, and with indifferent grace. On my telling him that I regretted not to see him in his own attire, he threw up his right arm for a moment, as though he were brandishing some heavy weapon, and answered as he let it fall again, that his race were losing many things besides their dress, and would soon be seen upon the earth no more: but he wore it at home, he added proudly.

"He told me that he had been away from his home, west of the Mississippi, seventeen months: and was now returning. He had been chiefly at Washington on some negotiations pending between his Tribe and the government: which were not settled yet (he said in a melancholy way), and he feared never would be: for what could a few poor Indians do against such well-skilled men of business as the whites? He had no love for Washington; tired of towns and cities very soon; and longed for the Forest and the Prairie.

"I asked him what he thought of Congress? He answered, with a smile, that it wanted dignity, in an Indian's eyes.

"He would very much like, he said, to see England before he died; and spoke with much interest about the great things to be seen there. When I told him of that chamber in the British Museum wherein are preserved household memorials of a race that ceased to be, thousands of years ago, he was very attentive, and it was not hard to see that he had a reference in his mind to the gradual fading away of his own people.

"This led us to speak of Mr. Catlin's gallery, which he praised highly: observing that his own portrait was among the collection, and that all the likenesses were 'elegant.' Mr. Catlin, he said, had painted the Red Man well; and so would I, he knew, if I would go home with him and hunt buffaloes, which he was quite anxious I should do. When I told him that, supposing I went, I should not be very likely to damage the buffaloes much, he took it as a great joke and laughed heartily.

"He was a remarkably handsome man; some years past forty I should judge; with long black hair, an aquiline nose, broad cheek bones, a sunburnt complexion, and a very bright, keen, dark, and piercing eye. There were but twenty thousand of the Choctaws left, he said, and their number was decreasing every day. A few of his brother chiefs had been obliged to become civilised, and to make themselves acquainted with what the whites knew, for it was their only chance of existence. But they were not many; and the rest were as they always had been. He dwelt on this: and said several times that unless they tried to assimilate themselves to their conquerors, they must be swept away before the strides of civilised society."

A snort sounded from the bed. Ruth Ann halted in her reading. She closed the book, fighting the indignation she felt. Even in her ill state, Mrs. Warren found a way to show her disdain.

"Perhaps you'd like to hear about the World's Fair. I happened to meet the First Lady there, President Cleveland's wife, Frances Cleveland. She's as lovely and charming as the reports say. She explained how she'd been told she was related to Peter Pitchlynn. But I'm sure you already knew that."

Ruth Ann bit her tongue, knowing her tone bordered on sarcasm. It was time for her to leave before she did anything foolish. She stood and picked up the basket.

"I brought bread. I'll leave it in the kitchen."

The soft carpet silenced her steps and allowed Ruth Ann to hear the whisper.

"Don't go."

She halted and sighed. She went to the other side of the bed so Mrs. Warren wouldn't have to turn her head. The phonograph continued to play the same sounds. Ruth Ann wondered if she should change the cylinder. Surely the same tune for hours, no matter how lovely, would drive someone out of their mind.

Mrs. Warren opened her eyes but didn't look at her. "Stay. I don't want to die alone."

Ruth Ann gasped and sat on the side of the bed. She placed the back of her hand on Mrs. Warren's forehead, all the memories of being at Matthew's side rushing over her.

"Oh, Mrs. Warren, you won't die! Why, you don't even have a fever. What did the doctor say?"

Mrs. Warren's glassy eyes stared at nothing. "He brought laudanum for the pain. I took it all."

Ruth Ann stared, blinked, and stared some more. "Mrs. Warren, do you mean…"

"You are so young and innocent. Your mother loves

you."

The woman pulled a hand from beneath the covers and reached toward the ceiling. Ruth Ann grabbed her hand and squeezed tight. The woman was as cold as death.

"No. No! Mrs. Warren, I'm going for the doctor. Don't die. Just don't you die until I get back!"

Ruth Ann sprang up and ran from the room, trying not to scream.

The front door opened. She took a sharp breath of relief. Lance Fuller must finally be home and…

Jake Banny's lanky frame blocked the door. He seemed as surprised to see her as she was him, but his presence didn't frighten her nearly as much as the room she'd just left.

"I have to get the doctor! Mrs. Warren is—"

Ruth Ann tried to push past him, but Banny shoved her back. She slammed into the hall table, gasping. The front door closed with a loud click.

"Well now. I came back to see if I could persuade that old crow to tell me where the rest of the money was hid. Looks like I found something even better."

Tears gathered in Ruth Ann's eyes, making it hard to see. "You don't understand, she's trying to kill herself! I have to get help."

She went for the door again. Banny hooked her easily around the waist with one arm.

"Maybe in a minute."

He sank his fingers in her hair and yanked her head back. A scream burst from Ruth Ann's throat and she stomped his foot as hard as she could, followed by a hard kick to his shin.

Banny threw her back again, toward the parlor. "I need to teach you some manners, little savage."

◆ ◆ ◆

After the talk with Lance Fuller and then Ruth Ann, Matthew stayed away from people as much as he could. Everyone continued having a jovial time, but he was tired. He was used to asking questions—not answering them. But people wanted to know how he was, wanted to hear the stories again about Mishaya and Lance Fuller and the mayor and on and on.

Matthew was tired.

He slipped between the wagons, looking for a shaded place to nap. He reached the wagon furthest from the gathering and had crawled halfway under it when movement at the edge of town caught his attention. A flash of brown, then the rump of the horse disappeared around the building.

What of it? Not everyone was at the picnic. Some people might already be leaving. Ruth Ann had. Peter told him she went to see Mrs. Warren.

A sick feeling overcame him and Matthew felt the urgency. Something was wrong.

He jumped up only to bang his head on the underside of the wagon. He dropped onto his hands with a moan and crawled forward. He stood and rubbed the top of his head as he walked. Faster and faster. His chest burned with each breath.

The back of the Warren home came into sight. Tied to a bush was a saddled horse, lathered like it had run hard. There was something familiar about that horse. Matthew walked faster, not waiting for his thoughts to catch up.

A muffled scream inside the house made him stumble. Then he started running, holding his chest in place with one fist.

Ruth Ann ran for the fireplace. She grabbed the iron poker and swung around to face Banny. Blind anger pulsed through her. "You're nothing but a coward!"

He stepped into the parlor. Behind him, the front door banged open. Ruth Ann screamed a warning, but he had already turned, drawing his six-shooter.

Matthew barreled into him, knocking the gun aside, but Banny didn't lose his grip. He kneed Matthew in the gut.

Ruth Ann ran forward and whacked Banny between the shoulders as hard as she could. He turned toward her and leveled the gun on her face.

Before she could blink, Matthew grabbed Banny's gun arm and shoved it up. He pushed back and pressed Matthew into the doorframe. Ruth Ann stumbled forward, poker raised again. Banny brought the gun barrel down to her brother's throat. Matthew twisted his other hand free and shoved the gun back. It went off.

Ruth Ann dropped the poker. She covered her mouth with both hands.

The room was still, filled with gun smoke. Matthew slowly knelt beside Banny's crumpled body, then looked away, eyes closed.

The former sheriff's face wouldn't be recognizable at his funeral.

CHAPTER THIRTY-SEVEN

CHOCTAW TRIBUNE

Publishers: Matthew and Ruth Ann Teller

MAYOR LEAVES TOWN ON A MULE

By Ruth Ann Teller

With the startling revelation that his partnership with Sam Mishaya had come to an end, Mayor Thaddeus Warren skipped town in the night. He stole a mule from Charlie Simms' stables and headed north. It is believed he caught the northbound train and traveled as far away as St. Louis.

Mishaya was placed in custody by Marshal Bass Reeves. The marshal had a writ for Mishaya's arrest on charges of conspiring to murder a white man, Will Hocks. Because of his Choctaw blood, the court in McAlester has issued a writ for Mishaya for conspiring to shoot Matthew Teller. He will be arraigned in Judge Parker's court in Fort Smith, Arkansas. If Mishaya survives the hanging judge's court, he will face Choctaw justice.

A writ had also been issued for Sheriff Jake Banny for allegedly being a part of the same murder conspiracy, but he met his death during an attack at the Warren home involving the publishers of this paper. Matthew Teller was cleared of any charges by Marshal Reeves. Mr. Banny's death was a result of self-defense.

Meanwhile, a writ has been issued for the arrest of Thaddeus Warren by Judge Parker in Fort Smith for conspiring in the murder plot of Mr. Hocks.

Though Mr. Warren is accused of taking part in the conspiracy shooting of Matthew Teller, he will not face charges in Indian Territory for the crime because he is a white man.

(Mayor and Mule continued on page 2)

CHOCTAWS AT THE CHICAGO WORLD'S FAIR

By Ruth Ann Teller

During a recent visit to the Columbian Exposition (Chicago World's Fair), this reporter was privileged to meet the popular First Lady of the United States, Mrs. Frances Clara Folsom Cleveland. President Cleveland's wife spoke about the importance of the United States on the world stage, and said that there was no better example of this than the Columbian Exposition.

In a more intimate conversation, Mrs. Cleveland expressed her pleasure of meeting someone from the Choctaw people. She shared an interesting story from her childhood of when she was told she is related to former Choctaw Chief Peter Pitchlynn. While this has not been verified, it created a unique connection with the First Lady and the Choctaw people.

(World's Fair continued on page 3)

SHOOTING AT WHITE TENANT'S HOME

By Matthew Teller

Two outlaws were killed in a shooting scrape near Dickens. Marshal Bass Reeves had ridden with the gang a short time, waiting for an opportunity to serve the arrest writs he carried. The opportunity came when the outlaws, Cub Wassom and Frank Bean, made a visit to a white family's home. In the ensuing shootout that involved Choctaw Pepper Barnes, both outlaws were killed. No other injuries occurred.

(Shooting continued on page 3)

CHILDREN'S CHOIR TO HOLD RECITAL

By Ruth Ann Teller

The Dickens Children's Choir is holding its first performance the Saturday before Thanksgiving at 6 o'clock in the evening at the First Baptist Church. The entire community and outlying areas are encouraged to attend and support the youngest citizens. They are the future community.

UPCOMING BAPTISM OF LANCE FULLER

By Matthew Teller

We urge you to join us in embracing Mr. Lance Fuller in our community. Following his recent conversion, he will be baptized this Sunday morning into the First Baptist Church in Dickens.

Join the celebration of new life.

CHAPTER THIRTY-EIGHT

THE LAST OF AUTUMN CAME in a rush, blowing in with the glory of gold and red leaves. A time of change, of sweeping away the old. A time for something new to take place.

Ruth Ann stood on tiptoe as she arranged a trio of pumpkins on a corner shelf in the school room. Or should it be considered the church right now? She eyed the hardbacked benches that served as pews or school desks—depending on the day—and decided there should be no difference between the two.

The platform where she stood had been cleared of teacher's desk and pulpit. It was ready for the scrubbed faces and shuffling feet of twenty-three children. Hopefully, they would all come as they promised. Hopefully, the entire community would come. They needed healing.

Beulah bustled between the small foyer and the platform, bringing autumn touches into the room with pumpkins, gourds and even fresh leaves of brilliant colors. Every other trip, she halted at the front bench and shuffled through the stack of songbooks. After ensuring all the songs were present and in order, she straightened the books and went to another task, only to return a few minutes later to the books.

Since it was only Ruth Ann and Beulah in the room, Ruth Ann chuckled. "You're nervous."

Beulah dismissed the comment with a wave as if shooing away a fly. "Nonsense. I merely want to be prepared. The children have worked hard for this."

Ruth Ann stepped off the platform and caught both of Beulah's hands in hers. She pulled her taller friend around to face her.

"So have you, and it means a lot. This is an important work."

She stumbled around for the perfect words, something to remind her Jewish friend about the lessons learned in Chicago, about the work they should all be about doing, about how the divides between races needed to stop. Ruth Ann couldn't put it all into words, but she didn't need to. Understanding shone in Beulah's eyes. Ruth Ann had never seen her so happy.

The sacred moment was disrupted by the door blowing open and Lance Fuller stumbling through with the backdrop of a darkening sky. The sun hadn't set, but storm clouds blocked it out. If anything would keep people away, it was an autumn storm.

But no matter. Those who would come, would come. God could do a work in them all through this. His hand was in it. The greatest evidence of that was the pure smile on Lance Fuller's face.

He kicked the door closed and showed off his armful of pumpkins. "What a harvest! People will be filled with thanksgiving as soon as they walk through the door."

Soon, children began to arrive with their parents. Ruth Ann helped pass out the songbooks and corral the children, but Lance Fuller kept them in hand. The children, white and Choctaw, had grown fond of him through his work with the choir, and the children respected their schoolteacher.

Ruth Ann left Lance Fuller and Beulah to their work. She took up a post by the front door to greet those who came for the evening. She needn't have worried about the storm keeping those in the town and on farms from coming. Her concern changed to how they would squeeze everyone in the building.

Pastor Rand greeted her with a hearty handshake and thanks for her work on the Concerned Citizens of Dickens committee. He winked. "You've done more than anyone could have asked for."

Before long, beloved faces of family appeared. Matthew and their mother had remained at home until now, serving a feast to their family that came in from the farm. They would stay overnight for church the next morning. Now they all arrived together, loaded with food and apple cider. There wouldn't be much sleeping tonight, only plenty of singing and eating.

◆◆◆

Matthew dodged through the light rain and mud puddles down Main Street of Dickens. When it was clear the success of the choir would cause people to stay and talk awhile, Della had asked Peter to return home and fetch the leftover cherry turnovers from the house to share with the children. Matthew took his cousin's place, glad to get outside. The crowded room bothered him. He had felt trapped, and tonight was a time to fill with hope. A trip to the house would remedy his mood.

But by the time he arrived home, the burn in his chest warned him he still had a ways to go to recover. It had been over a month since he'd taken a bullet in his chest, but he couldn't travel like he used to yet.

Rain dripped off the overhang on their front porch. Matthew climbed the steps and reached for the front door, but came to a stop. He sensed a presence nearby. Very near.

"Matthew Teller."

The voice was both sure and hesitant, but not familiar. Whoever it was knew him but he didn't know them.

He turned and stared into the darkness off the porch. "Who's there?"

A form moved out of the shadows and came to the edge of the steps. Her head was tilted and long black strands of hair fell over her shoulders despite the kerchief around her head. Even in the dark, Matthew knew the woman was Choctaw. And he had a bizarre feeling he knew exactly who she was.

The woman came up the porch steps and raised her head. When their eyes met, Matthew knew it was the first time he'd seen her. But he knew this woman.

"You're Takba?"

The woman nodded and brushed back the kerchief, revealing her face. She spoke in Choctaw. "My son tried to kill you."

Matthew sucked in a breath. "Your son. Cub Wassom?"

It explained a lot: why Takba had been on the road when Matthew was shot, and why she had saved his life; why she was at the Jessop farm; why she was here tonight.

She stepped closer to him. "There is something for you to know."

He fought down his anger. Cub Wassom had shot him. Had been a part of the gang who killed his father and brother.

Cub Wassom's mother stood here now.

Matthew calmed himself and continued to speak in his native tongue. "What your son did, he did. I don't hold anything against you. You saved my life, and I'm grateful. Nothing more needs to be said."

"The answer doesn't want to be found."

Takba's eyes bore into Matthew's. What was she saying? What was he about to get into now?

"Go to the coal mines in Krebs. Find Al Percy. Your journey will begin in Krebs, but it will not end there."

She paused. "He doesn't want to be found. But you will not rest until you find the answer about the man who killed your father. My soul will not rest until you do."

She turned and left. Matthew wanted to chase after her, but his feet wouldn't move. He stood in shock. *The man who killed your father...*

He felt like a boy who'd been told by an elder what to do,

and he had no choice but to obey. To follow the trail wherever it led.

God, You know.

♦♦♦

The building was filled with happy people after the choir performance. Beulah convinced the children to sing again.

The room had become stuffy with the whole town inside, and someone had opened the front door. But the air was cold with the rain, and Ruth Ann went to close the door. Before she did though, she caught sight of an ample figure tramping through the tangle of wagons and horses. Thunder boomed and the clouds opened on the figure—a woman—drenching her in the cold rain. She wore no raincoat, no hat, no protection against the onslaught.

Ruth Ann felt a sudden burn in her throat at the memories.

The doctor's grim words. *"Much will depend on her will to live."*

Late nights sitting by a bedside of hopelessness.

Tears in murmured conversations.

A past so painful death was preferred over life.

Ruth Ann opened her heart wide as the figure huffed her way up the steps, into the foyer, and shook off like a wet dog.

"My oh my, look at that downpour! It was just waiting to catch me out in the open, wasn't it?"

Mrs. Warren shook off her thin shawl. Her hair was askew, her dress rumpled, her shoes muddy. But Ruth Ann had never seen her look more alive.

"I'm glad you came, Mrs. Warren. I thought you were staying in with Mabel tonight."

Thankfully, the kind cook had taken pity on her boss and, with Banny's hotel shut down, Mabel had taken up residence with Mrs. Warren.

Mrs. Warren flapped her hands like a bird with short wings. "That woman thinks we are old and should stay indoors on a night like this. Why, she fell right asleep in her chair. It was my chance to sneak out and play."

She giggled, shaking her loosely pinned hair down and around her shoulders. Ruth Ann smiled and tried to help the woman compose herself by laying aside the drenched shawl and redoing the dripping wet hair.

Since her husband's abandonment and the suicide attempt, Mrs. Warren had become childlike. While she remembered her past and had said she was healing fine, there was something in her eyes that said she would need care a long time. Perhaps the rest of her life.

But she had that promise of care in Lance Fuller, who had taken charge of her like she was his own mother. And there was faithful Mabel, who understood and was ready to take care of Mrs. Warren.

And Ruth Ann knew she and Mrs. Warren were bonded. No matter how busy she was with the newspaper, she stopped in to see Mrs. Warren several times a week, often with her mother. Della was the gentle soul on a solid rock foundation.

Surrounded by a love from God Himself, Ruth Ann was able to smile at the dithering Mrs. Warren. The plump woman made her way up the crowded aisle and plunked down on the front row before the encore began.

Ruth Ann stood at the back of the room, surveying the crowd. It couldn't be more mixed than this. God must be smiling on them all.

And that explained everything.

Glossary of Choctaw Words

Chahta sia: I am Choctaw

Chihowa: God

Chi hullo li: I love you

Chi pisa la chike: I will be seeing you, or I will see you later

Chim achukma: How are you?

Vm achukma: I'm doing well. (Usually followed with: *Chishnato?* And you?)

Halito: A friendly greeting

Luksi: Turtle

Ome: Expressing a ready assent, agreement or acknowledgment

Pokni: Grandmother

Yakoke: Thank you

Author's Note

While these stories were presented in fiction form, they drew a good deal from actual happenings of the times. We strove for cultural and historical accuracy woven through this fictional tale.

Though the spelling today of the Council House area is "Tuskahoma," historical documents written in the 1890s by Choctaw tribal leaders spelled it, "Tushkahomma." This is the spelling I decided to use. Tushka homma is Choctaw for "red warrior."

The Choctaw Council House still stands in its original location in Tuskahoma, Oklahoma. I encourage you to visit there and walk the hall to see the displays, including one with the history of the Council House that includes photos and artifacts. Climb the stairs and visit the museum on the second floor. Be sure to stop in the gift shop (tell them I said *halito*!), and stroll the grounds to see the history trail and the traditional village replica. You can even make your way over to the old Tuskahoma cemetery and be carried back in time like I was to the old Choctaw Nation with Ruth Ann and Matthew Teller.

Bass Reeves was one of the first black U.S. deputy marshals west of the Mississippi River, working mostly in Arkansas and Indian Territory. During his long career, it's estimated he arrested over 3,000 felons. He served over 30 years as a deputy U.S. marshal.

The description of Beulah Levitt as a blonde, fair-skinned Jew may seem odd to some. However, this description, as well as the Jewish names, came from actual Russian Jewish immigrants who settled in Kansas and Missouri. Many migrated to Indian Territory. The Chicago Jewish names and histories were taken from actual records of German Jews and immigrants during the time period.

The excerpt Ruth Ann read to Mrs. Warren was taken from *American Notes* by Charles Dickens. While the original quote in the fifth paragraph reads "Mr. Cooper, he said, had painted the Red Man well" I did change it to Mr. Catlin for clarity.

The scripture verses are from Proverbs 17:27-28 and Psalms 120:7 (KJV).

Much inspiration about the Chicago World's Fair came from *A Proper Pursuit* by Lynn Austin and *The Devil in the White City* by Erik Larson.

The fictional town of Dickens was inspired by the history of two early towns in the Choctaw Nation—Hugo and Antlers, Oklahoma. The laws and politics follow closely the actual conflicts in Indian Territory before statehood.

Yakoke

They say writing is a lonely process, and at times, it is. But I could not go through it without many, many wonderful people who love and support me every word of the way.

Thank you to fellow author and Choctaw tribal member James Masters, who worked through the plot details and every line of this story. You analyzed my writing in ways I could understand. I hope this book shows the quality work you put into it.

Yakoke to Dr. Ian Thompson, Francine Locke Bray, Kay Black and Beverly Allen for giving me input on not only the settings for this book, but also the cultural, political and social structures of the Choctaw people. Try as I might, there are still things I overlooked or didn't think through when writing and revising. I needed the input you all gave. And thank you, Regina Green (Choctaw Nation Capitol Museum Director), for the fabulous new display in the museum about the Council House that gave me a broader vision of its history. Also, thank you for the Council House photo we used on the book cover.

Thanks to Kirk DouPonce (www.DogEaredDesign.com) for your hard work on the cover design! It's more than I envisioned. Thank you to Dori Harrell (Breakout Editing) for polishing the back cover description before it went to print.

At book signings and online, readers have supported my writing. I want to thank those who were a text, phone call, email or Facebook message away when I needed an encouraging word, those who read early drafts of this manuscript and gave me valuable input: Denny and Bridgett Huebshman, Barbara Grant, Mark and Deborah Potts, Jennifer Wingard, Shelia Kirven, and Kathi Macias. You guys got me through times when I wanted to quit. I also want to thank Elaine Alvarado for the splendid birthday gifts of souvenirs from the 1893 Chicago World's Fair! What treasures in my office during this writing process, and they were the perfect touch on the book cover.

I had a great time with the Chickasaw Nation employee book discussion for book 1, *The Executions*. Thank you for having me. I loved being able to give a sneak peak into book 2, though it was hard not to give away anything to you guys! I hope you enjoy *Traitors* as much as *The Executions*.

A very special thank you to my brother, James Hinz, who has read all my books. You have no idea how much fun I had talking about this story and characters with you (even though you wanted me to kill one of my favorite characters off!). Having family support is precious to me.

On that note, I want to give love and hugs to my aunts, Sherry McFerrin and Judy Ford. You supported me from near and far. Chi hullo li!

No one goes through more trauma when I'm working on a book than my mama, Lynda Kay Sawyer. She's lifted me off the floor more than once, and never wavers in helping me move forward. She's my editor and sounding board, and photographed the World's Fair souvenirs for the cover of this book. Did I mention what an amazing, beautiful mama she is?

The God Who gave her to me is the God who sees me through every word. I pray my words honor and glorify Him.

"In the beginning was the Word, and the Word was with God, and the Word was God." John 1:1 (KJV)

About the Author

SARAH ELISABETH SAWYER is an award-winning inspirational author, speaker and Choctaw storyteller of traditional and fictional tales based on the lives of her people. The Smithsonian's National Museum of the American Indian has honored her as a literary artist through their Artist Leadership Program for her work in preserving Trail of Tears stories. In 2015, First Peoples Fund awarded her an Artist in Business Leadership Fellowship. She writes from her hometown in Texas, partnering with her mother, Lynda Kay Sawyer, in continued research for future novels. Learn more about their work in preserving Choctaw history:

SarahElisabethWrites.com

Facebook.com/SarahElisabethSawyer

Choctaw Tribune Series, Book 1

Who would show up for their own execution?

It's 1892, Indian Territory. A war is brewing in the Choctaw Nation as two political parties fight out issues of old and new ways. Caught in the middle is eighteen-year-old Ruth Ann, a Choctaw who doesn't want to see her family killed.

In a small but booming pre-statehood town, her mixed blood family owns a controversial newspaper, the *Choctaw Tribune*. Ruth Ann wants to help spread the word about critical issues but there is danger for a female reporter on all fronts—socially, politically, even physically.

But what is truly worth dying for? This quest leads Ruth Ann and her brother Matthew, the stubborn editor of the fledgling *Choctaw Tribune*, to old Choctaw ways at the farm of a condemned murderer. It also brings them to head on clashes with leading townsmen who want their reports silenced no matter what.

More killings are ahead. Who will survive to know the truth? Will truth survive?

***The Executions* (Choctaw Tribune Series, Book 1) is available on Amazon.com**

Featuring the Native American classic, *Rising Fawn and the Fire Mystery* by Marilou Awiakta

SARAH ELISABETH SAWYER EDITOR

TOUCH MY TEARS

Tales from the Trail of Tears

FOREWORD BY JULIE CANTRELL
NY Times Bestselling Author

For this collection of short stories, Choctaw authors from five U.S. states came together to present a part of their ancestors' journeys, a way to honor those who walked the trail for their future. These stories not only capture a history and a culture, but the spirit, faith, and resilience of the Choctaw people.

Tears of sadness. Tears of joy. Touch and experience them.

Touch My Tears is available on Amazon.com

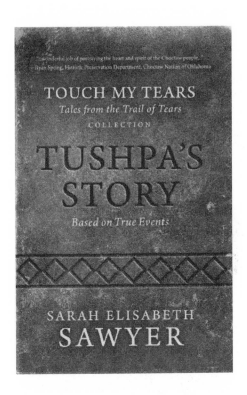

"Protect the book as you do our seed corn. We must
have both to survive."

The Treaty of Dancing Rabbit Creek changed everything.
The Choctaw Nation could no longer remain in their ancient homelands.

Young Tushpa, his family, and their small band embark
on a trail of life and death. More death than life lay
ahead.

Tushpa's Story (Touch My Tears Collection) **is available on Amazon.com**

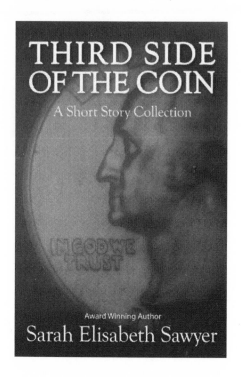

THIRD SIDE
OF THE COIN

A Short Story Collection

Award Winning Author
Sarah Elisabeth Sawyer

With the gift to find real meaning in a story, author
Sarah Elisabeth Sawyer creates tales to stir the heart and
evoke deep, often buried emotions. Not one to shy away
from tragedy or crisis of faith, she explores human conditions through engaging short stories.

Third Side of the Coin **is available on Amazon.com**